WHAT

LEGENDS

BECOME

When Legends Rise is an intense sci-fi thriller merged with sweet romance in a poignant redemption story. Fans of *Star Wars* or *Halo* will love this engaging story, and romance lovers will find a familiar dynamic in a new genre.

JAKE TYSON, author of *Vigilante's Light* and *Freedom's Fight*

When Legends Rise is a fantastic sci-fi thriller by Daphne Self. Combining elements of dystopia with assassins, interplanetary travel and themes of faith, it's a great read for the adult Christian sci-fi fan. The main character is a man running from an uncertain past into an even more uncertain future . . . and we're along for the ride. The minor characters are all interesting and greatly add to the story, which features jaunts to Mars and other galactic locales. Ms. Self keeps you guessing with every page, leading to an epic and unexpected conclusion well worth the read!

C.E. STONE, author of *Starganauts* and *Starganauts: Retribution*

Daphne Self's book *When Legends Rise* is a stellar blend of science fiction and Christianity. The story comes alive with personable, relatable characters, stunning descriptions, and gorgeous science fiction settings that will leave you excited to turn the page, but it also hits at the heart with a slow-burn romance, difficult decisions, and redemption for even those who have committed the worst of sins. For anyone who enjoys deep and realistic characterization, Christian themes without the preachiness that comes with so much of today's Christian fiction, and riveting science-fiction action sequences, *When Legends Rise* is a must-read.

ARIEL PAIEMENT, author of the *Legends of Alcardia* stand-alone series and the *Children of Chaos* duology

WHAT LEGENDS BECOME

DAPHNE SELF

LEGENDS OF LIGHT | BOOK TWO

AMBASSADOR INTERNATIONAL
GREENVILLE, SOUTH CAROLINA & BELFAST, NORTHERN IRELAND

www.ambassador-international.com

What Legends Become

©2024 by Daphne Self
All rights reserved

ISBN: 978-1-64960-509-2
eISBN: 978-1-64960-552-8

Cover design by Hannah Linder Designs
Interior typesetting by Dentelle Design
Edited by Katie Cruice Smith

AMBASSADOR INTERNATIONAL
Emerald House
411 University Ridge, Suite B14
Greenville, SC 29601
United States
www.ambassador-international.com

AMBASSADOR BOOKS
The Mount
2 Woodstock Link
Belfast, BT6 8DD
Northern Ireland, United Kingdom
www.ambassadormedia.co.uk

The colophon is a trademark of Ambassador, a Christian publishing company.

To my wonderful scifi nerdy sons, thank you for being my sounding board and helping with ideas.

And as always, all thanks are given to my Lord Jesus Christ.

AUTHOR'S NOTE

It is always darkest before the dawn.

As with most idioms, the saying changes over time; yet English theologian Thomas Fuller used the phrase, "It is always darkest just before the Day dawneth" in 1650 in his work, *A Pisgah-Sight of Palestine and the Confines Thereof*. It is possible that he rephrased an Irish proverb: "Remember that the darkest hour of all is the hour before day." Regardless, the saying shows that when all seems dark and lost, the light will surely shine.

This second installment of the *Legends of Light* series is a bit darker and deals with elements of drug use and sexual promiscuity, among other sins. Yet to understand the light, we sometimes need to know what the dark entails. I do not glorify the dark nor the sin, but I do want to show how one may fall into rebellion against God.

As John says in chapter one, verse five: "And the light shines in the darkness, and the darkness did not comprehend it." So, too, do those who rebel against God's Word not comprehend His love and suffer the consequences of their actions.

Even when the world was once void and covered in darkness, God said, "'Let there be light'" (Gen. 1:3). So, let there be light in the midst of the darkness and hope in the middle of despair as you read *What Legends Become*.

—Daphne Self

Chapter One

SETH

Seth stared at the dark gravestone. Age had weathered the stone, and ice had collected in the grooves of the words. No date. Never a date—a custom that had begun so long ago. Yet each year, they kept these that rested on the hill cleaned and repaired.

He stooped down and brushed away the dusting of snow that had collected on the top of his father's grave.

Julius Williams
Husband, Son, Brother, and Father
Child of God

It was one thing to have always heard his father's story growing up, even becoming his true namesake. Then there were the times he wished he knew the man who had fought for his freedom and given his life for his family.

The smell of fresh dirt invaded his nose, and Seth turned to the headstone next to his father's. Barely three days old. It gleamed in the soft Alaskan sunlight. Tears pricked his eyelids as he read the inscription.

Abigail Maureen Williams Marktov
Wife, Daughter, Sister, and Mother
Child of God

She had fought a brave fight; but even with their advanced medicines, not all illnesses could be conquered. So many times throughout his mother's illness and with his stepfather, Huey, at her side, Seth had wished he could have used his own advanced healing to save her.

When he had mentioned it to his mother, she had smiled, patted his hand, and said that when a person's time came, it came. And it was her time to go.

A shadow fell across the stones. Seth didn't look up. Today was Sunday. And that meant the shadow belonged to Michael, who came every week to visit his brother's grave.

Seth let his mind fall back onto that word: brother. His father had no biological brother yet had claimed Uncle JJ as his. Michael's brother, who was also not his biological sibling, was Peter, former Zulu assassin. Growing up, he had heard all the tales. The last of the Global Federated Territories assassins had arrived to the Coalition on the day they had gained their freedom and land—the day before his sixth birthday.

Seth rose to his feet and backed up from the headstones. There were no bodies here, just stones marking the area where their ashes were buried—another custom that had started when his father died. No one could take a chance that GFT would obtain his body and blood. Even now, the curse of GFT limited the movements of the assassin descendants.

"Thinking again?" Michael's soft voice drifted across the cold air.

Seth shrugged. "Always."

He turned and faced the aged former assassin. Heavy lines pulled at the man's face. His gray hair sported his trademark style: shaved head with tight braids on top. Yet his blue eyes still held a lot of energy and youth and a peacefulness that Seth wasn't feeling. He returned his gaze back to the headstones.

"She found it hard to live without him until you were born."

Seth whipped around. "What?"

"Your mother." Michael walked to the far end where his brother was buried and sank, cross-legged, onto the ground. "She and Julius were in love. Julius would do anything for your mother; and the weeks after arriving here, he did just that. The day he died . . . he knew he wouldn't survive. It was hard on your mother. Then you came into this world looking exactly like your father, and hope was rekindled in Abigail."

Rarely did Michael talk. In all of Seth's forty-seven years, he had only heard Michael speak this long a handful of times. Peter had once told him that Michael spoke only when there was something to say.

"You know a lot about love—especially from a man who never married."

"Granted." Michael gripped his knees and rubbed at them. "But love was never in the future for Peter or me. We had too many demons."

"As a child of God, shouldn't those demons have already been slayed?"

"For some." Michael smiled softly. "We focused what love we could give onto our families here. You are included in that."

Seth nodded and sank down beside the man. In front of them stood Peter's gravestone, its dark gray surface a shadow under the trees.

Peter Christian
Brother and Child of God

Christian. He and Michael had no surname. So, they took on the name of who they were, how they saw themselves. "Why wouldn't you let Mom find out when you and Peter were born? I've always wondered why you two refused to know more about your former lives."

The wind blew and stirred the leaves and grass around them. Overhead, a cloud passed in front of the sun, sending shadows dancing around them. A small shudder ran through Seth's body.

Michael sighed. "Our lives began the day we accepted Christ. What GFT did to us in Zulu was worse than what happened to Juliet. I do not care to remember those times. And I do not care to know who I was before then. Christ made me new. And I do not look behind me to the past." He looked over at Seth. "But that is my road to follow."

Seth nodded. "It still feels surreal."

"It will for a time." He closed his eyes and fell silent.

Seth stood, gently squeezed the older man's shoulder, and left him to his prayer. The trek back to the compound was a cold one. The weather was turning again. Their days should have been warming up, but the cold fronts kept their hold on their little home at the top of the world.

The sounds of the compound reached him long before he could see it—the idle chatter of workers in the fields, at the walls, around the domes and buildings; the drone of hovercrafts and children laughing. He caught the faint laughter of his daughter, Sierra. No mistaking that lilting chuckle. He always compared her to a delicate wind chime in the rain.

He ran their schedule through his mind. Today was her time with the small children, teaching them Bible lessons or, knowing

Sierra, incorporating the history into some fun activity. She would be with the school tomorrow, teaching the children herbology—and probably a bit of geology, too. Unlike her twin brother, Stephen, she had easily settled into a profession and study. His mother had said her green thumb came from her grandfather.

He smiled and hurried across the well-worn pathway leading to the side medical building. Today would have been his shift in medlab, but he had received a five-day bereavement. Still, whether he was working or not, he needed to run scans.

Being the child of the only GFT assassin that Serum Seventy-four had succeeded on meant monthly scans and bloodwork. The genetic manipulation that was done to his father had been passed along to him and to his children. And while the rest of the assassins had the serum in their system for many years, its effect never took—until they had children of their own.

Seth pulled opened the door. The pressurized air stirred his hair. The smells of medicines, electronics, and sterilized air surrounded him as his mind ran through the names of all those who were enhanced by Serum Seventy-four: Tamara, his wife, daughter of JJ; Donald, son of Mandy and Dan; Denise, daughter of Devon; Samson and Jade, son and daughter of James; and the last born, Peony, daughter of Jackson.

Although the effects of the serum were not as strong, a bit passed along to their children. Through his genetic research, he found the recessive genes that had been mutated by the serum. Given enough years, the gene would either weaken or be eradicated—but not so for his children and Donald's children.

For Donald, the son of two former assassins, he had gained the benefit of faster healing and advanced learning. His children inherited the same, yet at a more diminished scale.

Tamara had inherited from her father much of the same. But when they married, he had never thought that the abilities he had inherited from his father would bond with the genes she had inherited and create a new set of genetic mutations.

While his eyes remained white with green borders, their children's eyes were a deep green with flecks of white surrounding their pupils. Their comprehension rivaled his, as did their strength, speed, and healing. While Sierra stayed levelheaded, Stephen remained reckless and full of rage.

Seth crossed the empty lab room and entered his work area. The door clicked softly behind him.

"Lights, one eighth."

Dim illumination lit the room. Being at his mother's grave gave him extra incentive to solve the genetic equation. The Coalition would never remain safe if GFT knew about them. There had to be a code somewhere within that would stop the passing along of the serum's effects.

He activated his computer and entered the parameters for his search. The computer screen scrolled through line after line of code and ran results of scans and bloodwork. Seth pushed away from the counter and strolled to the full-body medscanner. As he stood on the platform, his door opened.

Tamara, her chestnut-toned skin shining under the harsh lights, smiled as she walked toward him, her silvery poncho swaying around her hips. Her curls had started sporting more gray hairs lately, giving her an ethereal look, almost exotic. His gut clenched at the sight of her.

The scanner beeped. Seth stepped off and swept her into his arms, claiming her mouth in a kiss before she could greet him. He pulled away, twisting a curl around his finger.

She smiled up at him. "How was your trip to the Hill?"

"Michael showed up." He held her hand as he walked to the other side to draw his bloodwork.

"He misses Peter." She sat on the stool and pulled a rolling tray between them.

In silence, they worked together to draw his blood and insert it into the spectrum analysis, then to run his medscan through all the set parameters.

She read the preliminary results. "Nothing has changed."

Seth shook his head. "I keep hoping that I will find some kind of cure to this."

Tamara reached out and gripped his hand. Her deep amber eyes softened with compassion. "Seth, this isn't a disease to cure. Our genes are a part of us. Don't become like GFT and manipulate us or them."

He shook his head as he ran a thumb over her knuckles. "I don't plan to do that. But if I can dampen the effects or at least stop the genes from being inherited, then I will rest easy knowing that we are safe. As it is, we are prisoners in our own country."

She sighed but kept quiet. For the last seven years, when the urge to do this hit him, she had tried to stop him. Then she had tried to distract him. Finally, she had decided to work alongside him. Although he knew, deep down, she was still hoping he would give up this fruitless effort. Only, he didn't find it fruitless.

The computer beeped. The results on the first search were finalized. He pulled up the readout and sagged in his seat. Nothing. It would take another six hours for the second set to finish.

"Come on." Tamara tugged at his arm. "You aren't supposed to be working today. And even if you were, you are scheduled for security and ops, not medlab."

"I had my schedule adjusted, so, yes, medlab would have been today." Seth allowed her to lead him away from his workstation. "I can do both, you know."

"I know." She pushed open the door and shot a quick glance over her shoulder at him. "But you really shouldn't. Why couldn't you just settle for one job? One career? Instead, you studied medicine, botany, military ops, and literature."

"Why settle for one when I could do it all?" He almost collided into her when she stopped suddenly and whirled around to face him.

"Really? So, are you not satisfied with me? One wife? One lover?"

Seth laughed and captured her face in his hands. "Can't banter with me, wife. You know the answer to that."

She rolled her eyes at him before releasing a soft laugh. "Come on, my stubborn husband. I came to get you because Huey left something for you at our quarters."

"What?"

"He said it was something your mom and he worked on for years. He said your mom wanted you to have it when she passed—an answer to many of your questions."

With his curiosity piqued, Seth found himself walking faster toward the far side of the compound where their quarters were. If

Huey and his mom worked on it, then it was important. And he had a good suspicion it dealt with his father.

"By the way, our son has been ignoring my calls for the last two days."

Seth sighed. He shook his head. "He's twenty-five, Tam. There's not much we can do at this moment. We can only pray he will come to his senses."

She huffed. "And when will that be? Dad had called him a moody monkey, and I'm beginning to believe it. He's chomping at the bit about something."

"Chomping at the bit?" Seth smiled and gently poked his wife in the ribs. "Have you been reading some of those classics lately?"

Tamara started laughing as they exited the main building and veered toward the seaside area. "The ancient books. Something that was called *Westerns*. Really strange reading something so old."

He slid his arm around her waist as she chatted about the titles and authors that were discovered in an abandoned building buried miles away. The excavation team had delivered loads and loads of books and tomes to the school and library. So far, he had made it through a quarter of the books. Some were boring as sterile dirt. Others invoked feelings and desires that left him wanting more to devour.

Tamara's soft voice floated along the air, drowning out his negative emotions, burying his fears and indecisions. Only she and her voice existed as they walked home.

Φ

Stephen stood at the window. The fused glass heated the sun's rays as it shone through and hit his bare chest. He curled his toes into the plush carpet and crossed his arms.

His visits with Danica were getting old. She had begun to demand more of his time and more of his attention. Time to move on. But not just yet. She still fulfilled a need.

Guilt at his actions tried to rear its head, but he shoved it down. He was tired of feeling guilty, of feeling shame. Tired of being the good man, the rule-abiding man. That man was boring. That man didn't live.

Slender arms snaked around his waist and up his chest. Danica purred into his ear. "What are you thinking? Why not come back to bed?"

He turned in her arms and leaned back against the window. His hands rested on her hips, keeping her close yet still away from him. Her long, black hair hung in soft waves to her waist. Dark eyes regarded him. "Have you ever ventured beyond our borders? That was what I was thinking."

She frowned and leaned back with her hands clasped around him. "Beyond our borders? Once. On a supply run. We went into Canadian Province. To Vancouver. Why?"

"What was it like?"

She shrugged. "Nothing special really. Even though Vancouver was a decent-sized city, it never recouped from the last war." She pulled away from him and settled down on the chaise lounge in her living room. Her plush robe fell open as she pulled her feet upon it. "Are you thinking of signing up for a shipment run?"

"No." He sat on the edge of the chaise and leaned over her. "I'm thinking of traveling."

Danica frowned up at him. "Why? You know we aren't to leave our borders—especially you and your kind."

"My kind?" Stephen snarled and straightened up.

She shook her head and gripped his arm. "I don't mean it that way. I just mean that you and the others are supposed to stay within our borders to keep you safe."

Stephen regarded the older woman. She worked as his father's understudy in the medlab. At fifteen years his senior, he had found her enticing and seductive. And from the first time they were together, he had discovered he could learn more about what his father was doing in medlab. Even though he could hack just about any system out there, his father had one advantage. He had used the GHOST, his grandmother's old program, to protect his research, effectively preventing any hacking into the system.

Stephen had not been able to get his hands on the program or its codes. He was never a part of the security detail or privy to the elders' meetings. In fact, he was shuttered from just about any meeting unless it was the general meetings.

Danica ran a finger over his brow. "Why are you so upset?"

He shook his head. "I feel . . . stifled."

"How so? You are the top hunter and guide. You range across all of Alaska. You teach the highest self-defense class, and the school calls you in to help with the higher mathematics. You are valued here, Stephen. You can do just about anything you want—even join your father's medlab study."

"No. Not that. He would allow me to train in medlab but not be a part of his research." Stephen twisted around so that he could stretch out beside her on the chaise. "Besides, I don't want to do those things anymore."

"What do you want?"

He smiled and began to show her what he wanted. A part of his mind was screaming at him for using her. When she fell asleep, like she normally would do, he would swipe her card to medlab. He would have his father's research, finally, and he would discover why he was subjected to medscans and bloodwork every three months. Then he would find a way to leave this hated place once and for all.

Seth inserted the antiquated data disk. From the looks of it, the recording on this one was decades old. He turned the data crystal that he held in his other hand around and around between his fingers.

"Are you going to activate it?" Tamara settled down beside him on the bench in front of the family console.

"Soon." He stared at the holographic hub. "I'm pretty sure about what is on this."

If he knew his mother well, then this data disk contained a recording by his father. But why wait for so many years to show him?

Tamara reached forward and pressed the button. "There."

His wife always knew when he needed the nudge. He wanted to activate it, needed to see it. Yet everything in him cried out in fear with the uncertainty of it all.

The holographic projection fizzled a bit before focusing into a man at least fifteen years younger than Seth. Scars ran down his face and neck. One prominent scar disappeared into his short, dark beard. His jaw was sharp and nose angular. Dark hair glistened in the lights above him in what looked like one of the older living quarters. Yet it was his eyes that were startling—half-white, half-vivid green. They shone with an inner light; yet behind them, Seth could also see the multitude of nightmares and demons.

His father steepled his fingers against his mouth. Light bounced off the dull scars that created a hatch-work design on his hands.

"Go ahead, Jules." His mother's voice sounded so youthful.

His father dropped his hands and took a breath. "My son or daughter, I don't know you yet, but I am praying for the day that we will be blessed by you and that I get to know you. You will be my legacy.

"I want you to know a few things about me. They will be hard to hear. They will be horrible to comprehend. Yet know that a few weeks ago, I accepted Christ; and He is making me new. My slate of blood and death has been wiped clean. I still battle the demons within me, but it is His strength that sees me through.

"I tell you this because what was done to me will pass along to you. And you will need to know the depth of what happened."

He took a deep breath. His demeanor changed. He became like a soldier during a debriefing.

"GFT abducted me when I was only five, the day before my sixth birthday. Killed my parents in front of me. Five years later, I was made to kill my best friend, Stephen, designation Sierra 7-N. That was when they took me away to Medlab Twelve. For days, I underwent neural biofeedback and torture designed to erase who I was, what I believed and thought—my very essence. And for a long time, they succeeded. I was their elite assassin, the head of Juliet squad. I'm attaching the mission files your mother was able to GHOST. You can read for yourself how I killed without prejudice young and old alike—men, women, and . . . " His voice faltered for a bit. "Even children.

"The last mission on record is the day I should have died. Instead, God kept me alive. And that began my journey to find your uncle JJ and to find my freedom from GFT. I was decommissioned, which in GFT terms meant to be killed, to be dispatched. I was no longer salvageable in their eyes. In other words, I was no longer their killing machine. And that was what I was—a machine with no emotions, no feelings, no memories.

"I escaped and met with Bishop Thomas, who helped me obtain my ship, *Nightingale.* You will see a lot of her in the houses and greenhouse. My one home was used to make another.

"And that is how my life truly began. Your mother and Huey plan to grab as much of the security feeds—those that survived—as they can and attach them to this video so that you can see a bit of my life.

"It was your grandfather and so many others—especially Evie, Danny, and CeeCee—that taught me what love truly is—what it means to have a family, what it means to follow Christ, no matter the cost. I don't know what the future holds. I don't know if I will survive because the GFT will always be looking for me—"

"You don't have to put it that way, Jules." His mother's voice filtered through. Her hand reached out and brushed at a wayward strand of hair on his father's forehead.

A long pause stretched through the video feed as his father regarded his mother. Then he gave her a slight smile. "It's the truth, Abby. Let me tell it my way." He turned back to the camera. "There were only two assassins on which Serum Seventy-four was successful. Juliet 7-A, which is—*was*—me. And it is believed, Juliet 2-Z, who is still hunting me.

"Our blood is valuable and holds the key into making men and women into a type of augmented soldier. Strength, speed, hearing, eyesight, healing, learning—I am far more advanced than anyone else. Yet I would gladly give it up for a normal life. I tell you this so that you will understand that if we—your mother and I and your family—ever put limitations on you, it is to keep you safe.

"It feels strange to say 'I love you' since you aren't even here, yet I do love you. I love the thought of God granting us a child. I love the idea of you and pray that I will meet you soon. Know that when I was searching for freedom, I didn't know the extent of what that meant. God has granted me more than I could have thought possible.

"These people I am with now, they are my family. You are my family. And I will love and protect you while I still draw breath."

He looked offscreen. "How was that?"

"It was good. Heartfelt." His mother came into view and sat down in his father's lap. She leaned against him as his hand wrapped around her waist. "Hi, my little one. It took a long time to get your father to do this. He preferred his greenhouse to the recorder."

"Really, Abby?" He half-rolled his eyes at her.

She laughed and kissed his temple before returning to the screen. "I want you to remember this: he was designed to kill . . . "

"Yet God had another design for him." Seth spoke the words along with her. She smiled and then leaned forward. The video ended, and the display dissolved.

Tamara brushed at her eyes and sniffed. "You look a lot like him."

Throughout his life, he had been told that. And now, seeing his father and hearing him, he could believe it. From dark hair to white-green eyes, facial features, and body stature, his father's genes had passed down to him—and from him to his own children.

Seth removed the data disk and inserted the crystal. The holographic display resolved into his mother's image. Age lined her face. Her freckles were lighter. Beside her sat his stepfather. Gray hairs had replaced the curly, dark hair. His brown eyes were weaker yet still held a youthfulness to them.

"Seth, we finally were able to track down the last of the feeds. GFT had kept them buried deep within their mainframe. Some were salvaged from our own files. The others were stolen from our Antarctica base and kept by GFT. They never gave up their objective in capturing your father nor the others until you were about five years old. The feeds are slightly corrupted. There's no audio, and some of them are only snippets of our time on the *Nightingale*, in Antarctica, and here in Alaska. The last bit . . . " Tears flooded her eyes. Huey, his eyes suspiciously wet, slid an arm around her and pulled her into his side. "The last file . . . just know that your father sacrificed his life for all of us."

She faded away, and in her place was a grainy feed of what looked like a hodge-podge of ships that were pieced together. Ice grew everywhere, and so many people walked around. There were children darting about and people working.

A man, his bearing and stature hinting at a soldier, came into view, holding a book—Seth's father. He walked and read as he rounded the corner of the walkway and started descending the stairs. His hand lashed out and caught an object midair.

When he looked up, a grin stretched across his face as he threw the ball back into the area below him. He closed the book and slid it between his vest and shirt before signing to someone off screen. *Not fast enough, my beautiful angel. Try again.*

Three children ran up the stairs and started pulling at him, dragging him off screen.

The screen changed. It was blurry, yet Seth could make out his father and a group of men apparently exercising. He recognized them all, from Dan to Devon and James to Jackson—former assassins. The image faded as they sank cross-legged to the floor.

The next one was a feed in a makeshift library of sorts. His father was nestled in the curvature of a window. His mother was seated in a small chair next to him. Uncle JJ and Aunt Trisha were on a small, cushioned bench, with his aunt reclined against his uncle's chest. They seemed content with each other's company as they read from their books. Seth zoomed in on the book in his father's hand and stifled a laugh. He was reading a psychology textbook. His father turned a page before reaching down and giving his mother an absentminded caress along her hair. A small smile flitted across his mother's face.

Then it changed to another feed, this one of his father screaming and bucking on a medlab table. Six men tried to hold him down. His great-grandmother rushed in and dosed him with something. Then his mother was there, along with Uncle JJ.

His mother's voice filtered through. "What you are seeing is when the serum repaired his neural pathways. All his memories came flooding back; and for five days, he was lost inside his own mind, reliving everything—from his parents' and Stephen's death to his torture to his missions. He told us that a voice told him that it was time to awaken. And that is exactly what happened. Your father woke up that day."

The video went on for long minutes. Then it fizzled into another grainy output of his father sitting on the edge of the bed and talking to his great-grandmother.

Seth sat through video after video. Some seemed to be out of order until he realized that the first batch was what they had on file. The second batch was what GFT had gained. His father was shown fighting on a catwalk, his moves so fast that they seemed to blur. Then he was on a ship—just glimpses of him moving about or sitting in the observation lounge.

One video gave him a few seconds of his parents' wedding. Then he was seeing his father at the compound—building the greenhouse; gardening and having a dirt fight with some boys; bringing in recent elk kills with Michael, Peter, and JJ, laughing at some of the children who played nearby as he watched.

There he was in the commons area talking and laughing with John. He was with Uncle JJ as they built the fishing pier. Seth smiled when he saw his father and mother in their quarters. They were setting up the recording, laughing. It had captured them playfully fighting with each other while setting it up. Then his father kissed her, pressing her back against the couch they sat on. His right hand held the back of her head as their kiss deepened; and with the other, he slapped the camera down to the floor.

Seth's face heated. He was quite glad there was no audio with that one.

His mother's voice filtered back through. "I wasn't sure about letting you see that. It happened right before he recorded your message. But I wanted you to see and understand that Jules really loved me. He cared for me. And I loved him, too. These were the good times. The other crystal contains the missions and the fight—the fight that cost him his life."

Her voice cracked. "I put them on a separate crystal so that you can look at them when you feel the time is right. Your father never did anything half-measure. He put his heart and mind into everything. And he really loved us all. Those few months he was with us—those were his happiest times.

"I've told you the stories growing up, Seth. You were named after him. And I waited until my death to let you see this because I wanted you to know the extent of why we kept you here behind our walls. We loved you so much, we wanted you safe—to be able to live and enjoy what your father had never had the chance to experience: life."

Chapter Two

SIERRA

Sierra looked around what they dubbed The Groove, a circular depression with intricate designs created to channel melting snow and rain into the grate in the middle. It had been dug in the middle of the courtyard where a grove of pine trees grew—trees that both of her grandfathers had planted. Under those tall pines were a variety of ferns and benches carved from stones.

Her gaze fell on the bench nearest to her. Her father had created that one when he was a teenager. Granddad always told her and Stephen that it was during her father's "restless days." A lot of statues, monuments, benches, and even arches that peppered their massive compound were made by her father's hands. They reminded her of the ancient days, when people mingled in what were called parks. But this one—the moss-covered bench—was her favorite. It was simple in design but elegant; a sunflower with its head full of seed stood over the three pine cones clustered together.

Her father had said the design had a specific message, but he never told her what it was. Maybe she should grab another of the old tomes from the library and learn about architecture. That was what her father had been studying way back then—that and art.

She let her gaze roam over the area. Most of the children had left. Only a few still mingled—chatting, laughing, and sharing stories. She had combined her class with an older class that was usually taught by Catherine Schau. And that had proven to be an interesting challenge.

Sierra stuffed the last of the books into her satchel. One of the children approached her as she slung her bag across her shoulder and down her side. "Yes, Stacey?"

The eight-year-old smiled up at Sierra. "Do you think it would be possible if I turned in the assignment early?"

Sierra almost laughed. Each week was the same question; and each week, she gave the same answer. "Of course. Just send it to my link." Her foot bumped a small pine cone. Out of habit, she plucked it from the ground.

Stacey walked alongside her as they left The Groove. "Okay. Mom said that we were heading out to Upper Bay this week."

"If that's the case, you can always send it in once you get back. You know there is no time limit on your Bible school assignments."

"I know." Stacey paused, placing a hand on Sierra's arm to stop her. "But Mom said she and Dad were thinking about staying in Upper Bay. I thought I should go ahead and finish what I can."

Sierra smiled. "Stacey, if you stay here or in Upper Bay, you can still send your assignment via link. But if you think you need to finish early, by all means, go ahead." She slid her arm around the girl's shoulders and began walking back to the central building. "I take it you are afraid that you will end up moving there."

A sigh escaped the girl. "Yes. All my friends are here. I don't know anyone in Upper Bay."

"Well, I do. And when you get there, go to the library. Ask for Jensen. And tell her Sierra sent you."

"Really?"

"Absolutely. Jensen will love to be your guide and show you everything." Sierra waved across the wide path at the girl's parents. "You go on now. I'll see you again."

Stacey gave her a quick hug before bounding toward her parents, who waited next to a rickshaw car. Once she climbed in, she gave Sierra one last wave before the automatic system drove them away to the east side of the compound.

Sierra turned away and mulled over her word: *compound.* They lived in a city now—Alaska Compound. It had gone from a small compound to a larger encampment to a small town to a city. Yet for some reason, most everyone here still referred to their home as a compound. She guessed habits do die hard.

At that thought, she looked down at the pine cone. Ever since she was a child, she would try to find an item that contained the Golden Ratio. It had started as a challenge issued by her brother, and now the habit continued. She studied the pine cone and then followed the closed seeds, trying to see what Stephen saw: perfect symmetry of the Fibonacci number shown in a spiral and something he once told her could be found in nature and in architecture.

A slight floral scent drifted across the air. The wind blew against her, and the scent grew stronger, mingled with a deep, spicy musk— Stephen. He had been with Danica again. Sierra shook her head, shoved the pine cone into her satchel, and adjusted her course.

Stephen might be her twin, but he was completely different from her. Her mother's voice drifted through her thoughts. *Your brother is a moody monkey. His rebelliousness will end eventually, but I pray it will happen before he does something stupid and drive me insane.*

Well, if she wanted to keep her mother sane, she would have to keep an eye on Stephen. There he was. His dark hair glistened under the bright Alaskan sun. With hands shoved deep into the back pockets of his tattered green military pants, he strolled through the throng of people milling about. He glanced to the left. His face had darkened from being out in the sun so much, yet she could see the brightness in his eyes. He was up to something.

She paused at the corner of commissary. He was blending in with the crowd yet staying to the edge as he meandered toward the medlab building. Sierra turned and skirted the far side of the commissary and hurried to the side entrance of Main Medlab. With it being Sunday, no one would be using this entrance as much.

She slid her card through the keypad and entered the darkened hallway. She leaned against the wall by the corner and waited.

It didn't take long. The keypad next to her lit green a second before the door slid open.

Stephen didn't glance her way. "Still stalking me?"

Sierra laughed. "I smelled you across the way. You were with Danica again."

Stephen rolled his eyes and kept walking, causing her to have to jog to catch up. "You going to give me a lecture on why I shouldn't? Do I need to remind you about Bobby?"

She scowled at her brother. Just like him to throw her one mistake in her face. "Seriously, Stephen?" Sierra fell in step with him. "You know Scripture just as well as I do. And you know right and wrong." She shrugged. "It's your life. Just be prepared for the consequences."

Her brother glanced at her. A small bit of guilt flooded his eyes before being erased by mockery. "Smelled me, huh?"

"Danica wears the jasmine perfume that Mary creates. And you haven't bathed lately, apparently." Sierra sniffed and then pinched her nostrils, her voice becoming nasally. "And it shows."

A deep, rumbling laugh flowed from Stephen. His smile softened his words. "You're a pest, you know that?" He nudged her with his shoulder, almost sending her into the wall. "And I did, too, shower, brat."

Sierra slid her arm around his waist. She could never stay angry at her brother for long. "So, tell me, what are you up to?"

Stephen let his own arm go around her shoulders and steered her toward the research division, lowering his voice. "I am going to look at my bloodwork today."

"You and Dad have the same obsession." For them to be so much alike, the way they butted heads over the tiniest of topics was an enigma. Yet their passions and obsessions ran along the same path.

"I know." He paused outside the doors and leaned against the wall to face Sierra. "There is a clue in there, a reason why we have to go through all this."

"Because we are enhanced, that's why." Sierra shook her head at him. "Our genes hold the secret to new medications and treatments. Think of it. We are the key to evolution and advancement. If what we carry inside us can help someone with an illness or a defect or heal them from a wound, think of how many we can help. Look at what Dad did for Auntie CeeCee."

"It didn't help Grandma Abby, now did it?" A bit of anger flowed across his face.

"Grandma Abby told Dad no. She didn't want him to do anything because it was her time to go." Sierra reached out and brushed a wayward strand from her brother's forehead. "Ven, you can only do so much. Now, tell me the real reason why you are here."

A ghost of a smile drifted across her brother's lips at her nickname for him. He stared at her. The white flecks in his eyes seemed to darken with the rest of the green. "I can never keep a secret from you." He pressed his lips into a tight line before replying. "I'm leaving."

"What?"

He turned from her, pulled a card from his pocket, and ran it through the keypad. "I'm leaving. Not today. Maybe not tomorrow. But soon."

"Why, Ven?" She followed him into the lab, casting a look over her shoulder. "Did you deactivate the security?"

"No, I used a loop."

Leave it to Stephen to hack the systems. Like a little puppy, she practically clipped his heels as he walked to the back stations. She settled down next to him and waited as he began hacking into their father's terminal. "You know he'll find out about this—and that you used Danica's card. I saw her print on the back."

He shook his head at her. "Eventually, he will. But I'll be gone by then." He glanced at the corner of the room and beyond the clear glass. "One of these days, I'll be able to get inside his work area. That's where he's keeping most of his research. For now, though, his general station will have to do." Stephen's fingers flew over the keys. Row after row pulled up on the screen.

Sierra watched as he highlighted a few, entered more commands, and switched from one line of code to another. She only understood the basics of programming and code. It never interested her as it did Grandma Abby, Granddad Huey, and Stephen. Even though her father dabbled in it at times, even his interests truly lay elsewhere. Like her father, she enjoyed studying biology, herbology, and history—her mother's interest. Stephen reached past her and touched the screen on the terminal.

"See that marker right there?" His fingernail tapped the screen and a holographic projection rose from the surface in front of them. The double helix rotated. Another rose next to it.

"You duplicated it?"

"No, apparently God did." Stephen cast her a brief glance before reaching into the projection and using his hands to zoom further, rotating it until the individual nucleotides could be seen. "Those are us. We share the same section in this strand."

Sierra reached into the projection and flipped it around. It was different. The bonds attaching the strands were normal, but the makeup of this section didn't seem like the others. "Is this the only one? And why does this one seem different?"

Stephen leaned back. "So far, yes. It's the only one. But in each of our bloodwork, Dad has found sections that are different from others." He brushed the projection to the side, erasing it, and pulled up another. The floating helix was red throughout one side and blue on the other. "He has been studying this one—T-C 574. I don't know enough about genetics, Si, but this is what makes us different."

"That's the manipulation?"

"Yes."

They stared at the floating helix for several long moments until Stephen broke the silence. "I've been coming in here almost every night trying to figure out what Dad has found. I can only surmise that this is a new genetic code." He leaned to his right and plucked a data crystal from the foam holder next to their father's research books. He tapped the console in front of them. Another projection superimposed itself onto the DNA section in front of them. Some of the nucleotides matched, yet a majority of the sequences were different. "We inherited what he has and then inherited what Mom has. That combination created something new."

"Meaning we are more than they are?"

"Could be. Maybe a lot more." Stephen propped his elbows on the table and studied the projections. "The key is there, floating in front of us—the reason why we are prisoners."

Sierra shook her head and stood. Her brother regarded her. "We aren't prisoners, Stephen. But staying here gives us protection. The world outside isn't safe for us."

"That's brainwashing, Si."

A sigh escaped her. Same argument every week. She leaned down and kissed the top of his head. "Ven, I love you. But this obsession with our blood and the outside will come to no good. Oh! I brought you something." She reached into her bag and brought out the young pine cone. "Golden?"

She always wondered how he could see the golden ratio in everything. From trees to plants to buildings and even people's faces, Stephen had once told her that it was like having the golden ratio diagram superimposed on the object. He could follow the lines and see its perfection.

His eyes crinkled in a smile as he accepted the gift. Slender fingers traced the scales one way and then the other. "It's a perfect Golden Ratio spiral. Thank you."

She left him smoothing his fingers over the cone while he studied the information in front of him. Sierra gave him one last glance. And in that glance, she saw sadness, a hardness to him, and something dark. Within him, a storm was churning.

He would come home tonight. Yet she felt it in her heart that it would be the last time.

She lifted a whispered prayer. "Where he goes, Lord, I will go."

Chapter Three
STEPHEN

Stephen placed the last crystal into the foam bed and closed the case. He turned back to the terminal and erased his tracks. His father would eventually discover the hack, but it would take a few days—unless he used the GHOST. But then, there was no reason to use that program. No reason . . .

He leaned back in the chair, one fingernail tapping against the table's surface. His grandmother had kept a copy in her quarters. When she was sick, she and Granddad Huey had moved into his parents' quarters. After her death, Granddad Huey remained and would so for the time being. So, her program should be in his room.

His gaze fell on the stack of flat data crystals by the terminal. It wouldn't take much to get a quick copy of the program. He would only need the portion to hack mainframes and security—and maybe communications.

He plucked one off the stack and shoved it into his pants' side pocket. Tonight, he would sneak into the room. Granddad Huey always left around ten to go see Granddad JJ or to visit with his cousin Alex.

Stephen pushed away from the table and headed for the hermetically sealed doors. His wrist monitor beeped. Only five minutes left before the loop program he sent to security would end. When he walked by Danica's station, he dropped her card on the floor near her chair. Let her think she had dropped it when she had left at the end of her shift.

Warmer air met him as he pushed through the double doors and into the quiet corridor outside the research rooms. A few whispered conversations flowed from around the corners to his right. Ahead of him, two of the medtechs walked, discussing the data on the datapad in their hands. Stephen veered to his left. No one paid any attention to him as he merged with the meager crowd in the lobby.

Once out the side door, his monitor beeped again. Security was back up. And his comm unit blared from his waistband.

Stephen glanced down at the caller and growled. Mom again. He inserted the earpiece and tapped it. "Mom."

"Stephen, are you coming home tonight? Dinner is about ready, and I—"

"I'm heading that way, Mom." He picked his way across the half-frozen pathway between the buildings. "Give me about five minutes."

A bit of relief sounded through her voice. "Okay. I'll set your place. Granddad Huey won't be here tonight. He and Dad are heading to Lower Town."

"What's in Lower Town?"

"Your granddad didn't say. But it has your father agitated even more. So . . . "

"You want me to distract Dad." Stephen smiled. "I can do that for you, Mom." He pushed down the twinge of guilt that started to rise as he continued. "In fact, I was hoping for Dad's help on something."

He didn't miss the curious lilt to her voice when she replied, "Great. Then I will see you in just a few. Love you, honey."

"Love you, too, Mom." He slipped the earpiece from his ear and reattached it to the comm unit on his belt. He really should grab the newer holographic units. But he hated to think about people being able to lip-read any of the conversations. Better they had just a one-sided eavesdropping session.

A cold wind bit into him as he rounded the last larger building and made his way toward the shoreline. His parents loved the sea and had claimed a spot nearest the shore. Although their sleeping quarters were underground with a view of the underwater life, he couldn't bear the thought of being surrounded by ocean water. His father had his sleeping quarters built above ground and with a skylight, so he could watch the sky and stars. And on those perfect nights, the aurora borealis would flow across, soothing him with the greens and blues of its lights.

A part of him would miss this place. But it was still a prison, no matter how much he loved the northern lights. No matter how much he enjoyed having Danica's attention. No matter how much he loved his family. Outside those gates was his freedom—and mystery.

And tonight . . . tonight he would start his planning. It would require precision to carry out: from slipping beneath his dad's and Michael's watchful gazes to hiding from security before finding the right spot to cross the wall—or cross under it.

He shuddered at the thought. No, he would find a way over it or through its gates. The next supply run should happen soon. He may be able to find a way to disappear with them.

His thoughts were interrupted when Michael stepped out of the shadows along the boardwalk leading to his home.

"Deep in thought?"

Stephen smiled and looked up at the taller older man. "Always. You eating with us tonight?"

"Your mother asked." Michael fell into step with Stephen. "Your father needs a distraction."

"What happened?" Worry laced his question. Rarely did his father become distracted or flustered.

"Nothing bad. But your grandmother left some data crystals for him. And he watched the last batch."

Stephen paused. Michael stopped and waited. "What were they?"

For a few long moments, Michael considered his words. Then the former Zulu assassin looked back at him. "They contained everything you ever wanted to know about your grandfather, Julius Williams."

With that answer, Michael continued down the street with Stephen following quietly behind him. They approached his home, smells of roasted meat and sweet rolls greeting them when the hatch slid open.

Throughout dinner, his father had kept up most of the conversation, with Michael inserting only a few comments now and then. Now Stephen was taking advantage of the lull between mealtime and sleep to begin his quest.

Stephen glanced over his shoulder as he set his dessert plate on the counter next to his father's terminal in the study. The sound of Sierra's movements indicated she had passed by and was heading to their parents' bedroom. Above him, the sliding door on the balcony clicked closed; and the footfalls of Michael and his dad faded.

He kept his head cocked to the side until a semi-silence reigned in the room. Only the muffled voices of his sister and mom sounded in the dark. Stephen pulled the chair from the far end of the desk and sat. The cushion sank from his weight as he twirled it around to face the terminal.

Several times, Sierra had made a few jabs at him, hinting at his relationship with Danica. His mom had raised a brow at a couple of her comments, casting a narrowed glance at him; but she stayed quiet on the subject.

Dad on the other hand . . . even though he was talking with Michael about the upcoming supply run, his hand had fisted over the napkin by his drink. Why couldn't Sierra just leave it alone? Yet he knew why. She didn't like the road he was traveling and wanted to get their parents involved to stop him without having to blurt out the truth about his affair. His sister was always looking out for his soul. Maybe he should remind her that he was the oldest, not her.

He chuckled at that thought as he sorted through the crystals. She would have only replied with a "by only nine minutes, amoeba brain" and then punch his shoulder. That spot on his shoulder had grown quite accustomed to her muscle-knotting punches. He paused at the pale blue crystal. It was marked with his grandmother's symbol. Stephen traced it with his forefinger.

All those years he had seen it, he never asked her what the Σ meant. Sigma? Enigma? Sum? He should have asked. And now his opportunity was lost.

He placed the crystal in the slot. The holographic display activated. His grandmother appeared, age pulling at her face; yet this was from at least five years ago. Beside her sat Granddad Huey, his gray hair peppered with darker strands.

His granddad spoke. "Seth, we placed these files in order. Many of them are corrupted. Some have sound. Others, we stripped the sound. Trust us, son, you do not want to hear what happened and what was done to your father. As you go through these files, you will see why we kept you here in Alaska Country and never allowed you to leave."

His grandmother covered Granddad's hand and squeezed. "It was hard to put this together. And that's why we placed it all on a separate crystal. It was our hope that you would watch this only after watching the data disks and seeing who your father truly was."

The image fizzled, and the first file began. Overhead cameras provided the angle. A man, stripped down to a thin, short-sleeved shirt and underpants, walked in the center of four guards. Scars covered his arms and legs. The feed switched to a medlab as they crossed the threshold. The man stepped up on a platform. Metal bands circled his chest, waist, and thighs. A neural relay was lowered onto his head. Then the feed switched to a full-frontal view.

Medstudies flowed around him. He suddenly strained against the bands as probes stabbed into him. Just as quickly, he quieted and stared straight ahead, almost as if he was glaring into the camera. Stephen paused the feed.

The man's face—he saw that face every day in his father and every morning in his own face. He zoomed on the polished, metal surface near his grandfather's head. It reflected a metal wall. Stephen pursed his lips. The camera was hidden behind the wall, so not metal but a mirror. He zoomed back out and allowed the feed to play.

He flinched when his grandfather suddenly broke through his bands and strangled the medtech, holding his lifeless body like a ragdoll before throwing him down. The stories that were told of his grandfather's strength paled in comparison to actually seeing it in action.

Stephen absorbed the information, pausing at times to study the readouts on the monitors. So, his grandfather was a beta, sub-alpha personality with delta-gamma traits. Delta for healing. Gamma for learning. The same as his dad but not himself. His was slightly different. Stephen reached out and pulled up his dad's medical files on them. He looked at the comparisons that were entered.

Julius Williams, β/α, beta-alpha, Δ/γ, delta-gamma

Seth Williams, β/α, beta-alpha, Δ/γ, delta-gamma

Stephen Williams, α/α, alpha-alpha, θ/γ, theta-gamma

Sierra Williams, β/β, beta-beta, θ/γ, theta-gamma

Tamara Salvatore Williams, β/β, beta-beta, Δ/θ, delta-theta

Was the difference between him and his sister because of their mother's genes? He made a mental note to check another time and see if that was the key. Maybe Granddad JJ's genes had more influence than originally thought.

He returned to the data crystal and sped through the files—days' worth of this. His grandfather was stripped, injected with the serum, and interrogated. He had killed a few medstudies at one point and held a broken stylus at the throat of a general, but he didn't kill the man. Instead, he twirled the stylus through his fingers and stuffed it into the general's breast pocket.

Stephen half-expected his grandfather to be punished. Yet the general nodded and strode out of the medlab, waving for the guards to take his grandfather back to the cells.

He sped up the next files. More torture. More training and conditioning. The feed fizzled once, and then he was watching his grandfather in a hospital. Surgeons worked on him as the general stood in the overwatch section above the surgery room. Then it monitored his grandfather in a recovery room with a bluish fluid in an intravenous bag that was hooked to him and flowing into his body. One feed showed Granddad JJ sitting beside his grandfather.

His grandmother's voice overlayed the next video. "These are just a few of the security files we could salvage of the fights when GFT invaded our Antarctica compound. The last feed, which you can only access with a bioprint, is the final battle we had here."

Her heavy sigh rasped across the mic. "Please remember, Seth, your father is a child of God. And his life here was quite happy. He sacrificed everything for us, for you. These files are only to show you why leaving here is so dangerous. GFT had never stopped looking for him, nor will they stop if they know he had a child. Or that the others had a child."

Stephen skipped the rest of what his grandmother said and went to the last battle that she talked about. He had heard the stories. Michael had told him some of it. Granddad JJ had told him a bit about fighting side by side with his grandfather.

The prompt for the bioprint flashed before him. He paused. Would his grandmother have included him and Sierra, too. Or even his mother? Stephen reached out and touched the virtual scanner. The bar ran down and then up before lighting blue.

When the holograph faded, he almost feared that he had tripped a deactivation code and would have to somehow gain his father's bioprint. But that fear was allayed as the file began. Apparently, his grandmother knew him well.

The feed was a bit grainy. Some of it seemed to be pieced together from different angles and different security monitors in order to create a whole image. Low-lying tanks advanced from the distance. His grandfather and the other former assassins had fanned out. Plasma bolts shot everywhere. Concussion bombs dropped from high above.

Stephen's heart pounded as he watched the images play out before him. The feeds barely kept up with the speed of the men that fought— and woman. He paused and zoomed in on a hill. Mandy stood with Dan, their rifles aimed at the advancing forces past the wall.

He restarted the crystal. A tear tracked down his face as he watched a plasma bolt slam through his grandfather, who fell to his knees while he kept his rifle pointed at his killer. The rest were rushing toward his grandfather as he fell to the side. Stephen paused the feed again and enlarged the grainy image until he was looking into his grandfather's eyes—half-white, half-green, bright, unfocused. There was a reflection of a light above him.

His eyes, though—Stephen reached to the side and pulled up the identification files of his father, his sister, and himself. The green color was the same—vivid, bright. The bone structure was angular and sharp yet softened by the curvature of their lips and nose. How much of his grandfather had passed down to them?

Φ

"I had been suspecting that he was seeing Danica. She would always light up in this smile whenever he came around." Seth propped against the balcony wall and listened to the lapping water on the shore.

Michael settled into a lounge chair near the wall and grunted at the audible pop of his joints. "Oh, I'm getting old. So, what do you plan to do about them?"

"I don't know. He's an adult. She's an adult—although a much older adult than Stephen. I'll just let it play out. I doubt it will last. I already know he's seen her today. Her perfume lingers in his hair." Seth glanced over his shoulder at the glass doors. "He keeps pausing the feeds."

Michael nodded and leaned back in his chair, staring at the stars above. "Do you expect any less?"

"No." Seth smiled. "Stephen is too curious. He wants answers."

"Why not give them to him?" Michael closed his eyes.

"Because, Michael, Stephen will never be satisfied with just one answer. He will want to know more about the studies and research. I can't let him know what I've discovered—not the whole truth. Probably why he's with Danica, thinking he can gain access to my terminal." Seth held up a hand to stop Michael's reply and cocked his ear toward the balcony door. "He's switched to the data disks."

"Ah, he wants to know his grandfather."

"He knows who he was, Michael." Seth peeked over the wall as the door below them swished open. Tamara and Sierra strolled underneath him and headed toward the small pier attached to their home. The two women linked arms and ambled at a slow pace. "Stephen wants to know why I won't allow him to leave. He doesn't know that I had installed a security program on my workstation—the one that isn't protected by the GHOST."

"You laid a trap?"

"I have to know why that rebellious son of mine is so determined."

"What did he find?"

"Only that which I allowed him to find—the genetic studies on our DNA code. I let him see that there was a variation in our blood." Seth pushed away and turned toward Michael. "The other descendants do not have it. Only my kids—a dual code, a dyad gene."

Michael opened one eye and regarded him. "Explain."

"They are fraternal twins. They share much of the same genetic codes; yet as with every individual, DNA is unique. They may carry many of the same alleles; but there are always a few that are different, gained from one or both parents. With them, Stephen and Sierra have one sequence that is the same; and I have never seen this variation before. The coding is different."

"So, you think Jules' manipulation that passed along to you and the diminished manipulation in JJ passed along to Tamara did what?"

"Created a new subset—a new DNA sequence and one that will not fade away. It's the dominant code. And the more I study it, the more I fear it."

Michael sat forward and stared hard at Seth. After a few seconds, he shook his head. "Don't play GFT nor God."

Seth plopped down on his lounge chair in the corner, ignoring Michael's statement. "Do you know what will happen if anyone finds out what my children carry?" He leaned his head back and folded his hands over his stomach. "It was just happenstance that I stumbled upon it. I keep trying to search to see if I can find the code in me or in Tamara. But so far, nothing. And now, learning that there's a faction that survived—one that has been continuing with the serum research . . . " Seth raised his head and glanced at the balcony door again. "He just finished watching."

Φ

Sierra smiled at her mother and lowered herself onto the end of the pier. Cold water encircled her feet. Maybe to others, it would have been freezing; but thanks to genetics, it didn't affect her as much.

"Did you and Dad have a hard time keeping your relationship a secret?"

For the last hour, her mom had been pressing her for her secret and then regaling Sierra with the story of how she and Dad began dating.

"We thought we did." Lines crinkled in the corners of her eyes as she laughed and eased down cross-legged by Sierra. "It was about two weeks before your granddad confronted us. I thought he was going to kill Seth. We had grown up together. But it wasn't until I was seventeen that I started seeing him as the man I wanted to marry."

"Was it weird to have Dad call Granddad 'Uncle JJ' and then start being with you?"

"It felt weird at first. But not because of that. It was because your dad and I had already shared so many secrets between us." Her mother laughed quietly as she apparently replayed some humorous memories in her head. Then she spoke so softly that the gentle, lapping waters almost drowned her out. "So many secrets."

Sierra smiled and studied her mom. She reached out and placed her hand next to her mom's. Chestnut skin contrasted with her light golden skin. "Why didn't I inherit your color? Or your hair?" She pulled a strand of her wavy dark brown hair over her shoulder. "I always wanted your curls."

Her mother slid Sierra's hand between her own and squeezed. "Honey, don't dismiss what God has given you. You have the shape of my eyes, the same hands." She turned Sierra's hand over in her own and traced the palm. "Just because you didn't inherit my coloring doesn't mean you don't carry it within you."

"But, Mom—"

"No." Her mom scooted closer and cupped Sierra's cheek. "Sierra, after learning more about your father's research, the genes you carry are strong. They come down from Julius Williams, your grandfather. Be proud of that. He was a fine man. You are my daughter, and I am so proud of you."

"I always wanted to look like you, though. Felt as though I wasn't what you wanted me to be. You know, not enough of you."

Her mother sighed and rested her hands in her lap as she gazed across the water. The stars reflected in her deep amber eyes. "I come from African Province blood and Ecuadorian Territory blood. I may have taken a bit more after my father, but I gained a lot from my mother."

She turned her gaze back to Sierra. "And you, Sierra, are a product of me and your father. Imagine all that: African, Ecuadorian, French, Romanian, and Irish. And that's just what we know. God created people to be unique. And you . . . you gained more from your father because what he carries is more dominant that what I carry. Don't belittle that. Despite all that, you are not the sum of your blood or genes. You are a child of God, a follower of Christ. Your essence is defined by Christ." She picked up a lock of Sierra's hair and twirled it around her finger. "Not in the color or texture of your hair. Not the tone of your skin."

Sierra sighed and lowered her gaze back to the water. "I understand. I just wish I was more like you."

"Like me?" Her mother started laughing. "Sweetie, you are more like me than you think. If you don't believe me, ask your granddad."

Maybe she should. But the words her mom said had hit hard at her heart. Maybe she had been overthinking the situation. She played with the end of her hair. There was a hint of curl to her hair, though. And it was the same shade of her mother's when she was younger.

Her mom uncrossed from her position and moved over until she was at Sierra's side and dangled her own sandaled feet into the water. "So, if you aren't going to tell me what secret you are holding, do you want to tell me about Stephen and Danica?"

Sierra whipped her gaze to her mother. "I thought my hints were falling on deaf ears."

"Maybe your father's deaf ears. But not your mother's." She kicked at the water, sending a few drops into the air. "I had been wondering where he was staying when he disappeared all those times for days."

"I'm not sure if he truly loves her or is just using her or if it's mutual on both sides. And if I mention it to him, he just throws my mistake with Bobby in my face." Sierra leaned back on her hands and arched a brow at her mom. "If I have a child, am I going to have these psychic mom powers you seem to have?"

Her mom chuckled. "I think it begins at the toddler stage."

"Oh, boy." Sierra smiled. "If I tell you what I suspect about Stephen, promise to not say anything to Dad—at least for a few days. Stephen is planning something."

"And you want to find out first." Her mom gave a half-smile. "Here we go again."

She nodded at her mom's statement. Yep, here they went again—another repeat of spying on Stephen. Figure out what he was about to do and then stop it before he put himself in danger. Ever since they were teens, she had been playing this role. And she was beginning to tire of it. Was she truly to be her brother's keeper?

Stephen leaned back in the chair and stared at the darkened terminal. Seeing those last few recordings of his grandfather smiling, laughing, and playing with children and then seeing the love between his grandparents . . . Stephen scrubbed his hands over his face and took a deep breath.

He wasn't nearly as ready as he thought to see what was collected on the disks and crystals. So much information, and it all began at Medlab Twelve. They had created who they were and who he was now.

Stephen tapped his forefinger against his bottom lip. Medlab Twelve. He could find the history on it in the main security building, though he would have to hack into the elders' mainframe for the more sensitive material. That was doable. And while there, he could gain the next supply run schedule.

Scrub the idea of leaving here and discovering what lay beyond the borders of Alaska Country. He needed to find out what made him . . . *him*. He needed the key to his genetics and who he was. He needed answers to why he was made and what made him—answers that would free him from his captivity and imprisonment, answers to why he had to be different and why he was referred to as "people like you."

Danica's words haunted him. She didn't mean for them to cut him. But they did, and they cut deep. He was different. He was an oddity. And sometimes, he could see the fear in other's eyes, wondering if he would be like what his grandfather was designed to be in the beginning.

He wanted normal. He deserved normal. And he would find a way to make himself normal. Or he would find a way to make himself more. One way or another, he would be what he wanted to be, not what others wanted him to be and not what God created him to be. It would be what Stephen wanted.

As he picked up his dessert plate, the slice of pie uneaten and cold, the thought of what he wanted to be played around in this head—a thought that had no answer. How could he answer a question that he still couldn't understand?

He climbed the short steps that led to the main part of the house. A quick glance out the glass doors showed that his father and Michael were still talking. Granddad Huey's room was just before the ladder that led to his topside room. He could quickly grab a copy of the GHOST and then go to bed without anyone being the wiser.

It was a plan. And he would begin it tonight.

Chapter Four

JSIN

The air from the ventilation kicked in. Alpha Zero, designation JSN-001, stood near the bars of his cell and waited. It was time. The midday allotment was on its way. Beyond the reinforced, titanium-steel alloy doors, footsteps approached. Hard soles. So, a guard then. Another set fell softer on the metal plating of the corridor. No cane—that meant a medstudy today.

Alpha Zero backed up a pace from the bars and glanced at the mirror that was set into the wall and protected by a fused pane of glass. Cyan eyes within a bronze face stared back at him. He touched his cheekbone under his right eye. The scar was gone. A small red mark was the only indication of the surgery that had happened three weeks prior.

That surgery had turned his eyes from hazel to cyan—stripped him of the melanin and added collagen to his stroma to help stabilize the neural implants. As he lay in recovery, his handlers spoke of the heightened vision. And he had to agree. His eyes were able to pick up almost every wavelength now. His world became a riot of colors and lines, as if everything was super-embossed upon each other. Yet cyan was unnatural.

He turned away. He had been through seventeen surgeries that he could remember; ten body enhancements giving him stronger muscles, denser bones, and much more; and thousands of injections of the serum. The biofeedback was supposed to keep him from questioning what they were doing; yet seven months ago, that had all changed. He began to remember the procedures, the surgeries, the indoctrination. Only, he couldn't tell anyone.

He touched his throat and cleared it. A guttural vibration was the only sound that issued from his mouth. Once, long ago, he could talk. Now, though, he couldn't remember the sound of his own voice.

Serum Seventy-seven had rendered him mute—permanently. Yet as he meditated on that thought, maybe it wasn't the serum. What if it was a surgery he hadn't yet remembered?

Alpha Zero stretched his neck to each side, loosening the tight tendons. Those thoughts could be visited later. He relaxed his shoulders and let his arms dangle to the side and rest against his bare thighs. The black underclothes they provided barely warded off the chill of the room—more of his conditioning.

The door at the end clanged open. Within moments, the guard stood at the bars with his meal tray. Medstudy Jankins motioned Alpha Zero closer.

"Move to the bars."

Alpha Zero stepped forward and slid his arm through the opening without being prompted.

The medstudy arched his brow at him but said nothing as he placed the hypospray against Alpha Zero's skin. The serum burned into him, heating his veins. "You may consume your meal now. Examination three-four-seven will commence in a half hour."

His meal tray was deposited on the floor. Alpha Zero waited until they backed up and walked away before he bent down to retrieve his food.

The Juliet Serum Initiative's logo was stamped on the metal lid. Alpha Zero frowned at it. This was the first time something like this was given to him. Another test, then. He retreated to his bunk and sat cross-legged on the hard cushion.

A spicy aroma wafted from the meat substitute that was rolled in a rice flour wrap. Small strips of green and orange vegetables stuck out the ends. Alpha Zero unwrapped the meat-like dish and poked through the ingredients. Nothing stood out. He picked up one sliver of orange and tasted it—carrot. Then he did the same with the green one—cucumber. Nothing was on them. A pinch of the meat revealed it to be three varieties of smashed beans with rice. Nothing indicated any other foreign ingredient.

He rewrapped his meal and began eating. Maybe they had learned the last time they tried to get him to ingest one of their substances. He had thrown the food across the cell and into the corridor. For two days, he had refused to eat a meal. It was worth the punishment he had endured.

From what he could hear while he was being subjugated to rigorous and seemingly endless experimentations, the substances were a concoction of various poisons and tranquilizers. Their hope had been to see how his body would break them down. They hadn't counted on him being so cautious.

As he chewed his bite, he reached out and traced the logo. JSiN. Jay. Sin. Once, a few years back, there had been a medstudy named Jason Richards. Alpha Zero had developed a rapport with the man, yet the medstudy was transferred within a few months. Orders had been issued that no one was to interact with Alpha Zero after that.

He took another bite and ran his finger over the embossed letters again. *Jason.* That would be his name from now on. No more Alpha Zero. He would call himself Jason after the friend that had been taken away from him.

Who would he tell it to, though? He glanced up at the camera in the corner. There was no one for him around here. But one day . . .

Jason took another bite. One day, though, he would be able to leave. He'd be what they want for right now. But the man in his dreams said that the day would come when he would be able to leave. He just had to wait a little while longer.

Jason drained the small cup of water, and then replaced the lid, collected the tray, and set it outside his cell on the metal plated hallway. He could do what the man said. He had endured this long; he could endure a little more.

Hard soles sounded outside the closed hatch. They were coming back for him. Time for his neural biofeedback and more experimentation. Jason closed his eyes and sent his thought to the dream man, asking for strength to endure another session.

Quiet and long moments passed before the hard soles echoed down the corridor. And the tap-tap-tapping of a cane followed. Jason backed up a step and waited. Fear began to eat away at him; yet he controlled his expression, keeping that fear buried deep down.

The guard walked into view, bent and collected the empty tray, and then stood to the side as the medtech approached. Her cane tapped against the bars of his cells as she hobbled into view. Her white hair pinned tightly at the back of her head nearly stretched her face.

Yet Jason believed nothing would ever erase the deep wrinkles of age on the woman. Her ice-blue eyes studied him before she turned to a second guard who appeared.

"Take him to Medlab Twenty."

Jason fought against the tremors that threatened to overtake him. Medlab Twenty? He had only been there once before, yet it still lived in his nightmares.

The door clanged open. Jason stood as still as possible as the second guard clamped fusion cuffs around his wrists before prodding him out into the corridor. The medtech's mouth was drawn in an evil sneer as Jason passed by him.

Jason sniffed as her scent reached him. The stench of death lingered on her—the smell of decay, of something rotting within. He glanced at her, and her eyes hardened even more. She was dying. That was what he was smelling. She was sick, a growing cancer within her.

Was that why he was being used and manipulated? Was she trying to cheat death? Afraid of her own mortality?

Those thoughts flew through his mind in that brief second of meeting her eyes. Then he looked away. There was more to all this, and he would find out. He only needed to bide his time and wait for his opportunity.

Her cane began tapping as she followed. "Add twenty cc's of Paxolin-X. He's beginning to awaken."

Jason closed his mind to her words. It didn't matter what they did to him. It never lasted. The dream man had said it wouldn't harm him for long and to suffer just a bit longer. Then all would be made right.

The corridors flooded hot, then cold, then frigid as they wound their way through the labyrinth of the foundation's research facility.

They halted him outside a narrow doorway. His breath hung in a white vapor as he waited for the codes to cycle through the locking program. Then he was ushered into the small, dark room.

Her cane tapped away as she retreated to the overlook area above. The lights blossomed to a bath of dull red. Before him on a solid platform was what he feared. The cuffs were removed, and pulse rifles aimed his way as the guard motioned for him to climb into the elongated cylinder that stood on the platform.

Jason swallowed. His hands barely shook as he climbed inside, sliding his body down through the narrow opening. Once settled onto the cold, metal surface, automatic manacles snapped over his wrists, biceps, thighs, and ankles. The guard fastened a respirator around Jason's mouth and nose. Then the cover slid over the opening, encasing him in darkness.

Jason's heartbeat skipped. Outside the cylinder, the monitor registered his reaction with a beep. A medstudy's voice reached him.

"He's showing apprehension but calmed down almost immediately."

The intercom hissed before Medtech Bastion spoke, her voice sounding even more aged than her face through the staticky feed. "Good. He's learning to control those reactions. Proceed with the experiment."

Hot fluid cascaded into the cylinder, covering his body, scalding him. Jason flinched at the sensation. But the manacles held him in place, minimizing his movements and preventing him from forcing the cylinder open in order to escape the pain.

"He's fighting against the pain. Registering beta three and beta two. Bounced twice into alpha."

The fluid began to cool. A hiss sounded beyond his feet, and more thick, scalding liquid flooded in. Jason closed his eyes against the force of the flow as it filled the tube he was in. Sounds outside his prison reached him, enhanced even more by the viscous fluid. His respirator rasped with his heavy breathing.

"Begin at three mils. Increase by a factor of three every five minutes for thirty minutes."

An electrical discharge zipped through the fluid and against his body. Jason arched against the pain.

"His vitals are stationary. Still at beta three."

Another round of discharge entered his body.

Medtech Bastion spoke again. "Initiate the serum."

He couldn't see the probes—not in his narrow confinement. But he felt them. The sharp instruments slid into his body—neck, arms, hips, legs, feet. Even his spine was pierced from probes underneath.

Agonizing pain surged through him. His mouth underneath the respirator opened in a silent scream. And as suddenly as it began, the pain ended. The serum still pumped into him, yet a gentle light lowered onto him, warming him like a soft blanket.

"Ma'am, he just entered gamma state."

"Good. What level is he at?"

There was a moment's hesitation. Jason barely opened his eyes as the medstudy replied, fear lacing his voice, "He's off the chart, ma'am."

Stephen waited, lying prone in the cramped maintenance ductwork above the command hub's main room. The skeleton crew, as his father referred to them, worked quietly at their monitors. Most of the room was encased in the dark dusk of the night sky that entered from the high windowpanes. In one more week, they would enter their dark season, and it was beginning to show.

A woman stood and whispered down to her coworker. "I'm heading to the commons. Want anything?"

The man rose from his chair. "It's a slow night. I'll come with you." He turned to their companion on the far side of the room. "Hansen, you want anything?"

"Yeah, man. Bring me some of that vanilla spice drink."

Stephen's mouth watered at the thought of the delectable drink. He should have grabbed himself some before climbing into the ductwork. It would probably be gone by the time he made it back to the commons—the price he paid for this excursion.

The door hissed closed as the two left. Hansen groaned as he stretched in his chair before standing and retreating to the extreme far side where the holographic table stood. Stephen waited and listened. A series of clicks indicated that he had activated the table. He glanced at his wrist monitor. This was the last security check of the outer perimeter before the morning crew took their stations. And no one would ever expect anyone but the technicians to be in the room. Why would they? There was no reason for anyone to slink around—no one except for him.

Hansen began humming quietly. Now was Stephen's chance.

He lifted the grate and set it to the side. Stephen poked his head out of the opening and quickly scanned the room. It was clear. Hansen's back was turned.

Stephen gripped the edge of the opening and flipped through. The sharp edge bit into his fingertips as he hung there, judging his landing. He let go and silently dropped to the floor. Hansen was still engrossed in the readouts.

Within seconds, Stephen had his copy of the GHOST out of his pocket and inserted into the mainframe by the wall. It cycled through the codes in two seconds. Stephen grinned and slipped his data crystal into the slot, downloading the information. As soon as it was completed, he disconnected the GHOST, pocketing both the hacking chip and data crystal. He pulled himself to the top of the tall mainframe machine and used it as a launching point. Stephen jumped up to grab the edge of the ductwork opening. It wobbled a bit and issued a soft pop from his sudden weight.

He pulled himself up and into the narrow venting. The cramped confines barely allowed him to move the grating back into place. It squeaked as it slid into the grooves, and Stephen froze.

Hansen whirled around. His gaze flowed around the room, over the walls, and then traced the ductwork. He frowned but turned back around to the table. Stephen blew out a silent breath and rolled his eyes. Too close.

He wiggled his way around and began the long crawl toward the back of the building. His wrist monitor beeped its warning. The security loop he had installed earlier and had used again was about to expire. He had three minutes before his presence would be detected.

Stephen suppressed a growl of frustration at his father who had redesigned the security program last week. It made getting in and out of the buildings more difficult now. Not impossible, though.

He pushed open the hinged grate that led outside. The lip above the opening, designed to keep water from leaking in, provided him a handheld as he dangled his body out of the passage in order to close and secure the grate. Once it clicked back into its locked position, Stephen let go and let himself slide down the slightly rounded twenty-foot wall to the ground. He landed hard, and a small plume of dust shot up around his legs, coating his black pants.

He glanced around as he dusted his pants off before hurrying between the main security building and the command building and onto a covered pathway that led to the center of the compound. And if anyone saw him there, especially Sierra or his father, they would think he couldn't sleep and took a late-night stroll through the area.

Stephen smiled as he gazed around him, taking in the few people who strolled along the various paths. Once he viewed the information downloaded, he would be one step closer to freedom. He slid his hands into his back pockets and ambled down the dark walkway. Soon, he passed from the covered pathway and onto an opened area, giving him an unobstructed view of the dusky sky above where the faint lights of the aurora borealis were fading.

The Groove, with its pine trees standing sentry around the cobbled circle, was unoccupied. Cold air bit into him as he sat on the bench under an archway. Hidden from view, Stephen pulled his small datapad from the side pocket of his pants and inserted the data crystal.

Undeciphered code streamed across the screen. He curled his lips. Hacking was not his favorite pastime. It was boring, uneventful. And yet he was having to do it at every turn in his life.

Stephen slipped the GHOST from his pocket and slid the chip into the side slot of his datapad. It was an older model built to handle data chips. Yet he had dismantled the datapad and built a new processor for it. Now it could operate like the newer versions and still use the more antiquated storage devices.

The program took a bit longer than usual. After ten seconds, the screen shifted; and files flooded across the screen. Stephen swiped at the files, closing most down, opening some, and accessing the subfiles within.

There! He opened the second subfile and frowned. Intech Juliet Serum Initiative. Medlab Twelve-twenty. That made no sense.

Stephen quickly scanned the file. So, Medlab Twelve had moved from Washington forty years ago and was now located deep within the Midland Expanse, a non-GFT nation. He scrolled down. Active war but a cold war. Negotiations in progress to combine Midland Expanse with the North Continent Territory, sans Alaska Country.

He minimized the file and opened the recent military file. GFT had lost three provincial lands in the recent years. One ongoing war with the Southern Asian Continent. Stephen harrumphed. That continent was nothing but a desert—a dry, bone-filled desert. What was so important about that place?

He shrugged and reopened the first file. It would be doable. He could travel down the coastline to the Westland Coast, then cross into Midland at their junction. He would need to have a citizen card created, though. And the program he held in his hand would allow him to do just that.

Stephen closed the files and searched for the supply run schedule. Tomorrow, they planned a scheduled run to Yukon to the

Food Bank Division and Citizen Mainframe in Canadian Province. It was a game plan.

A small amount of guilt rose in his chest at the thought of leaving his family. But he forced it down with a scowl. They would be okay. They would heal. And he would have his freedom.

He quashed the annoying warning inside his head. What he was going to do wasn't dangerous. No, not at all. It was exciting. Right?

"Right." Stephen answered his internal question. His voice mingled with the wind and blew away from him. Yet the nagging feeling of danger still remained.

Chapter Five
B≡YOND ΛLΛSKΛ

Stephen waited at his doorway. Granddad Huey's footsteps clicked against the floor. The door hissed opened, then closed; and the sound of his grandfather's boots faded. He waited for a moment longer. His mom's movements indicated that she was collecting the supplies she would need at the library excavation. Old tomes, their pages fragile and brittle, were found in a buried section. His mother's excitement was barely contained when they had contacted her last night. She was one of the few historians who were trained in repairing and preserving antiquities.

The door opened, but she paused at the threshold. "Stephen?"

"Yes?" He propped himself up against the hatch's frame.

"I'm heading out. Are you scheduled for anything today?"

The door closed. Stephen leaned out of his doorway and peered down the ladder. His mother's eyes questioned him as she gazed up at him.

"Yeah. I'm heading to the dojo today. Then I have a class at Level Five."

"To teach?"

"To present. Jackson Mills asked if I would show Shona's class how the golden ratio applies to nature."

His mother smiled before nodding. "That's great. Okay, sweetie. Will I see you at dinner tonight?"

"Probably." Guilt rose up in his chest at the lies. "I don't have anywhere else to go."

"Okay. Your father is at the main medlab today, and he said he has a meeting with the elders this afternoon. It will probably run late. If he is still there at Main Command, would you stop by and bring him home? He's not supposed to be working."

Stephen laughed and nodded. "Sure."

"And don't you get caught up there, too! We have dinner guests tonight, and I don't want any stragglers." She waved and threw him a kiss. "I would come up there to give you a kiss goodbye, but you probably aren't dressed yet."

He glanced at his bare legs, suppressing a chuckle. How his mom knew when he was clad in underclothes or fully dressed was a mystery. "I'll try to swing by the library after the dojo."

"Okay, sweetie. See you later."

Then she was gone. Stephen leaned back against the wall and waited. He didn't hear Sierra this morning. So, she must have left early. His father's departure had awakened him.

He waited.

The hum of the food unit, a buzz from the security light outside, and the gurgle from the underground pipes were the only sounds that filled the air. Stephen blew out a quick breath. It was time.

He yanked on his black, multi-pocket pants. The material clung to him as he buckled the built-in belt. It was the latest fashion, and he had ordered the new pants during the last shipment run. If he wanted to blend into the crowds in the GFT territories, he couldn't look like an outsider wearing homespun clothing.

He mulled over that word: *homespun*. Maybe that wasn't the right word. Their clothing in Alaska Country were too civilized and too practical. Their wool came from Lower Town, where sheep, rabbits, and even alpaca were raised for their fur and wool. Northern City grew silk farms in their enclosed domes. And on the other side of his town, Alaska Compound grew cotton in an older greenhouse. The artisans designed their clothing, fitting each and every person.

Stephen collected his pack and climbed down the ladder as his thoughts ran to the difference between their country and the rest. They had no monetary system. It was all barter or provided. Each person performed a service for the community, and the goods were on display for whomever desired or needed it. From artwork to furniture to clothing and even food, artisans, at times, would take on a special project in exchange for something they desired from another—such as the shirt he was wearing—black silk with gussets on the side to allow ease of movement and a seam pocket on the right. It was a design he had drawn and presented to Moriah. He, in turn, carved and built an intricate bench for her family dinner table. And that was the way of his people.

Stephen set his pack on the table and turned around the family monitor. In the GFT territories, he would need credits. He pulled up the global market reports and watched the numbers scroll down the screen, then browsed through the news to grab updates. The market was about to collapse again, easy to predict with the pattern that was flowing across the screen. So, credits would be worth less in about a month.

He clicked his tongue against his teeth. In order to fly under the scopes of GFT, he would have to contact Jinx. He pulled his copy of the GHOST from his shirt pocket and slipped it into the slot before entering her code.

"Stephen! How's life treating you?" Jinx's voice razzed across the connection. There was no video feed—never a video feed with her and her father.

"I'm doing good, Jinx. How about you and your father?"

"Well, I'm doing great, and you know my father . . . Batch is being Batch." She gave a small chuckle. "So, what do you need?"

He smiled. It was all business with her, just like her father. He activated the files he had obtained and the information he had collected last night. "I am sending you specs for a citizen card. Could you have it ready and with at least three thousand credits on it for me later today?"

"Hmm. Yeah. Can do. Where's the pickup?"

"It'll be in Yukon at the Mission Deli."

"Oh. That's easy." The clack of keys filled the room. "Okay. Send me your scan, and then I will have it ready. I can only do a Citizen Two status, but that will get you into every place but the ritzy ones. And stay away from the GFT official gov buildings. Their sub-hub will pick up the fraudulent card in no time. We have yet to access the new gov card codes."

"I can help you with that. Give me a day or two, and I'll send a link."

"Oh, no worries about that. We have a wave coming in soon. Thanks all the same. Though I may hit you up in the future for a little project, so keep that in mind. Anyway, go ahead and send me that scan."

Stephen sat at the console and activated the scan. The light ran down his face and then back up. When the prompt for his thumbprint came up, he set his right thumb against the screen and waited until it beeped green. "Okay. You should have the scans now."

"Yup. I got them. Hoo, hoo, you are looking good, my friend!"

Stephen laughed. "Stop flirting. And thanks, Jinx."

"Not a problem. Is this sanctioned or under scopes?"

"Under scopes." He fought down the guilt of telling another lie as he replied. "I'm heading to a newer facility in Yukon to check out possibilities. We want to keep it off records for the time being."

"You got it! Give me a connect when you reach the deli, and I'll bypass you through to print the card." Then she disconnected. Jinx was never one to waste words.

Stephen rose from the chair and removed the GHOST. He glanced around his home. The comfort would be missed. Yet he desired his freedom and answers more than comfort. The niggling warning that he was making a mistake refused to leave. He narrowed his eyes and pushed aside the wayward thought. Nothing would stop him this time.

He grabbed his traveling coat and pack and walked out. Bright sunlight hit his face. The sun was lower in the sky. Where he was going, he would be able to experience full days and full nights. None of the constant light, always day or dusk. None of the two months of pitch blackness.

A woman smiled and mumbled her pardon when she bumped into him. Stephen sidestepped to avoid the gaggle of children that followed her. Today was busy. For a moment, he paused at the water. No, the idea of swimming down and under the barrier was scrubbed as quickly as it rose in his mind.

He dodged and ducked around the moving throng of people as he made his way toward the front gates. The run to the Food Bank Division would be leaving soon. And he needed to make it to the auto transport before it left and somehow slip underneath.

No water. No ocean. That his fear was irrational and illogical didn't change the fact that his chest tightened at the thought of the deep, freezing water. The danger of the auto transport's undercarriage was preferable to a watery grave.

Seth rose from his chair and replaced the datapad he had been reading onto the stack in the center of the round table. Elder John clapped his hand on one man's shoulder, nodding at a comment from another, and then politely excused himself in order to approach Seth.

"Questions, Seth?" His father's old friend gave him a soft smile. Age had turned the man's brown eyes weak. Thick glasses perched on his nose. The treatments for his eyesight hadn't taken this last round, and he had resigned himself to antiquated equipment. His olive skin had lightened in the cold climate and from his bout with a serious illness last year. Yet strength still remained in him. "You didn't have to come today. You still have a couple of days left to your bereavement leave."

"Bereavement." Seth shook his head and stuffed his hands in the back pockets of his pants. "I find it odd that people need that time to grieve. My grieving was done while Mom was ill. By the time she died, I had come to accept that she was gone from my life now."

John crossed his arms across his chest and leaned his hip against the table's edge. "It's not designed only for grieving but also to adjust to life without having her in it." The man's smile faded. Deep wrinkles around his eyes grew as raw emotion filled his expression. "We all lost something when Abby left. I lost a wonderful friend and sister. Miriam lost her best friend. Huey lost his wife. You lost your mother. Now, there is a void left where her vibrant personality had been. And that's why we give others time to adjust. You can't bury yourself in work to ignore what you are missing."

"I'm not—"

"You are a lot like your mother and father, Seth." John's gaze softened as he looked across the expanse of the room as others who attended the meeting were leaving through the doors. "They would distract themselves when faced with sudden changes in life. For Abby, it was programs and tweaks to make things run better. For your father, during the short time he was with us, it was the greenhouse projects, the security of the compound, or his jaunts in the wilderness with Joshua."

Seth pulled his chair around and sat. Hearing John speak at such lengths was surprising. The history between his father and John was already known; from the time he was a little one to his teen years, he had learned everything he could about Julius Williams. He knew that while on a mission, his father had killed John's brother; then years later, he had saved CeeCee, John's adopted daughter, and eventually had become like a brother to John. If there was ever a story of redemption and forgiveness, it was the story between his father and John. Yet he never heard such wistfulness come from the elder when speaking about his parents.

"I concede to that fact, then, John." Seth rubbed his hands over his face, fighting against the weariness that seemed to pull at his bones. "But what am I to do? I can't sit idle. I can't mosey around the compound with no direction."

"Mosey?" John laughed. "Tamara has been using those old phrases, hasn't she?"

Seth let a smile show. "Yeah. And it's rubbing off. But I like the imagery. And that's what it would be like. I would be moseying."

"Well, since you moseyed your way into the meeting this morning, what do you think?"

"It's sound." Seth tapped his forefinger against the surface as he spoke. "Increasing the security is prudent in light of the cold war between GFT and Midland Expanse. And the impeding war between Southern Continent and Ecuadorian Province. Most of our supplies come from Midland and Ecuador."

"Yet there's something you want to say?" John sank into the chair next to Seth and turned it around to face him.

"Yes." His finger began tapping even harder. "I want to modify the GHOST. I've been studying it for years now. I want to install a newer version into the operations, security, and medical systems."

"Why medical?" John held up a hand before Seth could reply. "Does this have anything to do with your genetics research?"

How the man knew everything about what he did was always surprising. "What makes you ask that?"

John laughed again. "Seth, I told you. You are too much like your parents. They would want something but would always include more than their wants and needs. They would include others. And I've watched you grow. You look to your own wants and needs, yes, but you also include others. So, if you want, for example, to use the medical systems for further research and created a new program to help you, you will also examine what other systems would benefit, thereby helping those in the community."

Silence reigned for a few moments. Seth mulled over John's words before speaking. "You talked with Michael."

A hint of a smile drifted across the older man's lips. "I talked with Michael. And I already know that you've created a new GHOST."

Seth sighed and shook his head. He shouldn't be surprised. "Yes. I expanded the GHOST into a quantum program. It will provide multiple functions with less power input and with exponentially greater output. But unlike the other quantum programs we have devised, I chose a vector that will continue to oscillate between 2.005 and 2.006. The compression was a bit difficult, yet this would help us in many ways."

"By strengthening our security and response and giving us faster operation time and more computing power."

"And allowing us to increase our medical procedures, therefore reducing diagnosis time and treatment."

"Giving you more power and space to answer what?" The look in the man's eyes said he already knew the answer.

"It would give me the power to learn how to stop our genetic code from being inherited."

John huffed out a heavy sigh as he crossed his arms and hung his head. Seth waited and stilled his tapping on the table, allowing the rest of the room's sounds to filter back to him. The monitor on the far side of the room pinged with an incoming message. The ventilation overhead hummed. The *thump-thump* along with the small skip of John's heart filled his senses.

The older man shook his head. "Your obsession will not lead you to anything good, Seth."

"I want my children and grandchildren and the children and grandchildren of the others to know freedom—to be able to go beyond our borders, if they so desire, and not be sequestered behind fifty-foot, reinforced, fused titanium alloy walls!"

"You've lived this long behind our walls and within the borders of Alaska Country without complaint. Why now?"

"Because I found something in our DNA that I fear!"

Seth blinked at his own admission. He hadn't meant to state that. But talking with John always brought out his deepest hidden truths. The man was there throughout his teenage years when Seth had made so many mistakes. John had guided him, taught him, mentored him. Between him and Michael, Seth had unburdened a lot of secrets.

"The dyad code. Michael told me."

"It's more than that, John." Seth began tapping his finger again. "This gene . . . it is something new. And it is something that will create what this world doesn't need."

"Or it may be what this world needs. You don't know God's plan, Seth."

"There is no way this is God's plan! It was made by man, designed by man—"

"God's design is more than that of any man's."

Shame flooded through Seth. How many times had he said that phrase and its variations? God's purpose was stronger than any man's. His father was made by man, yet God had used him for a greater purpose. Could the same be said about the dyad?

"You found this code in Stephen and Sierra?"

Seth nodded.

"Seth?" When Seth met John's eyes, the man reached out and placed his hand over Seth's, stilling his tapping. "It's natural to fear for our children's lives and safety. This is where we must trust the Lord." He gripped Seth's hand. "Go ahead and install the program. Do the work you desire to do. But don't play GFT or God. Don't try to change who you or your children are."

The incessant beep from the console brought their attention around to the monitor. John gave his hand one last squeeze. "We will talk more about this. Let me go see what's going on. But promise me that you will only do research. No manipulation."

Seth nodded. "No manipulation." And that wasn't a lie. At least, he was granted permission to enhance the systems and do his more in-depth research. That was a plus. "And thank you, John."

The man smiled, clapped Seth's shoulder, and then shuffled his way to the monitor as the message went from green code to orange code. Another day in operations—there was always something going on.

As he rose to leave, John waved him to a stop.

"Seth, you were talking about your children being prisoners behind the wall?"

"*Prisoners* wasn't exactly my word."

"Semantics." John keyed the holograph projection. The supply run convoy filled the air, along with Sierra's face. "Your daughter is requesting to go on the Food Bank run and to update the citizen trading permits."

"She can see me?" Seth leaned against the table's edge.

"No. I have it on stand-by. Are you ready to trust the Lord? Let your daughter go?"

Seth's heart hammered. Now that he was faced with the possibility of one of his children stepping beyond the border, he couldn't allow it. This was another one of John's lessons, another one of his tests. Apparently, he wasn't too old for them. Seth didn't want freedom for his kind. He had used it as an excuse in order to receive permission to upload his program for his own gain. And once again, John had seen through him. No wonder the community had voted him as the lead elder.

John smiled. "This convoy will go to Yukon, stop at the Food Bank Division and at the GFT Citizen Mainframe Unit. It's scheduled to return by three o'clock this afternoon." He turned to the monitor before Seth replied. "Sierra?"

Her voice wavered a bit through the transmission. "I'm here, Elder John."

"You have permission to proceed. Keep with the convoy and do not stray from the designated route. And do not venture off alone."

"I have the rules and regulations memorized." She smiled, her eyes beaming. "Thank you!"

John signed off and turned back to Seth. "Go about your day, Seth. Everything will be okay."

Seth glared at his mentor. It didn't sit right, letting his daughter go beyond the border. He pushed away from the table and strode toward the door. He wouldn't be able to stop her, not with John's blessing already given. He could follow her, though, and travel with her to keep her safe.

"You don't have permission."

Seth's stride broke for a second before he recovered. He only nodded at John's statement, took a deep breath, and exited the operations room. It never failed that John knew what he was thinking.

Sierra touched the blooming shrub. The viburnum carlesii was growing nicely along the border wall. Its spicy vanilla fragrance permeated the air around her and mingled with the pine saplings growing nearby. Yet neither of those strong scents could override the lingering trail left by Stephen. An astringent smell overlaid his normal warm scent. She couldn't place the odor, but it seemed familiar.

She pulled a small tube from her satchel which hung down her side. Sierra popped the top off and raised it to her face. The gel glided easily above her upper lip and under her nose, effectively canceling the riot of odors around her. As much as she preached to Stephen about accepting being enhanced, her heightened olfactory sense was burdensome. From the small plumes of dirt to the slightest tang of sweat, she smelled it all. And that was why she preferred to work in the open, under trees, in fresh air, and near the water.

Apprehension filled her. She wouldn't have that fresh watery air on the transport. She'd be among the variety of bodies with their unique and probably rancid odors. But at least she had her gel with her.

Sierra left the blooming bush, and she followed the string of people heading toward the vehicle. Stephen's scent, along with the various other smells, faded as the gel neutralized the air with each breath.

"Sierra?"

She looked up and smiled at Donald, who slid his faded military cap up a bit on his forehead. "Hey, Don."

"They allowed you to come this time?"

"Yeah. Amazing, right? I asked to go to the Food Bank Division and to update our citizen permits." She handed him her card and waited as he ran it through the datapad. "I didn't think they would let me at first. You know, it has been an unwritten rule about our kind leaving the borders."

Donald nodded and handed back the card. "I know. But John has been advocating for us to be able to go beyond—as long as we stick with the convoy. As he put it in the meetings, it would do everyone good if they traveled at least once outside our borders and learned firsthand what is out there." He chuckled and shook his head. "I understand his logic."

"How so?"

They stepped out of the way to allow her fellow passengers to board the transport. He leaned against the side of the vehicle. "If we see what is out there—the hardships, the turmoil, the constant surveillance by their AIs, even the thought pattern scans in the cities—then we would understand that life here in Alaska Country offers more freedom and safety."

Sierra touched her temple, thinking about the drones that would patrol the larger cities. "They actually have the brain wave pattern scans? I knew they were testing that tech, but I didn't know they had perfected it."

"Last week—a few cities went online—Toronto, Floridian Port, all cities in Midland Expanse, Washington. I believe New Frandiego and New Vegas in Westland Coast went online yesterday. And that's just here on this side of the northern hemisphere." He motioned toward the opening of the transport. "But Canadian Province isn't online yet. So, you'll be safe."

"Now you have me worried, Don."

His dark eyes twinkled as he smiled at her. "We are enhanced, Sierra. We know how to control our thoughts and center our brainwaves on the beta and alpha. But you should have no problem in Yukon. Be safe." He held out his hand.

She placed her hand in his and allowed him to help her up onto the platform before stepping inside the brightly lit interior. Around her were seats bolted to the floor and bulkheads. A bar ran above them with air masks tethered to it, and poles ran from floor to ceiling between every other seat.

Danni, the daughter of one of her father's friends, waved her over. Her tightly curled hair bounced as she reached over and patted the seat next to her. "Here's an empty seat, Sierra."

She weaved her way through the crates stacked in the middle and sank onto the cushion. "What's with the air masks?"

Danni glanced up before answering. "We will travel through a tunnel that runs under one of the mountains. Sometimes, the air gets rank, so those are used. Once, we were ambushed, and toxins were in the concussion bombs. So again, we used the masks. But that was a few years ago. The path we travel is pretty safe now."

Sierra glanced around. This transport was a coffin—a metal, tube-shaped coffin. "No windows, I see."

"No. Too dangerous. Can't let those outside Alaska Country to see our numbers or our produce when we travel. But . . . " Danni pulled her datapad out and activated it. "I'm sending you a link. This will tie you in to the main cabin and into the vids. We are allowed to watch through the vid if we like."

A ding sounded from her satchel. Sierra reached in and grabbed her datapad. Soon, she had the video on her screen; and together, she and Danni watched the countryside begin to pull away as they began their long trek to Canadian Province.

What about Stephen? She frowned. Stephen would have found a spot underneath or on top—more than likely, underneath. There was less chance to be spotted. But would he have anticipated needing a mask?

With their speed, the air would quickly drop below freezing. Even with being an enhanced, he wouldn't be able to sustained prolonged periods in subzero temps. Although, he may have grabbed his traveling coat. Its thickness would protect him.

But what if they hit a pocket of rankness in the tunnel? Would he survive the putrid air? She closed her eyes and concentrated, listening to the sounds around her.

The *whirr-whirr* of the grav motors underneath rumbled. Muted conversations blended in with the coughs, sighs, and apparently a stolen kiss somewhere. Heat flooded her face as the sounds of their rapid heartbeats sped up even more. She tuned them out.

It was faint. And it was about six feet from her, under the center of the transport. His heartbeat was slow and steady, as if he was asleep. She opened her eyes and rubbed at her temple. Every time she concentrated like that, her head ached.

Her gaze flowed down the center of their transport. A few of the men sat on top of the crates, reading or talking in hushed tones. On each side of the crate was a convex groove, allowing their cargo to be nestled between and keeping them from sliding around. Each groove had support bars underneath that ran across the transport.

So, Stephen was using the underside of one of those to hide in. And it would be well-shielded from the cold. Sneaky devil.

She returned her attention back to the vid and to Danni as she regaled her with past trips and stories to Yukon and about the differences between Alaska Compound and Yukon.

"Tamara!" Seth set his datapad on the small table by the door as he stepped over the threshold. His wife peeked around the corner of the galley, drying her hands on a towel.

"What are you shouting for?" She quirked her delicate brow at him before disappearing back around the corner.

Seth stomped into the room and plopped heavily onto the tall stool by the long bar that separated the galley from the eating area. "Where's Stephen? Have you seen him?"

"Stephen?" She shook her head as she slid a pan into the oven. "He said he would be home in time for dinner. Said he was presenting at one of the Level Fives today."

Seth bit back a curse and pushed off the stool. Tamara followed him as he retrieved the datapad from the table. "Level Five. The man didn't have a presentation. That was last week. You want to know what he was doing?" He flipped the datapad around and shoved it at her. "Take a look! These are the security feeds sent to me after I installed the updated program and the only ones that were GHOST-retrievable. A loop program was used, effectively hiding all activity in the security hub."

Tamara's brows drew down as she watched the file of her son hacking into Seth's terminal the other night. Her eyes hardened when Sierra left and then when Stephen rose and dropped a card near Danica's station. She swiped for the more recent one that showed Stephen dropping from the overhead duct. "What did he do? Is he involving Sierra in this?"

"Just continue." He motioned toward the datapad.

Turning her attention back to the security records, Tamara's skin darkened with anger before she slammed the datapad onto the table and stalked to Huey's room. Seth followed, already knowing what she was planning. The door slid open. One side of the room was littered with wires, datapads, and mod units—apparently, more projects that Huey was working on. The other side was nice and orderly, each bin labeled and every stack in perfect balance.

Seth waited as Tamara veered toward his stepfather's workspace. He had thought they were the only ones who knew about the hidden compartment—the one that Huey had devised to keep the GHOST safe. She tapped the corner's hidden latch, and a small panel slid out.

Nestled in the black foam was his mother's program, one that she and Huey had redesigned and the one that he had reprogrammed. Yet this was the original.

"What's going on?" Huey's raspy voice filled the room.

Seth turned to find his stepfather leaning against the hatch's frame with an ankle crossed over the other. "Can you tell if the GHOST has been duplicated?"

"Yeah. It leaves a code each time. Looking for a recent dupe?" At Seth's nod, Huey pushed off the frame and joined Tamara at his desk. He plucked the data disk from its spot and crossed over to his bunk. Above his bed on a shelf sat one of the most sophisticated datapads developed—one of Huey's creations that he was designing for the elders. He settled on the edge of his bed and inserted the data disk into his pad.

It didn't take long for him to find it. Within seconds, Huey flipped the datapad around, showing Seth the coding.

Irritation was gradually giving way to fury. "He must have done it while you were out, and we were distracted." Seth ran his hands over his face and sighed. "I just installed a quantum GHOST in the system, Huey. It should be able to access what he did and where."

Huey nodded as he turned the datapad back around. Before Seth could leave the room, his stepfather called out to him. "Don't worry about finding it. I just pulled up the info. John said you had installed it earlier, and I already ran a Hi-Wave code to my stations. Give me a moment and let me see what I can find."

Tamara shook her head and smirked. Seth felt the same. Huey had always had a connection to the systems, which was the reason, as Uncle JJ said, that Huey was his father's right-hand man. John and Uncle JJ loved to tell the story of Huey's past. It was always a story he enjoyed hearing as a child—how Huey, after being released from the Siberian prison, had hacked the government systems and scrubbed all information on Huey Marktov and his parents, Vlad and Inga Marktov, plus the numerous Russian Coalition members who were hiding in the Black Sea within their ships, and then became the operations man for Julius Williams onboard the *Nightingale*. Huey hacked every system he came across, even the WeatherNet, always needing to know, needing to have the information at his fingertips. Seth suspected that it was Huey's insecurity of not knowing what was in store for him and his fear of being locked up in Siberia again.

Long ago, after his mother had married Huey, Seth had researched the Siberian Mining Prison. After gaining that knowledge—one that he wished he could stuff back—it was understandable. Only the grace of the Lord had kept Huey alive in that place.

When Seth was caught, he didn't get in trouble. Instead, many nights were spent with Huey, hearing the stories and tales and learning how to hack into programs and systems. His mother allowed it under one condition: that Seth would only use his knowledge to help and protect others and never for his own personal gain.

Guilt at his desire to use the newly created Quantum GHOST, which he dubbed the QG, for his own research ate at him. Yet it was quickly buried, and his runaway thoughts were scattered as Huey handed him the datapad. The age lines on his stepfather's face had deepened, and a weariness accentuated the sadness that haunted his brown eyes.

Seth read the screen. Tamara read over his shoulder. Dread ate at him. It would be fruitless to search Alaska Compound for his son. And now Sierra's request to join the convoy made sense.

Tamara looked at him. "He hacked security?"

"More than that. He knows about Twelve-twenty. And he has the convoy schedules—" Seth chucked the datapad to Huey, who caught it and set it aside. His stepfather and Tamara rushed after him. "Huey, I need the GHOST to see if he used our console to contact Jinx."

Huey brushed past him and slid into the seat at the communication console. He inserted the GHOST, entered a command, and then turned in his seat so Seth could view the readouts. "Yes, he did."

Seth entered his codes and waited. A couple of minutes passed by; and a man's voice, aged and weak, filtered through.

"Seth Williams. How's my favorite enhanced?"

"In a rage." Seth leaned on his hands and gave Batch a brief rundown. "Stephen is AWOL. And he has the GHOST. Jinx was his contact. I need to know what he requested."

Batch's sigh was heavy. "I warned you last month about your son, Seth. I could see the signs. I had Jinx put any comm from your household on a separate wave. Yeah, here it is. He asked for a citizen card with at least three thousand. She gave him a C-Two stat."

"C-Two? Why not the usual C-Three?"

"Let that boy run around with a C-Three stat? A C-Two would keep him localized. Seth, I may be on the outside, but I have eyes everywhere. I'll find them for you. Huey, you there, man?"

"Right here, old buddy." Huey twirled a stylus between his fingers. "I can set up a two-man ship. Give it specs to fly under scopes. Send an IF to me, and I'll prep it."

"On its way. And Seth, Stephen has already collected his C-Two card. And you aren't going to like the footage I have. Sending it now."

Their console beeped. Huey reached across and flipped a switch for the holographic projection. Stephen was shown with a hood pulled low over his eyes at the Mission Deli. He walked through the revolving doors. In the reflection of the glass and across the street stood Sierra. She browsed through a selection of clothing at a vendor's station. Every few seconds, she glanced in Stephen's direction and moved to hide her face.

So, she was not trying to stop Stephen but to join him? No, she was trying to stay hidden from him—to follow him, then.

"Jinx is keeping tabs on them. She set a tracking code into his card. I'll keep you updated."

Then he was offline. Huey swiveled his chair around to face them. In the galley, the oven's timer sounded.

Tamara placed her hand on Seth's arm. "I'll cancel the dinner party and contact John."

Huey looked up at Seth after Tamara left them. His hand landed on Seth's arm milliseconds before Seth could fling the contents on the desk into the wall. Seth heaved a deep breath. Anger wouldn't solve this.

"You tried, son. You tried to rein in his rebellion; but sometimes, you have to let them make their own mistakes in order to learn."

"Yet this mistake will cost them—and us—more than we can afford." Seth stalked across the room and then back, his hands clasped behind his neck. Tension pulled at his shoulders.

Huey shook his head. "No, it'll hurt. It'll change things. But remember, our future is never one of safety. I see now that it was our mistake in protecting you from the outside. We should have schooled you in how to handle the outside world and stay protected from it but not insulated. And that insulation we forced upon you has now affected your children." He pushed up from the chair and headed for the door. "I'm heading to the hangars to prep the ship."

"Wouldn't that be premature?" Seth dogged his steps.

Huey shook his head and slipped into his coat. "Nope." His brown eyes, weak and yet so bright, gazed back at him. "I know what will be decided. And either John or Michael will be with you."

Seth grabbed Huey's jacket and pulled him to a halt before he could exit. "You knew?"

Huey's gaze flowed from one side of Seth's face to the other before answering. "No. We suspected. No one knew if it would be you or one of my grandchildren."

His stepfather pulled away and stepped through the hatch, hitting the comm link on his wrist as he did so. "Joshua, we got . . . " His voice faded as he hurried down the boardwalk that led to the underground tunnels.

Him or one of his children? Was he that transparent? Did the elders think he would jeopardize his people? Did they think he would harm them in any way? Were they that mistrustful of him?

Tamara slipped under his arm and wrapped her arms around his waist, nestling her head against his chest. "They don't think bad of you, Seth. But your tendency to ignore authority has grown throughout the years. And our son is too much like you—too much like Julius, Dad said."

Seth studied his wife's amber eyes. Worry crinkled her brow. He cupped her face and used his thumbs to try and smooth the deep lines away. "I would never have put our people in danger, though, nor risked letting GFT learn about us."

Tamara captured his hands and stilled them. Something lurked in her eyes when she began to speak. "Seth—"

"I'll get them back, Tam." He engulfed her in his arms and rocked her. "I'll get our children home somehow."

She melted against him. "I know you will." Her muffled voice wavered, tainted with fear.

He felt the same—apprehension, dread. An ominous cloud seemed to descend . . .

Chapter Six
THE MISSION

Jason counted the seconds between his heartbeats. One. Two. Three. Beat.

Outside his confinement, the monitor beeped along with him. One. Two. Three. Beat. Beep. He closed his eyes as he listened. Medstudies murmured under their breaths. A keypad clicked to his left near the door. The static hiss as the holographic shut down. Soft-sole shoes tapped against the metal flooring. The buzz and zap indicated that the security perimeters had been activated outside the room and in the corridor.

Jason waited another minute. No other noise could be heard but the room's electronic hum and the gurgle of the serum components as it waited in the vials attached to his chamber. He took a deep breath through the respirator and tensed the muscles in his arms. His fists knotted. With a sudden flex, the bonds around his arms and wrists popped open.

It was tight, yet he squeezed his arms between his body and the top of the tube. His fingers bit painfully into his abdomen as he gripped the band around his waist. He snapped it apart, separating the catches that held the two pieces together.

The clamps on his legs were easier to detach. One flex with his legs and they parted. He opened his eyes, blinking against the thick liquid, and searched the pane above him. The fused glass would slide easily, and it wasn't sealed. Then again, why would it be? They would never have anticipated him leaving the experimentation tube. So, why secure the glass panel that allowed them easy access to him?

He pressed his palms against the warm glass and pushed. Warm? They had raised the temperature in the room. It slid into its recess, and fresh, sterile air flowed against his face as he ripped the respirator from his mouth. Jason gripped the sides and pulled. Inch by inch, tug by tug, he freed his hips from the band. Like a worm, he hunched and pushed forward, pulling himself one section at a time from the tube.

Once his knees reached the headspace, he twisted around and knelt to survey his surroundings. Twenty minutes remained until the serum was injected. He had fifteen to do what needed to be done.

Fluid dripped from his body and left a trail as he climbed down from the platform. He spared a small glance at the drops. The fluid would dry long before they returned. He approached the bank of monitors. All files were still active, which meant they were coming back later. Jason searched each readout until he found the serum file.

He activated it. The formula, his reactions, the positive and negative results scrolled past. Jason opened the formula file. He needed the Paxolin-X to be reduced and Serum Seventy-seven to be increased by a point three. It didn't take long for him to adjust the formula and erase his tracks.

For years, he had listened to the medstudies and medtechs talk about Serum Seventy-four and its redesigned counterparts and how Seventy-seven was the most promising formula. He had listened as they had the programmers come in and had learned the codes and language. And for the last few hours, while he had been in gamma state, he had created a computer virus—a quantum virus with codes and commands that oscillated using the same position and allowing less memory and processing usage—one that could stay buried deep within the system and would eliminate all records two minutes before his emergence from the tube. Then, it would allow the systems to come back online in twenty-seven minutes after initiation and then perform spots erasures for the next three hours, giving the appearance of down systems without the suspicion of tampering. Finally, it would go dormant before reactivating at sporadic intervals and downing random systems.

His fingers flew across the keypad. He gave a slight smile—one more step to freedom. This new formula would allow him to begin remembering. It would start to repair neural pathways. He began the program.

Jason hurried back to the chamber and grabbed his respirator. Warm fluid flowed around his legs as he sat on the edge to attach his mask. Climbing back into the tube proved more difficult. He squirmed, twisted, and pushed his way in. The bands scraped against him. As his legs settled into the groove, the bands clamped around him. He wiggled down another inch until his head rested back in his original spot. The automatics would seal the glass once the bands clamped around him. He closed his eyes and rested his arms back against his side. Metal bands snapped around his flesh. Sounds became muffled as the glass closed over him.

Probes shot into his spine. The serum raced into his system. Then all went dark. He sensed it more than anything. Through his eyelids, he could always see a hint of brightness—from the overhead lights to the reflections of the myriad monitors that glinted against the glass and the metal of his prison.

He relaxed and waited. Let his quantum virus do its job.

Seth strode through the tinted doors of security when they hissed open. Bright light stabbed at him, causing him to squint until his eyes adjusted. He nodded to Jackson, who sat at the bank of terminals to his right. "You wanted me to see something?"

The older man pushed away from the consoles and swiveled his chair around to face Seth. "It's been three hours since the transport arrived in Yukon. They will leave in the next hour. No trace of Stephen other than that which Batch had sent us." Jackson vacated the chair for Seth. "I have the coastline feed on terminal seven. That's what I want you to watch before you leave."

Seth settled into the chair and activated the holograph for terminal seven. He frowned as he viewed Stephen prowling along the coastal beach near the wall. His son hesitated at the edge before slowly backing away and retreating toward the transport gate.

"Looks like he had considered swimming under the wall." Jackson shook his head and leaned against the edge of the desk. "What was he thinking? I know your son is more enhanced than I or the others, and even more so than Peony, but he couldn't have believed he would be able to withstand such temperatures. Even your father suffered from his dive into the Southern Ocean when he saved CeeCee all those years ago."

Seth looked up at the youngest former assassin. Jackson was only twenty-two when he had defected GFT and joined the Christian Coalition. And now at sixty-nine, he was still one of the most active members and head of security. His full white beard gleamed in the harsh lights. Deep brown eyes studied Seth for long seconds before he crossed his arms with a huff. His talent for observation hadn't dulled, apparently.

"Stephen is more, isn't he?" He glanced at the feeds showing Stephen disappearing near the transports and out of sight. "I had hoped that what GFT did to us would fade. Peony shows a bit of the enhancements. Will her children have more or less?"

Seth shrugged. "I'm really not sure at this moment. From what I have discovered, the genetic manipulations on you and the others diminish over time, since you aren't on the serum. Yet—"

"With Jules, he had to have the serum to survive. And he was the only one that it was successful on." Jackson nodded. "So, Stephen and Sierra?"

"Something different. I don't know the extent of it yet." Seth closed down the feeds and opened the files on operations, medical, and security consoles. "As I told Michael, because my children are the product of two offspring from Serum Seventy-four assassins, something new was created."

Jackson straightened and tapped the screen in front of Seth, activating the more secured medical files. "Well, regardless, Stephen put us all in danger. John called a meeting with the elders."

"Did he say about what?" Although he asked, he had a reasonable deduction about what they were addressing.

Jackson nodded. "Yes, but I'll let John tell you." He swiped one file to the side and highlighted a line. "Looks like he hacked more than your medical files."

Seth sagged in his seat as he read the screen. The medical files were there as a trap—something that was hand-fed to his son to keep him reined in. But the loop program Stephen installed compromised their databanks, weakening their firewalls and quantum shielding programs. And Stephen's hack into the mainframe allowed him to find the information on Medlab Twelve-twenty.

Jackson read over Seth's shoulder. "If he found that, Seth, you know he will probably go looking for it."

"I know."

Medlab Twelve-twenty. The one rogue medlab that was hidden deep within Midland and still experimenting with the serum. GFT had been hunting down the faction; yet their corruption ran deep, and politics interfered with official GFT sanctions and decisions. Seth scowled at that thought. Always politics.

The doors opened. Seth and Jackson stood as Huey and JJ approached them. Seth met them halfway.

Huey held out a data crystal. "Specs and program to cycle your IF. You will take one of our smaller ships, *Depthfinder*. It has the more advanced sensors and is small enough to slip into the lanes undetected."

Seth slid the data crystal into his pocket. "Which route?"

"You will take the northern one. It'll bring you into Canadian Province on the eastern side." Huey angled his head toward Seth's pocket. "It's on the crystal."

"We just found out that Stephen discovered the file on Medlab Twelve-twenty."

JJ and Huey glanced at each other. Their expressions closed off, becoming unreadable.

Seth's father-in-law grabbed his arm and pulled him to the side near the doors. "I know I don't have to warn you about staying under the scopes on this, Seth." JJ's eyes darkened. "Michael will travel with you. And you need to bring that grandson of mine back as soon as possible."

"I know—"

"No." His father-in-law leaned closer. JJ's face hardened into black granite. "You don't understand how ruthless this faction is. Seth, listen, son. I never told you the full extent of their evil. I never wanted to burden you with this." JJ ran his hands down his face. All at once, the years and weariness aged the man who had helped raise him. At eighty-two, the man seemed ageless, always vibrant and energetic. Now, the worry made him look ancient.

"This faction, the one that is running Medlab Twelve-twenty, is the one that tortured your father, Seth. They were determined to gain his blood. And they were responsible for the battle that claimed my brother's life. They will stop at nothing to get what they want: our blood in order to create the ultimate death soldier."

"I knew about the faction, JJ. Knew they wanted us."

"But I never told you who was running it. And she will kill whoever gets in her way." JJ propped against the glass wall as Huey and Jackson talked and searched through the security feeds and commands. "What she did to Jules never left him. On many of our hunts after we arrived here, Jules confessed to having nightmares about his torture and how close he was to breaking. I need you to understand this. Jules never broke. General Hayden could never break him. But Anya almost did."

"Anya? Anya Bastion?" He recalled his father's eyes in the recording—that darkness hidden behind the light. Were those the nightmares?

"She's the head of Twelve-twenty." JJ closed his eyes and shook his head. "We never put that information in the files. We kept it from you because we never wanted you to know that the woman responsible for the death of your father still lived."

"You thought I would go after her." And he would have years ago.

JJ nodded. Shame flooded through Seth. He would have been like Stephen, leaving the compound and going after the woman who had taken so much from them and who held a cap on their freedom. Yet age had wizened him. He would never endanger his people now.

His father-in-law rested his heavy hands on Seth's shoulders. "You need to bring Stephen home as soon as possible. We can't let Anya discover that Jules had a child and that his child had children."

"Are you sure about Michael coming with me?"

JJ's hands fell away. He stuffed his hands in his pockets and glanced beyond the tinted glass at the people strolling by. "Yes. Huey and the rest of us cannot. Part of our treaty was that he, the others, and I would remain within the borders of Alaska Country. Michael has flown under the GFT scopes for a long time. GFT never knew about Zulu being with us."

"How was that possible?"

"Zulu was the covert squad. GFT needed plausible deniability. So, there were little to no record of them. And your mother made sure to keep it that way."

Huey approached, a strange look on his face. "Which plays into our favor." He swallowed hard before turning to JJ. "Joshua, I called John about this. We have a slight problem."

Seth frowned at his stepfather. "What did you find?" He pushed away from the wall and started toward the terminals, but Huey's hand stopped him.

"The convoy called in. Sierra's ID shows her logged in, but she's not on board. Looks like she stayed behind with Stephen."

A coldness ran through Seth. He walked a few steps away and paused near corner of the security wall. "I knew she was following Stephen. But . . . I didn't think she would be so stupid as to stay behind." Now, he had two to save. And she was too gentle for such a harsh world, a world that wasn't meant for her. She didn't know what was out there. If it wasn't for Stephen's arrogance and rebellion, this danger wouldn't be hanging over their heads—over his children's heads and their future.

All those years of protection was wasted. All the effort to stay hidden. All the research, the— With a guttural yell, Seth drove his fist into the thick, tinted security glass. Cracks spiderwebbed in the fused pane glass before crumpling into shards when his fist traveled through as his wrath consumed him.

Just as quickly as the rage rose, it fell away. His gaze traveled the mess of glass that coated the floor. He turned to JJ as Michael and John rounded the corner. They picked their way through the shattered glass. John shook his head at Seth. Disappointment was evident in his gaze.

JJ huffed at him. "I'm not cleaning that up."

John toed a few larger pieces. "I'll have maintenance notified." With a grim expression pulling his lips into a thin line, he looked at Seth. "You will have to control that temper and your thoughts if you plan to bring your children home. Many of the territories have the Pattern Recognition Scans active."

"They have the PatRecs online?" Seth fought against another wave of rage. He blew out a slow breath, pushing his anger back down. "We've been trained on how to center our thoughts in the beta and alpha brainwaves."

"But not if you let your rage get the better of you."

Seth flared his nostrils in frustration and looked out the shattered wall for a few seconds. He had lost control. It wouldn't happen again. He would make sure it didn't.

"How many are online?"

John held out a small data crystal. "Here's the schedule of when and where they come online. Canadian Province is still holding out; but hopefully, you will have them home before then."

"There's a problem with that, John." Jackson turned his chair around and crossed his ankle over a knee. "Stephen found out about Twelve-twenty. We doubt they will stay in Yukon for long."

John's gaze jumped from Jackson to JJ and Michael before landing on Seth. Anger flushed his complexion and brightened his eyes. "Get that son of yours back before he gets to Midland."

Φ

Sierra rose on her toes and peered over the heads of the crowd before her. Somewhere in there was Stephen. She had lost him, again. But his warm scent mingled with the various other smells—sweet, like orchids in the greenhouse. Sierra turned to her right. That aroma seemed to come from the group of women near a café—musky, petrichor—like the dirt near her home when the snow would melt. She glanced behind her. That would be from the market. Its sign read *Global Food Market*. There was a rack of baskets that held a medley of vegetables, many of them root vegetables.

Then there was an astringent smell—ozone, electronics. It floated all around her—from handhelds to buzzing signs above doorways. She pulled her tube of salve from her pouch and rubbed the substance under her nose.

The smells lessened. Sierra sighed as she stuffed it back into her satchel. The odors were beginning to make her lightheaded because on all those scents rode a varied amount of perfumes and colognes and the fuel from the ships overhead.

She followed a family as they threaded their way through the bazaar. Vendors called out their wares. People paused and purchased. The crowd thinned and grew, an oscillating wave of bodies.

A man bumped into her, murmured his apologies, and veered away. Sierra patted her pockets to ensure that her card was still there. It was.

As she passed through the courtyard, she eyed the clothing that were for sell. If she wanted to fit in and stay unnoticed, she would have to exchange her modest attire for something modern to the locale. Sierra stopped at the next clothing vendor. A huge collection hung from the racks.

She ran her hand over the silk and cotton shirts, touched the gauzy pants and flowing skirts. The seller walked up and greeted her. "Need any help deciding what to buy?" The woman's gaze traveled over Sierra's clothing. "You aren't from around here."

"No, ma'am, I'm not. Visiting family. Came from Metropolis." Sierra almost winced at selecting the most populated city on the eastern seaboard, a city that covered over 173,000 square kilometers.

"They are quite known for their varied styles. You must have come from the Manhattan region."

"I did." Sierra smiled and pointed to the green silk blouse. "I like that one. Would you recommend a skirt or pants with it?"

The woman stepped up to her with a scanner and took her measurements. "I would recommend the palazzos. You seem to prefer skirts; but around here, pants are in style. The palazzos would give you the best of both." She pulled a medium-sized green blouse from the rack and then walked over to the rack that held the pants and selected a black pair for Sierra. "These would be a great start."

Sierra smiled. "Can you add the blue cotton and another pair of pants, but in brown?"

The woman smiled and chose the garments. Within moments, Sierra paid for the items and was using the public changing station to switch into her new clothing. The silk slid against her skin, almost caressing it. It was a little lower in its cut than she was accustomed to. The pants flowed around her legs. As much as she loved her home's clothing, she had to admit the styles here felt wonderful—and looked good! She turned one way and then the other as she viewed herself in the mirror.

She slipped into her heavy jacket and stuffed her discarded clothing into the bag that held her extra outfit. Now, she had to find Stephen. Sierra left the public station. To her left was a lobby that held terminals. Many of the screens flashed with GFT headline news. Some hosted market reports, and others had advertisements that featured the local amenities.

Curiosity won. Stephen could wait for a bit.

Yukon was so different from Alaska Compound and the other Alaskan cities. She hurried across the paved center and into the darkened lobby. An empty terminal stood in the far back. She weaved her way through and stepped up to it.

"Welcome!" The automatic sensor began playing the promotional advertisement. "We hope you will enjoy your stay in Yukon. Established over one hundred years ago, Canadian Province is a proud member of Global Federated Territories. As the biggest northern province, our home offers a wide variety of shops, restaurants, hotels, sports arena, clubs, and historical attractions. Use the menu to the left to select your interest. If you would like to create an itinerary for your stay, please use the green icon at the bottom. For your convenience, we have uploaded your profile to our visitor log. You can create your account by selecting the upper right red icon. Thank you for visiting Yukon, and we hope your stay is extremely pleasant."

Visitor log? Sierra swallowed hard. Too late to worry about it now. She scrolled through the left side menu. So many options. The "clubs" was an interesting term. She pressed it, and the screen began displaying information on what they were. Using her finger, she scrolled through the options—drinking clubs, dance clubs, riding clubs. Riding? She selected it. It was a club for riding and racing horses—interesting.

She backed out and continued her perusal—tea clubs, historical clubs, pleasure clubs. Sierra paused over that one. Weren't all these a form a pleasure? What would make this one different? She touched the icon for it.

Heat flowed into her hairline as she soaked in the images. Absolutely not! What they were doing was vile, filthy. She would have to use sand to scrub the images out of her eyes. She backed out of the menu and hurried away from the terminal.

She had thought that Yukon was not that much different from home. The people smiled and laughed. They shopped. They walked together. They traveled to work on trolleys, rickshaws, and transports. Above her, ships flew in the lanes. But there was an undercurrent now that she was paying attention.

Sliding past some of the crowd, Sierra neared a section of the courtyard that was the least populated. She stopped under an overhang and studied the scene before her. Dark uniforms patrolled the area—GFT security forces. They traveled in groups of four. She counted seven contingents. People in crisp, dark gray uniforms hurried from building to building—protocol agents and workers who maintained the communication infrastructure in all GFT cities.

While she had noticed the smiling and laughing people before, now she could see the ones that wore hardened expressions—age-lined faces, stress, illness, lack of hope. If she had to calculate, they had the happy-go-lucky people at a two-to-one ratio. So, it was not that much like home.

Home. Sierra blew out a slow breath. She should have stayed on the transport instead of getting off as soon as she had logged in. She just had to be her brother's keeper, had to follow him into the city, and had to be determined on finding him. Yet maybe she could talk some sense into him and get him to go home.

She began to step away from under the overhang. A hard hand clasped over her mouth, gripped her jaw to keep her from screaming, and yanked her into the black recess behind her.

Chapter Seven
YUKON

Seth settled down into the co-pilot chair and flipped the two toggles overhead. The hull reverberated as the hatch at the back closed. Outside the viewport, Tamara stood with her father and Huey. Worry creased her brow. JJ wrapped his arm around her and brought her closer to him. Seth raised a hand to her, pressing his fingertips against the fused pane of the viewport.

He had never been apart from her like this—a couple of days spent in Northern City or in Lower Town, but never this far apart and unsure of how long. Tears glistened in her eyes as she waved goodbye; then, the *Depthfinder* was slipping beneath the dark waters of the bay. The waterline rose, erasing her from his sight. Seth let his hand fall back to the console.

Michael's hands moved effortlessly over the navigation board. Seth leaned back in his seat and let his mind replay John's last words as they had walked down the tunnel and headed for the bay hangar.

John had stopped him at the ramp. When Seth had faced him, the man's eyes held tremendous sorrow. "I wanted you to know this before you left, Seth. It was a hard decision we made, but I and the other elders have agreed that Stephen will be held on trial for his actions. His crimes—accessing official files without authorization and theft of official files—put us all at risk. He will have to face the consequences of his actions. But foremost, we want the twins home safe."

Seth ran his hands over his face. His son sent to prison. Their society used prison as a last resort for rehabilitation. Crimes were scarce. Usually, they involved domestic situations, destruction of property, theft, or battery. Murder was rare. Although, one did happen twenty years ago. That was their first execution, but the man was unreformed and had glorified in the blood he drew. Yet what Stephen had committed was a crime that his son gave no thought to.

His mind ran to the hacks he himself had performed when he was younger. He was caught, every time, usually by Huey or his mom. And he was taught why he couldn't do that and how to access information safely. He was shown how to use and write programs but for the good of his people, never to hurt them. If he wanted to know something, then he was encouraged to seek an elder. And that was what he did.

He could have easily gone the route of Stephen. Yet he had been guided back on the right path. Stephen had taken it an extra step, though. He had traveled beyond their borders with that information he stole. And the potential exposure of the enhanced loomed over them. Where along the line had he failed his son?

"We will be two hours from the north lanes." Michael glanced at him. "What's on your mind?"

"Stephen." Seth turned his chair to face Michael. "With him in the territories, the potential of GFT finding out about us has been elevated . . . " His words faltered at Michael's expression—the same that had been on Tamara's face. He thought it was apprehension about Stephen. But now? Apprehension about letting him know the truth was what he was seeing. "Tell me."

Michael's brow arched at Seth's hiss. "They already know, Seth."

"How?" He replayed in his mind every eventuality that could have led to them knowing, but none would have resulted in that outcome.

"There was a remote hack into our communications about three months ago. It infiltrated some personnel messages and our citizen roster. They discovered that whoever hacked our files were in the process of cross-referencing the information. Huey was able to stop it in time and set up some q-shieldings. Yet whoever hacked our systems was able to download a few GHOST codes and signatures."

Seth ran his finger across his bottom lip as he pondered Michael's words. So, that was why John had allowed the newer version of the GHOST. Why hadn't John told him? Had the hack grabbed more than the codes and signatures?

He lowered his hand and turned back to Michael. "It found us?"

"It found you." He sighed and activated autopilot before rotating his own chair to face Seth. "There are five families with the surname Williams. Do they know you are Jules' son? No one knows. But we are going with the scenario that they know about you and probably the others."

"Do the elders no longer trust me, Michael?" Seth allowed his gaze to follow the dark water as it passed over their viewport—cold and darkness. Above them, the blue-white floes of ice moved on the surface.

"They still trust you, Seth." Michael sank further into his chair and stretched his long legs out in front of him. "Yet you have been unpredictable lately—creating new programs, running your tests and researching genetics. Do they think you will be like GFT and genetically manipulate us in order to 'cure' us? I say no, but they are unsure. They had prepared for the possibility that you would travel outside the borders."

"Instead of me, it was my children."

Michael nodded. "And if they are discovered, GFT will know that we had hidden not just you and your children but also every descendant of the GFT assassins. Remember, GFT believed that we could not procreate."

Seth returned his gaze to Michael. Once again, the rare lengthy conversation with Michael—a blessing and a curse. That was what they, the enhanced, were, too. And they would be a curse to Alaska Country if they were discovered.

"So, it's imperative that we bring my twins home."

"And keep you and them flying under scopes in the meanwhile." Michael's expression hardened. "The towns and cities in GFT-controlled area are tamer than those outside of GFT. It's not a world you are used to, Seth. You may think you know the ways of the world, but you truly don't."

Seth nodded. "I've read about it, watched some vids."

"Those won't show you everything. We will have to travel some of the seedy areas. That's the only way to run dark." He swiveled his chair back around. "It'll be dangerous but follow my lead. No questions asked."

Sierra stood behind Stephen, who fought with an access panel. When he had yanked her back into the darkened alleyway, she had already begun fighting back. She had rammed her elbow into his ribs and begun twisting in his arms. But Stephen was a master fighting instructor. He had countered each move effortlessly. He had twirled her around, pressing his hand harder against her and flattening her against the cool brick wall.

It was only three seconds of action. By the time her shoulder blades had touched the wall, she had recognized her brother. Then she had given him an earful for terrifying her like that. He had only chuckled at her and chided her for following him. Then, he had pulled her card from her pocket, clucking at the status she was given before stuffing it into the breast pocket of her jacket.

That was how she had found herself hiding in a maintenance tunnel next to the Citizen Mainframe watching him hack into the system in order to change her bogus citizen status. Stephen muttered harsh curses as he bent over the datapad. A hot flush rose into her hairline as his curses became more bitter, viler.

"Ven! Seriously?" Her hiss sliced through the still air of the narrow alley of the maintenance tunnel.

He curled his lip, still engrossed in the readouts on the datapad. "What?"

"Language." She sidled a bit closer to him until her knee brushed against his shoulder.

"Curb the condemnation, Si. This isn't Alaska Country." He heaved a sigh and moved the trip-mod from one port to another. "I think I am in. They must have discovered a way to protect their cortex from the GHOST. That was over five q-shieldings."

A spark popped from the topmost port, hitting her brother across the cheek. A word, much harsher than any other, flowed from him. She gazed at him, soaking in what she was seeing. He was so different now. The light that had been in him was dying, being replaced by something darker, something more sinister. His eyes burned with a rage she couldn't identify. His body stayed in a constant tense and rigid state, as if he expected to have to bolt at any moment. Hands that had once danced across keyboards and created the most intricate designs were now curled into claws—strong but no longer a silent strength. He no longer conveyed safety and love but, rather, an aggressive strength. It was as if he would rip apart anything that stood in his way.

And that was what he was doing now. He yanked off the last panel on the junction, reached inside, and he pulled three wires from the depths. Sparks flew, but he ignored them and connected more trip-mods.

"Got it." He held up his hand and snapped his fingers. "Give me your card."

She pulled her card from the breast pocket of her jacket, yet hesitated. "Ven, I'm not so sure about this."

He snarled and stood, towering over her. He had more than six inches of height on her, but never had it seemed so menacing. His pupils dilated in anger. "Si, you have a Citizen One status. That will get you nowhere out here. Citizen One is akin to being an untouchable."

"But if you do this, not even the GHOST can hide the hack if they look too deeply into it."

He jerked the card from her hands and pushed her against the wall. His hand on her upper chest held her against the stones. "I didn't ask for you to follow me. You did that of your own accord. So, if you want to stay safe, you need this hack on your card."

Anger flared. She shoved him away. He stumbled back a step before laughing at her.

"Get angry, Si." He held up her card. Lights from above flashed along its surface. "Either let me hack this into a Citizen Two or go home."

She sighed. It was too late to go home. The transport had already left. He had already hacked into Jinx's core net for the codes. And he had access into the GFT Citizen Mainframe Unit now. "Are you sure it won't be detected? The GHOST program is pretty old now."

"It'll be fine." He stooped back down and inserted her card into the datapad. A few taps and swipes, and she was accepting it back from him as he held it up between his fingers. "Now, you are officially a Citizen Two."

As he replaced the wires with their trip-mods back into the junction, she scooted down the narrow maintenance tunnel and waited by the access hatch. Stephen would have to use the GHOST one more time to check their surroundings before they could leave.

She swallowed against the painful knot in her throat. Stephen had never slammed his hand against her before. He had always been the one who took the pain or hurt before she did—the one who shielded her, taking the brunt of anything heading their way. One time when they were teenagers, a storm had descended upon them. Chunks of flying debris had been hurtled about, and they weren't able to make it to shelter in time. Stephen had shielded her that day, blocking broken limbs to ripped pieces of roofing and even shattered fused panes from striking her. Medtechs had spent three hours digging shrapnel from his body.

Now, his normally warm scent had begun to turn. It seem more acrid. He eased next to her, paused at the control box, and plugged in the GHOST. As they waited for the patrol to pass by, Sierra let her gaze slide over him again.

Something was wrong with him. It had nothing to do with his rebellious nature. Something had unleashed within him, and it terrified her.

Tap. Tap. Tap-tap.

Jason rose from his bunk and stood silently, waiting. It was not his scheduled time. And why Medtech Bastion came today was baffling. Her withered form and that perpetual stench of death that radiated from her stopped at the corner of his cell.

Her icy, watery eyes flowed over his semi-clad body before she turned to the medstudy at her elbow. The medstudy was a new addition. Her gray eyes held contempt, much like the others; yet they also held a bit of hope. That would die pretty soon. There was no hope in this place for anyone—except maybe for him.

Although the dream man had said to wait a little bit longer, it was becoming increasingly harder and harder. His body still ached from the last round of experiments, and he didn't know how much more he could withstand.

"Give him the clothing."

The medstudy nodded and stepped forward. She held the small stack of clothes through the bars. Her eyes studied him as he approached and allowed her to transfer the stack into his hands.

As he dressed in the stiffly starched pants and shirt, the medstudy entered her code to slide open his cell door.

He clasped the last button and waited. If they gave him slippers and gloves, he was to be herded to the comms. If they left him barefoot, then it was to the medlab for more scans.

She dropped a pair of slippers and gloves on the floor. "Put those on."

Medtech Bastion motioned toward the four guards at the door. They surrounded Jason after he donned the articles. "Lead him to Main Comms."

A ripple of surprise flowed through him for half a second before he reined in the reaction. Main Comms? This was new. A test? Or a performance review?

He pushed his thoughts to the back and allowed the guards to escort him down the corridor and up three flights of stairs. Then it was a right, a left, and two more rights before he was led into a room full of consoles, holographic displays, and harsh lights that burned into his eyes.

His enhanced sight picked up on the glow of energy from the holographs, the pulsing waves from the consoles, and the halos cast from the lights above.

Jason glanced to his right at the bank of displays. Holographic readouts of the PatRecs in three of the nearby cities circled above the console. No blips, other than an occasional ding indicating someone slipped into theta band for a moment. Who was she searching for? One of the guards prodded his lower spine.

He increased his pace and followed the first set of guards to the back wall.

Medtech Bastion motioned toward the center monitor. "Have a seat. We want you to hack into the Alaska Country mainframes, particularly medical and security."

He tapped the console in front on him. His text ran across the screen: *The last attempt was unsuccessful. They had countermeasures activated before I reached too far.*

"Try again."

Jason shrugged. As long as she stayed at least ten feet away from him . . . he let his thoughts falter. There wasn't anything he could do, even if she didn't keep her distance. But his imagination conjured many scenarios ending in her death by his hands. He shouldn't hate. It felt wrong to do so. But when it came to her, that was all he had.

He settled in the swivel chair and began. File after file, program after program, code after code fell victim to his search. Before shieldings and firewalls could activate, he was already editing the codes to allow him entrance.

The sounds of people leaving and entering barely registered. The change of guards happened three times. The sparse food and drink that were brought to him remained untouched at his right elbow.

Alaska Country. The last time he tried hacking them, it had shut him out too quickly. This time, though, he hopped from Westland Coast; bounced from New Frandiego to Seattle; then bounced to Dakotas GFT, using Northfolk as the jumping point to bounce to Saskagina in Candadian Province, then to Yukon. He frowned and grabbed a data crystal from the pile by his console.

"Find something?" Medtech Bastion spoke from his left side. He almost jumped at her voice.

She had faded to the background to the point he had forgotten about her. Now, her stench returned threefold.

He nodded and copied the file onto the crystal before typing his reply: *There are some signatures that I recognized from the last time. I think it is their security codes or a program that is used for protection. I'm not sure.*

He copied the file and then had it pulled up on the holographic next to him. It began running through the lines. She read over his shoulder as he typed: *I have it set to run through some parameters for comparison.*

Then he returned to his own console. Nothing but red. No back doors. No weakened areas. They had something new.

He activated the holograph for his results and then pulled up his last results, creating a side-by-side comparison. Jason pointed to the red lines. Again, he typed, growing irritated at the lack of having a voice—all because of her. *These are new codes.*

Medtech Bastion shook her head. "What am I looking at?"

Let me create a 3D rendering for you. Jason created a file, converting the codes into a representation of the security wall around Alaska Country. He rotated the holograph so she could see the entire program and then highlighted a small section. *It has created a type of shell around their systems. It holds the codes of the program they had before, but it's more now. I can't access the new codes or see what it is. And there is no weak area.*

His console beeped. Jason pulled up the file and frowned. He ignored the hated woman's question as he pulled up the new results and the older codes from the last time. They were the same, and he had just seen those earlier.

Jason backtracked along his hacking line. Only one bounce—in Yukon. And there they were—the same codes from his last hack, the same codes that were stitched into the new program Alaska was using. And now, they were in Yukon.

These codes. Jason highlighted the lines. *These are the ones that were in the earlier hack and now here. These are the signatures that I found, same as the one before. They may have updated their program at the compound, but this isn't an updated one.*

"What did they do?" She motioned for one of the techs. "Give him a datapad with voice modulation. I tire of reading his statements."

After a moment, a technician handed him a small datapad. He typed in his reply, and a mechanized voice replied in his stead.

"Looks like a hack into the Citizen Mainframe. I can pull up the information that was obtained. Give me a few minutes." Jason followed the codes, searching. Within minutes, he activated the security feeds, diving into what was hacked and collected. He entered his reply, and the datapad AI spoke. "I have the information pulling up now."

Before them, the face of an extremely beautiful female materialized. Her citizen status had been changed from a one to a two. Jason leaned forward and studied her face—sharp nose yet softened at the end, full lips. Her jawline would have been angular if not for the slight roundness, and she had thick hair the color of light umber that flowed around her face, giving her an almost ethereal look with her golden chestnut-colored skin that offset her eyes. And those eyes captured him—green with flecks of white. Unusual.

He was so absorbed in the visage before him, it took a few seconds before he smelled the death-stench. Medtech Bastion hovered over his shoulder. Her breath was hot on his cheek. He cut his gaze over to her. Her eyes were lit with a fevered excitement.

She reached past him and enlarged the holograph. "Can you find where she is now?"

Jason nodded and typed. The datapad spoke. "I can download her specs and have it run through the mass comm. It'll pick up any scan made." Her breathing increased. Something excited her. "May I ask why, ma'am?"

Medtech Bastion's smile pulled at her thin lips and stretched her papery skin. She tapped the name underneath the holograph. "Williams. I know that name, and I know that face. She will be the key I need." She abruptly stood and motioned at the bank of consoles. "Keep tracking her. I'll have your meals brought in. I want to know where she's been and where she's going."

Jason turned back to the console as Medtech Bastion ordered a group of guards to stay and watch over him. Her cackling whisper reached him. "You've failed in hiding her, Jules."

The *tap-tap-tapping* of her cane faded.

Jules? Who was Jules? Jason reached up and traced the brow of the woman. She was the key? Why?

He bent down and began his own search. With him being alone in the room, he could devise a program that would search out who this Sierra Williams was and then find out what made her so important to Medtech Bastion. What was important to her became more important to him. First, he needed to find the woman's trail.

Chapter Eight
MIDLAND BOUND

Seth followed Michael through the narrow alley, pushing past dark garbed bodies and battered rickshaws. Buildings towered overhead. Ships flew in packed lanes. From the roar of the engines above to the voices overlapping each other, his ears had begun to ache.

After landing at the northern port, having their cards scanned and then rescanned when a blip appeared on Seth's, and then after an hour of waiting until they were given clearance, Seth had followed Michael as the man led them from the eastside port and snagged a public transport that had dropped them off at the center. Now, they were making their way into the main part of the district.

He held out his hands to keep a man from falling into him when he stumbled. After righting the old man, Seth patted down his pockets. Nothing was missing. He gave a small grin and glanced back at the bumbling fool. His hands were too clean, too smooth. There was no dirt. The hair stuck out as if it had been sculpted before having the tattered hat shoved down on it.

He was not an old man. He appeared to be a teenager by the gait—and a pickpocket. A card flashed in his hands as he bumped into a man dressed in a Nest Protocol uniform. The worker caught the "old man," helped to right him, and continued heading for the Nest Protocol building across the center.

Seth shook his head. He never understood the concept of stealing something. But the more he read—and now saw—about the world outside his country, the more he appreciated where he lived.

He almost bumped into Michael when the man stopped suddenly. "What's wrong?"

Michael glanced down at him. "We need to wait a moment." He waved at a bench. "Let's sit there. Enjoy the afternoon."

After a second's hesitation, Seth joined Michael on the cold, metal bench. He ran his hand over the smooth texture. Its ergonomic style gave a lot of comfort for such a hard surface. Michael shifted once, straightening his coat, which hid the shortened blade at his side. A hood had been pulled over his head, covering his braids—not that he needed to. Seth studied the people around him. They sported a number of hairstyles from bald to a spiked patch on top, from long, flowing tresses to shortened crops. There didn't seem to be a set style, except for clothing.

Most of the men—those not in workers' uniforms—wore pants that were tighter around the calves and ankles. Their shirts, in various colors, billowed as if a size too big. The women wore flowing pants. At first, Seth assumed they were skirts until a woman moved and the split of the legs could be seen. Their shirts were a lot like the men's, except cut deeper, showing more—perhaps a bit too much.

Seth averted his eyes as a woman sashayed by. He winced. The lenses he wore burned. He reached up and rubbed his eyes, trying to alleviate the irritation. John had insisted that he wear them to hide his white eyes and make them a blue-green in color.

Although, as Seth continued his survey, people around him had body modifications that included eye tattoos, giving them pink, chartreuse, and vibrant vermilion irises. He squinted. Were those purple eyes on that teenager?

He stifled a sigh. This sitting was doing them no good. It gained nothing.

Michael's voice broke his observation. "When I said on the ship 'no questions,' I didn't mean literally. What is it that is burning inside?"

"Other than these dreaded contacts? How is it that you and John seem to know what I'm thinking or about to do?" Seth shook his head. "I was only wondering why we are sitting on the bench, waiting, and not heading over to Mission Deli."

"We know that look on your face." If it wasn't for Michael's mouth moving, he would have looked like a statue as he stared straight ahead. "The Mission Deli has a signal to let us know when Jinx or Batch is online right there under the 'i' in Deli. It will turn blue. Right now, it's yellow, just as the rest—meaning that they aren't online, and the connection isn't secure."

Seth leaned back and crossed his ankle over a knee. "So, those who come here to do the updates and get codes from Batch . . . you've always had signals?" At Michael's nod, Seth shook his head. "I've never questioned how things operated outside the border. It was just a given for me. Convoy goes. Does what is needed. Comes back. We live on."

Michael rubbed at his knee. "Even though we had been given our independence, there are still sanctions and embargos against us. In order to trade and obtain that which we cannot make ourselves, we need updated citizen cards, hence the reason Batch,

Jinx, and the others stayed in the territories—to give us access to the codes needed."

Seth shook his head. "I've never realized how much went into our survival and how fragile our freedom truly is."

"And that is what Huey meant when he said the insulation imposed upon you affected us more than we realized." He suddenly stood in one smooth motion and waved for Seth to follow.

He did so, no questions asked. He marveled at the man. Time should have left Michael with aging bones and muscles, keeping him from moving quickly and smoothly. Yet the Serum Seventy-four manipulation that had been done to him during his years with GFT gifted him with younger looks and a younger body. He looked fortyish and moved like he was in his thirties; yet Michael called it a curse. His body defied God's design.

Yukon Marketplace Center—the banner that held that name ran the full length of the diameter of the center. So many people were bumping, walking, rushing. Some were smiling and laughing. Others were scowling and snarling. Then there were the security forces covered head to toe in a shimmering black uniform. Seth double-blinked as one seemed to fade into the shadow. His eyes adjusted and focused. The man would have seemed invisible to everyone else, yet Seth picked up a slight variation in the dark, a small sheen of an outline.

Intriguing. Seth glanced around. Now that he knew what he was looking for—there. And there. He turned a slow circle as he walked—five positions. Each was hidden in deep shadows, observing. And no one noticed.

The closest one to him lifted an arm and pointed. Two of the security officers rushed forward and grabbed an old man. Seth quirked an eyebrow. It was the teenager from the alley. There was a small scuffle, and then his view was obscured as he and Michael passed through the revolving doors of Mission Deli.

He had half-expected food smells, old grease, and the scent of sugary drinks. Instead, it was practically a sterile environment. People sat at partitioned cubicles. Their food was served in bento boxes. Drinks were set in circular depressions.

On the back wall were a bank of ordering terminals. Wait-BOTs trolled the area, serving and cleaning. Seth frowned. The customers seemed happy, but where were the people? Where was the interaction that came with meals?

Michael paused at the far corner terminal. "School your expression."

Seth closed off his thoughts. No need to allow anyone to read his expression. He needed to blend in. And no one questioned the culture they lived in. He paused by Michael and stood with his back to the room.

Michael motioned him to stand behind him, facing the terminal. "If you block the terminal, it will send a red flag."

Seth moved behind his mentor and watched. Michael inserted his card, ran through the menu items, and selected three: peach tea, lemon sorbet, and chicken sandwich minus the cheese. Then he entered three numbers: 117.

To the deli, it was an order being placed. But apparently, it was a code because the screen immediately switched to a 2D image on the viewscreen of a young woman with shoulder-length hair that curled around her jaw. The faux-face smiled.

"Mikey."

"Michael."

"Nope. Always Mikey to me." Jinx winked, causing a slight red patch to appear on Michael's cheek. "I am sending you an update on your card. Have Seth insert his."

Seth handed Michael his citizen card.

"And I will have to talk fast. Mission Deli may be compromised. Dad is tracking down the bounces right now. There was a hack on Sierra's card. Seth, it showed the old GHOST signatures. So, it looks like your boy has his hand on that program. Sierra's card was hacked from a one to a two. And Stephen's tracker has them on a rail transport heading to New Frandiego, where they will board another rail transport with an arrival at Midland border the next day. I'm uplinking the transactions now."

A cold feeling washed over Seth. He glanced over his shoulder. Three security officers entered and began heading to the far right terminal. Michael's touch brought him back around. Michael pursed his lips and slightly shook his head.

Stay put, apparently. Take no notice of them?

"Peach tea for you, too?" Michael's soft voice almost made him jump. Seth nodded. Michael touched the icon. The code was given. The staticky image of Jinx winked and fizzled. The man then ran his card through the slot and motioned Seth toward a nearby cubicle—Cubicle 117.

They settled down with Michael purposely ignoring the small contingent. Seth's back was to them, which gave him an uncomfortable feeling. He opened his mouth, but Michael held up a finger as a wait-BOT rolled up to their table. The bento boxes were placed before them, and their drinks were set in the holder.

"It's normal for people to ignore security. It's a common occurrence and such a normal part of life that no one gives a second thought to them. That's the reason I need you to ignore them, too." Michael sipped his tea.

Seth followed suit. "It's so different here. Did you see how many forces there are compared to people? The ratio is off." He began eating his sandwich, following Michael's lead. "The drink order—was that code to let Jinx know about the contingent?"

Michael nodded.

"In your past, you did this often?"

Again, Michael nodded. "We blended."

"I never asked, but I really would like to know. Was it just you and Peter?"

"No, there were ten of us. We lost two on a mission the year before we sought Bishop Thomas."

"The others?"

Michael spooned a portion of his sorbet and cut his gaze at Seth as he took a bite.

Seth returned to his food. Enough said. He and Peter had taken them out. It was written there in his eyes—a hardness. What did it take for him and Peter to leave that life? More than any man should have to give, apparently. He let his thoughts run back to his own father. His father had fought to leave that life behind—but only after he was decommissioned, and Uncle JJ had left. But he did it. He had left behind the killing, the destruction. Yet from watching the data crystals, his father had also been fighting to leave the demons behind.

The food no longer interested Seth. He picked up his drink and sipped at it as he thought more on his father, a man who had sacrificed his life for those he loved, a man whose genetic manipulation had been passed along to him. So, did the aggression and rage and detachment pass along as well?

For every action, there was an equal and opposite reaction. For good, there was evil. There was more than one side to everything. Light didn't exist without the dark. Actions had consequences. All those adages ran through his mind.

There was truth to those sayings. So, logically, it was possible that aggression and rage would have been inherited. Seth's rearing kept those tendencies from appearing. And he had raised the twins in much the same way. But now, beyond their border and in a place that offered more danger and temptations to them than they comprehended? What would happen if this world awakened the buried aggression within them?

Michael's comm beeped. He pulled it out of his pocket and glanced at it. "We need to head back to the ship. Jinx sent a Hi-Wave."

They stood. Michael pressed a small button on the table before they walked away. On the glass of the door, Seth caught the reflection of the waiter-BOT cleaning their table. Then he stepped into the bright Northern sun.

The trek back to the ship was just as slow. It seemed the afternoon pulled even more people out into the open. Seth kept his hands deep in his pockets, covering his citizen card and the QG crystal. John nor Michael knew that he had brought it with him. In hindsight, maybe he should have left it behind on the off chance it was stolen from him. Yet with his bioprint needed for access, it would be nearly impossible to hack. And as he had reasoned with himself, they may come into a situation where the QG was warranted.

The port was less populated than when they had first landed. Seth dogged Michael's heels. Michael waved toward the hatch's panel. Seth raised the ramp and secured the airlock before joining Michael at the front. Michael already had pulled up the communications hub.

"Looks like we are grounded until 0900 tomorrow."

On the small monitor below their viewscreen, the Yukon notice ran through the bands. An electrical storm was approaching. All ships were dry-docked until the morning.

"What about Jinx's message?" Seth removed his coat and threw it over the back of his seat.

Michael turned in his seat. "I sent it to your station."

Seth sat down. Priority alert flashed. He entered his name and set his hand on the bioreader. His blood seemed to congeal, and rage began to build.

Mid has bounty on Sierra. Came in an hour ago on all NP-Hi-Waves. Stephen's hack on card keeps her protected for now. Midland has different codes. We aren't updated on those. She will be flagged as soon as she uses her card. Connect @ Nelson's Hangar in MidC.

Stephen ushered his sister down the narrow aisle. They squeezed past bodies carrying small luggage bags, parents with children, and lone travelers frantically searching the berth numbers above the doors.

He nudged Sierra's back, guiding her to their immediate left to Berth 2310. The door slid back, and they stepped into the small confinement. Stephen turned a tight circle. Well, it wasn't that small—a twenty-by-ten room. Two bunks lined the corner of the room to his right. A faux wood table separated the lower bunk and the shortened couch nestled next to the window. Across from the shortened couch was a lengthier one with a long, cylindrical cushion. To his left was the refresher station.

Sierra settled on the shortened couch. She squirmed a bit before looking up at him with a smile. "It's quite comfortable."

He shrugged and stepped toward the longer couch yet propped his arm against the viewport and leaned against it as he gazed out. The transport began pulling away from the New Frandiego station. He hadn't gotten to see much of New Frandiego. Sierra had wanted to explore, but he had convinced her that Midland offered more. And they could come back. She thought he was here to explore. What would she think if she knew his real reason? And thinking of such, he needed to find a better card and hack it. His Citizen Two status wasn't going to allow him to get very far.

"Stephen? Did you hear me?"

He jerked out of his musings and turned to her as he sat on the couch's edge. "Sorry. Lost in thought."

"I was saying that they deliver food and drinks to the berths. Do you want anything?" She turned back to the viewport and watched the scenery race by. Tall, white buildings that gleamed in the light slowly faded away to more compact buildings and resident complexes. And just beyond those metal and faded terracotta buildings, the brown expanse of the desert began to appear.

Her eyes danced at the scene beyond, and a smile played at the corners of her lips. "The view is amazing."

"Yes. Amazing." He touched the arm of the couch and activated the amenities menu, selecting board mode instead of holograph.

"So, do you want anything?"

He shook his head. "Nah. I thought I would explore the galleys and see what they have. You know me."

"Yeah. I do. You can't bear to stay still in one place." She gave a slight chuckle. "Just be careful, yes?"

He gave her an absentminded nod and continued his scrolling: galleys, restaurants, dining halls. He paused at that one. It required a Citizen Three, Class Prime status. Stephen curled his lip in disgust. This class system of GFT's was ignorant and pointless. Yet it was a higher status he was going to need if he wanted to visited the better locales and travel undetected as he searched for that infamous medlab.

He swiped at "clubs." Those may hold what he would need. They would probably be packed with people, bodies bumping into each other. They would be easy targets to filch a card from. He closed down the menu and stood.

"I'm going to head out now."

She gave him a small wave and continued watching.

Stephen stepped out into the quiet aisle and headed west toward the tail end of the transport. Above him, the sound of the conveyor hummed as it transported the Citizen Three statuses toward the same direction. He shook his head. Why couldn't they be endowed with a Citizen Three? It would make life so much easier—especially his.

Still, this avenue offered some attractions. He paused at one of the art pieces framed in a gilded box that decorated the walls. The riot of colors swirled and blended in what would have appeared as an abstract to most people. But the red lines created the Golden Ratio within the medley. Did the artist intend for that to happen? He looked at the name tag at the bottom. The holographic readout stated her name was Denise Nicolosi. A prompt offered more information. Stephen tapped it.

A benefit was being held at Club Endeavors in C-Three Twelve West. Well, he was headed that way.

He followed the corridor, stepped through the couplings between the transport compartments, and drank in the crowded sight. Out of the all the people he saw, only three held the Golden Ratio on their face. There were two arrangements of flora that used ferns with Golden Ratio fronds. The rest of the world was nothing but chaos—sights, smells, and even sensations. He ran his hands against the sides of the booths as he passed through the galleys and restaurants—soft fabric, leather, wood, velvet. Then he felt the hardened steel-plast. Those were in the café named Harden Biscuits. Stephen shook his head at that name—absurd.

Then he was through and into a small club style section. An attendant held out his hand for Stephen's card. Stephen handed it to him as he surveyed the crowd. Lights danced above. There were no booths, just small tables bolted to the walls. People mingled with drinks in hand.

He accepted his card back and suffered through four more repeats before he made it to C-Three Twelve West. The door slid open, and a curtain pulled back. Stephen glanced over his shoulder. The curtain was holographic, a newer version, creating realistic images instead of blue and white lines peppered with green codes—not that most people saw it as such.

The attendant here waited patiently. Stephen turned his attention to him as he passed over his card. The quiet man scanned it and handed it back before gesturing toward the dimly lit area where people strolled along, pausing at times to view framed artwork or study the intricate sculptures.

He mingled among them. None of the art were as captivating as the one he saw earlier. Apparently, that was the only abstract. The paintings at the end of the row did capture the essence of mood and movement, such as the one with the two bare-chested dancers. Stephen frowned and stepped back in order to view the line of paintings that hung on the wall. These didn't capture the beauty of the human body—not like in the art books at home. Those paintings from centuries ago highlighted the beauty of God's creation. These? He let his eyes flow from one end to the other. They sexualized the body, removing the beauty. Stephen shrugged and moved to the next array of art.

The sculptures were excellent yet lacked the touch to make them realistic. Human bodies were not perfect, but these sculptures seemed to try and capture perfection yet failed. Perfection came in the imperfection of life, in the varied outcomes of personalities and features. On these sculptures, there were no wrinkles, marks, or bumps, just smooth marble and stone. They were lifeless. He paused at the last sculpture—except for this one.

The label said it was called *Eve Before the Fall*. Wavy hair hung down her body, appearing to float around her full hips. Strong yet delicate arms were reaching back to collect handfuls of her locks while her head was thrown back in obvious delight. And her face . . . Stephen had never seen such a perfect Golden Ratio. He allowed his eyes to travel over every inch of the sculpture. The exquisite talent rivaled the abstract from earlier.

"I see you know perfection when you see it." The mellow and languid voice purred next to him.

He smiled slightly and cast a hooded gaze over his shoulder. Her scent was intoxicating—a blend of rose, musk, and sandalwood designed to be an aphrodisiac.

"And what do you know of perfection?" He fully turned and studied the older woman, letting his gaze flow down her body. The black, shimmering dress hugged her lithe form. A small clutch on a golden chain hung at her side.

Dark eyes glinted mischievously from under glitter-coated lashes. Full lips widened, stretching the red stain that covered them. "Well, I created this piece. Actually, all of them that you see on this transport. In this compartment, it shows the progression of my talent from novice to master."

Stephen reached out and ran his hand around the sculpture, careful to not touch it. "And this is your last piece?"

"Why create more when perfection has been achieved?"

Stephen quirked the corner of his mouth at her statement. Perfection, huh? The woman was narcissistic and proud. She would be easy to manipulate. What would she think if she knew there was more than something like this sculpture? More than the regular humans mingling about?

He returned his gaze back to her. "Stephen."

"Denise." She waved toward the bar set up in the corner. "May I offer you a drink?"

Stephen offered her his elbow. A full smile slid across her face as she slipped her hand through the crook of his arm. He covered it with his hand and led her to the bar.

"I saw your abstract in one of the eastern compartments. Chaotic, but there was an order to it, too." He waited until she was situated on the stool before settling down beside her. "Was that an earlier piece?"

"Yes, but it was what spearheaded my sculpture line. So, tell me, Stephen, you like art?" She waved toward the wait-BOT. "Two martinis."

"I like beauty." He leaned toward her as she gave the wait-BOT her card. Her Class Prime status flashed in the lighting above the bar. He let his hand settle near hers. "And when I find beauty, I have to investigate it."

Her face blossomed as a slow red traveled from her neck to her ears. "Investigate it. As in . . . "

Stephen allowed his lids to lower a bit more. She was so much older than he—maybe closer to forty-five or fifty. Yet she was alluring. That beauty from her youth had never faded. Many women he had seen so far used artificial means to keep their youthfulness. But Denise . . . she allowed her beauty to age gracefully.

He reached out and used the back of his fingers to trace the fine lines at the corner of her eye and then smoothed it down her cheek, stopping at her jaw. His forefinger flowed across her chin and then down her neck as he spoke.

"I've always been intrigued with how beauty and perfection align—especially in nature. Some women carry this naturally—like you." He stopped at the recess of her throat at her collarbone, feeling the heavy pulse.

A deep rumble shook her chest. Stephen cocked his head in confusion.

"You are quite skilled, my young Stephen." She handed him his drink. "I'm experienced enough to know when a young man is trying to *charm* me."

As he sipped the alcoholic drink, raising a brow at the taste and lack of sensation, she continued. "But you need not try so hard. I had my sights set on you the moment you walked into the berth."

That took him aback. "Really, now?"

"You were hard to miss. Latest fashion. Dark, brooding. A man in search of something." She chuckled, reached to her side, and pulled her small clutch onto her lap. Stephen watched as she reached in and removed a small piece of film. She spread it on the bar's surface and peeled back the folds. Four tiny blue crystals laid on the surface. Denise pressed her fingertip onto one and turned to him.

He pulled back when she reached for his lips. A small pout issued from her mouth. "You wanted my time, right? Then do this. Trust me, you will enjoy it."

Stephen regarded her. He needed that card. That was the only way he was going to be able to get into Midland's central hub, since only Citizen Three status was allowed. And he couldn't risk hacking from a tunnel. Not this time around. It had taken too long in Yukon. No telling how long it would take in Midland City.

And he was enhanced. If alcoholic drinks had no effect, surely illicit drugs wouldn't either. He leaned forward. Her finger slid between his lips and placed the crystal on the tip of his tongue. Immediately, the room lit in a brilliant haze, pulling a quick gasp from him. Colors overrode his vision, highlighting lines and curvatures. People's faces became emblazoned with a bright glow and vibrant hues.

She laughed at his expression and slid a crystal into her own mouth. "This is how I create perfection." Her hands were cool against his skin as she captured his face and kissed him before he could react.

The riot of colors and enhanced sight were almost overwhelming. Now, the added sensation of her lips against his, forcing his mouth to respond as she deepened the kiss, awoke something within him. Then it began to fade.

He broke off the kiss and leaned away from her. Her eyes, hazy with passion and the effects of the drug, searched him. A part of him revolted at his behavior. Yet he *needed* that card. This was the only path to achieve it. Stephen swallowed hard against the guilt that tried to rise within him. "Give me one more."

"Are you sure?" At his nod, she grabbed his hand and tugged. "Follow me. You don't want to have a second one in public. Trust me."

Trust her? Definitely not but he would follow her in order to obtain his goal. The end—in this case, that card of hers—would justify the means.

His senses were returning to normal as he followed her through the west exit and through two more compartments. The Class Prime sections were opulent and identical in decor. Golden tones set into a faux teakwood wainscot. Soft, muted lights lined the aisle above them. A glass encased lift stood near the first berth, giving the passengers access to the conveyor above. Mauve carpet softened their footfalls.

She keyed open the second berth to the right. Dark lighting greeted them. Luxurious tapestries decorated the walls, and a plush coverlet draped the slender bunk to his right. As soon as the door closed behind them, she pulled the folded film from the depths of her clutch and then cast the purse to the side. It slid along a small table before coming to a rest against the wall and the corner of the bunk.

Stephen tamped down his excitement. It would be easy to grab that card.

She set the film on the table and opened the folded edges, pressed two fingertips against the crystals, and then turned, holding up her hand with two fingers suspended between them, offering him another taste of the mind altering experience. Stephen leaned down and accepted it, smothering the small voice in his mind as colors and heightened sensations exploded around him.

That small voice screamed louder at him, and a tightness gripped his heart and twisted it. He growled. She giggled. He would make that voice shut up. He was tired of it—tired of its condemnation, of it rearing its head when all he wanted was a bit of fun . . . and that card.

The voice began screeching as he allowed her to push his shirt from his shoulders, their lips never severing their connection. Aggression rose within him, and he didn't stop it. Her laughter filled his ears, and the voice faded as he allowed the most savage part of him to take over.

Φ

Sierra glanced up at the chronometer. Three hours had passed, and he was still gone. She closed down the holo-reader. It was time to find her irritating brother. After a quick check to make sure her card and salve were in her satchel, she stepped through the hatch and keyed the lock.

Smells assaulted her—cleaning fluids that were used on the carpet underfoot, oil from the walls, grease from the hatch's interior workings, ozone from all the electronics around her. She passed through the connection and into the next compartment—perfumes, colognes, food.

Her head began to ache from the various odors. She spied a short, polished steel bar at the far end. Sliding past the crowd that lingered around the small, circular standing tables, she hurried to the corner.

The stool molded to her weight and gave support. It was nice and comfy. She smiled as she pulled her salve from her satchel and uncapped it. The bartender approached as she rubbed the tube under her nose.

"Menu?' He held out the placard.

"Thank you." She accepted it and pressed the red icon in the upper corner. A holograph appeared above the card.

There weren't a lot of choices. Yet the food seemed to be specialties and delicacies. She perused the items before deciding on an egg hollandaise. They may have considered duck eggs a delicacy; but in Alaska Country, it was an everyday staple.

The drinks, though, were not familiar. She glanced at the bartender. "May I have plain water?"

"We only serve flavored spritz." He took the menu from her. "I suggest the strawberry. Easier on the palate."

Sierra nodded her thanks. He disappeared through a narrow door behind him as a voice drifted her way. She turned on the stool and scanned the area. Across the crowded expanse of the compartment, a woman dressed in a flowing, purple gown stood on a small stage. Her blonde hair was pinned at her nape, and a golden chain with a heavy pendant hung around her neck.

It didn't seem as though she was singing words—just inflections and octaves of sounds. Yet there was a pattern to it. She closed her eyes and let the song flow around her. No, those were words. She could catch the syllables and emphasis.

It reminded her of the dialect from Upper Bay. Some of the inflections and enunciations were the same.

"Here you are, Miss."

Sierra turned to her food. "What language is she singing?"

The server glanced up at the singer. "Oh, that's Katherine O'Hennessey. She's from the Gaelic Opera House in GFT North Isles. I think they use the ancient Gaelic language."

He moved down to the next customer. Sierra tried her food. It wasn't as fresh-tasting as home, but it was palatable. She moved her plate and glass around so she could sit sideways and watch the singer.

So many people seemed entranced by her songs. She was not immune, either. Sierra's heart lurched at the haunting melody. Did the words match the longing and heartache that the song seemed to create?

When the song ended, a hush filled the compartment for long seconds before everyone broke out in applause; Sierra joined in. She would have to find that song when she returned to the berth after locating Stephen.

Stephen . . .

She drained her drink. So engrossed in the song, she had finished her meal without truly tasting it. The bartender accepted her card when she handed it to him. He ran it through a reader. Sierra bit at her lip. This was her first use on the card since Stephen's hack.

The reader flashed orange, indicating funds were deducted. He smiled as he handed it back. "Enjoy your night."

"Thank you." She stuffed it into her satchel and slid off the stool. The next compartment was another restaurant. She strolled through it and another. And another. And another. How many places to eat did they need? She shook her head. The next compartment had better not be another restaurant.

A holographic curtain parted, and she stepped into opulence. The attendant scanned her card and then waved her in. She followed along the line of people viewing the artwork. The progression of art ran from novice to master yet were created by the same hand. She leaned toward one. The brushstrokes on them were unique—heavy to the right, light to the left, heavy again on top.

This artist enjoyed chaos on top of structure—an almost diabolic mind with its use of dark on light, letting the paints bleed into each other.

She meandered to the next line of exhibitions. The sculptures were hedonistic, too sensual for her taste, too lifeless—except for the last one: *Eve Before the Fall*.

Sierra smiled. If Stephen came through here, this would have been the one he would have been drawn to.

With a sigh, she left the compartment and ventured further west toward the end of the transport. These sleeping compartments were designed to show prestige. Yet the materials used were the same as theirs.

She bent toward the wainscot on her right and tapped it with a fingernail. Fake wood—it almost looked like teakwood. It was a quite good facsimile.

The door to her left hissed open. Stephen stumbled out with his shirt half opened; a dark shadow clouded his face and drew his brows downward. His eyes held guilt, along with a hardness. Sierra straightened and froze in shock. Surely, this wasn't her brother. She caught a glimpse of a half-dressed woman within. The older woman waved to him as the door closed.

He turned, and color drained from his face. "Sierra?"

Anger flooded through her. It was one thing that he did what he did with Danica. But a stranger? And not even two full days into their travels.

"Stephen!" Her lips curled in disgust, and her hiss cut through the suddenly cramped corridor. "Seriously? I can't believe you!" she growled in frustration.

Stephen's face darkened even more. Anger began to fill his eyes. "Curb it, Sierra. You don't control me. What I do is my own choice."

"I'm not trying to control you. But to give yourself—"

"Ach!" He clasped a hand over her mouth, pushing her against the wall of the compartment. "Stop. Just because you follow our people's beliefs doesn't mean I have to."

She batted his hand away, quelling the queasiness from the smell of overpowering perfume on his hand. "Why not? You were raised in it. It's who we are."

"Who you may be. But not me." Anger and bitterness hardened his gaze. "So, stop it with this—"

People around them began slowing and turning their head to curiously peer at them. Stephen noticed, too. His grip bit into her arm as he pulled her out of the compartment. She yanked herself from his grasp.

He was about to speak, but she slammed her hands against his chest, barely moving him an inch, and pushed past him, ignoring the odor that rolled off him as he twisted around to follow. He kept pace with her as she led the way back to their berth. When they stepped inside, she retreated to her couch and picked up her holo-reader.

"Si?"

"Patch it, Ven!" She angled herself away from him. "I don't want to hear your excuses nor your reasons. Nor do I want to know about your disgusting behavior. I can smell it on you."

"Si—"

"I can smell her perfume, the alcohol, and . . . What is that? It's foul. Smells toxic." She paused in her reading to grab her salve and run another path under her nose.

She refused to glance up at him when he took a half-step toward her. His sigh was barely audible. Then he turned, grabbed his travel bag, and disappeared into the refresher. For a brief moment, she wasn't sure if she heard retching or not. Then the water from the small shower unit began, drowning out any other sounds coming from the refresher.

Sierra dragged in a shaky breath and held her knuckles against her lips to keep them from trembling. She was way out of her depth on this. Something was wrong with her brother, and the feeling that it was only going to get worse wouldn't leave her.

Please, show me the way. She kept repeating her prayer until she had no energy to continue.

Outside, night began to fall.

Stephen stepped from the refresher and cast his travel bag onto the long couch. His reflection, dressed once more in the latest fashion, looked in her direction before he settled on the top bunk and turned toward the wall. Sierra set her holo-reader down. Maybe by the time she finished with the shower, he would be asleep.

Φ

The unit next to him beeped. Jason looked up from the Yukon Visitor profile of Sierra Williams and sent his chair rolling to the console. He halted his flight and activated the screen's readouts.

Her card had been used—Midland bound transport. Jason frowned. There was another signature but a different card. He pulled up the file to see a similar face to hers but more angular and harder. Stephen Williams. Her brother?

He glanced over his shoulder. Only one guard and he stood a step outside the opened hatch; boredom etched itself across his face.

With quick movements, Jason deleted the information. Now that he knew they were headed for his country, Medtech Bastion could wait. He still needed time to infiltrate Alaska Country and find the information on whomever Jules was. And she didn't need to know about the brother. Not yet.

He rolled his chair back to the main console. While he was looking at the other unit, apparently his initial program had finished.

Jason scanned the results. There was a signature similar to Alaska Country, yet different than the ones used in Yukon earlier and on the transport. So, that meant a third card. He recorded the data onto a crystal.

"Find something, Alpha Zero?" The she-devil *tap-tapped* her way toward him.

Jason turned in his chair. He typed his reply on the datapad. "A similar signature in Yukon, but it's different. Closer to Alaska Country."

"How far have you made it into their databanks?"

"Not far. The q-shieldings are more advanced."

She nodded and pulled up the results on the other console. Her thin lips pursed in thought. "I see your program is still running through the systems." She straightened and turned away. "Continue your search. And I want those databanks breached."

She didn't wait for his response. The door hissed closed, and then the locks activated. He turned back to the consoles.

How much longer? His thought rose to the surface and became more of a prayer.

And in his heart he felt the answer: *Just a little while longer. It will be soon.*

Jason closed his eyes and took a deep breath. His resolve was weakening. Yet he could keep himself distracted. Without anyone monitoring him, he could hack into Medlab Twelve-twenty's files. With Medtech Bastion preoccupied, she wouldn't suspect his actions. He opened the medical files and began searching.

While one program cycled through, trying to break the Alaska Country's defense walls, he dove deeper into the information at his fingertips. Minutes turned into hours. Jason rubbed at his eyes and leaned back. He had not found much other than the information he already had. He was about to close the program, but one command line caught his attention.

He clicked it. Lines flowed down. Jason ran the translation matrix. Soon, the face of a man with startingly green eyes and a scar down the side of his face stared back. He had seen that face—or, at least, a shadow of that face—in the man named Stephen and the softer version in the woman named Sierra. So, this was Jules. He read the file, absorbing the information. Jason closed down the file and erased his tracks before leaning back in his chair.

What the man Julius Williams was made into had apparently passed down through his family. And the serum used on Julius . . . had been redeveloped and used on him. After reading about the enhancements the serum created, Jason recognized the same in himself. But he wasn't to be a soldier. He was just a tool for extending that woman's life.

If he could somehow contact the brother and sister, would they be able to help him? He shook his head at the thought. Stupid idea. There was no reason for them to help. Yet Medtech Bastion would eventually catch them and experiment on them, too.

He shut down the fruitless attempt to hack into Alaska Country and set the program to surveillance mode on the Midland Central Hub and the Midland Visitor Hub. If either of their cards were used again, he would know and be able to pinpoint their location. And then he would let Medtech Bastion know about them possibly being siblings, maybe even twins, given how closely they resembled each other.

It was a risky move, but it would be his only way to escape. He would need outside help. And that required them to be captured and brought here. As his program scanned through the massive databanks, he pulled up the report on the Pattern Recognition System.

The system still had flaws, but it did the job at registering the theta waves and strong concentrations of alpha. If they were like him, then they would be in theta and beta or alpha. He narrowed the parameters and let it run.

A yawn crept up on him. Jason stretched and stood. It would take a long time for both. Midland City, the destination of the transport, was a sprawling metropolis—not that he ever had the opportunity to view the city he lived in. Yet he had seen the images.

He walked to his cot that had been brought in earlier in the afternoon. Jason settled down on the hard surface and relaxed. Now, it was a waiting game. And he had just moved his first chess piece of this dangerous game. One more prayer rose silently from his lips: *Please let my action stay hidden and please help us. Dear Dream Man, I believe we are going to need You.*

Chapter Nine
THE BOUNTY

Stephen glanced around at the expansive terminal as the transport with the newest load of passengers prepped to pull away from the platform. Bodies hurried and flowed around him, parting like waves against a rock. The loudspeakers announced arrival times and departures along with destinations nearby.

He thumbed the stolen citizen card that was stuffed deep into his pocket as he glanced back at Sierra, who stood at the border of the terminal and the plaza and was absorbed in the Midland City's holographic display of its directory. She had still been asleep when he had awakened. So, he had taken that time to hack the citizen card and download the Citizen Three, Class Prime codes onto his data crystal. Now he only needed to dump the card. He kept an eye on Sierra as he followed along the edge of the platform.

The grav motors activated. Station signals flashed their warnings to alert passengers to clear the platform as semaphores began to lower. He pulled the stolen card from his pocket and dropped it onto the rails before following the crowd away from the edge.

Heat from the motors should effectively destroy the card and any trace of the GHOST being used on it. His heart lurched in his chest, but he ignored it. Guilt wouldn't deter him—not this time. And that voice no longer badgered him.

Sierra looked up at him as he approached. Her eyes still held a bit of anger to them; but at least, she wasn't giving him the cold shoulder this morning. "It says there is a visitor's hub nearby."

"What about Central Hub?"

"We don't have the statuses for that." She frowned at him with narrowing eyes. "What did you do?"

"Do?" He scowled. "I did nothing. But I can use the GHOST to access the Central Hub. It'll give us better lodgings than the public visitor hub." He glanced at the holograph and located the direction of the Central Hub.

She shook her head as they strolled away from the directory. Keeping her voice low, she glanced around them. "If you keep using the GHOST, it will eventually be discovered. That program is too old now. Remember Dad mentioning that GFT had countermeasures against some of the codes. Nest Protocol created it. You know it wouldn't take that much time for them to find a way to supersede that programming, even with Grandma Abby's tweaks."

"I'm being careful, Si." He put his arm around her shoulders and steered her away from the center crowd and along the edges. "PatRecs are active. So, keep your thoughts centered on the now. Until we get a place to stay, we can't think beyond what we are doing."

She nodded and pulled away from him. A bit of hurt ricocheted in his chest. He caught himself and brought his thoughts back to the present and not on how differently she was treating him. He arched his neck to relieve the tension and centered his thoughts back on the present. Even though the PatRecs allowed the theta brainwaves, too much time spent in theta alerted the system to monitor the individual. And they needed to stay under the scopes as much as possible.

Ahead stood the circular, three-story building. Columns gave it a coliseum appearance. Twenty meters in were the scanners. Beyond that were the lifts that took people to the second floor. Stephen let his gaze roam over the second-floor balconies, where people were in their finery, laughing and drinking, gazing out among those who strolled through the area and sitting along the cushioned lounges. Whatever else was beyond them was hidden from view by the blackened glass exterior. Judging from their hardened expressions, he didn't want to know what lay beyond.

Stephen stepped across the white marbled threshold of the Central Hub. Sierra bumped into him when he paused and searched for an empty card scanner away from everyone else. He spotted one to his right in the far corner. He motioned toward it, and she followed.

As he walked, he pulled his citizen card from his pocket and inserted the data crystal into the top slot. The transfer was quick. Now, he had Citizen Three, Class Prime codes on a Citizen Two card. With the GHOST and his card working in conjunction, he should be able to access any information he wanted. He glanced up at the vaulted ceiling. At least here in Central Hub, the Pattern Recognition Scans were not used.

Stephen stepped up to the scanner, removed the GHOST, and inserted his card. As it cycled through the codes, he slipped the GHOST into a side port and waited. Sierra tapped his shoulder.

When he looked back at her, she pointed to a vendor near the outside edge of the center. "We skipped breakfast. Do you want anything?"

"Sure. Doesn't matter what. You choose."

She turned away from him and strolled back out into the sunlight. Stephen watched his sister for a moment. She paused at a few displays, touched a few plants that decorated the public terminal, and then fell into line at the vendor station.

Apparently, she was going to stay mad at him for a while. He sighed and turned back to the scanner. She would calm down soon enough. She always did.

The main menu opened. He ran through the files. How much information did they allow Citizen Three statuses? Apparently, a lot. Well, at least for Denise. Every file to every department was at his fingertips.

A green light flashed on the notification icon. His brow furrowed. It seemed Denise was well-connected. This one came from a Director Meachum on behalf of a Medtech Bastion. He touched it, and the messages displayed across the screen.

Enchanté Pleasure Club. 12-20 awaiting subjects. Confirmation on male subject: height, 5'11." Weight: 170. Need visual confirmation.

Payment for previous subjects pending.

Recert approved. Midland Expanse extending contract for one year.

He glanced at the timestamp. It was from last night, shortly after he left her berth. So, he would have been one step closer to finding the medlab had he stayed. But then, she probably would have dosed him. The drug she had given him had more of an effect on him than he wanted to admit. He had lost control last night. Only snippets of what had happened remained in his memory, and those turned his stomach. Yet he wasn't going to admit that to Sierra.

He shoved those remnant memories to the back of his mind and reread the message. Midland was more corrupt than he thought. Human trafficking seemed to be an evil that would never die. Yet what was Medlab Twelve-twenty using the men for? Were there women, too? Were they reinstating the Serum Seventy-four program or something different?

He would find out. Stephen scratched at the stubble on his jaw as he closed down the notification. He could go to the club and find out more. The medlab held the key to what he was. And if he had to perform unsavory actions to gain his information, then so be it. At least those actions were a bit exciting. And he would continue to ignore the thought that each action he committed was killing his soul.

Stephen opened the next file. The contact was a Robert at the club. Code to be given was "gold omega." And that would give him the location of Medlab Twelve-twenty in order to deliver the subjects, which, in this case, would be him.

Sierra's vanilla scent alerted him well before she approached. He quickly shut down the files and opened the visitor information menu.

"I bought you a small shake and a breakfast bar." She set the two items on the console lip and peered under his arm at the screen. "What have you found so far?"

He stepped to the side to allow her a clear view. "Which hotel would you like to stay at?"

She glanced through the high-end hotels as he picked up his bar and began nibbling at it. Her eyes blinked a couple of times before she gazed up at him. "We don't have the funds for these."

"We do. I have already taken care of that, Si. I have the funds on my card. So, pick your stay."

Her eyes narrowed at him. Yet she turned back to the screen and selected a hotel near the central plaza in the Golden Sector. He browsed through the amenities as he picked up his shake and sipped it. This one had a performance show every night, a restaurant on the top floor that overlooked the metropolis, and a recreation area on the ground floor. He shook his head. Sierra and her restaurants. Her metabolism ran so high, she had to eat almost every hour or two. Thinking of which . . .

He entered their reservation information as he asked, "Did you bring your metabolic pills?"

"Yes, I keep them on me. Stop worrying."

"I can't help but worry, Si. If you don't take them, you'll have to constantly eat."

"Well, we are in a place where the food is abundant." She glared at him when he shut down the scanner and faced her. "I'm more worried about you. I know you are up to something."

"Not at the moment." He wrinkled his nose at her and motioned outside with his shake in hand. "Shall we? It's a bit of a walk to the hotel. Or should we take a rickshaw?"

"Walk, please." She brushed past him, flipping her hair over her shoulder. "I would like to see a bit of the city before you sequester me behind walls."

Frustration flared through him. He would ignore that barb. She was itching for a fight, apparently. "Beta, Sierra."

"Keep yourself in beta, Stephen."

They passed from the darkened interior of the Central Hub and into the bright sunlight of the public terminal. He followed Sierra as she strolled along the walkway, taking in the sights and smells around him. There was no rush; so he allowed her to stop whenever something caught her eye, murmured his appreciation at something whenever she showed him a product from nearby stores or vendors, or gave a small smile when she laughed in delight at the sight of plants and trees and flowers. She even bought a few bouquets.

He curbed the impulse to tell her they wouldn't last long. But she seemed to brighten with each step as they traveled further into the city. And her anger at him also seemed to fade a bit at a time.

Her happiness was infectious, though. Soon, he found himself slipping a sheer scarf over her head, causing her to giggle. He paid for the delicate blue material and handed it to her. She gave him a slight smile before she stuffed it in her travel bag. He laughed with her as she tried on an oversized shirt and then was caught up in a musical performance at the center of one of the plazas.

Through it all, he was dimly aware of the black garbed forces that moved amongst the crowd. The gray-suited individuals flowed from building to building. The ships flew in their lanes above. The PatRec drones buzzed through the air. And a malevolent undercurrent surrounded everyone.

When the performance ended, Sierra clapped along with everyone else. She grabbed his hand and pulled him along the walkway, continuing their exploration. With her anger at him gone, she chatted away. He soaked it in—and that small voice returned, telling him to turn back, to go home. But it was more subdued now, barely heard. Or maybe he was choosing not to hear.

Φ

Seth ground his fists against his eyes. Even with the lubricating drops, the lenses still itched. He paused along the walkway and called out to Michael. "Hold up."

An alleyway allowed him to slip into darkness, away from the PatRecs. Michael leaned against the stone wall of the building. "Drops aren't helping?"

"No." Seth thumbed one of the contact lenses out and blinked away tears. The itch was beginning to subside, but the other eye was still going to drive him insane. "Do I have them in wrong?"

Michael grabbed his jaw and turned his head one way and then the other. "No. Try putting the drops directly on the lenses instead of in your eye."

Seth sighed. Shades would have been better—or darkened goggles. But John and Michael felt as though it would be too noticeable. And it would have been. No one wore them in Midland. While those items were normal attire in Canadian Province, it was not so here.

He pulled the bottle of drops from his pocket and placed two droplets onto the contact then reinserted it. Seth blinked a couple of times, feeling the contact float around before settling against the tear film of his cornea. He repeated the steps with the other eye. All this was just another reminder that he was different. He was accepted at home. No one thought much about his eyes. When he was growing up, the girls flirted with him and thought his eyes were attractive. Tamara had told him once when they began dating that she used to threaten any girl who wanted to venture into a relationship with him because, as she said, *He's mine. Those beautiful whites are only for me.*

A drone buzzed by.

"Beta, Seth!" Michael's hiss cut through his thoughts as he recapped his lubricant drops.

Seth cleared his mind and stepped out of the shadows, along with Michael. The drone buzzed around them for a moment before continuing down the narrow walkway.

"Watch your thoughts. Keep them on the now."

Seth nodded. That was much easier said than done. Michael was trained for this, and he didn't have a wandering mind like Seth. He caught himself before his thoughts ventured down another memory.

"The problem, Michael, is that this walk is boring. I'm not seeing anything but darkened alleyways, dirty streets, and dilapidated buildings. With nothing to occupy my mind, I tend to think back on things." He stuffed his hands in his back pockets and strolled beside the taller man.

This side of Midland City was sparsely occupied—warehouses and loading ports, docking hangars and trading buildings—the backbone of the city, yet the darkest and dirtiest part.

"Always thinking." Michael held up his comm and read the display. "Jinx said Nelson's Hangar is just up ahead, right around the next corner. Once inside, the PatRecs won't read you."

"Good."

Seth struggled to keep his mind on the present. Maybe the itchy contacts were a good thing. They kept his mind from wandering as he constantly rubbed at his eyes. Above them, a black transport began lowering, kicking up dust that coated the road and walkways. Around the area, yellow lights began flashing on the lampposts; and people halted what they were doing.

Warehouse workers laid down their tools. Drivers on hoverbikes stopped and stood next to their vehicles. The trolleys slowed to a standstill, and the people on board disembarked. Michael let out a low hiss between his teeth and motioned Seth to his side.

He spoke low as the transport landed in the middle of the wide street. "Midland Security Forces. Have your card ready to be scanned."

Black-garbed men flowed down the ramp. Two stood at the entrance. Three broke off and headed toward the corner where Nelson's Hangar was located. And four separated into each section of their area.

Seth copied Michael in stance and behavior—head slightly bowed, and eyes cast down, hands in full view with one holding his citizen card. Once a person was scanned, the security personnel waved them on. Another transport flew into the area and landed near the intersection where they were heading.

Michael's hand flexed once. Nearby, a PatRec issued a beep, but it kept its course down the walkway. Seth reached up and rubbed at his left eye just as the security officer stopped in front of him.

"Problem with your eye?" He held his hand out for Seth's citizen card.

"Just dust from your transport landing. It'll clear."

The officer nodded and held his hand out for Michael's card. He gave Michael's card a quick glance before running it through the scanner. The light at the top lit green, and the officer handed it back. "It expires within the month. Make sure you renew before then."

Michael nodded as he pocketed his card.

The officer studied Seth as he ran his card through the scanner. "Are you sure your eyes are okay? They look red. This is a high drug-trafficking area. Do I need to run your blood for illicits?"

Seth shook his head. "No, it's just the dust."

"Uh huh." The officer frowned at the scanner and pulled out Seth's card. He wiped it against his pants and reinserted it. The top lit with green and then immediately turned yellow. "Your card has been flagged. I will need you to come with me."

Michael held out his hand to stall the officer when he reached for Seth. "Could you run it again? He's been having trouble with the scanners since arriving in Midland City."

"Coming from where?" The officer pulled Seth's card out for another try. He narrowed his eyes and held up a hand to stop Michael. "I think the man can speak for himself, yes?"

Michael straightened and cast his gaze back down, yet Seth caught the tension in his muscles and the slight shift in his stance.

Seth gave the officer a lopsided grin. "Just arrived from Yukon this morning."

"Yukon? GFT territory. What brings you to Midland City?" He inserted Seth's card.

"Prospects for trading high-yield plasma torches for the shipyards. My family owns a mining vein in Yukon and seeks to expand our business."

Michael gave him a side glance and arched his brow in surprise. Seth suppressed a smile. All those years of sitting in on the meetings and listening to the trading committee had paid off, it seemed.

"Midland City offers the best." The officer nodded when the top of the scanner lit green and was about to extract it when it turned yellow. "Yeah, I'm going to need you to follow. We can quickly corroborate your story at headquarters."

He began to turn. Michael gave one nod, and Seth leaped forward and yanked his card from the man's hands as Michael sent a right hook into his jaw. The man crumpled.

Around them, the PatRecs issued their shrill alarm. Officers raced their way, weapons drawn. Seth ducked as a plasma bolt shot at him. It skimmed above his shoulder and bored into the building next to them.

"This way!" Michael veered away from their area and down a narrow path near a canal.

He ran down the walkway behind Michael. The officers were no match for their speed; and soon, he and Michael had outdistanced them. They entered a darkened alley on their left. Still, they didn't stop. Through two more alleys deeper into the city, across three streets, and then into another alley. He and Michael slowed to a walk as they approached a public plaza.

With the overhangs in the alley, the drones were not able to fly close enough to register their escape. Seth glanced up at the last overhang. That was a blessing. He slipped off his coat in order to cool down as he followed Michael to the benches surrounding a water fountain.

Sunlight gleamed on the white concrete, burning into his eyes. Around him, people strolled, sat on benches watching the Holonews. Some, dressed in gray, ate and drank with others—Nest Protocol workers.

Michael pulled his datapad from the side pocket of his pants and activated the Holonews. He kept the audio muted, but the ticker gave the story. Seth leaned a bit closer and read it. Nelson's Hangar was bombed two hours ago. Three fatalities. Evidence of illegal trading of citizen codes was discovered, and authorities were now flagging any and all codes that matched those on the list.

Seth forced the lump back down his throat. His card—he didn't use the QG on it; and now, in hindsight, maybe he should have. "Stephen has the GHOST. If I know my son, then he used it on his card and probably Sierra's. That should keep them protected for a while, at least."

"For a while." Michael closed down the datapad and leaned back against the bench. "But he has the old program, doesn't he?"

Seth nodded. "He doesn't know that the NP has a new program that detects the GHOST signature. That's the reason Mom and Huey always tweaked it."

Michael's comm beeped. He opened it and then turned it around to show Seth.

Batch and Jinx were on the run, having gone silent an hour ago. Their contact was dead. And they were to dump all codes. Seth checked the transmission. It ran through all the sub-bands. So, Alaska Country received the same information. That meant they were truly on their own now.

"Michael, I need to show you something, and I need you to go along with me on this." Seth pulled his data crystal from his vest pocket. The small, flat blue disk shone in the sunlight. Then he slipped it back into his pocket. "I brought my Quantum GHOST. It's bioprinted to me. Just get me to the Central Hub. I will be able to find out where they are."

Above them, two drones zipped by, flew a circle around the fountain, hovered for a moment, and then zipped away. He concentrated on watching the people around him and emptying his mind of thoughts.

Michael rose and stretched, causing his back to pop. "I'm getting too old to run like that. Come on. Central Hub is this way."

A PatRec drone hovered nearby. Seth smiled and glanced up at his friend. He only needed to think of something trivial to deflect the drone. "Find a nice hotel this time?"

The drone rotated and slowly ventured down the plaza, irritating some of the people and causing others to stand and flee inside. He stood and walked with Michael as he led the way across the plaza toward an amphitheater-style building. As they approached, Seth studied the architecture. No, this was more coliseum, reminiscent to the ancient Roman structures. And above him on the second floor stood those who gazed down upon the people with haughty attitudes and disdain smiles. Definitely ancient Rome.

He pushed passed Michael as they crossed the threshold and chose the first empty scanner. Seth held out his hand. "Give me your card. It's not flagged yet."

"It will be soon."

"The QG will hide it." He took Michael's card, slid the QG into the slot at the top, and inserted the card into the scanner. It didn't take long. Files opened at his command—directories, sub-files, coding. He located the security section and began his search. It took three seconds for his QG for find the information.

"That was fast-thinking earlier." Michael propped against the partition between the scanners. "And a good job on deflecting the PatRec drone."

"Thanks." Seth pulled a data crystal from his pocket and inserted it into the terminal. The file copied onto the crystal; then he pulled Michael's card from the scanner. The man studied him for a moment before accepting his card sans the QG, which Seth slipped back into his pocket.

"How many data crystals do you have on you?"

Seth frowned. "Two. I always have two on me. Why?"

Michael shook his head slightly, turned, and waved Seth to follow. "You have so much of your parents in you." They walked along the edge of the threshold of the Central Hub. "I take it you need to run a deciphering matrix?"

"It was run as soon as I downloaded it onto the crystal. The QG does that. Just need to get somewhere safe to read it."

Michael pulled his ship lock cylinder from his pocket and glanced at it before motioning toward a restaurant across the plaza. "We'll go there. It's inside and populated enough to stay hidden."

They took their time in crossing the plaza. It was easy enough to do with it being crowded. Once they entered the restaurant, he and Michael found an empty table near the back. They settled into the booth. Michael activated the holographic menu as Seth used his datapad to read the crystal.

To anyone else, it would seem he was reading the Holonews but in text format. When Michael asked what he wanted, he just nodded. The older man paused, shook his head again, and ordered.

Seth clamped his jaw against the curse that rose to his tongue. Stephen's card was used. The GHOST signature was attached to it along with a Citizen Three, Class Prime status imprinted over a

Citizen Two. Red colored his vision, and his nostrils flared at the stupidity of that move. Seth forced the burning anger down and breathed deeply through his nose.

Where did Stephen get a Citizen Three, Class Prime status? It had been scanned at Hotel de Ville. He swiped that information to the side. They would head there next and collect the twins.

The next file caused his hands to shake before he could rein in his reaction. Midland City Security Force had issued a bounty for Sierra Williams. That, he knew about. But the text underneath sent a surge of anger through him; a warrant had been issued for Stephen.

Seth's hands gripped the datapad. "Michael, we need to get back to the ship."

"Can't. It's monitored." Michael reached into his vest. He passed Seth the thin ship lock cylinder. The small, liquid crystal display was red.

Seth slid it into his datapad's port. The ship's outer cameras showed a contingent of security forces around the ship. He sighed and handed the ship lock back. "Then get me somewhere where I can access a console—anywhere that has security that is hardlined to Central Hub. High-end hotels or recreation clubs. Belay that. The twins registered at Hotel de Ville. We can go there."

"What happened?"

"There's a warrant out for Stephen. And I need to trace the origin. It's not showing Midland City codes."

It should have been a curse, him being able to remember things in explicit detail. Yet now he considered it as another blessing. Every code, signature, and file that he had read earlier was burned into his memory.

Their food arrived, and Seth forced himself to eat some of it.

Michael leaned forward. "Let's eat our food. That will give enough time to blend in with the shift change when we leave. Go with the flow toward Golden Sector until we reach the hotel."

Seth nodded and sipped his tea. But the anger was slowly rising within him. He ignored Michael's watchful gaze and picked at his food.

Chapter Ten
ACTIONS AND CONSEQUENCES

Jason swallowed against the pain. Barbed bands encircled his biceps, waist, thighs, and ankles, holding him against the heated, upright metal bed that stood on a grated platform. On the far side to his left stood the hated tube. It would have been preferred. At least, he knew what to expect with that treatment.

Above him, bright lights burned, causing tears to flood his eyes and run down his face. They had turned the illumination to maximum as punishment, knowing that his ocular enhancements could not handle the onslaught.

A Medlab Twenty medstudy next to him rolled his chair around to Jason's left side and studied the readouts before continuing his rolling journey in front and to the other side.

"The serum is ready, ma'am." He rolled back to his station and out of Jason's peripheral sight.

MedTech Bastion tap-tapped toward him. Her withered face peered up and studied Jason for long moments. She was standing six meters from him, yet her stench was still overpowering. "I'm disappointed in you, Alpha Zero." She hobbled to his left. "Did you think I wouldn't be monitoring you? You accessed my files. Tell me, what was so interesting about Julius Williams?"

When he didn't answer, she nodded at the medstudy. The bands tightened, and the ones on his biceps punctured muscle. One drop of blood hit the grating with a soft splat.

She drew closer and disappeared around him. Her *tap-tapping* stalled for a second and then continued until she came into view on his right. "Julius Williams was a fine specimen. The serum worked on him. And he was more than what any other assassin ever was. I used that same serum that he had on you. Did you know that? Then I used your serum-laden blood to create Serum Seventy-seven." She smiled and nodded. "Yes, I know you found that information about the serum. And I know that you tried to hide the information on the young man and woman."

Jason cut his gaze to her. Young man? He thought he had deleted all the files about Stephen Williams.

"I have a sub-routine, Alpha Zero. It monitors and records all that happens here." She hobbled in front of him. "You are my prized and most coveted possession." She stepped forward and placed her hand on his abdomen. "You have been the best, and I'm not going to punish you too severely. I do not want to damage you, in case this Stephen and Sierra are not want I need."

What she needed? Jason suppressed his frown and kept a blank stare on her as she continued. "I will have them delivered to me shortly. As I said, I know that face. I've touched and kissed that face. They are either his children or his grandchildren. And if grandchildren, then that means there is another out there. And you have brought me a prize above all prizes."

She waved her hand at the medstudy. "Proceed."

Clanking sounded behind him, a whir of machinery, the sound of a drill. His heart raced for a second before he forced himself to remain calm.

"I still have need for you, Alpha Zero. But your insolence was unexpected. We will have to repair that." She approached him again and ran a hand down his leg. "It won't take long, I promise."

Then she left.

The bands tightened even more. Blood began dripping from him and onto the grating below. A hiss issued from behind his head. Jason squeezed his eyes shut as the automatic injections pierced his thoracic spine. The three probes released the sedative and serum into his system followed by the Paxolin-X.

He bucked against the bands, causing them to tear his flesh as the drugs burned into him. They were going to make him forget again. The bands tightened even more as the sedative began working, weakening him.

Jason let his head fall back and gazed at the ceiling, ignoring the harsh, scalding lights. The strength within him waned. His lids grew heavy. The buzzing and drilling began. There was a slight pressure against his lower spine, but he felt nothing else. What were they doing to him? He let his gaze flow back and forth over the smooth, reflective tiles above. His reflection was blurry, as were the instruments behind his bed.

Another round of Paxolin-X entered him. As it burned through his body, he closed his eyes and called out a silent plea to let him wake up soon. Next time, he would be more careful about what he was doing. What was he doing, anyway? What did he do? Why was he being punished?

His thoughts fell away as blackness claimed him.

Stephen stepped into the lift. Beyond the glass enclosure, the world beneath rose to meet him. Light along the walkway and around the center plaza blossomed to life as the night began to fall. Rickshaws, hoverbikes, and low-grav vehicles moved along at a leisurely pace. His comm beeped. He glanced down at where it was attached on his belt before silencing it.

He'd had another row with Sierra. This time, his anger getting the best of him pricked at his conscious. But he ignored it. He had to ignore it. If he didn't, then he would allow her to talk him into returning home. She always had been able to cajole him into doing her bidding. Not this time, though. He'd make it up to her. He may be able to find the ingredients for her salve in the morning when the stores opened.

The lift doors opened, and he merged with the rest of the hotel crowd as his thoughts continued to stay on his sister. He hadn't meant to cause her to drop her tube of salve over the balcony wall. He hadn't meant to shove her aside. Yet she had blocked his path, wanting to prevent him from leaving. She had shown him the clubs and how they used chemicals sprayed into the air. Even the argument that they were enhanced and the drugs would have no effect hadn't dissuaded her from badgering him. And that was when the fight had begun.

Stephen raised the hood of his overshirt and shoved his hands into his pants as he strolled along the concrete. He could take care of himself. He could handle anything that came his way.

The club was located around the block, conveniently close to the hotel. His mind ran back to Denise Nicolosi. If he had stayed with her and Sierra had not been with him, would she have brought him to the very same hotel he was at now?

He glanced back at where he was staying. The building towered above the Golden Sector Plaza. It was possible that it was one of the hubs for human trafficking. He could find out later if he so desired. At the moment, his only concern was to find this Robert guy and discover where Medlab Twelve-twenty was located. Then he would figure out the next step.

Stephen turned the corner. Across the small plaza, the pulsing sign of the club shone in the dark. He hurried across the plaza, noting that PatRecs drones were curiously absent in this area.

The man at the entrance held out his hand for Stephen's card. When he scanned it, he quirked an eyebrow, yet only gave it back and then opened the door for Stephen to enter. Harsh music battered his ears. Lights strummed against him, causing him to squint until he could adjust to the glare.

All around him were people in various states of undress. Morbid curiosity took hold, and he surveyed them for a few moments. With a shake of his head, Stephen weaved his way through swaying bodies, dislodged roaming hands, and stepped up onto the raised platform where the bar was located.

He pulled his citizen card and the GHOST from his pants pocket and slid them into the hidden pocket of his black silk shirt. The bartender, a woman with smooth skin and blonde hair pulled into a messy bun, paused in front of his spot.

"What will it be?"

"What's the strongest you have?" Stephen flashed a smile at the young woman.

"One Oasis Drought coming up." She disappeared behind a small partition, while Stephen spun on his stool and surveyed the room once again.

The floor contained a center area with lounges, couches, and chairs that were big enough to hold two people. All were in use. He swallowed against the scene and allowed his gaze to travel to the upper level. The tinted glass above the rails allowed only blurred movements to show. Yet from what he could tell, they were doing much more than what was happening on the floor.

"Here you go. You will have to pay now."

He turned around, gave her his card, and then took a small sip. The fruitiness of the drink was pleasant. The heat of the alcohol burned for about a second before fading. And that was it. A strawberry-and-peach-type of flavor served with some alcoholic liquid over ice. She handed him his card.

"Anything else?"

"Yeah. I'm looking for Robert."

"There are a lot of Roberts here."

Stephen took another longer sip before replying. "This Robert I'm needing to see . . . just tell him 'gold omega.'"

Her eyes narrowed and scrutinized him for a moment before she turned and disappeared through a door at the end of the bar. He continued sipping on his drink, watching the reflection of the action behind him. It wasn't long before she came back, followed by a man dressed in a form-fitting black suit.

Silver glasses perched on his head; and a small, black cane topped with a silver eagle head helped him balance his gait as he limped toward Stephen.

He paused and studied him before speaking. "Follow me, and I'll take you to Robert. Mister . . . "

"Williams. Just Williams." Stephen slid off the stool. Around them, bodies parted out of the way, giving deference to this stranger.

Knowing gazes from a few of the women followed them. Stephen made note of those. He would steer clear of them when he was ready to leave.

A small lift took them to the next level, where the music was just as raucous as below and where the hallway was packed with writhing bodies. Stephen followed the man through it all and into another lift. He counted the bumps—only two. So, they were on a fourth level.

When the lift opened, golden opulence met him. Gold omega was a fitting code. But if gold had a logical meaning, what was meant by omega?

Stephen took in the sight. Holographic curtains hung from each wall. Chandeliers six feet in diameter and with crystals the size of his hands hung from the ceiling that depicted erotic scenes. He recognized a few from the ancient classics, including *Dante's Inferno*. But these representations were more modern—and viler.

Red velvet couches littered the area. Plush, white carpet with golden strands softened their footsteps. To his right, a formal table was heavily laden with food and desserts. Stephen catalogued each person as they passed by. Men in tight-fitting trousers, much like his guide, and women with short skirts that hugged their hips lounged around. Scarves were the only tops they wore.

The tips of his ears heated. He wasn't a stranger to carnal pleasure, but this was beyond anything he had ever experienced. He suddenly had the urge to shower. The smells were already overpowering. From the food and sugary desserts to the perfumes and pheromones and from the alcohol and something that smelled acrid, he began to second-guess himself. Maybe this wasn't such a good idea after all.

But that thought was allayed as a heavy orange curtain parted, and the man waved Stephen through. The curtain fell back into place, and Stephen stood before an amply fed man seated on a white, overstuffed chair. He looked up from the datapad he was reading and gave Stephen a smile.

He stood and motioned him to an identical chair next to his. "Have a seat, my friend."

Oily—that was the thought that popped into his mind as he perched on the edge of the chair. The man reseated himself, shifting a bit in the chair before he reached forward and placed his datapad on the circular table between them.

"I'm Robert, as you may have guessed by now. Josiah said you gave the passcode. So, I take it you have a few deliveries for medlab?"

Stephen nodded. "Just one."

Robert's gaze glanced at his datapad before he pressed a button on the arm of his chair. Immediately, Stephen's guide stepped through the curtain. "Josiah, bring two drinks and send in two, please."

The man nodded and left, prompting Stephen to lean forward and ask, "Two?"

"You'll see." He grinned, causing Stephen's skin to crawl. "To make sure we are on the up-and-up, describe the package."

Package? Stephen narrowed his eyes. The man's vernacular was strange. Was this how they referred to the people being delivered to the medlab? "About five eleven. Weighing in around 170 pounds. Dark hair. Slender. Young."

"Sounds like you, my friend." He laughed. "The message we received described the package as the same—dark and slender." His gaze traveled up and down Stephen. "You must have excellent taste."

Stephen curled his lips and sat back. "Pardon—"

"Your clothes." Robert interrupted with a chuckle at Stephen's confusion and apparent misunderstanding. "I noticed you're wearing silk. That's a material that is hard to come by these days."

Stephen raised his chin and forced a smile. "Bartered for it. Pretty high price, too." The curtain opened, and Josiah brought in two drinks on a tray. He set it on the table and left just as silently.

"Ah. May I?" Robert reached out. At Stephen's nod, he ran his hand down Stephen's arm, caressing the silk sleeve. "That is excellent craftmanship. Wouldn't happen to want to trade, would you?"

Stephen laughed. "No."

"No matter." Robert picked up one of the glasses and handed it to Stephen. Then he grabbed his own. "With the compensation that I will get from Medlab Twelve-twenty, I will be able to buy my own swath of silk—maybe even five. How soon can you have the body delivered?"

"Morning." When Robert took a swallow of his drink, Stephen followed suit. Unlike the last one, this one wasn't fruity nor alcoholic. It had a vanilla-like ether essence to it with a hint of a burn. But otherwise, it was just a carbonated drink. Stephen took another pull of it, finding the flavor intensifying.

"That's good. Medlab is only ten miles west of here underneath an old medical facility. You'll recognize it right away. The entrance for your delivery is on the south side." Robert replaced his glass on the tray. Only a quarter of it had been consumed.

Stephen glanced down at his drink. He barely had any left, yet he didn't remember drinking that much of it. His words sounded slurred when he spoke. "Will there be need of a code?"

"No, they will be expecting you." Stephen squinted at Robert as his face wavered. The lights pulsed in and out around the man. When Robert spoke again, his voice echoed as if he was in a hollow tube. "Since you don't have to be there until morning, might as well enjoy yourself, young Williams. I started a credit line for you. Enjoy yourself for the night."

Stephen smiled and tried to focus through his muddled mind. He could play along with the man, although he would have to figure out how to burn off the effects of the drink. Robert snapped his fingers. Josiah stepped in. Two women followed him. Each of the females took Stephen by the arm and led him through the curtain.

Another drink was pressed into his hand and guided to his mouth. Stephen swallowed the carbonated beverage and marveled at the colors around him. Above him, a puff of mist blew into the room. Like the low-lying fog on the bay at home, the mist hung above them. Hadn't Sierra said something about an addictive concoction being in the air of the club?

The next thing he knew, he was stepping out into the hallway with the women. The one on his left, her scantily clad body leaning against him, placed a crystal on his lip; and another drink was encouraged. A riot of explosions happened around him. Colors. Sensations. Everything breathed, bled, and blended. No, here was his addiction: the new sensations and the sin. A blast of thick mist fell from the ceiling.

He needed to get out of the club. Too much was happening, and he couldn't keep a coherent thought in his head in this toxic air. He smiled as they led him to a couch in the corner. He just needed to play along, so no one would suspect. He could wait for a bit longer before leaving.

He shook his head to clear the cloudy haze that seemed to be draped through his brain. No, they did suspect. They made sure he had been drugged. The drugs would burn off soon enough. He was an enhanced. Stuff like this didn't affect him like others. Yet the slowed perception of movement and muted sounds around him gave evidence at contradicting that belief. Stephen's mind pulsed with the music, and he blinked hard against the haze. He'd just leave now.

Stephen started to push the women off him, but the dark-haired one pressed herself closer and rubbed at his lower lip. A coarse and gritty substance smeared underneath the pad of her thumb and onto his lip. Before he could stop her companion, she had another drink at his mouth.

He pressed his mouth closed, trying to turn his head away. But a pair of hands held his head still; and the fluid combined itself with the substance on his mouth, soaking through the thin membrane of his lips.

Stephen gasped. His world fell away into a hazy aura of red and orange as his strength waned, and his body seemed to melt into the cushions. Sounds became muted. Smells began to fade. And the sensations intensified and burned before he was washed away from the world with his last thought: he never should have come here.

Sierra paused in the center plaza and, for a moment, watched the people flow in and out of Enchanté. When Stephen had left, she had used his datapad to view what he had been looking at. Most of the information was in his cipher, and she didn't know the command code to translate the files. Yet the pleasure clubs and hotels had been highlighted, and this one was the closest.

Before she had shut down the datapad, a message on one of their sub-bands had come through. She had pinched the bridge of her nose after reading it. Their cards were no longer valid. As soon as she used it, it would be flagged as a noncompliant citizen. She huffed out a breath. She couldn't prevent that, and she needed to get her brother out of there.

Sierra squared her shoulders and marched toward the club. The man held out his hand for her card, scanned it, raised an eyebrow, and handed it back. She accepted her citizen card as he opened the heavy slab of metal and waved her through.

Loud, raucous music slammed her eardrums. Sierra gasped. Sodom and Gomorrah.

She forced her mouth closed and averted her eyes at the scene before her. Everywhere she looked, there was some form of debauchery happening. Bodies bumped into her. Drinks splashed against her legs and arms. It was worse than the images she had seen on the Yukon kiosk about the legal clubs that were set in all the GFT and former GFT nations.

She wasn't naïve to what was in the world. But this was . . . wrong. So wrong.

She stepped forward and weaved her way through the atrocious smells, trying to ignore the sights and sounds. The dizzying effect of the haze that hung around their heads created a trippy feel to the club. Flashes and colors pulsed in and out of her vision.

Voices and laughter seemed weirdly warped. Echoes rose and lowered in pitch. Halos of light danced through the veil of smoke. She cast her gaze upward to ignore the couple in front of her. They swayed to the harsh music that played. Yet they were doing more than swaying and weren't hiding a thing.

Sierra sidestepped through a throng of people and squeezed into an area near the tables along the wall that was less congested. She scanned the crowd. How was she ever going to get this sight out of her head?

Disgust rose within her, but she forced it down. She couldn't let anyone pick up on her distress. People came here came for this. She needed to blend in as much as possible but not that way!

Stephen's laughter rose above the noise. Sierra searched to her right. Ten yards away, in the middle of a group of women, he laughed and—

"Oh, boy!" Sierra swallowed. What she had just witnessed was now forever burned in her memory—one that she didn't want to have or need of her brother. "The idiot!"

She pushed her way toward him, elbowing women and men out of her way. When she reached the table, she slid past one woman, who was holding a glass of blue liquid to Stephen's mouth. Sierra grabbed it and threw it onto the table.

At first, she thought the woman was going to fight her. But as quickly as the anger rose, it died within the woman's eyes as she smiled. Her drug-laden attention drifted to another man standing nearby, and she wobbled away.

Stephen glanced up at her. Two other women leaned against him, hands roving. "Si?"

"Go away." She pulled the smallest woman away from her brother as he fumbled with straightening his clothing.

The woman pouted; but whatever drug was used in this club, no one fought. They just accepted whatever happened. More people began crowding around them. Hands touched her, touched Stephen.

She shrugged them off and slipped Stephen's arm around her neck. "Come on. We have to leave. There was a communiqué on the sub-band. Your card has been flagged. So has mine."

Stephen barely moved his feet, his hands patting down his shirt and pants as if he had forgotten something. "You have to try this! I thought it would dis . . . dissap . . . go away with our enhancements. It's not as strong, but it makes you feel good." His breath reeked of a mix of sweet and sour. Ketones, alcohol, and synthetic drugs filtered through.

Sierra rolled her eyes. She reached over and pulled his unbuttoned shirt closed. "So, now you want drugs? Seriously, Ven? First, you tried the drinks and went to a stranger's berth. Now, you try the drugs. I've already witnessed what you allowed to happen back there. Did you even stop to think about what you were doing?"

He straightened and tried to disengage from her grip, his gaze roaming around the people surrounding them. When she tightened her grip, he slumped against her. "I don't need you to control my life. I didn't ask you to come here."

People danced, swayed, and meandered in their path. For every two steps, she had to squeeze past rank and vile bodies. She should have packed two tubes of the salve. Anger at Stephen causing her to lose her blocking salve almost caused her to dump him on the floor and leave him to his revolting decision. Yet she couldn't do that.

He suddenly stopped and retched. Liquid splashed against the floor and her boots. She curled her lips. This was repulsive. The sooner they left the club, the sooner she would feel better. The haze was sickening. The odors were worse.

Clean-BOTs hurried towards their spot. She took a firmer grip on his arm and hauled him toward the door, ignoring the bodies she plowed through. Stephen's head lolled weakly against her shoulder as they stumbled through the door and into fresher, albeit just as dank, air.

"The aerosolized drug should start to wear off immediately."

He straightened from her and looked around. His eyes began clearing as she led them down the walkway and into an area behind the corner of the club, where a brightly lit courtyard blocked the stars in the sky. He rubbed at his eyes and mouth with his sleeve, following her to a bench on the far side.

"Sit down. I'll be right back." She left him looking around in slight confusion on the bench and hurried to a vendor nearby. Keeping one eye on her brother, she paid for two drinks and a small sandwich. Stephen would need something to help push the drugs from his system.

The green in his eyes darkened as she approached. "I thought it was some kind of dream." He accepted the drink and downed most of it, almost sighing in response. Then he devoured the sandwich in two large bites.

He spoke around a mouthful of food. "I remember feeling euphoria at first. Then it melted away, and everything was moving, blurring. The colors . . . " His hand waved as he talked. "And it felt so good. I wanted more—and then more. So many sensations, Si. But I couldn't stop it. It was if, for every step I took toward the door . . . "

His voice trailed off, and he shook his head as if to clear it.

"The drug creates a temporary addiction." Sierra sat next to him. "You knew they used a drug concoction sprayed into the air to control the people in that club. I showed you the information on it. It was one of three legal pleasure clubs here in Midland City."

It was a bitter laugh that came from him. "I thought with my enhancements it wouldn't affect me as much."

"You seemed more aware than the others." Sierra glared at him. "You made me wade through horrid and wicked people who were doing things that no one should ever do—vile and disgusting things! Unnatural things! And you . . . " She shook her head at him. The image of him in his drugged stupor rose to the surface. She closed her eyes against it, willing it to go away. "You were doing some of the same. How could you? What was the purpose for all this? To rebel? To try a new experience? I'm trying to understand you, Stephen."

Hurt flooded his eyes as he watched her stand and pace away from him. "Si, I'm sorry."

"No, you're not! You're just sorry you were caught." She whirled, jabbing a finger at him. "Come home, Stephen! This has gone far enough. We can't live in this kind of place. You are only going to get yourself killed."

He rose, throwing his arm out to balance himself as he wobbled slightly. His eyes were slowly becoming clearer. The drugs were definitely wearing off. "You can go home. I'm not. You didn't have to come get me." He began to walk away.

"Didn't you hear me earlier, Stephen? Your card is flagged."

His steps faltered. His hands clenched at his sides before he turned back to face her. "Flagged? How?"

"The codes were discovered, according to the file. Batch and Jinx are running silent now. When you entered the club, it automatically flagged the system as a noncompliant citizen. And the same happened when I entered the club. Midland's system has a quicker response time than a GFT one." She stepped toward him, offering him her hand. "We have less than an hour before they come to collect us—just enough time to make it to the border. If we can cross over into Westland, we can make it undetected to Canadian Province."

Stephen hesitated. He glanced back at the club, watching scantily clad people enter and exit, laughing with each other and leaning onto each other to remain upright. A desire burned in his eyes, but it was more than that. She narrowed her eyes and studied him. It was some kind of burning drive that had brightened his gaze. He took a few small, backward steps toward her before turning his back on the club and its scene.

"Fine. Let's go."

She accepted his hand and allowed him to pull her through the alleyways. Something deep inside his expression caused a mistrust to rise within her. They made it part of the way down an alley that led away from the hotel and the clubs before he collapsed to his knees and began retching.

"Ven?"

He waved her away and then spat one last time before rising to his feet. His hands shook as he ran his sleeve over his mouth. "Drink, please."

There wasn't much left, but she shoved her drink into his waiting hands. Stephen drained it before handing it back. But the drink didn't stay down long. He fell to his knees again, expelling all he just took in.

"Ven!" She knelt next to him. When she put her arm around his shoulders and gripped his bicep with the other, his body was shaking itself apart. Another wave had him doubled over and dry heaving.

After a few seconds, he pushed away and propped himself against the alley's wall. "I'm sorry, Si. Really, I am. This wasn't by choice. The club, yes, but not the drugs." He squeezed his eyes shut and huddled tighter into a ball. "I can remember snippets—the drinks, the drugs, the women who gave them to me. Then it was just lights and sounds, touches. Then you were there."

She frowned at her brother. Confusion lined his face. "Why did you go there to start? If not for the sinful and horrible amenities they provided, then why?"

He leaned his head back with a sigh. With his eyes still closed, he bit at his lip. "I wanted to find Medlab Twelve-twenty. I needed to find it. And that was the only way to do so."

There was more to the story, apparently. They needed a better place to talk away from the mess near them. She grabbed his hand and pulled him to his feet. "Let's go. We can't go back to the hotel with our cards being flagged. Let's just get to a nicer spot, and then you can tell me everything."

Stephen only nodded. Apparently, the drugs, the sickness, and the weakness had temporarily killed the fight within him. He stumbled along next to her, his arm around her neck and the other arm clenched over his stomach. "Did you grab anything of ours?"

"Just your datapad."

Ahead was a small fountain under a gazebo. The esplanade seemed to be an outside eating area. Tables and chairs dotted the cobblestone ground. Tall, thin trees overlooked the gazebo. Sierra led him under the covering and settled down beside him on the edge of the fountain, which was a tribute to the founder of Midland City.

The statue stood above them with water flowing down its cape and into the pool behind them. She turned toward him.

"Tell me."

He leaned forward and propped his elbows on his knees, holding his head as if it would roll away from him. She sat through his confession, tamping down her anger at him. So, Medlab Twelve-twenty was the source of the serum and run by the woman who had caused the death of their grandfather. And he wanted to discover more about the serum and find out what made them who they were. She closed her eyes when he related why he did what he did with the woman on the rail transport. Her brother—the thief and fornicator.

She forced herself to take a deep breath when he admitted the reason for going to the pleasure club. And then her heart ached at learning how they had drugged him. He could only relate snippets of his time there; but it was obvious that with all that was forced upon him, he was struggling to remain sober, even with his enhancements. Yet it was his stupidity that had brought it upon him.

"I know you think it was my stupidity that caused this." He steepled his hands against his mouth and took a deep breath. "And you're right. It was."

Finally, some sense had come to the man. "Then can we go home? Use the GHOST to hire a ride or somehow contact home?"

Stephen mulled over her words for a long time. His whisper filled the silence. "Omega. The end."

Sierra frowned. "What?"

Stephen shook his head. His body seemed to wilt. A variety of expressions flowed across his face, showing the battle that waged within him. He blew out a breath before squaring his shoulders and standing. Sensibility won. He held out his hand. "Let's go home."

It wasn't repentance that was in his bright green eyes when he finally looked over at her. It was terror. She began to reach for him, her heart hammering in her chest. Only one thing frightened Stephen—deep water. But the look on his face was worse than that fear. Whatever he knew or suspected was enough to frighten him beyond anything else.

Her hand slid into his at the exact time a shadowy movement registered in her peripheral. She gasped as a dart hit her chest.

"Si!" Stephen grabbed at her before jerking back as a dart embedded itself into his left shoulder.

She hit the stone floor hard enough to make her teeth rattle. The dart burned as she yanked it from her. Stephen, a blue dart falling from his hand, stumbled to his feet as two men rushed into the gazebo. She twisted and swept her leg under one, sending him crashing back through the opening and down the steps. Stephen, rage contorting his face, grabbed the other and hauled him through the air and into the fountain. The man's head hit the centerpiece with a sickening thud.

Sierra scrambled to her feet. Stephen suddenly shoved her behind him as five darts whistled through the air and hit with meaty thuds. His body began sliding to the ground; but she caught him, pulling him away from the opening and to the other side, grimacing as men in black once again appeared in her peripheral.

A piercing stab hit her between her shoulder blades, and then another hit her in the lower back. She fell across her brother's body. Her weight jarred Stephen awake enough for him to yank her over his body, roll with her in his arms and against the edge of the fountain, and shield her from another onslaught. But it was too late. A dart had hit her in the thigh. A whistling pierced the air, and a heavy grunt issued from Stephen. Then she was sliding into darkness.

Muffled voices reached through the inky black. "Bastion warned you they were strong. The loss of your man was your own fault. Now, get them into the transport. But gently! She doesn't want them harmed."

"Watch out! He's still awake."

A pop sounded. Stephen's arm fell across her stomach. Then everything became nothing.

Michael pushed open the sliding maintenance door and peered out. He waved his hand at Seth, and they slipped into the hallway of Hotel de Ville. Seth glanced at his datapad and pointed down the silent corridor.

"Third door." He clicked the icon in the corner and checked the security feed. "The loop is still running."

The dark, mahogany door looked like wood. Michael tapped it as Seth pulled a hand-sized panel lock from his pocket and inserted the QG into the top port. Metal reverberated from Michael's fingernail. "Once inside, you'll need to check for security recordings."

"On it." Seth placed his instrument over the keypad, and the door swung in. Once through, Seth keyed the door to the locked position. He stuffed the panel lock into his pocket and then pried the cover off the inside unit near the door. Sparks flew out as he yanked a white wire from the back. His fingers fumbled with the thin trip-mod when he dug it from his pocket before splicing it onto the wire. Seth brought his datapad back around and used the QG to run through the recordings. "Yeah. There's a lot here. The twins arrived late this morning."

He paused the recording and zoomed in on the datapad in Stephen's hand; but it was angled, and the screen couldn't be read. Michael finished his inspection of the room and stood behind him, watching over his shoulder as Seth resumed.

"Looks like they are arguing." Michael huffed at Stephen's shove against Sierra. "That's the first time I've ever seen Stephen treat his sister so poorly."

Seth had to agree. When his son turned around, rage had filled his expression. Then he was stalking out of the room with Sierra scowling after him. "Let me play this back with audio."

They watched it one more time. The twins' voices never rose above a heated whisper, but it was apparent that Sierra wanted her brother to return home. Seth hooked his foot around the leg of a nearby chair and pulled it closer to him so he could sit down as he continued watching the recording.

Sierra had picked up Stephen's datapad after using the console. She read it, and anger flooded her face. She grabbed her satchel, stuffed the datapad inside, and left.

Seth frowned and disconnected his device. "I need the visitor console."

Michael moved out of the way as he rose from the chair and strode across the deep, luxurious carpet. Seth sat at the small monitor in the corner. It took only seconds with the QG. Stephen had used it, then Sierra. Seth sat away from the console.

"What did you find?"

"He went to a pleasure club in Golden Sector right across the plaza." Seth stood and frowned at Michael. "It doesn't make sense. Stephen may be rebellious. I know he's done things, but this is not him. He went there for a reason. And I'm sure Sierra followed."

"Then let's go find out the why."

When Michael reached the door, a ping issued from Seth's datapad. "Hold up, Michael. The security loop is gone. Let me put a black-out on this floor, so we can leave."

Seth reconnected his datapad to the door's unit and broke through the firewalls and q-shieldings of the hotel. They weren't recorded coming in; and if the door opened without a record of someone arriving, then the hotel would initiate a lockdown. And they did not need that. He ran through the codes in security and highlighted their floor and the two above.

"Give it a count of three."

He stuffed his datapad into his coat pocket as Michael counted down. The lights in the room blinked once. Electrical hums silenced. Seth nodded, and then they were heading to the glass-enclosed lift at the end of the hallway. Once inside, Michael selected the plaza entry on the controls.

Seth turned around and viewed the people outside enjoying the night's activities. Their objective stood towering at the furthest corner where people crowded around the doorways, alleys, and that side of the plaza. The lift opened. He and Michael raised the hoods of their coats and strolled across the cobblestoned center.

He gave a quick glance upward. No PatRecs at night? That was curious.

Michael angled his head toward the small alley on the side. Seth veered to his right, sidestepping a tight huddle of scantily clad young people. He curled his lips at the smell of the noxious fumes of some drug that rolled off their skin.

No one paid attention as they slipped under the overhangs and into the narrow alley—more of a pathway, it seemed. They had to angle slightly to keep from brushing up against the stones of the buildings. Michael paused halfway down and glanced up.

Seth followed his gaze. A ledge about a foot wide jutted from the building a little over ten feet above them and under an octagon hatch. "That's what we need?"

"Your card is flagged. We need to gain entrance without being seen."

He wiped his hands against his coat and jumped. His fingers grabbed the lip, and he pulled himself up until he was balanced on his palms. With his left hand, he felt along the edges before dropping back down. "There's a small keypad underneath the bottom."

Seth nodded. He pulled his panel lock back out, inserted the QG, and held it in his teeth as he gauged his jump. With a grunt, he launched himself up, grabbed the lip, and wormed his way up until he was propped on his arms. He used his toes against the stones to balance himself as the panel lock clicked over the keypad, and then the hatch's cover slid back into its recess.

Seth squirmed up and into the maintenance tunnel. Michael's grunt barely echoed in night air. Once inside, Seth keyed the hatch to close.

Michael's penlight flashed around the tunnel. "We need to find an access port."

Seth knelt next to the hatch and used the panel lock for the codes. "I have the codes downloaded. Let me do a quick adjustment. Give me some light."

The penlight shone his way. Seth dumped his datapad, panel lock, and two trip mods on the floor of the tunnel. He needed the ability to hack without switching between tools. His fingernails dug into the corner of the datapad. The cover popped off. He set it aside and twisted the panel lock's sections. The two halves split. He reached into his coat's inner pocket, pulled out his slender toolkit, and selected a tool spike from the options that were nestled in their foam.

He glanced up at Michael. "Shine the light on the datapad, please."

Michael squatted beside him and held the light over the makeshift work area. "What else are you carrying in your pockets?"

"Hmm?" Seth held the panel lock's cover between his teeth as he concentrated on removing the core drive from the datapad. He spoke around the object. "Datapad, trip mods, panel lock, data crystals, small toolkit, and my QG."

The core drive separated, and he unhooked the wires. Then, he took the bottom half of the panel lock he dismantled and slid the core drive on top of it. The tool spike tapped the leads into place. Next, he grabbed a trip mod and slid it into the empty section at the corner of the panel lock. With the leads of the trip mod now connected, he slid the cover to the panel lock back on.

He threw the datapad pieces to the side and stood. Seth held up his new toy, brushing at a collection of dust on the small screen. "It won't show as clearly as the datapad did, but it'll give us an idea of what is happening. Plus, I will be able to read the code and know what's going on."

Michael pointed at the discarded datapad items.

Seth shook his head as he replaced his tool spike in the kit. "Useless now without the core drive."

Michael's gaze lingered on him for a moment, studying him, before he waved for Seth to follow. Long minutes passed before they came to a hatch labeled "Security Floor." There wasn't a keypad on this side. Michael shone his light around them, but nothing hinted at this hatch being locked or monitored.

"I find that odd."

Michael nodded. He reached out and pushed the hatch opened a crack. Darkness greeted them. He shoved the hatch door to the side.

Seth stepped out behind him and glanced around the darkened, circular corridor. It ran around a central area, where only a few people sat at monitoring stations on the far side. His whisper seemed overly loud as the hatch closed behind them. "Definitely not much security."

Michael moved toward their left. "Probably not needed, considering their trade being hidden by what happens below."

A door hissed opened behind them. He and Michael ducked around the curve of the central wall. The footsteps faded away in the opposite direction. Seth turned and peered through glass at the men working at the stations. He scanned each one before tapping Michael's shoulder and pointing to the monitor nearest them.

"That one will do. Looks like that one is hooked to the wall. I don't need to be inside."

They made their way through the dark and to the portion of wall by the monitor Seth needed. He knelt and ran his hands around the wall panels. A small groove was the only indication where the access port was located. Seth pulled his tool spike back out and pried off the small section of the wall panel.

The QG slipped easily into his updated panel lock, and Seth clicked it into place. In three seconds, he was in and watching a staticky view. He cycled through the floors and through the security logs. The twins' cards had been flagged.

"Cards were flagged. I found Stephen—on the fourth floor." Seth switched the files. "He was meeting with a man—Robert Assuage. Hold up. I'm downloading information on Medlab Twelve-twenty."

Once the file downloaded, he switched back to Stephen and the man—drinks, two women. Seth studied the movements. They were slipping something into Stephen's drink and then leading him out of the room. He closed his eyes to what was happening on the couch and pushed his anger back down. He would deal with that later.

He sped through the feeds. Sierra had come for him. They disappeared outside. The outside feeds had them on the far side of the plaza for a while; and then, they disappeared from view, heading toward the westward side.

Seth opened some other files. His blood seemed to congeal. Michael must have registered his change in mood. The man's hand landed on his shoulder.

"What did you find?"

"Assuage contacted Medlab with info on Stephen. A bounty and warrant were issued by Medtech Anya Bastion. A contingent was sent to collect the twins. How did she find out about them? It looks like funds were paid to a Josiah Donaldson." Seth snarled. "Sorry, Josiah. Your funds have just been diverted." He entered the necessary codes, sent the payment to various people's cards that were in the system, and then erased his tracks. Seth yanked the connection away and replaced the panel. "I have the codes we need for Medlab and its location. The twins are in danger, Michael. They were last seen heading toward the westward side of the plaza."

Above them, the lights flicked on. Boots fell heavily against the flooring on the far side and headed their way. Michael tapped his shoulder and pointed at another maintenance hatch. Seth hurried after him, slapped the panel lock over the keypad, and then jumped through when it opened. The hatch clicked closed behind Michael. They leaned against the side, listening.

The group walked past, but a voice filtered through. "I want two groups on this floor and above." Rustling against the wall indicated that security had been stationed next to the hatch.

Seth pinched the bridge of this nose for a moment, thinking. When Michael began to motion toward the end of the tunnel, Seth shook his head and viewed the screen on the panel lock. He turned it around and showed Michael.

Security was at all exits but not at the front, where patrons flowed in and out. Michael moved away from the hatch and near the ladder that led to the lower tunnel.

"Using the Hi-Waves?"

"Sub-bands. Once I gained the codes for them, it stays connected." He followed Michael down the ladder. "We won't be immune to the aerosol, you know."

Michael's sigh was the only answer he gave.

Seth glanced at his readouts again. "Down two hatches. It's the only one that is away from the others—less chance of being spotted."

Chapter Eleven
THE CAPTURE

Jason. My name is Jason.

Jason stood between the two beds watching over its occupants. The restraints had been triple-checked. When they awoke, they would not be able to break free. Those metal fusion bands were too strong. He kept his gaze on the empty space between the woman and the man as Medtech Bastion drew their blood, placed neural relays on their heads, and hobbled away.

His mantra repeated inside his head: *Jason. My name is Jason.* There was something he was forgetting. It was there on the edge of his mind but too vague to grasp. He shifted his stare to the woman and allowed himself to view her smooth skin, which was a light chestnut color, golden in hue. With his enhanced sight, the waves of heat from her body and the electrical field she emitted combined to make her skin shimmer like silk under the lights. Waves of thick, dark brown hair surrounded her shoulders. Her eyes would be green.

How did he know that? She hadn't opened them. But he knew. Just as the man's eyes would be green, too.

"Alpha Zero," Bastion called to him from across the medlab, "I need you to remain here and watch over them. Alert me if they begin to rouse."

She didn't wait for his reply, only shuffled in arthritic steps out the door, leaving one guard to watch over him. Jason glanced out the corner of his eye at the guard by the door. The man yawned in boredom and then leaned heavily against the wall, holding his pulse rifle across his midsection. Jason ignored the guard.

Minutes passed. Jason let his attention settle on the man on the bed before him. He was younger than Jason, maybe by a couple of years or so. His face still held a bit of youthfulness to it. Yet there was a hard edge to it, too. This man would be dangerous.

The woman moaned. Jason whipped his head around to her and stared as she slowly turned her head to the side. Her eyes flickered open for a second before closing again. He turned on his heel and approached the guard.

"Alert Medtech Bastion the female is awakening."

Without waiting for a reply, he returned to his station at the end of the beds. The guard exited out of the room and stood outside the door, talking into his comm. His conversation was cut short as the door slid closed.

Jason took a step toward her bed but stopped. They would be monitoring the room. He backed up a pace and stood with his hands at his side. After half a second, the man groaned as he awakened. His legs jerked against the restraints. Green eyes glared at Jason as he thrashed against the bed and bands. The neural relay's information displayed on the console to Jason's right. He glanced at it.

The man was in alpha—and gamma. Who were they? Only those like him could stay in gamma and in beta or alpha brainwaves simultaneously. Jason frowned. A memory of something he had read flitted through his mind. When he returned his gaze to the man, he was staring at Jason with pure hatred. Yet his expression softened when the woman began moving against her restraints.

"Stephen?"

"Sierra, I'm here." He spoke to the woman but continued glaring at Jason.

She turned her head and stared at her brother. Jason dropped his gaze to the floor. *Brother?* Yes, they resembled each other, but why would he think the man was her brother? When he looked back up, they were both watching him.

She spoke first. "Who are you?"

When he didn't answer, the man tried to kick at him. When he couldn't lift his leg, he thrashed around but could only move centimeters. Then he growled when the restraints proved unbreakable. He let his head fall back onto the cushioned bed.

His green gaze bored into Jason. "She asked you a question."

Jason gave her his full attention. She studied him, letting her gaze run up and down his body, taking in his thin, black uniform. Her observation of him stopped at his bare feet before returning to his face.

"Can you tell me who you are?"

Jason shook his head.

"Where are we, then?"

Again, Jason shook his head.

The man—Stephen—wiggled his arm around before relaxing a second. Then he repeated the motion. His sister was doing the same thing. Jason waited. They wouldn't get far. No one ever got too far—not even him.

He frowned. In his mind, he was pushing memory after memory aside. He had been in this room, strapped to a bed. But his wasn't a cushioned bed like theirs. It was a heated metal bed.

These two... he had found them when he had been stationed at the monitors. He had tracked them down, discovered them at Enchanté, sent the contingent as Bastion had ordered. Jason straightened with a deep inhale as his memories rushed back to him.

The woman—Sierra—had been quietly observing him as Stephen fought to free himself. Her eyes searched his. She began to speak, but the door to the room hissed opened.

Jason clasped his hands at his lower back and waited.

Bastion *tap-tapped* their way. Stephen stilled and studied her as she slid past Jason and stood in between the two beds. Jason's nostrils flared at the death-stench that rolled off her skin. He clamped his jaw and noticed that the woman was having the same reaction as he. Stephen only glared.

"Stephen and Sierra Williams." Bastion hobbled to Sierra and leaned over her, reading the results on the neural relay. She then turned and approached Stephen. "Tell me—children or grandchildren of Julius Williams?"

When they refused to answer, she motioned toward the guard. "Send me a contingent."

The guard nodded and spoke into his comm. Stephen and Sierra watched them. Stephen's eyes had narrowed into slits, the green becoming hardened emeralds. Sierra's eyes had widened, taking in all that was around them; her gaze darted from Jason to Bastion to the banks of consoles and tubes.

Bastion was still talking. "It doesn't matter. After viewing your DNA, I have deduced that you are his grandchildren, which means there is another out there with Serum Seventy-four altered genes." She ran her hand along Stephen's shin, causing him to buck against the fusion bands. "You favor him greatly, young Stephen."

She slowly moved up the length of his bed, letting her hand travel over him. Her fingers trailed along his jaw and cheek, despite him trying to turn his head away. His lips curled in disgust as she ran her hand though his hair.

It was the touches that seemed to sicken Stephen. Jason mentally noted the man's reactions. He glanced at Sierra. Concern flooded her eyes as she could only observe. Bastion paused with her hand still buried in Stephen's hair and peered over her shoulder at Sierra. A small grin filtered across the medtech's mouth, and she hobbled over to the sister.

When her fingers gripped Sierra's chin, turning her head from side to side, pure anger and hate poured from Stephen. He strained against the bands, yet they held.

"Get your hands off her!" His hiss sliced the sterile air.

Behind Jason, five guards and a medstudy entered the room. The guards fanned out around the beds as the medstudy held out a hypospray to Bastion. Without pausing, Medtech Bastion grabbed the tool, approached Stephen, and placed it against his neck. A quick hiss from the hypospray indicated the delivery of the drug. Veins stood out against his forehead, neck, and hands as he arched in pain.

Jason swallowed. Pure Paxolin-X. He remembered the burn through his veins as the drug had coursed through his body. It was designed to make one forget, increase obedience, and fuel rage. It never lasted long on him. Would it work on the man, Stephen?

She stepped back and motioned for the guards to release the bands on Sierra. "Alpha Zero, take hold of her."

Sierra leaped off the bed and took half a step toward her brother before Jason wrapped his hands around her biceps and yanked her to him. His arms clamped around her, holding her against him. When she began to fight back, using her legs to kick back and stomp, he squeezed, compressing her ribcage.

She gasped in pain but rammed her head backwards. He was prepared and moved his head to the side. With his left arm around her chest, squeezing even harder, he slid his right hand under her chin and gripped her neck. His fingers at her arteries applying pressure caused her to pause.

It was only seconds. Her muscles bunched underneath his arms. She would fight them. But she wouldn't win—not yet. Medtech Bastion laughed at Sierra futilely fighting and at Jason's annoyance before turning back to Stephen. Jason took that opportunity to tap the carotid artery twice. Sierra's breath froze mid-intake, and she cut her gaze to him.

Keeping his eyes on Bastion as she injected another round of Paxolin-X into Stephen, Jason mouthed a message to her, *Not yet. Trust me.*

It was asking a lot; he knew that. Her green stare bored into him, delving deep into his soul. Whatever she saw, she cut her gaze back to her brother and stopped straining against him. Yet she remained rigid under his arm.

Bastion motioned the guards to deactivate the restraints. They popped open; and Stephen immediately shot upward, shoved a guard aside, and grabbed another. Three others rushed in, battering at Stephen with electro-probes and rifle butts.

Sierra flinched when a guard went flying through the air and into the wall of holographic displays. He fell into a limp pile on the floor. There was a crunch of bones, and another guard collapsed, his head at an odd angle.

Two down. Jason backed up a step, pulling Sierra with him, as one more guard went down in a heap, blood seeping around a knife protruding from his neck. Stephen had used the guard's own weapon against him—impressive.

Only two remained; and they had backed up from Stephen, who stood with blood covering his hands and splattered across his face. He whipped his gaze to Jason and Sierra. Rage poured from him as he advanced.

"Stop." Bastion held a pulse gun aimed at them. Stephen didn't falter in his steps. Bastion adjusted her aim and fired the weapon at Stephen's feet.

Stephen stopped and regarded the scorch mark before resuming his advance toward Jason. Bastion moved closer and aimed the gun at Sierra's temple. Stephen stumbled to a pause as the last two guards cautiously approached him from both sides.

"One more step forward and I will kill her."

Jason tapped Sierra's artery again. She needed to make her brother stand down because Bastion would kill Sierra without pause. With Bastion's gaze concentrated on Stephen, Jason tapped again and drew his finger along her skin spelling out *stop*.

Her throat contracted once. He couldn't let up, though. Bastion couldn't know that he was awake.

Her voice was hoarse as she called out to Stephen. "Ven, stop. Please, stop."

Stephen's eyes studied his sister, his hands clenching and unclenching. His gaze began to cloud over until his eyes became empty, and his breathing began to slow into a deep rhythm. Jason pulled her tighter against him. The Paxolin-X was now in full effect. He was Bastion's now.

Bastion walked over to Sierra and pressed the gun to her left temple. "Stephen Williams, do you see the guards beside you?"

Without turning his head, he nodded.

"Kill them."

It was a slight pause, just a half-second of hesitation. Then Stephen moved. To others, it would have been a blur. To Jason, he could see each movement as the man whirled to his right, gripped the guard around the throat, and continued turning, bringing the heel of his hand to meet the throat of the other. As the second guard collapsed to the floor, choking, Stephen wrapped his arm around the other man's neck and jerked. Bones cracked, and the man's body hit the floor with a thud. Stephen stooped and pulled the knife from the belt of the other and drove it into the guard's back, through his tactical vest, and into the heart.

It was over in seconds—too fast for the guards to react to Bastion's command.

Stephen returned to his original position. With a vacant gaze centered on a point somewhere along the wall behind them, the brother stood immobile.

Bastion laid the gun on Sierra's vacated bed and approached Stephen. "The Paxmedlin took to you better than I had hoped, even though it took two doses. I'll have to adjust the strength a bit for you."

Jason frowned. Paxmedlin? A new derivative? Bastion *tap-tapped* around Stephen, allowing her gaze to flow up and down him before facing Jason.

"Alpha Zero, escort her to the cells and remain there until called." She snapped her fingers, and the guards outside the medlab flooded in to escort them.

Sierra stumbled when they jerked her away from him. Two flanked Jason while four surrounded her.

Her voice cracked when she called out. "Stephen? Ven!"

Jason glanced back as they were ushered out the door. Stephen never responded. His empty expression remained as Medtech Bastion ran a portable scanner over his body. Then the door hissed closed, hiding away what she was about to do to him.

Yet Jason knew—experiments, control, drugs pumped into the system. Stephen had replaced Jason.

Seth hunched over, propping his hands on his knees, as the last remnants of the aerosolized drug faded. His head pounded in time with the queasy roll of his stomach. Michael leaned against the wall of the alley and waited.

"How are you not affected as badly by that stuff?"

Michael shrugged. "Probably because I'm not as enhanced as you."

That made sense. Seth's body would have been trying to purge the drug at the same time his cells were absorbing it and breaking it down. He straightened and drew in a breath. "This alley should lead us in the direction they went."

Michael pushed off the wall and led the way down the narrow alley, glancing up every few seconds at the overhanging balconies. Seth peered back over his shoulder as the echo of raucous laughter bounced off the bricks. A group of women dressed in diminutive clothing and surrounding a man swayed and stumbled past the alley's opening.

Seth shook his head at the scene and tried to push the memories of what he had witnessed in the club from his mind. Seeing what had happened on the feeds was one thing. But as he and Michael pushed and shoved their way through the hordes of bodies, what he viewed was now emblazoned in his mind. He would not have had to deal with any of that kind of depravity if it hadn't been for his rebellious son and his determined daughter.

The effect of the drug that was spritzed every five minutes into the air had almost had him in the middle of the action. Seth snarled at the thought. Only those few seconds of clarity kept him from betraying his Lord and his wife, but he had come close. A worse thought was that his children had been there. Did they—

"Hold up."

Michael's whisper cut through his disturbing thoughts. Ahead of them and across the esplanade, a gazebo and surrounding area was occupied by a security force. They slipped back into the darkened recess of the alley and watched as soldiers collected items from the ground and from inside the gazebo. Three men patrolled the area, walking a tight perimeter around the small sitting area.

Michael touched Seth's shoulder. "Can you see what they are picking up?"

"Give me a second." Seth thumbed the contacts out of his eyes, pocketed them, and blinked to clear away the tears. He squinted and focused on the gazebo. Gloved hands reached down and grabbed two blue darts from the cobbled floor. A streak of blood marred the centerpiece of the fountain. A man stood behind the gazebo, issuing orders. "Darts."

"Then they must have the twins."

"I will be able to tell once they leave."

Michael's assumption was probably correct. The twins had been found and collected. How did Bastion learn about them? Seth reined in his emotions and buried them. There would be a time to deal with that later. First, he needed to wait.

Seth leaned his shoulder against the bricked wall. Twenty minutes passed. Soldiers congregated near a transport. Another fifteen minutes and the leader, talking into a comm unit, stepped from the shadows of the gazebo and stalked to the transport near the street. Seth caught snippets of his conversation.

"All has been collected. Body is in transport now . . . one hour."

Body? He clenched his fists and restrained the fear that threatened to rise. *Please let it not be one of my twins, Lord.*

The transport pulled away, yet they waited a full minute before stepping out of the dark. He and Michael rushed across the open esplanade and into the gazebo. Seth held out his arm to stop Michael.

He sniffed the air. "They were here. I can smell Sierra's vanilla scent and Stephen's smell, overlaid with toxins. It's faint but there." Seth eased around the center fountain, looking for anything that would hint at what had transpired.

Michael knelt near the fountain and ran his finger over a slight score in the concrete. "Looks like a dart hit here."

Seth nodded and toed another one on the cobblestone near him. "And here, too." He walked back around to the front and studied the fountain where he had seen the bloodstain. "There's a bloodstain above the waterline on the centerpiece. That must have been the body the leader was mentioning."

A golden flash caught his attention. Seth knelt on the edge of the fountain and plunged his hand into the freezing water.

Michael joined him. "Find something?"

Seth straightened and held up a small, golden keycard. "Looks like whoever was thrown in the fountain lost their card." He angled it so that Michael could read the inscription: Intech Juliet Serum Initiative.

"Medlab Twelve-twenty." Michael turned his attention in the direction where the transport had gone.

"Has to be." Seth pocketed the card and stood next to Michael. "It will take an hour by transport—an hour and half for us. Once there, I'll find a way in and—"

He and Michael froze as a scuff sounded behind them and across the plaza. No, it was three scuffs. Then a voice called out to them.

"Raise your hands and place them on the back of your heads!"

Seth and Michael complied. He forced himself not to clench his fists as anger and frustration began to rise within him. Now was not the time to have to deal with security forces. And by the sound of their hard soled boots, these were Midland Security Forces.

"Turn around."

He turned. The officer waved his men to fan out around Michael and him before holding out his hand. "You two are in a restricted zone. Citizen card."

Seth cut his gaze to Michael, who gave a barely imperceptible nod. With slow movements, Seth reached into his side pocket of his cargos and pulled out his now-defunct card. He held it out to the officer.

When the man reached for it, Seth grabbed the man's wrist and yanked him forward, driving the heel of his hand into the bridge of the man's nose. The officer dropped to the floor with a heavy thud. Michael held his officer in a headlock, slowly cutting off the man's airway as the last officer—a burly, towering bulk of muscle—rushed Seth.

His rifle was raised and primed. Seth batted the rifle to the side, the shot burying itself into the fountain's water, and grunted as the man's fist plowed into his ribs. Seth grabbed the barrel of the rifle and yanked. The weapon clattered to the cobblestones as he slammed his hand onto the back of the officer's head. With a quick jerk, Seth sent the man's face down toward his rising knee. The man's hands grasped Seth's knee, softening the blow, and shoved at Seth's leg. He pushed away from Seth, drawing a slim dagger from his belt. But Seth closed his hands over the man's and plowed into him, pressing him into the wall. Little by little, Seth angled the blade toward the officer, forcing the tip deeper and deeper into the tactical vest.

The man strained against Seth's leverage. With a grunt, he butted his forehead against Seth's, causing stars to spiral in Seth's vision. Seth's grip loosened; and the officer pushed, sending Seth stumbling back half a step. Yet it was enough to give the man an opening.

The security officer gripped Seth's hands and began squeezing, trying to make Seth relinquish his hold. Fury and a bit of maniacal humor rose from Seth. What did the man think he was going to accomplish? That trick may have worked on a regular human. But his enhancements and all those years of labor had made his hands and arms stronger than titanium alloy.

He grinned and drove his shoulder into the man's chest, sending him back against the wall and breaking his hold on Seth. Shock poured from the guard's face as Seth repositioned his hands on the hilt and drove the dagger deep into the man's chest. For half a second, their gazes met; and Seth viewed his own reflection in the man's widening pupils as his life drained from him. A hardened, white gaze, one that burned with fury and diabolical glee, stared back at him from those black depths.

As the man slumped to the floor, the fury faded, leaving Seth to stare at the dead man in horror. He looked at his hands. Not a drop of blood on them yet they had just killed. He had only meant to render the guard unconscious.

Michael eased past him and pulled the weapon from the body. "Can't let them get any evidence off this." He quickly wiped it down on the man's clothing and slid it into his belt next to his short blade. Michael's blue gaze studied Seth for a second. Then he grabbed Seth's arm and pulled him out of the gazebo.

Seth freed himself from Michael's grasp and followed. This could be dealt with later. He arched his neck from side to side, stretching the tendons and relieving the tension, and shoved what had transpired deep down within his mind.

With a clearing of his throat, Seth unclasped the hidden pocket on his vest and removed the QG. He slid his small panel lock from his side pocket and inserted the QG into the top. "I may be able to find a quicker route that will keep us hidden."

As the panel lock ran through the downloaded information on the medlab, Seth's mind replayed the fight. So much for burying what had transpired. Where had the fury come from? It hadn't been there before. Anger, yes—at his twins, at the rebelliousness of Stephen, at . . . . He paused in his thoughts, following Michael through the darkened alleys and streets.

His anger had started a little over a year ago as he had begun his deeper research when he had become agitated and restless seven years ago at being stuck behind the walls of their country. He had discovered the dyad gene, and then his mother had died. But he was handling that, sorting through the emotions and reasoning with himself, applying logic and counseling and cognitive techniques. He was even reading Scripture to learn how to control the uncertainty that the future was presenting. Surely, he was handling it well. Wasn't he?

Yet that fury he had felt during the fight—it was freeing, but also terrifying. It was . . . Seth paused, causing Michael to stop and study him. The fury unleashed within him was always a part of him—a part of being enhanced. A part of what? Of his father?

Later! Seth shook his head and brought up the display of the new route to the medlab. He turned it around so Michael could see. "Rail transport. That will cut our travel by at least twenty."

Michael nodded and waved him forward. Yet there was a question in that blue gaze. Seth's dilemma hadn't gone unnoticed by his friend.

Chapter Twelve
REVELATION
OF JASON

Sierra studied the man in the cell across from hers. He sat on the bench that was built into the back wall, one that was identical to hers. For the last twenty minutes, he had not moved, only studied her as she was studying him. He was tall, at least three inches over six feet. His black hair shone in the harsh light of their cells.

After being shoved into the stark cell where the bright light burned her eyes and after they sealed the outer hatch to their corridor, Sierra had stood at the bars of her containment and waited. The man was different. When she had awakened to find herself trapped on a medical table, he had, at first, seemed like an empty shell. But as she continued to watch, there was a battle raging in him behind his strange, cyan eyes and across his bronzed-tone face.

Then, within moments, an awareness had flooded through him, as if he, too, had just awakened. She had seen that on people before when she assisted during one of her internships in the medlab back home. People awakening from the anesthesia always had that emptiness to them until their consciousness caught up. And when

Aunt Evie's son had gone through a seizure, it took a while before his mind caught up with reality.

Even when he had grabbed her around the throat, the man's fingers were positioned slightly off her arteries, therefore not able to cause any permanent damage to her. When he mouthed to her "not yet" and then later when he spelled out "stop" along her skin, she had to consider that there may be more to whom he might be.

That woman—a woman from her grandfather's past because, logically, who else could have known how their grandfather had looked—had called him Alpha Zero. So, he was a test subject, then—one of hers.

Sierra approached the bars and gripped one of them. "What's your name? The medtech called you Alpha Zero, but that isn't a name."

Silence answered her. The seconds stretched into minutes as they stared at each other. Then he stood and walked to his cell bars yet didn't touch them. He only remained an unmoving tower.

"How long have you been here?"

Again, he didn't answer. His brows drew down in a slight frown. His hands flexed into fists before uncurling and flattening against his black uniform.

"You didn't answer me in the medlab. I had assumed it was because you weren't allowed to talk to me. Are we monitored in here?"

He pointed to the side of his cell and then at the ceiling between them. Sierra glanced across her cell. A small monitoring unit nestled quietly above a covered mirror. The one in the corridor was just as quiet.

"Monitoring, but not now, I see. So, they don't always watch?"

He shook his head.

"But you still won't talk." Another frown creased his face. He wanted to talk. That was it. He desired to talk. "Oh, you can't talk, can you?"

He shook his head again. Then he reached up and touched his throat.

"Something they did to you?"

He nodded, his eyes never straying away from her face. They narrowed into slits as he cocked his head and mouthed, *Can you read lips?*

Sierra stepped closer to the bars. "Yes, I can. I learned from my aunt CeeCee. She was deaf most of her life; and we learned early how to read lips, then how to sign."

His puzzled gaze roved across her face. *Sign?*

"A form of communication using the hands and gestures. I can teach you, but it takes time."

I learn fast. Like you. Faster than any other human.

"You are enhanced?"

I don't know what you mean by saying enhanced, but if that means more than, yes. They made me into something more.

"How long have you been here?" Sierra leaned against the bars. The cool metal pressed against her forehead.

He stepped closer, draped his hands through the bars, and let them rest on the crossbar. *Since I can remember. All my life. I'm hers. I'm Bastion's.*

Anya Bastion. A woman from her grandmother's past. She shook her head at his statement. "No, no one belongs to another. Do you have a name?"

Alpha Zero is what they call me. But I call myself Jason.

"Jason." Sierra smiled at him. When she did, he cocked his head and touched his own lips. "I like that. Tell me, Jason. Do you know why we are here?"

I'm sorry. It's because of me.

"You?"

I was made to search for you. At first, I hid you. I wanted to figure out a way to bring you here safely because I was hoping you could free me. But she found out. I was punished. And she knew where you were and captured you.

Silence descended upon them as she mulled over his words. Free him? So, he was a captive, too. How desperate was he? He searched for them, found them, hid them to figure out a way to get them here. Yet it was a dangerous game, and he was caught.

She allowed her gaze to travel over him. If he was enhanced, that meant he probably had the same abilities as they did. She already knew he was strong. His muscles had felt like carbon steel against her back in the medlab. He studied everything around him, so she had to believe him when he said he was a fast learner.

Those cyan eyes studied her as she examined him. "What did they do to your eyes?"

Augmentations. I see in more wavelengths than normal eyesight.

Interesting. If Bastion was using the Serum Seventy-four, added with the serum's augmentations, then he would see better than she or Stephen, maybe even her father. "You are on Serum Seventy-four?"

Jason shook his head. *No, she made a new one, Serum Seventy-seven.*

Interesting. Sierra gripped the cell bars. "You mentioned punishment? What did they do?"

He huffed out a heavy sigh and looked away. For a moment, she didn't think he would respond; but then he turned and lifted his shirt. Across his lower back was a flexible, flesh-colored electronic patch around a tiny, round, metal tubing that was flush against his back and had been inserted into his spine. The light next to the tube blinked green.

Jason dropped his shirt and turned back around. *If I step out of line, they inject more Paxolin-X into me. And then I forget who I am. I become hers again.*

"So, you have to pretend when you wake up?" He nodded. Sierra was about to reply, but the light above the monitor in the corridor turned red.

Jason stood at the entrance of his cell—no expression, no movement. Sierra arched her brow at him as the hatch hissed open. She grimaced at the death-stench that rolled across the air. The smells had been there before but not as strong. Now, without her salve, anything more than the sterile air seemed to magnify a hundredfold. She glanced at Jason, noting that his nostrils had flared momentarily.

Bastion hobbled her way toward Sierra's cell. Her cane tapped against the metal floorplates in an ungainly rhythm. Behind her, two of her medstudies waited at the hatch. The aged woman stopped at Sierra's door, and Sierra backed up a couple of paces.

"Sierra Williams." Contempt poured from the woman's ice-blue, watery eyes. "You have a bit of your grandmother in you. I can see her. But you favor your grandfather a great deal. Tell me, does your father have the same strong genes?"

When Sierra didn't answer, she chuckled. "It doesn't matter. I have what I need from Stephen. But you . . ." She waved at one of the medstudies. "Bring it to me."

The medstudy handed her a vial and injection gun. Bastion inserted the empty vial into the gun and smiled at Sierra. "Don't worry. I modified this for extraction." With another wave, the medstudies opened Sierra's door and trained two tranq pistols at her. "Go ahead and extend your arm."

Sierra swallowed. It was better to play along for a while and wait for a chance. Right now, she didn't have the advantage. Her mouth dried, and her tongue stuck to the roof of her mouth as she held out her right arm. Stephen was better at strategy than she was. Stephen . . . what was happening with him?

Bastion positioned the gun against Sierra's skin. A quick prick, a small hiss, and the vial began filling with her blood. Then Bastion was stepping back, and the door was closing. Behind Bastion, Jason flattened his hands against his legs. His nostrils flared again, and the pulse at his neck beat heavily.

Sierra took a half-step toward her closed door; but the tranq pistols whipped up, aiming at her chest. Bastion glanced at them before turning to Jason.

"Alpha Zero." She pulled a small datapad from her pocket. "I see that this dose of Paxolin-X wasn't enough. I'll have to adjust that. You are building a strong immunity to it. If the Paxmedlin in young Stephen shows as much promise as it seems to, I will start using it. As it is . . . " She stopped short of his cell door and ran her gaze up and down him. "I cannot have you waking up."

Bastion pressed a button on her datapad. Jason suddenly arched. His body became rigid, straining against an unknown force. Then he relaxed. Like Stephen, an emptiness filled him.

"Go lie down until called, Alpha Zero."

Jason turned and retreated to his bunk. Bastion once again turned her attention to Sierra. With a flick of her wrist, the medstudies fired their tranq pistols. The darts hit Sierra in her midsection. Then, she was sliding to the cold floor. Her last view was of the metal-tipped cane tapping its way down the corridor.

His world was a blur of movements through a red haze. His vision pulsed in time with his heartbeat. The room in which he stood breathed along with him. Fear pricked against his mind. He was underwater. Had to be. The sounds and voices were muffled and garbled as if he were underwater.

But he couldn't be. He could see the computers, the consoles, the wall that mirrored his body back to him. Medtechs and medstudies swarmed around him as he stood manacled to the upright bed.

"Give him one more cc of Paxmedlin and the serum."

The words reached him, yet they made no sense. Pax what? What serum? His grandfather's? Stephen let his head fall back against the bed's hard cushion. The ceiling swirled in a kaleidoscope of colors. One of Sierra's words bounced through his mind—phantasmagoria. That's what it was called.

Sierra. Where was she?

A hiss from behind him and a puncture into his spine erased that last thought. Stephen arched against the burn and then relaxed as it faded.

His gaze settled on the hazy woman standing in front of him. She wavered in his red haze, issuing orders. He had begun to grow weary of her. She demanded him to obey her: do this, do that, kill him, torture her, hack that. And he did it just to make her shut up and to silence the demons yelling at him. No, not demons. It was them—the people around him.

The bands around Stephen retracted, and he stepped off the platform. No matter how hard he thought about it, he couldn't harm her. He wanted to, if for no other reason than to wipe that smirk off her face and erase the stench that clung to her. Did she know she was dying a slow death, rotting slowly from inside?

"Stephen, your designation is now Alpha One." She walked around him, her cane at times tapping against his body that was clad only in his underpants.

The room should have been cold, but an internal heat raged through him, keeping the frigid air at bay. The white puffs from their breaths drifted upward.

"Repeat your designation."

Stephen heard the hardness in his voice. His mind thought *Stephen*, yet his voice said, "Alpha One."

"Excellent. I had feared the mix of Paxmedlin and Serum Seventy-seven would not work. But it seems as though it has. T-agent just may be the key I need." She tapped her way back into his line of sight. "Alpha One, I need you to repeat after me."

Stephen willed his hands to move, to reach out and grasp her throat, to strangle the remaining life from her. Yet nothing obeyed. He was trapped in his own mind. The rage that covered him— the one that flowed through him and that colored his vision— was claiming him, slowly and bit by bit. In his mind, he beat against the wall that trapped him inside.

"I am Alpha One." She waited for him, leaning a bit closer.

Stephen stared at the mirrored wall behind her. "I am Alpha One."

"I am Medtech Anya Bastion's design."

He couldn't say— But then, he heard himself repeat, "I am Medtech Anya Bastion's design."

She walked to the console next to them and accepted a uniform from one of the medstudies. "Put this on."

"Put this on."

Medtech Bastion chuckled. "Stop repeating after me and put this on."

Stephen accepted the uniform and slipped into it. The thin material clung to his body, warming his skin. A pair of boots were dropped at his feet; and he donned them, stamping them onto the floor twice to settle them into position.

When he straightened, she handed him a tactical vest. He was not given any weapons—just an empty, pocketed vest. He shrugged into it and then waited.

She left him standing in the middle of the room near his upright bed. Rattles from the corner indicated she was rummaging through the instruments she had used on him. Those were faint memories from not so long ago. The instruments brought him torture, but he couldn't remember the pain of it. Then he had to use them on others. Or . . . or what? There was something lurking in the back of his memories, something she had used against him to make him do her bidding.

The *tap-tapping* of her cane alerted him a second before the hypospray was pressed against his neck. Another round burned into his system. Then she was ordering the medstudies to increase the dosage another twenty cc's.

She stopped short of touching him as she walked back to stand in front of him. The last time she had touched him, the fury within had unleashed; and he had sent three medstudies flying across the room, killing two of them. There was something about being touched, about hands touching and roaming over him, that unleashed a rage he had never known. But like the other memories, it laid buried beneath the blood-red haze.

"You are showing a resistance to the Paxmedlin. But the increased dosage should work this time around." Medtech Bastion leaned against her cane. "Do you know what you are, Alpha One?"

He shook his head. Human? Not human? More than human? He didn't know what he was anymore.

"You are an abomination—an abomination to humankind. You shouldn't exist. It should have ended with your grandfather, yet he allowed the abomination of your kind to be born." She grinned, displaying white teeth and pale gums. "He and the others were good for one thing and one thing only: killing. Only, he defied that. But I will use your abomination for a greater purpose, for our goal."

Stephen mulled over her words when a medstudy handed her a datapad and she perused it. Abomination? Yes, that was what he was now—and had been. His kind shouldn't have existed. Humans weren't meant to be this evolved.

"What are you, Alpha One?" She never looked up from the datapad.

"An abomination."

At her nod, the medstudy accepted the datapad back and left the medlab. "Good. I think you will do just fine. A few more adjustments to the system and dosage, and I'll have you ready for Sector Gray." Her hand patted and then caressed his forearm, sending a red rage through him. With a knowing smile, she headed for the door, yet paused on the threshold. "Alpha One, only I and Medstudy Johannsen have clearance for Medlab Twenty from now on. See the rest?" At his nod, she turned and began walking away, speaking over her shoulder. "Kill them."

The hatched closed. The panel next to it turned red: locked.

Around him, the medstudies began panicking. They huddled behind consoles. Some rushed the door, trying to force it open or to hack the panel.

He reached over, picked up a stylus from a console, and ran a finger down its length. Strong metal. Rigid. It would work well.

Inside, Stephen screamed, wanting himself to stop. But on the outside and on the surface, only Alpha One existed. And the blood that began to color his hands matched the red haze in his vision.

"The time is soon arriving, Jason." The Man sat cross-legged on the floor before him. As with all the previous times, Jason could see Him, yet a light obscured his face.

Jason propped his hands on his own crossed legs and sighed. "How much longer?"

He knew he said those words, but he couldn't hear his voice. It was always like this, sitting cross-legged in the middle of the floor of his cell and talking with the Man dressed in white. He would speak, actually say the words, but there was never a sound. And the Man's voice . . . it sounded like a thousand waterfalls—like the ones he had seen and heard on the learning videos from years past.

"Not long. Sierra will show you the way."

"Does she know of You? Should I tell her about You?" The words rushed from Jason.

"She knows Me. And if you ask, she will tell you of Me. Now, time to awaken, Jason."

With a gasp, Jason sat up on his bunk and looked around his darkened cell. He had been ordered to lie down and wait until called. And now that the dose had run its course and been purged by his body, he was back to being Jason, not Alpha Zero.

After a few moments in the refresher and a quick splash of cold water against his face, he resettled on his bunk and gazed at the woman in the cell across from him. Sometime during his sleep, they had moved her from the floor to the bunk.

She had one arm across her stomach and the other hanging off the edge of her bunk. Her head was tilted at an odd angle. They must have dumped her, not caring about her comfort. He let his gaze travel down her body. She was thin—not skinny to the point of bones poking out, but quite thin. Her hair fanned around her in thick waves. The lights played with the wavelengths, and a riot of color danced across her. She was a golden beauty with velvet hair under the shimmer of silver and blue.

The hatch to their cell block hissed just as she moaned and opened her eyes. A medstudy carried a tray to Sierra's cell. Jason frowned. It wasn't time for the daily allotment. As Sierra sat up, she felt her pockets and then began to panic. Noticing her panic, the medstudy set the tray and a small vial on the floor.

"Medtech Bastion ran your blood and noticed your abnormality with your metabolism. She still has use for you, so your pills were

allowed to be returned; and a plate of food has been prepared to help."
Then the medstudy left.

Sierra stood and wobbled a bit on her feet before collecting the
tray and settling down cross-legged in front of the bars. Jason waited
and watched.

She popped the top off the vial and fished out a blue capsule. She
removed the lid to the tray, which held a small glass of water next to
a plate of bread, cheese, and fruit. After a quick perusal, she used the
water to wash down the capsule and then proceeded to eat the food.
Bit by bit, strength and clarity seemed to return to her.

Once she finished the small meal, she set the tray back on the
floor and pushed it through the bars and into the corridor, yet she
remained seated on the floor. Her eyes met his. He was taken aback
by the intensity of the green—green with those small flecks of white
near the pupil.

"Are you ready to learn how to sign?"

Jason glanced at the monitor. It was offline. He rose from his bunk
and sat on the floor in front of his bars. *Do you have a metabolism condition?*

"I do. It runs higher. I have to take medication to slow it down." She
moved her hands in conjunction with her words. Jason followed them,
picking out what each one may mean.

He held out his arm and moved his other hand up it. *Slow down?*

"Yes. And this is 'medicine' or 'medication.'" She touched her palm
and then her mouth. "We also use this for 'eat' or 'taste' by using
three or four fingers instead of one. Remember, I said our version
is different than others. We modify many of the words to keep our
conversations private to others in different territories."

So, "metabolism" is this? He touched his mouth, then over his heart, and made a circle in his cupped palm.

"Yes. You weren't joking when you said you were a fast learner."

He watched her hands and then mimicked the words. It was a hybrid way of speaking: *You no joke. You fast learn.*

So, to speak in sign, I take the words and apply them to our speech patterns to get what is being said?

"Exactly. Sometimes, a gesture can mean a multitude of things. It is the rest of the sentence that determines what is being said."

Jason tried out a few more of the words she used. Feeling how his hands and fingers flowed in the patterns she displayed felt like a dance, and it was freeing.

I have a question for you—something that I understood that you may be able to explain. Will you use sign to answer?

She nodded, curiosity lining her face.

I dream about Someone. A Man in white. I call Him the Dream Man. He said you know Him. And all I have to do is ask you about Him. He is the One Who has kept me holding on and believing that a day will come that I can escape.

It was a fear of his that she would laugh at him, think him mentally unbalanced. But a strange look settled in her eyes. A light flooded the green, and a smile brightened her face. "It reminds me of a story my grandmother used to tell us. My grandfather, Jules, once saw a light on the battlefield—a fight that should have left him for dead. It was the light that kept him alive. Then he saw it again. And at times, as he told my grandmother, he would see a Man in white, usually when he was about to fall asleep or in a dream."

Who is He?

"He is the Son of God, our Savior Christ Jesus." She leaned forward, excitement flowing from her, causing her hands to move faster. "He is the One Who died for us, atoning for our sins—past, present, and future—in order for us to be reconciled with our Creator, God. You've never heard of Him?"

Jason shook his head, enthralled by the story. *So, He is real?*

"More than ever. We have a book called The Holy Bible. It has survived many centuries. It's still illegal in GFT territories. But in this book—our Bible—it speaks of the history of mankind, our fall from God's grace, and our reconciliation through Christ, Who came to earth to walk among us. Imagine that: God walked among us as one of us!" She smiled at him. "So, this 'Dream Man' of yours may be Jesus or an angel, guiding you and preparing you for what is to come."

And what is that?

Her hands stilled and fell into her lap. "I don't know. But we will know when it happens." She reached out and gripped the bars in front of her. "How much do you know about this place?"

I learned the schematics long ago. I know every corridor, every tunnel, every shaft. He tried his hand at signing: *I will make sure we . . .* His hands faltered.

Sierra smiled and signed, holding her hand flat and moving a finger underneath it and away. "Escape."

A buzz issued from the monitor. Jason glanced up. The monitor was blinking red. He stood and waited. Sierra followed suit, her eyes flicking from the hatch to him and back. The door opened; and a contingent of guards trooped in, aiming their pulse rifles at them. Two medstudies approached and opened their cells.

"Follow us."

Jason motioned for Sierra to follow first. She stepped out, and four guards surrounded her. The remaining two flanked Jason as he followed them into the corridor and through the maze of turns. Sierra's fingers on each hand would at times tap against her thigh as she counted the turns. Jason had done the same the first time he was marched through the facility. Even though she had to be scared, even terrified, she hid it well. Only the tension in her shoulders hinted at her emotions.

A guard called out for them to halt. They were in Corridor F, Medlab Fourteen—the biological division, the room he had been in the most during his teenage years and where he was administered the newest serum that Medtech Bastion called Serum Seventy-seven, examined, prodded and probed, and injected with substances that changed his body.

They were led across the threshold and to the far right side, where two medical beds were positioned under a scanner. Sierra was instructed to climb onto the second one. Then Jason pulled himself up on the first, lying back on the hard surface.

The medstudies strapped the restraints across their wrists, ankles, hips, and necks, giving each one a violent yank to ensure their secureness. Sierra cast a worried at Jason. He raised a finger, motioning for her to remain still. She swallowed and stared at the ceiling. Her lips moved silently: *Lord, be with us. Please, give me strength and still my fear. Amen.*

Jason mulled over those words, then repeated them in his head. Maybe her God would listen to him, too?

Medtech Bastion approached them. Not a word was said as she positioned the scanner over them. He squinted his eyes against the onslaught of the bright light as it ran up and down their bodies. She read the display as it scanned, periodically clicking at her teeth with her tongue.

When the scan was completed, she strolled to Sierra and took another vial of her blood. The *tap-tapping* of her cane traveled to the other side of the room and then back to Jason, where she removed a vial of his blood. Moments passed. Consoles beeped, and machines whirred.

When Medtech Bastion returned, an evil, little smile played at her lips. "You two are compatible. I told you, Alpha Zero, that I still had use for you."

She motioned toward a medstudy. A mask was slipped over Jason's face. He cast a look at Sierra. The same was happening to her. Gas hissed underneath him. Sierra turned her head, and her green gaze met his. Tears pooled in her eyes in a silent plea as fear and anxiety took hold. The same emotions coursed through his heart, too.

She blurred in his vision. Then, the world blackened.

Chapter Thirteen
THE SECRETS WITHIN

The PatRecs slowed their movements. Seth had assumed that once morning came, the drones would be back out in full force; but he had assumed incorrectly. By the third hour, each section had dozens of the drones zipping through the air. The rounded black machines periodically paused above someone who walked the area in the wee hours.

He peered around the corner as they waited. Michael thumbed his datapad, searching for updates on the sub-hub. Across the roadway was their next destination: a rail transport to the edge of the west side of the city. The sprawling building stretched for hundreds of yards. The darkness of the hour should have bathed the streets and plazas in shadows; but the bright lights of various signs, glow of the ship engines above, and the overhead rail system's pulsing beams lit the scene and scorched his eyes.

Seth arched his head to the side, popping tight tendons. How could one live in such a place with constant commotion and constant noise? He blinked against the beam of an automatic rickshaw as it zipped around the bend ahead. Seth scowled. He needed the fresh

214

pine air of home, the soothing sounds of the bay, and the soft Alaskan sunlight.

The buzz of a drone reached him. Seth ducked back under the overhanging balconies and reached up to grasp one of the lower bars. He leaned against his arms as they waited for an opening. The black machine paused at the alley's entrance, beeped once, and then veered off toward the plaza.

Beta or alpha. He had to stay in beta or alpha brainwaves. He propped his head against his forearms. *Please help me find my twins so we can go home, Lord. I hate it here.* A heavy sigh became his amen as he ended his silent plea.

"Here." Michael handed him his citizen card.

Seth straightened and accepted it. He fumbled for the QG and then inserted it into the top, downloading only the q-shielding program from the QG. Now, the card was a ghost in the system. It would keep them hidden.

He pocketed the citizen card and slipped the QG back into its hidden pocket on his shirt. After the fight and along the walk here, he had moved the data crystal from his vest to his shirt. It might be safer, though, if he moved it to the hidden slit on his waistband.

Michael motioned for him to follow. An opening in the thick throng of people and rickshaws had presented itself.

Seth cleared his mind. As they stepped out onto the pavement, he kept his head down, watching his feet take step after step across the roadway and onto the next walkway—a step in a small puddle, a step on a broken stone, a step up on the concrete, a step to the right to avoid a suspicious, disgusting mass. No telling what that was. Then he was near the open platform of the hub.

A drone buzzed by, paused, and circled back around to them. It hovered for a second as Seth read the poster attached to the fused-pane glass with travel times, costs, and destinations. The drone whined once and zipped away.

Then he and Michael stepped over the threshold and into the interior of the rail transport hub. Seth stuffed his hand into his back pockets and took a silent deep breath.

Keeping himself in beta and alpha wave was taxing. He scanned the area. Not many people were around. There were token booths nearby. About eight people lounged on the benches, waiting. The sterile, bright environment boasted no décor.

The HoloNews ran a ticker on the overhead display. The bodies in the esplanade had been found, and authorities were conducting an investigation. Railways were being monitored. Rickshaw rentals were suspended. Personal rickshaws were subjected to periodic and random scans. Anyone traveling along the west-central side would also be subjected to periodic, random scans.

Seth suppressed his snarl. That would put a kink in his wires.

Michael veered toward the nearest booth. When Seth stepped up, Michael slipped behind him and stood, watching the surrounding people, as Seth inserted the citizen card. Only one transport ran the length of Midland City. Another stopped about half a kilometer from the western sector. The first wouldn't leave until two hours from now. The other one would give them about thirty minutes of downtime.

Now that daylight was coming, he and Michael wouldn't be able to run the distance and stay unnoticed. Flying under the scopes was imperative. Yet half a kilometer of travel . . .

Seth selected the second option and accepted the tokens that dropped from the dispenser. He passed one over his shoulder to Michael and pulled up the Midland City visitor map. The west area was sparse—residential apartments, manufacturing facilities, three shipyards, more citizen housing, two medical facilities. And the one they wanted had been marked as a reconstruction project, date to be determined, not open to the public.

He clicked on it. A message popped up on the display: no information to display due to reconstruction. Well, then, they would have to wait to figure out how to get in.

Michael tapped his shoulder. "Let's grab a drink as the others are doing while we wait. No one is staying at the booths as long as you, so let's not draw undue notice."

Seth nodded and followed Michael to a nearby vendor set up against the wall. He bought the drinks, settled down on a bench next to Michael, and waited. A waiting game—this was all it had been. Get one step closer to getting his children back home and then they were forced to wait, losing that precious momentum they had gained.

Anger at the situation hammered around inside his chest. Seth sipped his drink to still the erratic beating. He couldn't let his emotions overtake him this time. The fight still burned in his memories—the look on the officer's face as the knife slipped between the ribs, the feeling as it slid through cartilage and muscle. Every motion, every tug and tension, had been felt by his hands. But the eyes of the man, the dilation of the pupils as his life drained from him . . . Seth mentally shook his head.

The horror of what he had committed was there, but no other emotion—no regret, no guilt—just the horror of killing.

Seth gave Michael a side glance. The man had picked up a nearby public datapad and was reading it, sipping his drink, leg crossed over his knee. Michael had killed for years. JJ and every other former assassin had. They had been trained for it. Huey had killed but never again after his release. At times, he saw the haunted looks in them, the former assassins. But a light covered that.

Did he still have that light in him? Seth reached into his side pocket and removed his small toolkit. Inside was a mirror that he used to peer behind consoles and other tight spaces. He held the thumb-sized item up and looked at himself. He had forgotten to put the contacts back in.

White eyes bordered by a thin green and set into a hard face stared back at him. Dark eyebrows were pulled low over eyes that were underscored by deep shadows. A bearded face twisted in a scowl. His lips were curled. Seth arched his head from side to side and again popped tight tendons. Slowly, his face smoothed out as some of the tension released, but the hardness in his eyes remained.

He sighed and slipped his kit back into his pocket.

"When faced with your first kill, it isn't easy." Michael swiped at the datapad and continued reading. Nothing else was said as they waited. What was there to say?

Seth crossed his arms and closed his eyes, breathing deeply and steadily. He would deal with it later. He had his twins to rescue. That was the top priority and the only thing that required his attention. Sounds of the hub increased as more people flooded in. The distant hum of the grav-motors of the transports rumbled through the air and above them, the electrical sizzle of the lights and holodisplays. Michael's soft heartbeat thudded. A woman released a sigh behind them. A child cried in the far corner. A ping sounded from a datapad, indicating a message was received. The drone of a multitude of conversations cascaded around him; and somewhere on the eastern side, a siren wailed.

A bell chimed, and the speakers announced their transport. Seth opened his eyes, stood, and followed Michael to the departure gate at the far left end. The meditation had centered his mind; yet for some reason, his hands still slightly shook.

Incessant beeps from a nearby monitor woke her. Sierra blinked against the harsh lighting of the scanner above her. She turned her head to the right. No one was in sight. The holodisplays ran through their vitals, genetic codes, and bloodwork.

Their records were side by side. She was right about Jason being different. He had the TC-575 gene. Her record displayed the TC-574, exactly what her father had found. His bloodwork wasn't much different than hers, although her sugar count was lower. She grimaced. It was a lot lower than it should have been. And that would account for the lightheadedness she was experiencing.

The heartbeat on Jason's readout suddenly spiked and then lowered. She turned her head and found him watching her. A hazy look filled his gaze before his eyes fluttered closed. Footsteps padded toward them. She shut her eyes and slowed her heartbeat and breathing as the people approached—two of them by the sound of their footsteps.

"She was awake for a few moments." The person's comm issued a staticky hiss as he continued, "But she's back asleep. I don't expect them to awake anytime soon. And it looks like the procedure took. We will know more by tomorrow."

Bastion's voice filtered through. "Good. I've initiated another round of Paxolin-X into Alpha Zero. Go ahead and replace the tubing for the Paxmedlin. Alpha One has adapted well to the higher dosage. So, it should work on Alpha Zero. Give me an updated report in an hour." The woman's tap-tapping faded into the distance.

Hands checked her restraints. A voice spoke from her left, near Jason. "Help me roll him."

The person left her side. They spoke in hushed voices as they worked.

"Here. Hand me the old tubing."

"Looks like his body is trying to heal from the tube's opening. I had to cut away some of the flesh."

"Here's the new one."

"Okay. Give me one zap here. Yeah. That will do it."

"The Paxmedlin is too thick for this tube. Let me get another."

The soft-soled shoes padded away. Trays rattled. Drawers opened and shut. Then the person returned. "Here's the better one."

"Yeah. Much better. The hole will have to be bigger. We will have to let Medtech Bastion know that he will have to stay away from open electrical panels, and no shock sticks can be used on him like we have used on Alpha One. It will short-circuit the patch. We have to let the skin and flesh heal around it first."

"Go tend to her. I'll finish patching him up."

The medstudy stopped by her bed. Behind her eyelids, the light grew brighter and hotter. The scanner hummed. Then it pulled away. Fingers tapped on the consoles. A monitor clicked. Then their footsteps faded to the far side. The hatch opened and closed. Darkness descended.

Sierra waited a full minute before she opened her eyes. The red, blue, and yellow lights from the nearby consoles blinked in the dark. Holodisplays had been shut down. The bluish glow from their medbeds were the only other lights in the room.

She craned her head to glance at Jason. He was still unconscious; yet at times, his body would flex as if in pain. A sudden heat flowed into her veins. She tried to peer at her arm but couldn't raise her head high enough.

Bending her wrist as far as the restraints would allow, she used her fingers to grope around the beginning of the heat source. A medicinal tube was attached to her intravenously, dispensing something into her.

Her head began to clear a bit. That meant there was glucose in it. With the drowsiness that was overtaking her, they had also dosed her with a sedative—a heavy one, at that. She grimaced. Unlike Stephen, she was more susceptible to sedatives.

She floated away from the dark and the soft lights of the consoles. Her thoughts flowed around Stephen, praying that he would be okay and that, somehow, they would be able to escape—all of them. It was then the small aches became noticeable around her abdomen and hips.

They had the bands too tight. That would account for the ache around her hips. But the ache that ran around and through her abdomen? That, she couldn't explain. Was that what Jason was feeling, too?

The question fell away as she continued floating along her soft, white void. Her lungs rose and fell. Her heartbeat slowed. Then there was a *tinking* sound that seemed to echo hollowly in her ears. Over and over, it played, growing stronger and more obnoxious.

Sierra opened her eyes with a gasp. Her hard bunk was under her. The lights in the cell were a soft red. She sat up and looked around. The monitor above her stood dormant. Across from her, Jason stopped thumping his fingernail against one of the bars.

She rose from her bunk. The ache in her abdominal region had diminished to a slight pang, fading with each step she took toward the bars. Sierra flattened her hand across her stomach. What did they do to her?

The questions about their time in the medlab fell away as she noticed the apprehensive expression on Jason's face. He wrapped his hands around the bar and pressed his face closer.

She leaned against the bars. "Are you okay, Jason?"

He let go and signed to her, *I'm fine. Had some strange pains in my lower torso region. It's gone now.*

"Yes. Me, too." She pointed toward him. "I heard them speaking about your implant. They changed the substance on you."

His fingers spelled out the word. *Paxmedlin?* When she nodded, he signed again. *What did they say?*

"No shock sticks can be used on you until it fully heals and to keep you away from electrical panels." She twirled her finger in the air. "Turn around and let me see what they did."

He raised his shirt and turned. His flesh had already healed, leaving a raised scar around the border of the patch. The green light flashed near a small readout, which indicated the next dose would be released in ten minutes. The medstudies were right, though. It was a rudimentary design. An electrical current would short-circuit the automatic injections and loosen the seal of the patch.

"Your patch is a lot like the ones that were used a decade ago. A quick electrical charge in the center and you should be able to remove it. You have nine minutes remaining before the dose is injected."

Jason turned around. *And I lose myself to Bastion.*

His eyebrows lowered until his cyan eyes became hooded and filled with hatred. He turned from the bars and began prowling his cell, running his hands over the walls, over his bunk, and over the enclosed mirror. Then he turned his attention to the ceiling and the monitor in the corner.

"If you use the monitor, what will they do when they realize you disabled it?"

Jason glanced at her and nodded. He disappeared from her view and into his refresher. If his was like hers, there would be an automatic dispenser for the cleanser. It could provide enough of a shock to dislodge the patch. She mentally counted down the minutes as she waited.

After two minutes passed, the shrill shriek of metal on metal filled the air, then the acrid stench of ozone and burning flesh. Heavy, meaty thuds against a wall reached her. She grimaced. Those heavy thuds sounded like punches, much like what Stephen used to do when he was in pain.

After a few long seconds, Jason stumbled back to the bars. Sweat matted his hair and rolled down his face and chest. His shirt was wrapped around his right hand. Dark spots dotted his wrapped knuckles.

He leaned heavily against the bars and breathed in deep, ragged breaths. *I used the dispenser. But I can't remove the patch on my own.* He tapped the door to his cell. *If you are like me, then you are strong enough to break the hold.*

Sierra nodded and followed his lead. She gripped the furthest bar of the door, positioned her body against the bars, and leaned back. Sparks flew from the control panel at the lock, but she was only able to pull the door centimeters apart. Jason grunted, released his hold, and reached toward the bar nearest the lock. She let go and did the same. He jerked back, his muscles straining and sweat beading along his skin.

Moisture slicked her palms as she grasped her inner bar near the lock. Pressure built in her head as she strained against the magnetic field of the door. Two crackling pops echoed in the small enclosure; and Sierra barely caught herself as the door slid open, almost dumping her onto the floor.

She hurried through and met Jason in the narrow corridor. "Turn around. Let me get it off you."

He turned and leaned against the bars of his former cell. Sierra ran her fingers around the patch, loosening it from the skin. He jerked a bit when it pulled at his flesh. His hands gripped the bars until his bronzed skin on his left hand turned white around the knuckles and the shirt wrapped around his right hand released heavy drops of blood.

She prodded the tubing. It pierced the spine between the L3 and L4 and entered his spinal canal. "Give me your shirt. As soon as I remove this, you are going to bleed; and some spinal fluid will leak. You may get dizzy until your body seals itself."

Jason unwound his shirt from his hand and slung it over his shoulder. His grip on the bars resumed. He began taking slow and even breaths.

Sierra gripped the patch and gave it a small pull, judging the resistance—none. With a quick pull and a deep hiss from him, the tubing slid from his back. Blood and a bit of clear spinal fluid flowed down the curvature of his lower back and into his pants. Sierra pressed the shirt against the wound and held it there.

Jason sagged against the bars. He let go with a grimace and pressed his hands against the sides of his head. She kept pressure on his back and glanced at the patch in her hand. The tubing was five centimeters in length. His body would be able to heal quickly.

"Do you have extra shirts?"

He shook his head and quickly signed. *No. They are brought to me.* Then he returned to grounding his fists against his temples.

"You'll have a headache for a while. But if you are as enhanced as us, you should be fine in a few moments."

He nodded and turned around to face her. She found herself inches from his face as she continued pressing the shirt against the wound, causing her to hold him in a slight embrace. His gaze flowed over her, studying her, and confusion crept into his eyes. Then he reached back on either side of him and grabbed his shirt, pulling the ends tightly around until he could tie them. It made a simple, yet effective, bandage.

Sierra stepped back a pace. "You said you know this place. Ready to leave?"

He gave her a small nod and signed. *Thank you.*

She smiled. "You're welcome."

Jason motioned to the door and led the way. Her first thought as she followed him was how they would get past the door. No control panels were on this side. And the fused-pane glass inset would be unbreakable, even for them.

But her question fell away as he stopped at the wall near the left side of the door. His fingers dug into the metal panel. With a grunt, the three-foot section popped off, revealing a narrow tunnel filled with wires, tubing, and pipes.

He looked over his shoulder at her, so she could read his lips. *This runs parallel to the maintenance tunnel. It'll be tight, and we'll get singed; but twenty meters ahead is a junction that will lead us to an unused portion that has the hatch leading to the subterranean tunnels.*

"Unused?"

They shut down that medlab years ago. Turned it into a bio-reclamation unit. He swallowed. A haunted look crossed his face as he nodded to the access hatch. *You'll understand soon.*

"The initial results are promising. More tests and simulations will need to be performed in order to ensure the serum adheres to the host. There's an 83 percent efficacy on subjects containing the T-C 574 gene, a 65 percent efficacy on the subject containing the T-C 575. Proposition Gemini may be the key we are searching for to further Sector Gray."

Proposition Gemini. Those words stuck in Stephen's mind. Gemini. Two. Twins.

So, she was working on two subjects—him and the one she called Alpha Zero. Yet there was something missing, buried deep within him, but he couldn't place it. It was there looming in the dark recesses of his mind and behind the infernal red haze. A small movement broke through his thoughts.

Stephen cut his gaze toward the guard nearest the door. Medtech Bastion had assigned five guards under his command. Two more were stationed in this room. Yet the one that stood at the door was suspect. Another of Bastion's tests? She constantly tested him—tested his obedience, his speed and strength, his aggression and rage.

He had already dispatched three guards who refused to follow his orders. They were replaced by the three who stood on the far side of the room. The fourth man, Zander, stood on the other side of Medtech Bastion—her favorite lackey, it seemed, a man who held contempt for Stephen. It was there, written in his eyes and micro-expressions.

The fifth guard—the one in question by the door—shifted his weight and dropped his arm to his side—a newer recruit named Nelson. The man's fingers slid into the side leg pocket. An audible yet soft click reached Stephen. The buzz of the electronic frequency filtered through the air, unheard by everyone else but him. Stephen kept his gaze on Medtech Bastion as she wound down her report and watched from his peripheral as the guard resumed his rigid stance.

"If you have dead men at Section 314 that were killed shortly after the capture of my subjects, then it is safe to assume that there is another one out there. I agree that all transports should be checked, all cards scanned. And when found, I want that subject brought here, too. Keep me informed." Bastion closed down the communiqué and stood, leaning heavily upon her cane. "Alpha One, lead the way to Medlab Twelve. I want to run one more additional test on your blood. You may choose one man as your subject."

His subject. She always made him choose a person to be injected with the plasma serum. And each one died. Only half a second was needed to choose, and he wanted to choose her favorite guard, whom she called Zander. The man was impudent. He never crossed the line, but Stephen couldn't have anyone under his command question him.

He raised his hand and pointed with his index toward the door, indicating for his men to leave. The guards fell into formation, three ahead of them, Zander behind him. Stephen kept pace with Bastion, allowing her arthritic steps to control their speed.

She used her cane and pointed at the opened doorway, stabbing the air for emphasis. "When we arrive at medlab, there are a couple of things that must be completed before I begin the testing. I know, Alpha One, that you abhor being touched. Yet I must, in this instance."

Stephen inclined his head. "Yes, ma'am."

The treasonous Nelson stood aside, waiting until they passed to close the door and fall into formation, as usual. Once he was half a pace from the man, Stephen slid his blade from its sheath on his belt and sent it flying. It embedded into the man's chest.

With his face frozen in shock, the guard slid to the floor in a heap.

"Alpha One!" Bastion whirled on him as the contingent of guards brought their weapons to bear on him.

"Ma'am?" Stephen ignored his team and bent over his victim, patting down his vest and pants.

"You were not ordered to kill." Her cane slammed down on his shoulder. The click of a button sounded; and a blade appeared at the end, the tip pressed against his neck.

Stephen kept his head angled away from the blade and pulled the comm device from the side pocket. The room's light glinted along its surface as he held it up between his fingers. "Hi-Wave band link."

Long seconds filled the room. The blade retracted. Bastion slid her cane from his shoulder and snatched the device from his hands. Stephen stood and turned around, clasping his hands at his back as he waited.

She spun the link around in her hands, examining each side. "GFT Hi-Wave LinkSystem 9VN. Government issued. Military Division." Bastion passed it off to the guard next to her. "Download any information you can and then destroy it."

The younger man nodded and disappeared out the door and down the hallway with the device. Bastion poked the dead man with her cane. "When did you suspect?"

"Two minutes before you disconnected. Heard the activation of the link. Was not our frequency."

"Frequency." She gazed up at him and pursed her lips. "Hmm. Alpha One, I want to run one more test on you. The serum seems to be increasing more than just strength, speed, and aggression. What else can you sense?"

He looked at her. Her death? No. That, he would keep to himself. But the man next to her—the infection within him permeated through his skin. Stephen pointed at him.

"There's an infection within him. Virus. Non-lethal."

Bastion glanced at the guard and smiled. "Glenn, go to bio and get your next dose."

The guard nodded and left, leaving Stephen with only two men.

"Well, Alpha One, you are exceeding beyond my expectations. Let's continue to medlab, shall we? And we will test out these new abilities." She swept out her arm, inviting him to lead the way.

He gave her a small nod, turned, and stepped into the corridor. Stephen grasped the shoulder of the man in front of him and pulled him back, motioning with his thumb for the guard to join Zander at the back of the line.

Leading the way, Stephen wound their way through the labyrinth of corridors designed to confuse a person, to keep them disoriented. Except they didn't work on him. He had the corridors memorized from the first moment he walked them—even the dead-end areas on the west side and two levels below.

A hiss and pop sounded from the wall. Stephen froze, holding out his arm to steady Bastion as she hobbled to a stop. He held his finger to his lips and cocked his head. It had come from the walls two, maybe three, corridors over.

"Alpha One?"

He gave her a small glance and then shook his head. "Probably heat expansion in the ventilation in Area Five. I will run a quick scan after the tests."

She nodded and reached out to hold his shirt sleeve as he resumed their march to medlab. Perspiration began to bead along her hairline, yet she refused to acknowledge her condition and give the appearance of weakness. That was his only deduction of why she would not use a hoverchair.

He turned the last corner and palmed open the door. It slid to the side. "Tomas, stay here in the corridor. Zander, with me."

Bastion shook her head. "Zander is one of our best guards, Alpha One."

"Then hope that he takes to the serum."

With no more than a glance at her, he stepped across the threshold and into the stifling environment of Medlab Twelve. Stephen slipped off his vest and hung it on the hook by the door. Then he pulled his shirt over his head. He folded it and placed it on the shelf beneath. His boots slid off easily, and Stephen tucked them under the shelf.

"Weapons, too." Bastion motioned for the guard to start stripping.

Stephen removed his belt and hung it by his vest, then pulled the various knives from his pockets. He dropped those onto his folded shirt before striding to the metal bed. He stepped up onto the platform and settled against its hot surface. Bands snapped around him. He let his head fall back and began to relax.

Zander would not survive this, and Stephen would have taken out his one threat in the unit. He needed men who would do his bidding with no hesitation, men who feared him.

Next to him, the monitor began its long checklist: serum components, vital signs, brain waves—always the same.

This had become commonplace in the last few days. Days? It felt like years, not days. But was it even days? Stephen opened his eyes and stared at the ceiling and his reflection in the polished tiles. No, it hadn't been that many days. He had only been here for two—

A sharp jab quickly entered his spine. The serum burned into him. And whatever it was he was thinking about vanished like whisps in the wind.

"That made a full twelve hours before the next dose had to be administered." Bastion *tap-tapped* her way to him. "I've increased the dosage once more. It will need five minutes to incorporate itself into your bloodstream." She motioned for Zander to climb onto the platform next to Stephen. "Zander, I believe this round will be the progress we need."

The man glared at Stephen but complied by stepping up on the platform and grunting as the bands snapped around him. Fighting would have been futile. Bastion would have killed him and chosen another. Stephen ignored the man's bitter stare.

Bastion retreated to the far side of the room where the bank of vats bubbled, and monitors displayed their holographic readings. Stephen narrowed his eyes. One of the holographic displays showed a pairing of the T-C 574 and T-C 575 genes.

The T-C 574 was in him, yet that wasn't his genome in the holographic. Someone else shared the same gene with him. The thought that there was someone else out there badgered him. *Gemini.* The word bounced around in his mind. But who had the other gene, the T-C 575?

He concentrated on that question, yet it was a flimsy thread that withered and dissolved in his mind, leaving him empty of thoughts. Stephen settled his gaze on the wall in front of him. Its metallic coating reflected himself and Zander.

Whatever he was thinking about seconds before couldn't have been consequential. He leaned his head back and allowed Bastion to withdraw his blood, to measure his body. She shone a vital pen into his eyes. Her hands poked and prodded different areas of his body, checking muscle tone and reflexes. Then she held the new tests of what he detected in each vial at his nose—iron oxide at .001 milliliters, sulfur at .02 milliliters, and ozone.

Stephen scowled at the next one. The strong, bitter taint of a crystalline substance reached him before she held the vial under his nose. He turned his head away. "Quassin."

"That's impressive. Now, let's try the auditory." She slipped the headset over his ears and backed up to the unit nearest him. When she activated it, Stephen raised his finger. Her eyebrows furrowed. "That's five hertz below normal. What about—"

He raised his finger again when she turned the dial.

"Again, impressive. That's 250 percent above normal." Bastion deactivated the test, stepped up onto the platform, and studied his face before removing the headset. "You are so much like him." With a *tsk-tsk*, she smoothed her hand across his head and cupped his cheek. "But you are so much more, Alpha One. Let's see if the plasma will work on a non-enhanced. Go ahead and dress." With a small pat on his cheek, she eased down off the platform and pressed the controls that released his bands.

Stephen stepped down and strode to his clothing, acutely aware of Bastion administering the plasma serum into Zander. The man's guttural cries of agony rose in volume as the serum flowed through his system. Stephen quietly dressed and watched. As he buckled his boots, Zander's yells finally died. With a stamp against the floor, Stephen reached behind him, grabbed his vest, and shrugged into it.

Zander was a bag of sweaty meat when Stephen approached Bastion, who stood before the guard. Red lines traveled across the man's body, branching out from the injection site on the left side of his neck—a blood infection. His body was rejecting the serum.

Bastion slid past Stephen and retrieved a hypospray from the medical tray. She pressed it against Zander's neck. Immediately, the man sagged against the bands. His head lolled almost lifelessly on his neck. "Alpha One, release him and place him on the medical bed. I want to run a scan on him."

Stephen did as she requested. Even when he dumped the larger man onto the hard bed, the guard never responded. His dilated eyes remained fixed on the ceiling. His breathing was shallow. Stephen leaned over him. The man was as good as dead—no life, no reactions.

Bastion placed her hand on Stephen's arm and pushed him aside. He glanced down at the spot she touched, but there was no rage this time. Wasn't he supposed to fall into a fury at the slightest touch?

Stephen stood at the head of the medical bed studying her movements as she pulled the scanner over Zander, slipped a neural relay over the man's head, and hooked a monitoring device onto his wrist. She kept the monitors from displaying the results, reading them on her datapad instead; but her gaze said enough.

Would Zander die, or would he become zombified like the rest? No matter, she always had him dispose of the people, anyway. And he had run the equations through his head the last time she'd had him choose a subject. The plasma serum would not work on anyone but an enhanced. They had to have the genes or traces of Serum Seventy-four in their genetic code.

Serum Seventy-four . . . no, he had Serum Seventy-seven in him. Right? That was what she gave him. Where had the other thought originated from?

Stephen remained still as she worked over the guard. The man's heartbeat slowed even more. The space between breaths lengthened—then, nothing. Bastion collected blood from his right arm and vitreous from the eye. She waved her hand at the body and walked away.

For a second, Stephen stood gazing down at the lifeless man. He caused this. He needed the man eliminated, but the reasoning behind it was lost to him. Stephen hoisted the dead man over his shoulder. The bio-reclamation had seen a lot of additions the last two days. Now, it would have one more. And while he was there, he could study the vats one more time. Although, why the urge to do so still escaped him. And there was another thought, there on the edges of his mind. Its shadowy arms flicked around the edges of his consciousness. Something important—or someone important.

"Wait, Alpha One. I will join you."

He suppressed his grimace. What was her game plan? She never accompanied him to the bio-reclamation unit. Was she sensing a change in him? Stephen blinked against the red haze that seemed to be a permanent addition to his vision as he waited for her hobbling gait to catch up to him. He palmed open the door, ordered the guard to remain, and escorted his owner and her latest victim to the other side of the facility.

Jason swiftly wormed his way through the tangle of wire and tubes. A junction box at his elbow sparked when he accidentally brushed against it. Small sparks slammed against his cheek, yet he ignored their burn and continued his steady squirm. Ahead of him, Sierra slithered through. Unlike him, her thin frame gave her ease of movement.

She paused to push aside a bundle of wires, stuffing them behind relay tubes. The blue lights from the readout units bathed her in an ethereal glow. Sierra glanced back at him and waved him forward before she began sliding further down the tunnel.

The access junction would be just ahead. He racked his memory for the schematics. It had been so long ago since he had read those files. But most all the access tunnels were designed the same. Jason pulled himself along. Sweat coated his palms and glistened along his forearms.

Heat from the tubes and junction units created a stifling, humid atmosphere. And the closer they approached the bio-reclamation section, the hotter it became. Sierra suddenly gasped as she slid down the short grade that led to the junction that connected the western and eastern section of the facility. Her foot hit the side of the tunnel causing it to reverberate down its length.

Jason grabbed the edges of the opening and slowed his descent. Once his feet cleared, he twisted around and landed softly beside her.

"Which way?" She turned in the small enclosure. Her arm bumped against his side, and she stumbled slightly as her foot clipped his. He steadied her and pointed to his left.

Sierra nodded and gazed up at him. The low lights from the tunnels accentuated her eyes, causing the wavelengths to dance around her face. Jason swallowed against the vision. Did she know how beautiful she was?

"Maybe you should lead, Jason. Looks like this access tunnel is taller, yet more narrow." She had turned to peer down the dark, metal shaft.

Jason tapped her arm to gain her attention and signed, *It will be tight. We will have to go sideways, and there will be a spot where the units will hamper our movements.* Some of the words he had to mouth when he didn't know the sign. Sierra placed her hands over his to still them.

"Hamper. Difficult. Hinder. Slow down. You can use 'slow down' for hamper."

Jason grinned and signed it to her. *Slow down. Well, that's what it will do. Need to be careful. There are exposed wires.*

She nodded and moved aside to allow him to squeeze by. His body brushed against hers. Heat burned his ears at the accidental touch. Yet she seemed unaware of his distress.

He slid into the accessway, sidestepping, and used his hands against the opposite wall to brace himself. Sierra mimicked him, and they began their slow and arduous shuffle in the dark. Behind them, the dim lighting began to recede more and more. After a few more minutes, the dark completely encompassed them.

Her whisper seemed overly loud in the narrow confine. "Are you sure they won't be able to register us in here?"

Jason paused and glanced down at her. She bumped into his side when he stopped. The dark almost concealed her face; yet with his enhancements, the smallest amount of light that bounced down the tunnel allowed him to see her questioning gaze. Could she see as well in the dark?

He reached for her hand and held them against his lips. *Can you see as well as I can in the dark?*

"I can see the shape of you—a bit of your face and mouth, but not much. There isn't enough light in this shaft. You can see?"

His lips moved against her fingers. *Like what a person would see at dusk—dim, lacking in detail. I ask so I will know whether to sign or just mouth the words.*

"Until we reach a better-lit area, let me feel you mouth the words when you need to say something."

Then you need to know that there is a quantum virus installed. It is dormant at the moment but will reactivate in probably a couple of hours. I had it programmed to randomly shut down systems. And to answer your question, these shafts are unmonitored.

"You wrote a quantum virus? Impressive."

Jason smiled, dropped her hand from his lips, yet threaded her slender fingers through his as they resumed their shuffle down the tunnel. It seemed so much longer, but it could have only been around ten minutes, fifteen at most, when a soft red light began to appear, brightening with each sideways shuffle they took.

He brought her hand to his lips. *It will get narrower as we come upon the relay units. And hotter.*

When he let go of her hand, she reached out and pressed her hand against his bicep, holding on to him as they continued. The protruding square units pressed against his chest as he squirmed past. For Sierra, she only had to slightly duck to avoid the units. Once past the first set, Jason leaned forward and squeezed past the next one. A sharp edge caught his makeshift bandage and caused him to stop mid-shuffle.

"Hold up and I'll free you." Her fingers worked at the knot, and then the shirt fell away. Warm fingers slid across his lower back. "You're healing quickly. But we can't risk the unit puncturing you." She flattened her hand against him, covering his wound.

At her nod, he resumed his tight slide through the limited opening. Her gasp of pain filled the air, along with the smell of fresh blood. Sweat coated his skin, allowing him to slide the rest of the way. She followed. Once through, Jason held up her hand in the light of the units. A deep gash marred her soft skin.

"It'll heal. Don't worry about it." She pulled away and handed him his shirt. "How much further?"

Jason donned his shirt, grimacing at the stench of dried blood. *Probably about twenty meters. Then inside the room, there will be an access hatch situated near the vats.*

"Vats?"

You'll understand soon enough. He suppressed a shudder and reached again for her, even though there was enough light for her to see now. She threaded her fingers through his and tightly clasped his hand. Her heartbeat rose. He didn't blame her. Even his heart began beating heavily in his chest. But was it because they were about to enter a hellish nightmare or because he found the touch of her intoxicating?

Chapter Fourteen
UNLEΛSHΞD

Seth pressed his forehead against the fused pane and craned his neck to view the front of the rail transport. They sat too far back to see the front section of the massive transport. Moments earlier, he had felt the tremble of the retro-brakes engaging. Outside, the blur of the buildings began to sharpen in detail as the transport decelerated. Within seconds, the underside stabilizing motors activated, and the rail transport began lowering itself onto the ground tracks.

They were in the western industrial district. Smoke billowed from the factories. Steam hissed from vents in the bricked walkways. Few PatRecs hovered around the area. And across the walkway in the plaza beyond sat a sleek Midland government ship. Seth frowned. So many plazas in the cities.

He leaned away and toward Michael, keeping his voice low. "Can't view far enough ahead to see why we are stopping fifteen minutes early."

Michael jerked his chin upward toward the mid-hatch of the compartment they were in.

The door hissed opened, and a group of Midland Security flowed into the aisle. They split into groups, demanding cards and scanning them. Two went to the front; two made their way toward them.

Seth glanced at the back of their compartment. A pair of guards stood outside on the connectors, while two others made their way up the aisle. He turned back around and ran his hands over the window. There was no way to open them; so, there was no escape. Michael touched his thigh.

Seth glanced up at the guard who stopped at their seats.

"Citizen card." He held out his hand. His hard eyes studied Michael and then Seth. His blond brow arched as he stared at Seth. "Nice augmentation on your eyes. Get that done here in Midland?"

"Westland Coast."

He ran Michael's card through the scanner. It lit green, and he handed it back. "You need to renew soon." To Seth, he replied as he held out a hand, "Yeah. They are known for body mods. Card?"

Seth slid his defunct card from his jacket and glanced around as he passed it over. He would have to play along. No way out of this one at the moment.

"Nervous about something?" The guard slid Seth's card through the scanner. Red light. He slid it through once more with the same result. His hard gaze zeroed on Seth as he raised his weapon. "If you will come with me, sir."

Too many people were around him to fight back and not enough room, either, to maneuver without harming innocents.

Seth and Michael stood. Another guard pulled Michael to the side as Seth stepped out into the aisle. The rest of the guards surrounded him as fusion cuffs were fastened over his wrists. One of the guards pressed the fob in his hands, and the cuffs snapped together. Hands patted down his body, pulling his panel lock, his last remaining trip mod, and his toolkit from his pockets.

Seth counted the men—two behind him, two at the back exit, two beside him, and two in front. He spied the guard slipping the fob onto his belt as another guard turned toward Michael.

He motioned to Michael. "Are you together?"

Michael shook his head. "No. Only struck up a conversation with him out of boredom."

"We will confirm that at headquarters." He waved at the man beside him. "Cuff him, too."

Seth shrugged off the hand that grasped his bicep. "What's the charge?"

"Your card is flagged with illegal codes." The guard grabbed his arm and jerked him the rest of the way into the aisle. "Move."

Seth hid his scowl and began following the man in front of him. He would have to wait for his chance.

Around him, the other passengers kept their gazes downward or slightly turned toward the window. Fear was pungent on their skin. There was something else, though, an undercurrent that flowed around them.

He cocked his head and listened. The heartbeats of the guards had increased. Their breathing was ragged, indicating anxiety. The creak of a glove tightening on the grip of a weapon. That came from the guard behind him. Whatever orders they had been given, they apparently knew who they may have captured.

Static from a headset. Murmur of an affirmative. The muzzle of a weapon pressed against his spine.

"Turn here and step down off the transport."

Seth obeyed him. He stumbled slightly on the last step. The guard beside him steadied him and jerked him upright. Seth fell against him, allowing his finger to hook the fob on the man's belt. He cupped the item in his clasped hands. The guard yanked him to a stop as Michael was escorted down. Once Michael and his guards descended, the stairs retracted; and the transport's engine began priming, prepping to pull away.

The guard who scanned his card walked around and stood in front of Seth. "You will be taken to headquarters and processed before being transported to Midland Prison to await your transfer." He waved at the guard next to him and pointed to Michael. "Take him to the hub and run his card and background. Verify his story."

Michael slid Seth a sidelong glance and gave a slight nod as they led him away to a black transport ship near the corner of the walkway. Seth's guards prodded him forward and surrounded him as they escorted him toward the larger ship that sat in the center of the empty plaza. Around them, the few PatRecs hovered in standby mode.

Seth ran his thumb over the fob until he found the switch. He used his fingernail to push the small button. The connection on his cuffs shut off, but he kept his wrists together. Behind him, the rail transport pulled away, picking up speed and whirling dust into the air. The two guards at his side raised hands to shield their eyes from the debris.

Seth leaned to the left, lifting his cuffed hands to shield his own eyes from the cloud of dust, and stumbled against the commanding guard. The one on his right reached for him, dropping his hand from his eyes. When his gloved hand landed on Seth's forearm, Seth flung his arms out to the side, knocking both men backward and to the ground. He bent at the waist and reached up with both hands as the guards behind him whipped up their weapons. His hands wrapped around the barrels of the pulse rifles.

He knelt and pulled them forward just as the bolts shot out. The blue plasma slammed into the backs of the men in front before they had the chance to turn. The man beside him began to recover; Seth spun on his knee as he ripped a rifle away. One shot from the rifle slammed into the man at his left. The butt of the rifle rammed against the face of the next man. Then he stood and drove the muzzle into another guard's midsection. Seth pulled the trigger. The man's eyes bulged as his spine and organs melted from the bolt that shot through him. Seth turned, dropping the weapon as the remaining guard stumbled to his feet. His hand closed around the throat of the guard who had scanned his card. His fingers dug into the arteries on the side of the man's neck as he lifted him inches from the ground.

Fingers futilely plucked at Seth's fingers, and his legs kicked at air. Red colored the man's face, matching the red that filled Seth's vision. He squeezed harder, feeling the cartilage under his fingers crunch. A gurgle issued from the guard's mouth.

"Seth!"

Seth looked over his shoulder as Michael ran toward him. Blood dotted his friend's shirt. A pulse rifle was slung across his chest.

Seth's captive weakly slapped at him before slumping. The man's heartbeat pulsed faintly and slowly against Seth's fingertips.

Michael slowed and approached Seth. His hand landed on Seth's forearm. "Let him go." Michael's blue gaze hardened as he repeated his command. "Let. Him. Go."

Seth snarled and dropped the guard. The man landed hard on the brick ground. Seth unclasped the fusion cuffs around his wrists, and they clattered onto the cobblestones. He bent and snagged the scanner from the man's belt. Then he searched the pockets of each until he found his panel lock and trip mod, yet neither of them had his toolkit. Michael nodded toward the darkened alley to their left.

"Let's get in the alley before the PatRecs come back online."

Seth nodded and followed. The red haze had begun to fade. He glanced back at the group of dead bodies he left in the plaza. It had only taken seconds for him to kill them.

"Did you kill your guards, Michael?"

The man ignored his question as they passed into the shadows of the alley.

"I think one of your guards had my toolkit."

Again, Michael ignored him as he held out a hand. "Let me see the scanner."

Seth passed it to him. Michael activated the screen and read the display. "Looks like there was an order to check all rail transports. Apparently, our fight at the gazebo didn't go unnoticed. How far are we from the medlab?"

Seth pulled his panel lock from his jacket. He studied the display before turning it around to show Michael. "We can follow this alley for a while, cross the street here." He tapped his fingernail against the screen. "And then follow the walkway the rest of the way. We will have to stay in the crowds the closer we get until we arrive here." He angled the panel lock to view the readout. He enlarged the map. "Right here is where we can go through one of the buildings. It's a business sector. So, we can blend easily. Once through, the medlab will be straight ahead."

Michael paused and squinted at the map. "Where is the entrance we need?"

Seth shrugged. "Not sure. But we can assume our little golden keycard will open whatever entrance we find."

With a nod, Michael turned from him and began the long walk. Seth followed, pushing the memory of his fight to the back of his mind. Right now, his twins were the only thing he needed to think about—not the fight, nor the kills. And not the red haze that overtook him. Yet something was wrong inside. Something was beginning to be unleashed within.

Michael glanced over his shoulder. "Use this time, Seth, to recenter yourself."

Seth scowled and drew in a deep breath. Recenter himself. It was becoming increasingly difficult to do so. Scripture—he would use this time to run Scripture through his mind—anything to help him bury the bloodlust that gnawed at him. Yes, that was what he was feeling: bloodlust.

Psalm twenty came to mind. *"Now I know that the LORD saves His anointed; He will answer him from His holy heaven With the saving strength of His right hand."* He let his thoughts roll from Psalm to Isaiah fifty-three. *"And He bore the sin of many, And made intercession for the transgressors."*

Seth arched his head to ease a tension knot developing in his neck as he continued thinking upon verses from the Bible. *Proverbs twenty-four: "Deliver those who are drawn toward death, And hold back those stumbling to the slaughter."*

The third verse in the third chapter of Ecclesiastes rose to the surface: *"A time to kill, And a time to heal; A time to break down."*

Seth ground the heels of his hands into his temples as those verses echoed in his head. And in the shadow of those echoes were two more: he was becoming what his father used to be. And what would happen to him when the time to break down finally arrived?

The body sank into the bubbling, noxious, gelatinous fluid in the vat. Stephen flared his nostrils at the odor that rose from the greenish solution. He stepped back and pressed the only button on the control unit. The cover slid from the recesses and closed over the rectangular vat.

He stepped off the platform that held the bio-reclamation unit and retreated to the far wall to wait for Medtech Bastion to finish her work. She hunched over the monitor across from him. Holodisplays rotated above her station. Stephen studied the readouts, scans of Zander's body.

The extracted plasma would be sent to the biolabs and Medlab Twenty. Blood had been extracted and would be filtered and stored in here. The rest of Zander would be broken down into individual protein sequences and distributed to various sections of Sector Gray.

He let his gaze roam around the small room. Two-foot vats lined the back wall near his position. Most were empty. Only one contained an occupant. Yet it was dead, floating in the semi-opaque blue liquid as the leads attached to it continued monitoring the small body. The fluid gurgled, and bubbles rose from the bottom of that particular vat. Then a red bloom flowed into it, surrounding the body before the vat opened at the bottom and the contents emptied into a small bio-reclamation located underneath.

Deep down, he knew he should have felt horror at the scene. Yet all he felt was detachment. A nozzle dropped down and began rotating in the vat, spraying the sides with a light mist. Stephen turned away from the cleaning process and resumed his study of his owner.

She rolled her chair down to the end and propped against the desk as she read the stream of data that scrolled on the flat display. With a harsh sigh, she turned from the workstation, glanced at the portable monitor attached to her forearm, and faced him.

"Alpha One, I will return shortly. Stay here until I return." Her cane *tap-tapped* as she shuffled across the room and out into the corridor. The door slid shut, and red lit the panel—locked.

Stephen arched his shoulders, releasing the tension, and resumed his stare across the room. On the opposite wall, the blurred reflection of himself stared back—a man in a black uniform, hands at his sides and clenched into claws. His eyebrows were drawn down in a perpetual scowl that shadowed dark eyes. Was that him?

He stepped forward and studied his reflection. Behind him, light glinted along the edge of the vent. Shadows seemed to move around and behind him. Stephen shifted his weight onto his left leg and watched his reflection mimic him. Another wave of darkness flowed behind him.

Stephen looked over his shoulder at the wall behind him. Nothing. Only a black, polished metal wall, a wall that reflected another image of him. He quirked his eyebrow and turned from his mirror image. Why was he looking at himself? A dark curtain seemed to drape through his mind and between him and his reflection.

Stephen strolled to the back wall. The vats. He remembered he wanted to look at the vats. But the reasoning remained elusive. He ran a finger over the cold, thick glass surface, tracing the curvature of the container.

They all stood empty now. The last time he was here, they had been occupied. With what? It looked like bodies, yet they were misshapen and hidden in the murky, blue fluid—except for this last one.

He walked to the last vat and activated the display on the control panel. Icons peppered the screen—ancient zodiac symbols, numbers, shapes. It seemed like a child's education display. He touched the Gemini sign, and a holograph appeared.

It triggered a memory, and that memory fought to rise to the surface. Then like smoke on the wake of a violent wind, it dissolved. Stephen reached into the double helix that floated in front of him. He zoomed in on a strand of the DNA displayed. He had seen this sequence before. It was a combination, a blending.

A tap down the hall echoed. Stephen shut down the display and retreated to his original position. Within moments, Medtech Bastion hobbled over the threshold and waved to him.

"Come here, Alpha One."

He met her halfway and stopped before her, waiting.

"Remove your vest and shirt."

Stephen complied. Once the items fell to the floor, she reached into her lab coat pocket and pulled a small, square patch from its depth. Without comment, she slapped the patch against his skin and sealed it to his side. Her finger pressed a small button on the surface, and a cannula entered his muscle.

He grimaced against the burn, and then all seemed to fade away.

"As I said, Alpha One, you are an abomination to mankind. Yet you will soon be ready for Sector Gray. It seems, though, that there must be a continual administration of Paxmedlin, unlike the daily dose of T-agent that you receive." She smoothed her hand over the patch. "I think this will work well. Get redressed."

He bent and collected his clothes. As he slid the shirt over his head, something tickled the back of his mind—something about two, about genes, and about the vats. Then the heat of another small dose of Paxmedlin entered him. He frowned as he fastened his vest. He would need to count the time between doses. Yet the reasoning behind that escaped him.

Bastion moved from station to station, downloading data, and shutting down the consoles. Then she motioned for him to follow her, and they left the bio-reclamation. Stephen glanced back once more and scanned the room. There was something about that room. Something he was missing. Something he had seen.

Paxmedlin burned into him. Five minutes, and it felt as though it was two cc's.

Φ

Sierra stumbled. Jason tensed and steadied her as she regained her footing in the tight confines of the access tunnel. Heat created a humid blanket around them. The smell of the blood on his shirt mingled with the ozone of the electrical units above them. Sweat from their bodies permeated the air around her.

She flared her nostrils at the smells and fought against the lightheadedness. Fresh air was what she needed, not this stifling, muggy atmosphere that surrounded them. She bumped into Jason's side when he suddenly stopped.

The units above barely lit his face when he looked down at her. He didn't bother to sign this time.

We are at the bio-reclamation, but there is someone in there. We must wait.

She nodded as he led her to a section by a narrow vent. That area was slightly larger, allowing them to settle down on the floor in a semi-comfortable position. Jason wrapped his arms around his raised knees and leaned back against the tunnel wall. She copied him; and together, they waited, listening.

It was Medtech Bastion's voice that spoke. The slats of the vent warped her words.

"Alpha One, I will return shortly. Stay here until I return."

Alpha One—that was what she called Stephen. So, Stephen was in the room! She began to rise to her knees to peer out the vent, but Jason's hand on her arm stalled her movements. Sierra turned to him.

His finger was at his mouth. *We can't do anything for him right now. He's too dangerous.*

She shook her head and leaned toward him, mouthing her words. *We can't sit and do nothing.*

We must. Trust me. We can find a way to help him here in this room. This is where most of her research is done.

Sierra sighed and relaxed against the wall. He was right. If Stephen was more than what she had witnessed the first time he was injected, then he would be extremely dangerous to himself and to them now.

The slats of the vent provided them a blurred visage of her brother, who stood not too far from their position. He remained statuesque for long moments before turning and staring at the wall.

She swallowed. It seemed as though his hard, dark gaze bored into them. After a few seconds, he turned and walked away.

Sierra maneuvered to her knees and peered through the vent. He had retreated to the back of the room, where small, empty vats lined the wall. What was he doing? He ran his hands over a vat and accessed a control panel. Minutes stretched by as he continued his reading and manipulating of the holograph.

A bump in the corridor had him closing down everything and retreating back to his original position in front of their vent. Jason tugged at her arm, urging her to sit back and wait. Sierra nodded. She couldn't let them see her through the slats. His eyesight would be even more enhanced with the serum they gave him.

She settled against Jason's side and waited. They listened to Bastion call her brother an abomination and talk about a patch and Sector Gray, and then Bastion and Stephen left. Sierra and Jason waited long moments after the hiss of the door.

What seemed like an eternity, Jason finally twisted to his knees and felt along the bottom edge of the vent. With a grunt from him and a pop from the metal, the vent swung out as the bottom detached from the seam. He motioned for her to go first.

Sierra slithered through the opening and onto the warm, metal flooring. She stood and surveyed the room as Jason crawled through and caught the vent before it slammed down. He eased it closed and rose to his feet.

She thought the heat from the tunnel they left was oppressive, yet this room was similarly as stifling. The overhead lights had been left on. Sierra ran her gaze over the low ceiling and corners.

"No monitors, Jason?"

He shook his head as he crossed the room. She joined him, and he quickly signed before turning to the consoles. *Bastion wants no record of what she does here.*

"And what is that?"

Jason's shoulders hunched and tensed. He shook his head and trailed a finger along the surface of each station until he came to the last one. All of the controls were dead, shut down. He flipped a couple of switches. Nothing happened. He pressed a few buttons—nothing.

A bio-print reader sat nestled in the top corner of the upper console. Jason cocked his head, biting at his lip before turning to her, mouthing the words, *In the tunnel, near the units, you should see the repair kits. A small box, barely the size of your palm. In it are two items: graphite for the tubing and a roll of adhesive. I need them.*

Sierra nodded. There was no need to ask what he planned to do. It was an archaic method, yet effective. If they could find even one small trace of a fingerprint, they may be able to access the consoles. She hurried to do what he asked. The grate creaked as she lifted it, and it painfully clipped her ankle while she crawled through. Underneath the boxy units was the kit he had mentioned.

She ripped it from the wall and pried it open—a small squeeze container of graphite dust and a roll of white adhesive. Once she grabbed them, she squeezed back through and rejoined Jason. He puffed a small mound of graphite into his palm and motioned for her to do the same. Together, they bent and gently blew the dust over the surfaces. Sierra squatted until her gaze was level with the flat areas. There was only one print with enough ridges. She tore a piece of adhesive from the roll and gently placed it over the small dusting of graphite.

Jason snapped his fingers. She glanced over at him and rolled adhesive into his waiting hand. He ripped a piece away with his teeth and slowly, meticulously placed it over one of the flat crystal datadisks. She caught the roll as he sent it back to her.

With precision and bated breaths, they peeled the adhesive away. Sierra flipped hers over. It was an almost perfect print, a collection of ridges and oils.

"How does yours look?"

He stood and angled his piece in the light. His was more crisp, more detailed. Apparently, Bastion had held the datadisk for a while. Sierra laid her piece on the console's edge and hurried back to the tunnel. She lifted the grate and chucked the bottle and roll inside.

Jason had already collected the pieces and stood at the bio-reader. He started to turn his piece around, but Sierra stopped him.

"It'll read the size of your finger. Let me." She gently took the small scrap of adhesive and held it to the reader before using her index finger on her left hand to press it against the screen. A red light ran up and down twice. Then it paused before lighting green. The consoles at each station blossomed to life.

Jason tapped her shoulder. *Need to clean off the stations. Leave no evidence. I'll look for the files on Stephen, since I know what to look for.* He removed his shirt and handed it to her.

Sierra nodded, taking his blood-stained shirt. She began to dust each surface, removing the graphite. Once through, she rejoined him at the last station and read over his shoulder as he bent close to the screen. He grabbed a datadisk and inserted it, downloading the information. Then, he was swiping at commands and files.

She stopped him from going to the next one. "What's that one?" Sierra tapped the icon at the bottom of the screen.

Jason pressed it, and a holograph of a double helix appeared. She studied the image. It was similar to the one she had seen when she was strapped to the medbed. Jason reached out and rotated the holograph. The data that scrolled beside it was in a cipher they couldn't read. But the image gave them a good idea of what Bastion was doing: she was reimplementing the serum program.

"I've seen those genes before." She enlarged the holograph onto two sequences. "While in that medlab and strapped to the medbed. T-C 574 is mine and Stephen's. My dad had that in his research. And I'm going to assume T-C 575 is either you or something she was creating."

Overhead, the lights dimmed before returning to their original luminescence. Jason cast a quick glance upward and began shutting down the consoles. She read his lips as he worked.

Bastion was doing human experiments. Those vats . . . they contained bodies at one time. I was her stem cell source. I don't know my genes. I just know I have what is needed to help your brother on the disk, but I need a place and a way to access it. We don't have much time. The virus is about to activate.

His quantum virus.

Sierra swiped at the console with his shirt once he stepped away and then handed it back to him. He slipped it over his head as he headed to the back wall near the vats. Next to the first vat was a narrow hatch. He stood near the control panel between the hatch and vat and pried off the cover.

As he worked with the wires within, Sierra studied the vats along the wall—small, for tiny bodies. Openings were at the bottom to flush away whatever was held within. Tubing and leads hung against the sides. All but the last one had begun to show signs of unuse. Mold grew along the edges. Tubing was cracked. The last one still had a bit of liquid beading along the curved glass. Yet the back access port was wide open.

Sierra forced a swallow past her dry throat and clenched her hands to keep them from shaking. It was pure evil. One had to have no conscious for conducting such experiments. Tears pricked her eyes at the thought of the lives destroyed by that woman's hands.

Jason snapped his fingers to gain her attention.

She turned from the vats and the terrible horrors it once contained. As she followed Jason into the darkened and constricting corridor where the light slowly faded behind them, one thought flitted through her mind: why did Bastion no longer have any use for the vats?

No answer to that question. Her thoughts were interrupted by a soft bang up ahead. Jason gently pushed her behind him, and they waited for whatever was heading their way to appear.

She gripped the back of his shirt, praying that they hadn't been discovered.

Φ

Seth knelt next to the control panel, mentally cursing the jumble of wires and nodes he had to navigate in order to hook his last trip mod to the relays. He closed the clasp on the trip mod and then attached the lead. He hissed at the slight pain as sparks flew and singed his fingers.

Michael glanced down at him as Seth grabbed the thin cord and plugged it into his panel lock. His QG quickly cycled through the codes. The hatch slid open.

Seth ripped the lead from the panel, replaced the cover, and slipped into the dark corridor behind Michael. He hit the door's control with his palm. The hatch slid closed, and they were washed in a dim red light illuminating the corridor.

"Do you see any security measures?" Michael ran his hand over the smooth surface of the corridor.

"No." Seth scrolled through the readouts on his panel lock. "Looks like this section is unmonitored and on limited power. Fifty meters ahead is a junction. Take a right and it should lead us to a medlab . . . um, yeah. It's designated bio-reclamation."

"Don't like the sound of that."

Seth nodded. "Me neither."

He followed Michael as the man led point and continued to scroll through the information on his screen, letting his mind fall back on their journey to get here and would be needed to leave. After arriving at Medlab Twelve-twenty, he had found all entrances heavily guarded. They had prowled the perimeter until he had found an access hatch on the far side of the facility and practically hidden in rubble. The keycard hadn't worked, yet the Hi-Waves allowed him to access some of the data, showing that main power output was located deep within.

After a slow and arduous climb through the hatch and down four levels, they had come to the entrance that would lead them into the bowels of the building, deep underground. They just needed to get to an active console, and he would be able to find his son and daughter. Then, they could go home.

Michael slowed. Seth looked up, casting his errant thoughts aside, and pointed to the dark corridor to the right. It was narrow, almost blending in with the shadows. Michael barely fit; his shoulders brushed against the sides. Seth paused over the threshold.

"Hold up. Let me check." He opened the command line on his screen. "Yeah. This should lead to bio-reclamation. But it shows a recent activation."

Michael resumed his slow, stealthy pace. The red light behind them faded until it was a pinpoint of light. The screen on his panel lock hardly penetrated the blackness. Seth's eyes adjusted to the dark. He nudged Michael to the side and squeezed past.

"Let me lead. I can see better in the dark than you."

He kept part of his attention on the screen of his panel lock as his free hand trailed along the sides of the corridor. Every five feet, his fingers brushed over a raised seam along the wall. After five of those, his fingernail caught on an indentation. He studied his screen. That would be another hatch. Yet it didn't show on the schematics he had.

Five more. The sixth was another notch. Engrossed in trying to make sense of the hidden accesses, he almost missed the pungent scent that traveled toward them—blood, sweat, and a slight vanilla essence.

Michael must have caught the change in his stance when he dropped his hand from the wall and straightened. The man shifted his weight as he tensed, preparing for whatever might happen. Seth shoved his panel lock into his pants side pocket and then began his measured advancement.

Two figures began to materialize in the dark—the tall build of a man and, behind him, the slender arm of a woman. The vanilla smell was slight, overpowered by the other harsh odors; but he would have recognized Sierra's scent anywhere.

His whisper seemed overly harsh in the near blackness. "Sierra?"

"Dad!" She pushed passed her companion and rushed toward him. Her body plowed into him.

Seth crushed her to him, holding back an unexpected sob. Her slender frame shook against him as he tucked her head against his chest. "Stephen?"

"He's been captured." She pulled away. Tears caught what little light was in the corridor. "Dad, she used a new serum on him and some drug. She created something she calls T-agent."

Seth closed his eyes. *Her.* Anya Bastion.

Sierra looked passed him. "Michael?"

Michael reached out and ran his thumb across her cheek, erasing the tears. "Are you unharmed?" Concern laced his voice. Seth glanced back at him. The tenderness in Michael's voice was unmistakable.

"For the most part." She wrapped her arms around Michael's waist in a brief, hard hug before turning and motioning toward the figure that stood still in the corridor. "This is Jason. Anya called him Alpha Zero."

Seth approached Jason, which caused the young man to shift slightly into a defensive position. Jason stood four inches over him. Even in the darkness, Seth could see the augmentation to his eyes. "How long have you been here?"

"He can't talk, Dad. They did something to him. But he said he's been here as long as he can remember."

Seth regarded the man as Sierra returned to Jason's side, grabbing his hand and propelling him forward. "I see. You can give us an update later; but right now, I need to get to the lab beyond."

Jason grabbed Sierra's hand and held it to his mouth. Seth frowned. His question about that motion was answered when Sierra began speaking.

"Jason said don't bother. He downloaded Bastion's files onto a data crystal, and his quantum virus has already run through this section, eliminating all files. There is a backup in a small room two levels down." She dropped her hand and accepted something from Jason.

Quantum virus? Impressive.

When she turned, she held out the crystal. "He wants to leave, too."

Seth nodded and grabbed the crystal, inserting it into his panel lock. Holding his thumb over the bio-reader, he ran his QG. Immediately, the screen started displaying the information—Serum Seventy-seven, Paxolin-X, Paxmedlin. He frowned and angled the screen so they all could see it.

"This isn't everything. Are you sure this is where she keeps her data?"

Jason shrugged. He grabbed Sierra's hand again and held it to his lips.

"He says she walked out with a data crystal. She could have downloaded the information to send to Sector Gray. And there's one medlab that she uses for her experiments and to contact Sector Gray—Medlab Fourteen. That's the one two levels up. Two levels below are the back-ups and Medlab Twenty." Sierra paused and let her arm fall to her side. "Above us, is that the room we were in, Jason?"

His gaze fell on her before nodding and looking away.

Michael turned and waved them forward. "Jason, if you know the way, please show us."

Jason glanced at Michael and then squeezed past them. When he passed, Seth caught a whiff of dried blood and the faint odor of spinal fluid. Sierra followed behind him, but Seth noticed the patch of dark at the young man's lower back.

What did he endure in this place? There wasn't enough light in the corridor to read his expression clearly, but he was sure it was horror that etched itself across the young man's face in that brief moment while Sierra was relaying his words.

Michael brought up the rear as they slowly followed Jason until he stopped at the first hidden hatch. A gentle pop sounded, and he set a section of the wall to the side. Once again, Sierra's fingers were at his lips.

"We have to crawl through this section to reach the ladder that will take us up. The area is heavily monitored, so we have to stay in the shafts."

Jason and Sierra climbed in. Seth motioned Michael to go next and then followed. He twisted around and grabbed the inside handles of the panel to snap it back into place. It clicked closed, and all light was washed away.

He listened to their laborious breathing and trailed behind them.

Chapter Fifteen
FATHER'S SON

Stephen. Stephen. Wasn't he called Stephen once? Long ago? No, only recently.

The burn of Paxmedlin ran through him. Alpha One—no, Stephen! He grimaced. He'd call himself Stephen; but to her, he was Alpha One. Didn't she call someone Alpha Zero? Logically, there had to be another. In binary, there needed to be a zero along with the one.

He allowed vague images to filter through his mind: a tall man with strange eyes, holding onto a woman with green eyes—a woman who seemed familiar.

"There is still a need to monitor him for several more days. Efficacy is up to 93 percent, yet he shows a resistance to the serum."

"Didn't you create a new serum, Bastion?"

Stephen rested his head against the metal bed and stared at his reflection in the wall across from him. For the last ten minutes, he had been listening to her update and debate with the head of Sector Gray. What was his name?

Crawley? Hawley? Creston Hawley? Crawley was more apt. There was something about Sector Gray, something he heard but wasn't supposed to have known, something that made his skin crawl.

"I have. T-agent. Using Serum Seventy-seven and Paxmedlin, I introduced the sedative Medolin into the formula. Medolin, in the dosage I administered, should keep the subject complacent and obedient. Paxmedlin should suppress long-term memories through altering the hippocampus chemistry. Serum Seventy-seven has increased the enhancements inherited via the gene manipulation of Serum Seventy-four. No one took in account the mRNA structure. I have that running through analysis."

"And this Paxmedlin can be used only on the enhanced? If so, that would be counterintuitive."

Stephen cut his gaze toward Bastion as she replied, "I do not believe so. If Julius Williams procreated—and his own offspring did, as well—then it stands to reason that there are descendants of all GFT assassins who escaped decommission. And that is where the T-agent will come in."

"There are treaties with the Christian Coalition, Islamic Alliance, and Buddhist Sangha. Gaining the subjects we need will expose us."

"Once you have Alpha One, you may be able to infiltrate. I have a sub-indoc ready."

"Alpha Zero?"

"I have other plans for him. His genetics have proven to be useful . . . "

Stephen let the rest of her words fade away. He had been right. There was another, and that memory had not been a false implantation via indoctrination. He thought back upon her words: descendants? Of whom? This Julius Williams?

Williams. He knew that name.

A burn coursed through his system. It didn't matter from where he came. As Medtech Bastion said, he was an abomination to mankind. And soon, he would be unleashed upon the world. He would lead them.

Sector Gray would soon control the non-GFT territories. Sheer power and ruthlessness would topple the giants. He was their David.

Stephen inwardly frowned. Their David? Why did the story of David and Goliath enter his mind?

Another scathing burn flushed those inconsequential thoughts into oblivion. The motors behind him activated, and his bed began to lower and tilt. Probes entered his spine as the bands around his extremities tightened. A neural relay lowered over his head and face.

Another round of videos and audio, all designed to bend him to her will. Yet he had learned to shunt those images and sounds and dive deep into his own thoughts—thoughts on the images of himself, the man with cyan eyes, the slim woman with honey skin, and a man with white eyes.

He was supposed to know them. As the propaganda of Sector Gray played out before him, Stephen studied the features and details of the mysterious figures buried in his mind. The one with white eyes . . . he saw an almost identical appearance in the reflection of his own face on the wall and in the mirrors.

Another burn coursed through him. Angles, curves, sharp features—his progenitor? No. According to Bastion's remarks, this man must have come from the other man she had mentioned: Julius. So, the one with white irises—Father?

Another abomination. Abomination bred abomination. To gain control, he needed to understand who these entities were.

One more burn flowed into his muscles.

The disembodied voice of a medstudy called out, "Ma'am, his gamma is higher than Alpha Zero's."

"Double the Paxmedlin." Bastion's voice seemed muffled.

"I have, ma'am." Hurried taps on the consoles. The harsh staccato of a cane. "He's remaining in gamma and climbing."

"Sedate him!"

The neural relay retracted. Bright lights from the scanner overhead seared his eyes. Scalding fluids rushed through his veins.

Stephen didn't fight the pull of the drug and let his head fall to the side to rest against his shoulder. His last view was her haunted face—withered, skeletal, dying. His last thought as he faded into darkness: he would soon no longer be hers. She could call him Alpha One all she wanted, but he would be his own. Then he would be able to erase the abominations.

Φ

Jason paused in the narrow confines of the access tunnel. Sierra's hand landed at the small of his back. Heat from the tubes that ran between the walls and from the intermittent relay boxes added to the stifling atmosphere. When her hand hit his back, the shirt clung to the sweat that ran down his spine, creating an even more uncomfortable setting.

"Jason?" Her whisper cut through the silence.

He turned and held her fingers to his lips. *Countermeasures are up. I can see the infrared along the plating near the hatch.*

When she relayed his words to her father and his friend, he eased toward the hatch and studied the security measures. A dampening field muted the words from inside the room, yet he caught one utterance: *gamma*.

A touch that was not Sierra's on his shoulder startled him. Jason whipped around and found himself staring into the strange white irises of Sierra's father. Seth, was it? Seth raised a finger and motioned back toward the midpoint of the tunnel. With a jerk of his thumb, he indicated for Jason to follow.

He glanced back once more at the hatch before retracing their journey. The murmurings within Medlab Fourteen rose yet remained garbled. Something critical was happening in that medlab.

Within moments, they stood around a small junction box. Jason grabbed the panel cover when Seth handed it to him. His curiosity piqued, Jason leaned forward and studied the man's movements.

Nimble fingers stripped and spliced wires, hooking what looked like a redesigned panel lock to the access drive of the relay box. Jason placed his hand on Seth's to stop Seth from activating one of the nodes. When Seth frowned and looked at him, he quickly tried to sign to him.

That one won't—

"Mouth the words, Jason. I can see in the dark almost as well as you."

Jason nodded. *That node won't work. It's connected to the main security command. One of Bastion's deceptions is to have nodes mislabeled. She's highly paranoid.*

"I have a program that will prevent any alerts."

It won't work. It is designed to set off an alarm as soon as it is accessed, despite any programming. The blue one, tucked into the back, is the one you need if you are looking for a way around the countermeasures or an alternate route into Medlab Fourteen.

Seth regarded Jason for a moment. "Okay, help me out here then."
He moved aside, giving Jason room to work the relays. Sierra's
father continued watching him as he plucked aside longer wires,
tucked away smaller relay tubes, and then used his fingernail to
pull out about seven centimeters of the blue wire from the back
of the junction.

This is only how far it can be pulled out without alerting the facility.

"You know your way around these junctions quite well."

*I had many years to study the schematics, and I listened to the technicians
as they talked. I learned.*

Seth's eyebrows furrowed over narrowed eyes as he studied Jason.
With a short nod, Seth nudged him out of the way. His fingernails
worked a bit of the insulation from the wire before clipping his panel
lock onto it. Seth's hand flashed toward his belt. What faint light
bounced through the dark tunnel caught on the data crystal as the
man inserted it into the top of the panel lock.

Immediately, lines of code and commands began scrolling
down the display. He recognized the main signature at the top of
the display—the same as the Alaska Country security protocols. He
touched Seth's arm.

Seth never looked up. "Yes?"

Jason tugged the man's sleeve. With a slight scowl, Seth cut his
gaze toward him. *I saw those signatures when Bastion ordered me to
attempt to breach Alaska Country. I had thought I deleted the information,
but she had a sub-routine. She has those codes in the database, though I
doubt she knows what they are.*

For a moment, Seth regarded him before turning back to the
display. "I can erase them later. For now, we need that medlab. And . . ."

He tapped the controls once and then disconnected the panel lock. "I have the entry codes. And I've set the security to shut down on this floor; but unfortunately, the security within these access tunnels are not accessible through this relay, so I can't shut down the field. Is there another place we can exit?"

Jason shook his head. *Security will still be up. My virus probably won't hit this level for another hour or two.*

Seth flipped his panel lock around. On the display were the security feeds for the floor. "We have access now. I'll know when it shuts off—and when Bastion leaves the medlab."

For a moment, Jason regarded Sierra's father. There was more to this man. It was written there behind those white eyes—a hardness, a lethalness, and an intelligence that spoke volumes. He could see the signs of enhanced strength in the man's bearing. And Stephen carried much of the same features. Unlike Stephen, though, there was a trust that seemed to emanate from Seth.

Jason angled his head toward the tunnel's entrance. *This way. Down about fifty meters. A smaller access tunnel runs perpendicular to this one. It'll lead us to a corridor over from Medlab Fourteen.*

Seth flattened against the wall as Jason squeezed by. Sierra slid past her father and, with her hand at his waistband, began shuffling after him. Barely a sound issued from Seth and Michael as they followed him through the increasing dark.

Jason's thoughts bounced back to the men that followed them. Sierra's father looked a lot like the image file of Julius Williams. But the other man . . . there was a coldness behind the light in his eyes. And though he looked around the same age as Sierra's father, those chilling, blue eyes were older and more hardened. He ran the man's actions through his mind. Michael never stumbled in the dark, never squinted. He moved just as silently. So maybe he, too, was enhanced—as Sierra called them?

He glanced over his shoulder. Seth followed at the back, his eyes bouncing up to them and back to his panel lock display. Michael continued his steady pace behind Sierra; at times, his hand moved to her side yet never touched her. Blue eyes zeroed in on Jason. A small flare of compassion flowed from Michael before being replaced by an aloofness.

Confusion ran through Jason. His only contact with people were those here in Medlab. He had no family. Was this how a family was? A subtle connection that bonded each individual together? Every movement and gesture from the three that followed them hinted at this.

Maybe he would be able to learn and experience this, too. The thought fell away as they approached the needed section. He stopped beside the panel and pried it from the wall. Small, recessed lighting every ten feet ran along the upper part, bathing in a dull red light the clumps of tubes and wires banded together.

Jason turned to Seth. *We follow this for about twenty meters. It leads to a corridor that is seldomly used.*

"You know this facility well."

There were numerous times when I was left alone and unmonitored for many days. Sometimes, weeks. I would use that time to explore the tunnels—until I was caught.

Sierra's hand tightened at his waist. "Caught?"

They punished me, then put me into the cell—the one we were in. That had been my home for the last ten years.

Jason turned and began the journey down the tunnel, grateful that it was a bit wider than the previous one. No one said anything else. Yet he could feel an almost tangible undercurrent flow amongst them. Not sympathy, it seemed. He had caught the flash of empathy in their eyes before he turned away.

Seth studied the display. Codes and commands flooded the upper half, while the lower portion gave him a view of the corridor beyond. He glanced behind him where Michael stood with Jason and Sierra, waiting.

The travel through the access tunnel had been uneventful, other than a few snags against his head from the wires that were above them. Once they came to the corridor and he hacked the control panel next to the hatch, they had found themselves alone in a sparsely lit corridor. Dust had flown upward when Jason removed the wall panel, and they stepped out.

From the data that scrolled, this was one of many unused corridors. And from what he read, there was a reason: the last skirmish with GFT had wrecked a lot of the facility's infrastructure. These corridors along the outer perimeter had lost many of their functions; so apparently, Anya Bastion had most of the power rerouted to the innermost corridors and labs, effectively creating a type of medlab cocoon.

On the display, the door to Medlab Fourteen slid open. Seth swallowed hard as Stephen led Anya, her medstudies, and a couple of guards out and down the westward passage.

He turned to Jason and mouthed, *What's west of Fourteen?*

The lift that leads to Medlab Twenty below and main communications above. There are a few other labs, but they're hardly used.

Seth turned back to his display: no movement. A faint hum of motors indicated that the lift had activated. He peered around the corner. All clear. With a wave, he hurried down the short corridor and paused at the right corner. Another glance at the display showed security was still active.

Jason leaned over his shoulder. Seth held up the panel lock, so the young man could watch. He had noticed Jason's innate curiosity earlier. And the more Jason learned, the more he could help if needed.

Seth slipped his QG into the slot and ran the decryption codes. Within two seconds, the security programs in a fifty-meter radius shut down. He switched to internal communications, entered the false data to show that security was still up, and installed a loop.

"Jason, once we get inside, can you grab schematics of the facility? Particularly, the closed portions. We need an exit well away from this area."

Jason nodded.

Seth straightened from his hunched position. "Let's go."

Their soft footsteps followed him down the corridor and to the one that led to Medlab Fourteen. Seth turned the next corner and glanced around the brightly lit passage. Only one medlab graced the corridor. Jason pointed at the control panel by the door. Seth nodded and placed the QG over it. Immediately, it cycled through, and the door slid open. Jason's bronzed skin blanched, but he swallowed hard and led them into the room.

Seth listened to Jason's heartbeat. Heavy. Rapid. Then it calmed.

"Jason?"

The man turned to him and signed. *I am okay. I don't like this room—torture, pain. Memories I don't understand flood my mind.*

Jason turned from him and led Sierra to a console near the back, so they could tap into the schematics of the facility. Seth scanned the room. The left side held a bank of holographic consoles. Vats of liquid, some bubbling, lined the far back wall. And to his right were three stasis pods and a metal, bedlike platform. Close to the right wall, an enclosed tube was situated on a raised dais.

He hurried to the consoles. Michael began prowling the room, checking the pods and vats and studying the readouts on the panels near them. As he inserted the QG into the main console, Michael spoke from the back wall.

"These vats are full of Paxolin but a different formula than what we know."

Jason snapped his fingers for their attention. *It's called Paxmedlin, stronger than regular Paxolin and Paxolin-X. It makes all memories disappear, alters people, makes them rage.*

Seth frowned. "Did she use that on Stephen?"

Sierra's eyes filled with tears. "On Stephen and Jason, Dad. She had a patch on Jason, but we were able to remove it. An electrical discharge did the trick."

Jason signed and mouthed his response. *It doesn't last. Must be given every day. The reaction is strong, but the medicine is weak for enhanced.*

"We'll figure it out as we go. Sierra, you and Jason get those schematics. We need a way out of here once we grab Stephen." He turned back to the console and ran through the decryption. Codes and commands flooded the screen. Seth activated the holograph and began searching. He swiped one way, zoomed in further, and twisted the image around. Codes and pathways highlighted and disappeared. *There!*

He reached in and grabbed the command line. Before him, the holograph shifted into text. The serum had been altered, dubbed the PAX. Serum Seventy-seven? She had created a new version and had combined it with Paxmedlin and the plasma of the blood of an enhanced—specifically, in this case, Stephen. She had created something called T-agent.

Anya was close to developing a drug that would . . . what? Every indication seemed to suggest that she was searching for a way to slow the aging of the human body. And . . . Sector Gray? No, Stephen's formula, T-agent, was for Sector Gray. So, what was she using for the anti-aging drug?

Michael leaned against the console beside him. "She's looking for an anti-aging drug?"

Seth shrugged and pointed to the blue text on the side. "Maybe. But it goes beyond that. She's trying to find a way to make herself enhanced, slow aging, eliminate disease, and increase strength and healing. But looking at these results, it shows that rage and aggression are heightened, as well as lack of rational thought." Seth slipped a data crystal into the console and downloaded the information. "Looks like there are some vids from one of the labs—"

Sierra interrupted him. "Those would probably be Jason's experimentations, he said. But he does know that Stephen was taken to Medlab Twenty."

"I'll download them for later perusal. We need to find Stephen— wait." He activated a file. "The formula. Jason, we need a quick route to a lab, preferably one on the far side, one seldomly used. Michael, grab a sample of the Paxmedlin and Serum Seventy-seven. The clear one is the serum. I'm going to need it."

Michael frowned at him. "What did you find?"

"A way to reverse what was done to Stephen. And it requires my blood—specifically, my plasma." He sent the data to his crystal. "I'll explain in a bit."

He pulled the QG from the slot and walked over to the main console in the center. Michael returned and handed him two vials: one with greenish tinted fluid and another so clear it seemed as if nothing was in the bottle. Seth shoved them into his breast pocket. He hesitated before inserting his program into the console.

"Sierra, do you two have the files?"

"Just finished downloading them onto a datapad. And we have a clear pathway to one of the lesser medlabs in what is labeled 'yellow corridor.' Jason said security will need to be disabled before we get there."

Seth gripped the edges of the console. If he did this, then it would sound the alarm. Yet it would destroy all within the system. The growth would be slow. They would have about fifteen minutes to make it to the medlab. Then everything would become havoc.

"Sierra, Jason, you two wait by the door. Jason, you will lead us. Michael, I need you here."

The older man approached him and gazed into his face. "Your plan?"

"My QG is bio-coded. If it's not me using it, then a virus is released into the system. And this virus replicates and expands exponentially until the cortex and core are eliminated." Seth held out the Quantum

GHOST crystal. "I need you to activate it, Michael. You don't carry any of the genomes we have."

"What do I have to access?"

"Any file in the system. This is mainly medical and experimentation files. Pick one, activate the QG, and then remove it. The damage will have been done within a second."

"That's a dangerous command you put there."

"I did it while we were on the ship. Couldn't take the chance that the QG would fall into the wrong hands."

Michael accepted the chip and turned from Seth. As the former assassin pulled up a file, Seth joined his daughter and Jason at the door. Jason flipped a small datapad around and pointed to the highlighted route.

"It's done."

Seth turned at Michael's voice, hearing the catch in it. A worried look flashed across the man's face as his gaze flowed over Sierra and Jason, but then it disappeared and was replaced by his hardened exterior.

It was barely a half second of an expression but enough to know that Michael had found something in the files, something that not only worried him greatly but caused great pain.

Seth accepted the crystal back and slipped it into the hidden slot on his waistband.

Stephen stood near her chair. The frigid atmosphere surrounded him, yet his internal temperature kept the cold at bay. White puffs of air, tinged red by his vision, flowed around them. She cursed. She complained. She railed at the system.

For the last five minutes, systems had been going down sporadically, with no pattern or indication of tampering. The topmost levels experienced the blackout. Then it flooded down a level. It didn't last long; but once it all came back online, the system in communications had been wiped. So far, the level they were on had remained untouched.

Her vile comments about GFT and Midland filled the air—their lack of funding, their indifference in her need for new technology and a better facility. She unleashed more curses about the unfairness of having to remain hidden, even in a non-GFT territory.

Irritation flowed through Stephen—such inconsequential things to complain about. Complaints without action were meaningless.

She rolled her chair back and strode to the far end of the bank of consoles. "Alpha One, we are going to try this new formula on Alpha Zero. Have two of your men collect him."

Stephen turned to two of his newer guards. "Go. Take Medstudy Johannsen with you. Bring back Alpha Zero." He glanced at Bastion. "Do you need the female?"

"No, just Alpha Zero." She turned her back to him and activated the holographic display.

Stephen dismissed the men. They left the medlab, and the sound of their boots receded down the corridor. Bastion stood and approached him, circling around to his left side. She pulled the hem of his shirt up and probed the serum patch. A burn washed through him. She nodded and resumed her place at the end of the consoles.

There was something he was forgetting—something that dealt with the patch.

Above them, the lights dimmed. Around them, consoles flickered. Then it all shut down. Harsh language poured from her mouth as a clatter filled the room. Stephen glanced down at her when she stumbled in the dark when her cane caught the lip of the raised platform. For a moment, he considered leaving her to lie there; but with a sigh, he stalked to her and jerked her to her feet.

"This way." He placed her hand at his elbow and guided her to the closed door. Her skeleton fingers clutched at him as Stephen pried open the door.

"This lab is on a separate security protocol. I want you to take five men and search the area—"

The two guards stood there. One of them had his hand on the control panel.

"What's wrong?" Her voice cut through the freezing air.

"Alpha Zero and the female are gone. The bars are open, but there's no trace of them anywhere."

The shorter of the men stood back as rage filled Bastion's face. She whirled around and poked Stephen's breastbone. "Find them! Do not kill the female. I need her. But kill Alpha Zero. I will make do with you for the new T-agent. Alpha Zero has defied me for the last time!"

Bastion hobbled down the corridor, heading toward the lift. "Tomas, get me to Secondary Command. Something is downing our systems. I want to know what."

Stephen waited until they disappeared down the corridor. The lab behind him stood silent, just as silent as the man before him.

Something was taking down the systems? Could be possible that it was a program set to randomly activate.

He quirked an eyebrow and turned toward the far end of the corridor. That lift would take him further down into the bowels of the facility and near the seldom-used medlabs. He keyed open his comm. "I want four men to meet me at junction delta-three."

A click confirmed the order. Behind him, the remaining guard followed. Bastion wanted Alpha Zero found. And he would find them, yet not the way she intended. For once, she left him to his own devices. Now was the time to lay his own strategy. He would no longer be her pawn. She would be his.

He entered the lift and pressed the button for the bio-reclamation level. He would head down later. There was something he had missed earlier in bio-reclamation. And if he wanted to find Alpha Zero, then that would be the place to start.

His comm hissed. "Sir, we are ready."

Stephen tapped his earpiece. "Bio-reclamation."

A click signaled their response. The lift stopped. Stephen stepped out into the dark corridor. No lights—*odd*. Guards flowed around the corner at the end and met him halfway.

Stephen entered his code into the control panel. Nothing happened. He motioned for two of the guards to grab the door and help him force it open. With heavy grunts, they slid open the dead hatch. Pure darkness greeted him.

"Stay here." Stephen entered the black room and scanned it. Nothing seemed out of place . . . there. The grate for the vent had been moved. Its corner stuck out as if it didn't latch properly.

He strode to it and bent down. It swung up with ease. Inside were two items that had been cast aside: tape and a tube. Stephen crawled in and peered down the access tunnel. This was the point of entry.

The grate clipped his shoulder as he backed out and stood. On the wall near the vats was the other access hatch that led to the inner tunnels that were used for maintenance. He walked to them, calling over his shoulder, "Grab your lights and follow me."

Small beams of light flashed around the room as they followed him. Stephen removed the panel and paused. A faint vanilla scent lingered in the tunnel, along with dust and sweat. This tunnel had been used.

He led his men into the increasing dark. Long moments passed; and he stepped out into a larger corridor that was littered with refuse, rubble, and downed, dead wires. Stephen backed up and retraced his steps, dragging his hand along the wall and counting the indentations.

The vanilla essence hit him again. He paused and retreated a couple of steps—another access. He motioned for the men to remove the panel and then stepped into an accessway lit with red light.

Behind him, the corridor suddenly blossomed as the lights above reengaged. In his corridor, the red lights dimmed, flickered, and then disappeared. No pattern. It was random. It was designed to be random. He keyed his comm.

"Yes? Have you found him?"

"No, ma'am. We are in an access tunnel. Lost power in one of the relay areas as another near bio-reclamation came back online. This was designed to seem random. But it is too random." Stephen squeezed past a protruding junction box and ducked under a low-hanging bundle of tubing.

"Alpha Zero. Had to be him." Harsh taps on a console filled his earpiece before she came back online. "Continue your search and expand to the perimeter. They could be using a smaller medlab or office."

"Yes, ma'am." Stephen keyed off his comm and shoved it in his vest pocket. Ahead was the opening to Medlab Fourteen. He frowned. The vanilla scent had long disappeared. But they couldn't have gone this way. The security measures would have been active.

He pushed opened the hatch and stepped into the lab. Vats bubbled along the wall. The vanilla scent grew stronger. So, they didn't use the tunnel but had been here—and recently, judging by the strength of the scent.

He furrowed his brows. The vanilla scent belonged to her, but he couldn't determine how he knew that. Stephen stepped up to the console when around him all the systems shut down, darkness doused them, and the facility-wide alarm began shrieking.

His comm buzzed against his chest. His men pried opened the door. Stephen joined them as he slid the comm over his ear. "Ma'am?"

"All systems are down. My work is being erased. Take me to the lower junctions. We are still in Secondary Command. Get me out of here!"

"On my way." He closed down the comm and stood for a moment in the black corridor. No, he would leave her there. This was the advantage he needed. He turned to his men. "Wait here."

He retreated into the medlab. The tools he needed were on the raised dais—that hated bed, the one that caused so much pain. He grabbed an electrical probe, turned it to maximum power, and jabbed it against the patch on his side. Scathing heat surrounded him, and agony swept through his abdomen. The pain intensified, and he drove his fist into the side of the metal bed, leaving a deep dent.

If the patch was anything like he had seen at home, then it would deactivate with no problem. Stephen froze. The probe continued its searing zaps into his side, but his mind fell into a memory that had no form: *home. Snow. Trees. A woman with green eyes, laughing and smiling.* Then it blinked out of existence as one last burst of Paxmedlin—a large dose by the way it burned—entered him.

The patch's automatic unit fizzled. Stephen gripped the edges and ripped it away from his side, hissing at the pain. He let the patch fall from his hands. Stephen arched his neck one way, then the other, popping tight tendons, releasing tension.

He rejoined his men and motioned toward the far end. Time to begin the hunt.

Chapter Sixteen
HUNTER AND PREY

"Wait!"

Sierra stumbled to a stop and looked up from the datapad's display of their route. Her father stood at the entrance of a darkened corridor.

"What's down here?"

Jason replied, signing and mouthing his words, *A small storage area at the end. Contains small weapons that have been either depleted or not in use.*

Her father and Michael glanced at each other before venturing into the black. She looked up at Jason, who waved for her to remain with him. Sierra squinted down the hall as the vague shape of her father operated the control panel before disappearing inside. Within moments, he and Michael returned, each carrying a sword slung across their backs and two plasma pistols strapped to their waists.

"Let's go."

Sierra handed Jason the datapad and began following him as he led them to one of the medlabs on their level—one that was a seldom used area, according to Jason. "Do you expect trouble, Dad?"

"Always, Sierra. These last few days have been nothing but." Her father shot a hardened gaze toward her. "We'll speak about it later."

She swallowed the hard knot in the throat and nodded. With all that had happened since their capture, she hadn't given much thought to what she and Stephen had committed. She had only had to return home and let the elders and her family know where Stephen was, and they would have collected him without any troubles. At least, she hoped that would have been what happened.

Yet with her remaining . . . it caused even more complications. And now, Bastion knew about them. Probably Sector Gray, too. It was only a logical deduction that they knew or suspected that there were more of them in Alaska and the other sanctuary territories.

She gave her father a surreptitious, sidelong glance. There was a hard edge about him now. His face seemed like stone. His eyes were cold. Michael's touch on her shoulder was featherlight. Sierra turned to him.

Concern and compassion filled his eyes. Michael had always known her thoughts, so she wasn't surprised that he could read her now nor surprised that he caught her glance at her father.

He leaned toward her and whispered in her ear, "Do not fret about your father. He will be all right. Let's concentrate on retrieving your brother."

Then he straightened, pushing past her and joining Jason at the front. What had he seen while he and her dad were following her and Stephen?

Jason paused a few steps from a door on the left in the middle of the corridor. *This is it.*

Her father stepped up and began to place his panel lock over the controls but paused. "Michael, this shape is familiar." He pointed at the small, rectangular indentation on the panel.

Michael turned to Jason. "You said this was 'yellow corridor'?"

At his nod, her father reached into his pocket and pulled out a small, golden item. He flipped it between his fingers, studying the surface before sliding it into the slot. A green light shone at the top of the control panel, and then the door slid open.

"So, not for the outer doors then." He shrugged and entered the dimly lit room. "Sierra, check the panel near the door and see if the illumination controls are there."

He and Michael prowled the room while Jason surveyed a small workstation to her right. Sierra located the controls and dialed the lights up a few levels before joining Jason at the station.

Her father called out from the back wall, where he was browsing through the supplies in the floor-to-ceiling cabinets. "Sierra, Jason, I need a blood extraction tool, three vials . . . and see if there is a centrifuge over there."

She and Jason rummaged through the drawers and holders. Jason removed a small centrifuge unit from the workstation's right cabinet. She found three vials in a sterile box in the left drawer. Michael approached and laid an extraction tool on the surface.

Her father stepped up and dumped more vials, tubing, and a micro-eyepiece onto the workstation and then removed his coat, letting it fall to the floor. "Si, grab the extraction and prep it. Jason, I need you to keep an eye on the security feeds."

Sierra fed a vial into the extraction tool, located the bio-wipes and cleaned the end as her father rolled up his sleeve. With a few quick, hard wipes against his inner elbow, she positioned the tool and pulled the trigger. Unlike the one Bastion used on her, this one caused less pain, though her father never seemed to feel as much pain as others.

Red blood flowed into the vial. Once it reached the max level, she pulled the tool away and removed the vial.

While she placed it into the centrifuge, her father began using the adjustable pipettes to remove some of the serum and Paxmedlin to a small petri dish, which he set under the scopes. He strapped the micro-eyepiece around his head and adjusted it until the small lens was situated over his right eye. She reached over and activated the holograph, allowing him to look up periodically and check his work as he manipulated the strains.

The centrifuge spun to a stop. She lifted the lid and removed the vial, handing it to her father. He used another pipette and carefully removed the clear plasma from it and inserted it into a vial on the rack holder.

He never looked up from the scopes and hunched even further over the workstation. "Michael, bring me the darts."

It would be a few more minutes until he was through, so she joined Jason at the door as Michael placed five darts on the workstation. Jason turned the datapad around for her to view.

Beyond the walls of the medlab, an alarm began shrieking. They all winced at the slight pain it caused. After a few long seconds, it ended. Jason frowned and slid the door open to peer out.

Red light strobed through the corridors. He ducked back in and turned to her. *Alarm must have been deactivated by someone. Systems will start failing pretty soon.* He flipped the datapad around. *There is a way out. But . . .*

"There's a 'but'?" From his expression, it wasn't good.

Security in this corridor—he enlarged the feed—*hasn't been deactivated. It seems to be on a separate grid. It'll have to be shut down before we can go further.*

"How will we do that?"

I'll do that. Jason swiped the screen and traced the blue line with his forefinger. *This is the path you will need to follow. I've been monitoring internal comms. Your brother is on this level here.*

She looked at the map. The lowermost level had interconnecting corridors and one exit at the very end, on the other side of the complex. "What about you?"

I'll be up one level, near Secondary Command. There's a small monitoring room adjacent. I may be able to access Secondary Command in there. I can follow once I deactivate the security. These corridors have basic, but rustic, methods. A hold over from long ago. Bastion never used them that much. She reasoned they were enough of a deterrent for anyone trespassing.

A clatter at the workstation brought their attention around. Her father was sliding the darts into the gun and placing two vials into a small, metal container. Michael shoved the gun into his waistband and followed her father as he rose and headed their way.

"Let's go." Her father's gaze was tired and hard.

Jason placed his hand on her father's arm and shook his head. He quickly gave them the rundown and then waited. Michael glanced at her father and nodded.

"Here, take this." He passed Jason a plasma pistol. "And meet us as soon as you can."

I'll send a quick message to this datapad. He passed the device to Sierra.

Sierra looked up into his cyan eyes and held his gaze for a moment. Indecision filled his eyes, and a haunted look crossed his face. His dark eyebrows furrowed for a second before smoothing out. Jason straightened and palmed open the door. Her hand on his bicep stopped him.

"Be careful, Jason."

I will.

Then he was gone, disappearing down the corridor and around the corner. Her father's hand at her elbow prodded her in the opposite direction. "Come on. He can take care of himself. And we will wait for him before we leave."

She hoped so. Jason may have been the initial cause of their capture, yet she felt as though no one held him accountable for that. And he deserved to leave this place that had imprisoned him his whole life.

As she followed her father, with Michael bringing up the rear, her thoughts fell back upon her grandfather's story. Jason's life paralleled her grandfather Jules'. Except, Jason was only a tool, a means to an end, whereas her grandfather had been designed as a weapon.

Hopefully, Jason would be allowed to live a life of freedom a bit longer than her grandfather had. She lifted up a small prayer for her newfound friend. Jason deserved a new life, but his haunted expression and sad eyes wouldn't leave her mind. Jason knew something that he wasn't sharing with them.

Around him, the overhead lights dimmed before shutting down. Emergency backups flared, bathing everything in a sickly yellow.

Jason paused at the corner and listened. About a corridor over, the thumps of heavy boots grew louder. The hiss from one of the comms announced a contingent arriving at the secondary command room. Bastion's yells grew louder.

Jason eased around the corner, squatted against the wall, and waited. Her command for Alpha One to come to her ended with a few piercing curses. Then her shouts about her work and Sector Gray ricocheted against the metal walls.

Minutes passed by. Jason rose and eased down the corridor, pausing at the end. Secondary Command stood around the corner, first room on the right.

A hiss from a comm floated through the air. Then Bastion's voice issued orders. "Take five men and see what is keeping Alpha One. Could be he found Alpha Zero. Meet us at level ten, junction eight."

"Yes, ma'am."

The lift she would need to take would be at the opposite end. Jason pulled away and slinked back until he stood by a small maintenance closet. He pried open the hatch and slipped inside, leaving a small gap between the door and the frame. Beams of light bounced around the corridor as the guards rushed by.

He waited a few seconds and listened to Bastion's footsteps hurry away to the lift. Silence greeted him as he hurried back to the corner and peered around. Nothing. Only darkness awaited him when he stepped into the abandoned area, glad to not have to figure out a way to access the consoles through the adjacent room.

Was it Seth's program that had initiated the shut-down in this sector or his quantum virus? If his quantum virus, then it would reboot in a few moments. Jason spun a chair around. The memory gel conformed to his weight when he sat.

Long minutes passed. Then the console flickered, then another. The electronic hum grew as systems began rebooting. Jason smiled. He reached forward and pulled up the schematics for the facility. A few keystrokes deactivated the security protocols along the route Sierra was taking. Most were straightforward, except level twelve. The program had been corrupted. Hopefully, it did shut down, yet he would warn them to be safe.

He keyed communications to the datapad's frequency and typed his message: *systems down. Beware of level twelve, the corridors near the exit. The subroutines were corrupt. Some may still be active. The last two corridors are disabled. On my way.*

Jason stood. The quantum virus wasn't designed to erase the data. But Bastion had screamed about it. Was it possible that the quantum virus and Seth's program worked in tandem? He bent over the console and searched the perimeters of the core. It was all blank—no data, only the subroutines for security. Interesting.

He grabbed a data crystal from the holder near his hand and inserted it. The base codes of the newly erased core downloaded with ease. A few command lines stood out. They could be studied in detail later, though. He slipped the crystal into his pocket before retreating to the door.

Jason shoved his hand into his pocket and ran his thumb over the edge of the crystal. Why did he feel compelled to download the codes? He had no answer for that other than he felt the need to do so. Instinct? Gut feeling? He'd trusted those feelings for all these years.

He would continue to do so again. And his gut feeling was saying that he needed to follow Bastion.

He made his way down the now brightly lit corridor and into the lift at the far end. He pressed the holographic icon for level ten. Junction eight was near one small research lab, a place where she had conducted a few horrendous experiments long ago. Although the room was sterile, in his mind it still reeked of death, decay, and blood.

The lift opened. Jason stepped out into a corridor that flared intensely for a second before plunging into darkness. He hurried toward the end of the corridor but slipped into shadows along the wall as men flowed from the research room.

Bastion stepped into the corridor, calling out to them. "If Alpha One has found them, then he will need the reinforcements. Bring the female and take the blood from the older male before killing them."

She didn't wait for their reply. The door to the room hissed closed as the men rushed away down the corridor and around the last corner. Silence descended.

Jason waited for a moment before he strode to the room. The door swished open. He stepped through. Bastion looked up, shock rocking through her, and her hand flew toward the comm unit on the console.

Jason covered the area in two strides. He ripped the comm from her hand and crushed it in his fist. His other hand caught her cane on its downswing. He tore it from her grasp and brought it down over his knee, breaking it in half. Poison from the interior part seeped from the shattered compartment.

He cast the broken pieces aside and shoved her down into the chair. Her watery, icy gaze held scathing contempt and hate. "You'll die for this, Alpha Zero."

Jason ignored her and studied the console she had been reading: transmissions, research data. A program had been executed to compress it all to fit onto a crystal. Jason pulled up the holograph and then shoved her back down onto the chair when she tried to stand.

Her gasp of pain didn't faze him. He felt the bone, probably the third or fourth rib, fracture under his palm. The pain would keep her immobile for a few seconds. Jason reached out and enlarged the holograph. He highlighted the middle command line. With a few keystrokes, he entered a new line.

"What have you done?" Her pain-filled hiss filled the room.

He smiled, closed down the holograph, and then ran the new program. Immediately, every file she had created began to disappear, but his program didn't stop there. It began to flow into the databanks and into the cortex. Eventually, it would make its way into the core drive that was attached to this console system.

She tried to stand but gasped. Her hand gripped at her chest. When she tried to reach for him, he shrugged out of her way.

"Alpha Zero."

Jason grabbed a datapad and quickly typed out a message: *My name is Jason.*

He flipped it around for her to read. Her eyebrows lowered into a scowl, yet she looked up at him with curiosity.

"You named yourself?" Moving with exceptional sluggishness, she rose from the chair but didn't try to reach for him. "You can't leave me here, *Jason*. I'll die. You caused my rib to puncture a lung. Please, you must help me."

Her voice reeked with false compassion. He studied her as she gazed back at him, a hand held out in the space between them, imploring him with deceptive kindness. She was the source of all his anguish. The source of many deaths. The deaths of those who would have been like brothers and sisters to him. She was the evil that continued to thrive, like the cancer within her. Did she believe he had forgotten what she had done, or that he would have pity upon her?

Jason leaned forward and sniffed. Confusion danced across her face at his movements. He pulled back, typed on the datapad, and stepped away from her. He placed the small device on the edge of the console before heading to the door. Her footsteps hobbled to the datapad, and he paused on the threshold as she read aloud.

"You are already dying. I can smell the stench of death in you. You will die here. Alone." The datapad clattered to the floor. "No!"

Jason stepped through. As soon as the door closed, he ripped the control panel off the wall. Wires and internal circuitry sparked when he plowed his fist into it. Pieces of metal, wires, and nodes flew through the air, hitting against him, bouncing off the wall, and spinning along the floor as he tore it all away.

Her muffled yells and dull thumps filled the room beyond. There was no way out. Even if she tried to flee through the maintenance shafts, she would become lost in the dark. He backed up and heaved a sigh. The heavy weight on his shoulders had finally lifted.

Jason turned from the room and began backtracking along his route—time to regroup with the others.

Stephen rounded the corner. Darkness flooded the corridors. Behind him, the yellow emergency lights engaged, bathing all with an orange hue in his reddened vision. He paused and keyed his comm. He wouldn't go to Bastion but let her think she was still his. More men were needed if he was to flush them out.

"Alpha One? Where are you?"

"Still in pursuit, ma'am. I'm closing in but need more men. Junction twelve, level eleven."

Static filled his ears before she replied. "I'm sending the last of the guards your way. Systems are going down too quickly, so hurry."

"Yes, ma'am."

He keyed off his comm and slid it into his pocket. Then he motioned for his men to stand down as they waited for the reinforcements. Short minutes stretched into long moments. Eventually, the heavy thuds of boots reached him as the lights flickered back on.

The new men approached. One stopped in front of Stephen. "Message from Medtech Bastion."

Stephen studied the guard. "Proceed."

"She wants the female and the blood of the older male before they are to be terminated."

Stephen narrowed his eyes and waved the man away. So, she wanted Alpha Zero and the older man, the one with white eyes, to die. He shrugged. That was fine. They were abominations. But so was the female. Bastion must have a use for her, which meant she would be the bargaining chip he needed.

He pulled the plasma gun from his belt and motioned his men to follow. Catlike, he stalked down the corridor, his head cocked to pick up any errant sounds.

A thump issued from one corridor over, near the lift. Stephen rushed down the hall and around the corner. Ahead, Alpha Zero skidded to a stop. His bronze face paled a bit, and fear entered those unnatural cyan eyes. Stephen whipped out his gun and fired.

The back of the lift sparked and melted as the man dodged the plasma bolt. Alpha Zero raced away down the short corridor on the right. Stephen gave chase. These levels were mazes, with interlocking intersections. This level had two lifts. He needed to keep him from escaping into the next one.

He shouted over his shoulder. "Five of you head down section three and cut him off at the lift!"

Alpha Zero disappeared around the next corner. Stephen followed and then ducked as a metal pipe whipped above his head. His shoulder rammed into Alpha Zero, sending him flying back and sliding along the polished floor. But the man twisted midflight and crouched into a fighting stance.

Stephen smiled. They would be evenly matched, for sure, if they were fighting. But he was to kill the man. He raised his gun and fired. Again, the bolt shot missed Alpha Zero as the man ducked and rolled.

"Argh!' Stephen swerved to the side as a plasma bolt narrowly missed him.

Alpha Zero was too swift for the plasma gun.

Stephen shoved the gun back into his holster as the men with him caught up. He reached over and snatched a sword from the nearest one. Without a word, he took off after Alpha Zero, who disappeared around another corner.

Stephen skidded around it, expecting another swing. But the other man was rounding the far corner. Heavy thuds echoed and a scream from a man. A shot sounded from a plasma gun, then the unmistaken fizzle of the battery pack on the gun. Stephen rounded the bend, kicked the discarded gun out of the way, jumped over the fallen guard clutching his left arm against his stomach, and raced after the abomination. He passed his guards, who were struggling to keep up with Alpha Zero.

The lift was just ahead of them. Stephen skated into a slide. His momentum sent him barreling into the man, knocking his legs out from under him. Alpha Zero toppled back. Stephen palmed his knife and sliced at him, but Alpha Zero had begun to roll away before his body even hit the floor.

The tip of the blade tore through the shirt, leaving a tiny rivulet of red on the man's back. Then he was up and running. Stephen flicked the knife toward Alpha Zero's lower back. With a twist, Alpha Zero spun out of the way and jumped through the lift doors.

Stephen grabbed his gun and pulled off three shots. They hit the back of the lift before the doors slammed shut. With a heavy sigh, he clambered to his feet. He had underestimated the man. He wouldn't the next time.

His guards finally caught up. One hit the return button for the lift.

"Don't bother. He would have destroyed the control panel." Stephen turned from them and began counting the sections. He needed the eighth one.

"Where do you think he went?"

"Down to the twelfth level. It's the one that leads to the only exit on this side of the facility." Stephen stopped at the eighth maintenance tunnel section. He shook his head. The design of these facilities was horrendous. He gripped the edges and yanked. The panel separated with a pop. "Let's go. Twenty meters ahead and down the ladder."

His men followed him into the dark. Penlights lit up the area and bounced around them. In moments, they reached the ladder; and Stephen led them down into another darkened tunnel. Without waiting, he turned left and hurried to the end. His kick sent the panel flying outward.

As he and his men piled out, Stephen spotted Alpha Zero standing down the corridor. Four faces turned toward him and his men. Stephen paused. The female had her hand on Alpha Zero's arm.

Alpha Zero signed. Stephen frowned. Sign? Why would Alpha Zero sign? The man's mouth moved in conjunction with his hands. *Go. I'll lead them away. Don't wait for me. I'll find you.*

The female gave him a quick kiss on the cheek. The man with white eyes grabbed the arm of the female and pulled her away. A memory of the man floated to the surface: his fist gripping a napkin, his face scowling at Stephen.

Alpha Zero cast Stephen one look before sprinting in the opposite direction.

Stephen shook the errant memories away and motioned with his hand. "Seven men. Follow Alpha Zero. Kill him. The rest with me."

No reason to hurry. Level twelve had countermeasures. And no matter which way they ran, it all led to one junction—the one junction between the facility and the exit. Stephen turned left down the corridor the three had fled. But before he reached the next corridor, he took a right, a path that would parallel theirs. His prey would not escape him.

Φ

Seth ducked. A plasma arrow embedded itself into the metal wall. He slid to a stop in the intersection. Sierra and Michael almost collided with him. He studied the area where the plasma arrow hit. The arrow left a small hole in the wall. Around them, the corridors were peppered with those holes. Some were rusted. Some had lost their sheen of metal. The new ones created by them had melted edges around a ragged hole.

Sierra shook her head. "Jason said that some of the security measures may not be deactivated."

Three corridors over the sounds of boots pounding against the floor reached him. Seth glanced around him. "We have three intersections to go through. The corridor before the fourth intersection is perpendicular to the corridor that leads outside."

"We can't leave without Stephen, Dad. Nor Jason."

Michael placed his hand on Sierra's arm. "Jason said he will catch up. We will wait as long as we can once we leave here."

"Jason knows we cannot wait indefinitely, Sierra." Seth turned from his daughter and stepped into the corridor ahead. No reaction from the defenses. He took another and ducked back, as a bolt shot from the top of the wall. "Try that corridor, Michael."

Seth stepped back into his corridor, then another step, and a puff. Then he was ducking and jumping back. "I approximated barely half a second."

"Same." Michael motioned down the corridor. "We can move fast enough to make it to the next junction." Seth nodded as Michael turned Sierra around to face him. "Just as I taught you, run. Listen. React. You will hear the puff. Duck and keep going. Don't look back."

His daughter swallowed hard. Her face paled a bit, but she straightened her shoulders and faced the corridor ahead. Seth rubbed his hands against his pants and released his pent-up tension through a deep breath.

He allowed one more inhale. "Let's go!"

He sprinted. A puff sounded. Seth ducked, then slid along the floor. He rose to his feet, ducked the next puff. The arrow melted the wall next to his elbow. Then he twisted to the side as another shot in front of him. Then he was sliding again, feet first into the intersection.

His daughter collided into him. Then Michael was next to them. Seth glanced at them. "Two to go."

With a quick exhale, Seth ran through the corridor. Behind him, the puffs echoed. He jumped out of the path of one and skidded to a stop in the next junction. Sierra stumbled to a stop. A small gash marred her arm.

She rubbed at it. "Superficial. Guess I wasn't fast enough."

Michael arched his shoulders. "Those came a bit faster."

"I noticed." Seth waved toward the corridor ahead. "Ready? Last one."

Before he entered the corridor, the arrows began firing. Jason wasn't exaggerating about the program being corrupted. The first two showed signs of slowed response times. But this one . . . Seth dodged a bolt, felt one rip through the sleeve of his coat, and then ducked as another shot at his head. He tucked his shoulder and rolled into the intersection.

"Michael!" Sierra's shout along with the sound of a plasma arrow ricocheted in the stark, metal hallway.

Seth whirled and began to run back to them, but Sierra had Michael under the arms pulling him away from the edge of the corridor.

Michael sank against the corner of the empty intersection, his hand pressed against his abdomen. A slow trickle of blood pushed

through his fingers. Sierra ripped Michael's gun from his belt and
fired at the top of the wall. Above them, melted metal hissed where
the plasma bolt destroyed the automatic defense.

"Let me see." Sierra knelt beside him and pushed at his hands. The
older man slumped against the wall with a grimace.

"It's deep. I can feel it." He hissed as Sierra tore his shirt to view
the damage.

Seth probed the wound. The small arrow *was* deep. Dark blood
indicated that it had punctured or nicked his liver, possibly his spleen.
He grabbed the med box and opened it. "Sierra, when I say, reach in
and yank the arrow from him."

"That'll kill him, Dad!"

Michael shook his head. "Sierra . . ." His words fell thickly from
his mouth, and his hand shook as he cupped her face, smearing dark
blood onto her skin. "Do as your father says. I know what he plans
to do."

Seth arched his brow at Michael's gesture. He had never seen
Michael display such affection before. There was something more
to his action—a deeper meaning. Sierra's hands gripped Michael's as
tears coursed down her face, and Michael's thumb wiped at them.

Michael relaxed; his body slid down to the floor, and his hand fell
away as unconsciousness claimed him.

"Grab a vial."

"But, Dad, those are for Stephen!"

Seth dumped the supplies on the floor. Distant thumps four
corridors over indicated that Stephen and his men were on the way.
He had to be quick in order to save Michael.

"Rip his shirt away. Yank the arrow out."

Seth slipped the vial of his plasma-enhanced serum into an injection pen. Sierra's sobs strengthened as blood flowed around her hands and onto the floor after she pulled the arrow from Michael. "Pack it with the coagulant and bandage it. It'll bleed for a while; but with him passed out, the plasma will work faster."

Blood slicked his hand. Seth wiped his palm across his pants and then jammed the injector against the older man's stomach and pushed the plunger. Michael's body stiffened; his muscles became rigid, and veins stood out as the pure formula coursed into his body.

"Dad?"

Seth ignored her as she wrapped the bandage around Michael's abdomen. "He lost a lot of blood. I don't know if he will survive, but Sierra . . ." He looked into his daughter's eyes. "You will have to protect him until the plasma takes effect." He surveyed their junction. Near the eastern corridor stood a hatch. Seth pointed to the vent across from them. "Pull him back into the ventilation tunnel. Stay there until I come back."

"Dad?" Her green eyes shone brighter with unshed tears.

Seth stood, ignoring her. "Protect him, Sierra. Protect him."

He left her there with the man who had watched Seth grow and mature and then watched as his own children did. And in the back of his mind, the memories of Michael and how he stood over his children, especially Sierra, like a dark, guardian angel were vivid. Michael had been with them throughout all the years. He couldn't let the man die now.

Seth shook his head. It was a good thing he had made two enhanced serums. At the time, he hadn't even thought about it, just felt as though two would be needed on Stephen. He arched his

neck one way and then the other. He stepped into the corridor—
no arrows.

It was faint, the sound of the duct's grating clicking back into
place, but relief filled him knowing that Sierra and Michael were
out of danger for the time being. And now, he would have to face
his son.

Seth stopped at the junction of the hallways and waited. No
cameras. No security. No way out. Jason had assured them that these
corridors held no security. And the way out was the way they had
been traveling.

He pulled the pulse gun from his belt and held it by the barrel.
This fight would be without firearms.

Boots echoed. Then Stephen and his men rounded the corner.
His son skidded to a stop; his eyes pierced Seth. The white in his
irises had expanded. Jason and Sierra were correct. Anya had used the
new formula on his son.

Seth held his gun out and then flicked it to the side. It banged
against the furthest wall and bounced to the floor. Stephen's gaze
followed the movement. He grinned and then followed suit with his
own gun, signaling his men to do the same.

When Seth pulled his sword around, his son copied him. Yet it
was a flick of Stephen's finger that sent his men toward Seth.

Movements slowed as Seth met them. He seemed to split in
two. One part of him recognized that time had not slowed, and his
movements were swift and almost instantaneous. The second part
could see every motion and change, every subtle shift of stance in
the men. His blade met each. A swipe down the chest of one, a thrust
between the third and fourth rib of another, and a slash across the

throat of one more. Light flashed on his blade as it met each adversary. Blood splattered the walls, him, and the floor.

Within moments, Seth stood in the center of the carnage. Stephen gazed at each of the men that were either dead or dying on the floor. Rage burned in his son's eyes.

Seth whispered a prayer, the first he had said out loud since leaving Alaska. "Lord, let him not be an Isaac. I would gladly sacrifice myself in his stead, yet I know he needs to be stopped. Give me strength and wisdom, Lord. I am Yours to do Your will."

Stephen sneered. "God doesn't care about us, *Father*. We are an abomination. And you have to die."

"This isn't you, Stephen." Seth loosened his grip on the hilt. "It's the Paxmedlin and T-agent. You know this."

"I know that you have to die." Stephen rushed him.

Sparks flew from the blades when they met. Seth spun and met his son's blade as it came from the other direction. Block, parry, and repeat. They moved in a blur. Striking with precision and strength so rapidly that the blades began heating. Stephen struck high; and Seth met him, stepping back with his left leg to keep from falling from the brunt of Stephen's hit. Their blades met again, the red glow growing along its edge; and sparks flew around them, stinging into Seth's cheeks. Their blades collided once more. Block, swing, thrust, parry, repeat.

Stephen's eyes burned with a wildness and evilness that had filled him, pushing him. Seth leaned into his thrust. When it was parried, he reached out, grabbed Stephen's wrist, and threw him back. His son staggered a half-second before righting himself.

Stephen roared. His blade came down at Seth. Seth's blade met it, and the two fused along the heated edges. With a jerk, Seth sent the swords twirling down the hallway. Rage consumed him. Bloodlust flowed through him. Stephen's eyes reflected the same.

Before Stephen could react, Seth had him by the throat and against the wall, his short blade from his belt in his hands and aiming for Stephen's chest. A thought emerged as he began to thrust his dagger toward his son: they had become what his father had once been.

His son grabbed his wrist, but it was too late. The blade began sinking into Stephen's chest . . . Suddenly, Seth was thrown to the floor. His body skidded into the wall, and he smacked his skull against it.

He shook his head, clearing the stars from behind his eyes. Stephen had been thrown against the opposite wall and was trying to rise up from the floor. His son's arms shook and barely supported him. Stephen collapsed onto his back with arms sprawled to the sides. His chest heaved as he fought for breath. Three darts had been embedded in his chest, in the spot where Seth's knife had begun its journey.

Seth pushed to his knees. Sierra stood in the middle of the slaughter, a tranq pistol in her hand and Seth's dagger buried in her shoulder. "Sierra?"

"I couldn't let you kill him, Dad." She aimed the pistol at her brother and pulled the trigger one more time. A dart hit her brother's neck. Stephen jerked once and held his hand out to his sister, a pleading look flooding his eyes before his arm fell heavily to his side.

Seth crawled to his son and felt his pulse. It was heavy and slow. His breathing was deep. He thumbed back Stephen's eyelids. The eyes were rolled back. Seth sighed. His son would be unconscious for a long time.

He looked back at his daughter, who stared wide-eyed at the bodies around them.

"You did this, Dad?"

Seth ignored her and stood. Sierra gazed at the knife that protruded from her shoulder. "I didn't even feel it." Wonder filled her voice as she slid it from her body. "Minor, it seems, Dad. Doesn't feel like it hit anything vital."

She held the knife out to him. Blood dripped from its blade. Seth stepped closer and examined her shoulder. Blood flowed from the wound, but it was healing. It looked like it had slid between the muscles. He accepted the blade, wiped it on his pants, and slipped it back into the sheath at his back.

When he reached for the gun, she relinquished it. The chamber held the last dart. Seth popped it out. It wasn't the standard, and the color was wrong. Bloody fingerprints marred the side. Seth held it closer. He had considered it a curse to be able to remember everything, yet now . . .

"These are Michael's fingerprints. What did he do?"

"Michael added fifty cc's of Medolin to your enhanced serum and put it in the darts. He told me this would stop Stephen and keep you from having to kill him."

"And Michael?"

"Still in the tunnel waiting." She held out the datapad. "Jason must have reached another console. He sent some schematics. There's another corridor we can take that will lead us closer to a tarmac undetected." When Seth took the datapad, refusing to meet his daughter's eyes, she spoke again, softly. "I heard your prayer, Dad. I couldn't let Stephen be an Isaac. I asked God to let me be the ram for you."

Seth's hands shook. He had almost killed his son—almost. He turned from Sierra but held out a hand to stop her when she stepped toward him. He couldn't deal with this right now. Too much had happened in such a short period of time. The most important, though, was they now had Stephen.

"Let me grab your brother, and you lead the way."

Chapter Seventeen
THE ESCAPE

Jason skidded around the corner and paused in the dark corridor. Boots pounded against the floor, growing in intensity. He squared his shoulders and eased down the corridor, searching for anything.

Dust and nothing else kept him company in the abandoned hallway. He resumed his position at the corner and waited. The first guard rounded the corner. Jason plowed his fist into the man's face, grabbed his vest, and shoved him back, causing the two that were behind him to topple painfully to the floor. Another guard whipped out his plasma gun, but Jason gripped the man's wrist and twisted. The bolt shot harmlessly across the hall.

The guard pulled the trigger again as one of his companions rounded the corner. The plasma hit him in the chest and sent his body flying into the opposite wall. Jason snapped the man's wrist and ripped the gun out of his hand. A quick bash on the bridge of his nose had him unconscious. The two who had fallen earlier began to struggle to rise, yet Jason sent a kick into the sides of their head, rendering them unconscious.

The two more guards flooded around the corner. One jumped a downed man, while the other stumbled over the inert frames. Jason lashed out and clutched the vest of each. Meaty thuds and a crack of bone filled the air as the two were bashed into each other. Jason let go, and their bodies fell into a heap next to their companions.

He surveyed the fallen men. Only one was dead—and not by his hands. Jason knelt and searched the nearest one. He found two knives, which he pocketed; a keycard; and a citizen card. Jason turned the citizen card over in his hands. It would be flagged once it was discovered to be missing. He slid it back into the man's pocket and searched the dead man.

Jason slid the dead man's citizen card into his pocket, removed the comm unit from his ear, and slid another knife into his waistband. He paused, his hand on the man's vest.

He couldn't leave the facility with his tattered clothing. Jason glanced around at the rooms. A small medlab stood opened nearby. He rose, seized the dead's man arm, and dragged him into the room. He was approximately the same size and girth as Jason.

In moments, Jason stripped the man of his clothing and boots. He couldn't hide the small, burned hole in the shirt, but that was okay. He may be able to find a coat or vest on his way out. When he slipped his feet into the boots, the sides pinched; yet they would make do for the time being.

Jason held the comm unit to his ear. Static met him. He cycled through the channels. Nothing. With a shrug, he slid the unit into his pocket and stepped out into the corridor.

Hopefully, the others had already made it to the exit. He began to pick his way through the jumble of bodies. Midway through, light caught on the edge of a datapad. Jason stooped and grabbed it, activating the screen.

Schematics. He scrolled through them. There was a different route, one used by the guards on their subject retrievals. Jason smiled. He entered the frequency of Sierra's datapad and sent the new directions. He would meet them as soon as he could.

He was halfway through the lower level and almost to the exit when her reply was sent. *We have Stephen. At the tarmac now, in front of a transport. But there are security forces. We are waiting on you.*

Jason grimaced. Did Bastion send a message? Or was there a security sub-routine that they didn't know about? Regardless, the guards posed a new threat and complication. He hurried through the corridors; but when he reached the ones with the corrupted defenses, he paused.

For them to escape, there would need to be a distraction. He backtracked along the corridors to the lift. He would need the main communications room for this. As the lift took him to one of the upper levels, he sent his message to Sierra. *I'm creating a distraction. Leave without me. I will join you soon. Don't wait on me.*

Her reply was immediate. *We will not leave you, Jason!*

You must. Jason sighed. The lift doors opened, and pitch black greeted him. His enhanced eyes barely registered any light. The dim illumination from the datapad cast a weak glow in the corridor. *Give me the coordinates to Alaska. I'll be right behind you.*

He stepped into Main Communications. Consoles were dead. But along the back wall, near the bank of processors and holographic projectors, was the tiny, black box. He removed the keycard from his pocket and strode to the box.

The datapad in his hand dinged. Jason looked down at the message and smiled. Her father had sent the message, ordered him to be safe, and suggested taking a northern country route. At the end were the coordinates that would bring him to the main gates of Alaska Country.

Jason burned the coordinates into his memory, snapped the datapad in half, and stood before the box. Emergency reset. He needed Bastion's card. He only had one try. Unauthorized use would activate the one failsafe she had—a bank of explosions set far underground which would implode the building. The alarms would draw off any remaining security guards in the facility.

It would be a cascade once activated; but he could make it through the tunnels and to the south entrance, grab a transport, and begin his escape. With the decision made, Jason strode to the maintenance hatch and tore the panel away, then returned back to the box.

Jason bowed his head. *Be with me. Give my feet wings!*

A sudden warmth filled his heart. Jason inhaled a deep breath, lifted the covering, and inserted the keycard. The air seemed like a cool breeze against his face as he raced into the tunnel and fled down its darkness and up its ladders. Around him, klaxons sounded.

They waited. Once Jason's last message had come through and Seth sent his reply, it wasn't long before klaxons pierced the air. Guards had rushed the entrances, and he and Michael rendered the remaining three unconscious. With the Midland official logo plastered to their highjacked vehicle's side, they fled down the streets unimpeded.

The rumble was felt more than heard. A mighty tremble shook the transport, causing Michael to lose control for a moment. Seth almost jumped at the sudden pings when the onboard display began issuing alerts. All traffic was suspended for citizens—official transports only. Seth craned his neck to peer out the small window. Above them, the lanes began to clear.

More alerts flooded the display. An explosion occurred, destroying everything within a 183-meter radius. Seth leaned back as more updates poured across the screen.

"We can make it to the port, but it's going to be tricky to get on the ship." Michael turned the corner and eased down the street. He steered the vehicle behind another and set the speed to match the one in front.

"I can use the QG to clear away security." Seth selected an alert on the display and pulled up the holograph. Reports of the abandoned medical facility that had collapsed, indications of medlab officials trapped, orders to evacuate the area as containment crews arrived. Seth ran a hand down his face and pressed clasped hands to his lips.

His thoughts centered on Jason. The man was enhanced. He would have been able to escape in time, surely. Seth sent a small plea to the Lord asking Him to keep the man safe and to guide him, for Sierra's sake. He had seen the attachment that had formed between the two.

"I'm sure he made it." Michael winced as he veered the transport down a narrow street, reached forward, and activated the clearance codes as they approached the checkpoint, before relaxing back into his seat. He placed his hand over his wounded side for a brief moment before letting it rest on the console.

Seth ignored Michael's statement. What was there to say? He rose from his seat and retreated to the back area. Seth paused at the opening that led to the rear compartment and surveyed the scene before him. His daughter bent over his son, hooking leads to his chest and head and, at times, adjusting the portable monitor. Shadows underscored her eyes, and her shoulders drooped with weariness.

On the padded bench against the side of the vehicle, Stephen remained in his induced sleep. The harsh lines had been smoothed from his face, yet nothing hid the bruises along his cheekbones and jaw nor the reddened shadows that surrounded his eyes. Small cuts and burns disappeared into the thick growth of Stephen's beard.

She had removed his shirt, and on his son's chest and abdomen were faint marks—wounds from an electro-probe that were almost completely healed. Seth leaned against the frame of the opening. What had happened to his son? And what had Michael seen in that medlab? He stuffed his hand into his pocket and ran a thumb over the crystal. There wasn't time to read it, not yet. But once they arrived home . . .

Sierra noticed his presence and spoke over her shoulder. "I increased the Medolin, inducing a medical coma."

Seth eased to her and squeezed her shoulder. "Did you already administer the plasma?"

"I did." She looked up at him. Unshed tears glistened in her eyes. "I don't know if the one dose will work, though."

"It worked on Michael almost immediately, so I believe it will be enough until we reach home. Then I can replicate some more." He sat on the corner of the bench and laid his hand on his son's stomach, feeling it rise and lower in a steady rhythm. An undercurrent of tension flowed from his daughter. "Are you holding up well?"

Sierra shook her head. When he held out his arms, she fell into his embrace. Seth buried his hand into her hair and cradled her against him as her body racked with sobs. Her speech was garbled. "I'm so sorry, Dad. I thought I could help Stephen. I almost succeeded, but we were captured. I feel like if I had only returned home, Stephen would not have suffered all this. John and the others would have found him sooner."

"Shh, shh, shh. We can't change the past. What's done is done." He rocked her gently. "We are heading home now. Let's concentrate on the next step, then the next. Okay?"

She hiccuped once and nodded.

Michael called to him. Seth kissed the top of her head before letting go of her and rejoining Michael at the front.

Without looking up, Michael spoke as he steered the transport into the far corner of the port. "We're here."

The *Depthfinder* stood, gleaming under the harsh sunlight, at the furthest dock, nestled in an open alcove away from the others. Midland had moved their ship and stationed a small contingent of Midland Security around it. Michael pulled his ship lock from his pocket and passed it to Seth.

When Seth stuck it into the panel lock, the status of the ship scrolled across the screen. "It's been tagged. I can take care of that once I get on board. This is the only contingent." He passed the ship lock back to Michael and inserted the QG into the top of the panel lock and connected it to the transport's communication hub.

Michael nodded. "Any way to get past them?"

Seth shook his head. "No, their orders are to remain at their post. No other orders will supersede the ones issued unless the code is given. And unfortunately, the code is not mentioned." He scrolled through the information. "We have another problem. This transport has been flagged as highjacked. We need to abandon it. There's a new squad heading this way."

Michael pointed to a small docking station near the *Depthfinder*. "We can make it to that station. Were there any uniforms back there?"

Sierra called out to them. "Yes. Three medical uniforms, two security, and one portable medbed."

Michael motioned Seth to the back. "Sierra, don the medical uniform. Your dad and I will grab the security ones. I'll help you enclose Stephen in the medbed."

They worked quickly. Sierra pulled the medical uniform over her clothing, tied back her hair, and shoved a cap onto her head. He and Michael removed their coats and pants, yanked on the security uniforms, and then pulled on the vests. Swords were slung across their backs and into the sheath attached to the back of the vests. Plasma guns were shoved into the holsters.

Seth emptied his coat and pants and placed all the various items into the vest pockets as Michael helped Sierra transfer his son into the medbed. He slipped his QG into the hidden pocket of his shirt, fastened the uniform, and then readjusted the vest.

The lid of the medbed hissed closed, encasing Stephen behind fused glass and plasti-steel. Air hissed as the automatic ventilation system activated. Sierra lowered the bed's hover-skids as Michael opened the back hatch. The ramp dropped, and they began their descent. He and Michael led the way toward the station. Sierra followed, pushing the medbed in front of her.

Around them, a few curious bystanders glanced their way. Three Midland Security looked at them but continued down the walkway. They were one of many groups entering stations or walking to their destinations. Seth spied a similar group across the port—three guards around two medical personnel pushing a medbed.

They arrived at the station without incident. Michael pulled opened the door, allowing Sierra to push the medbed inside and toward the back, where she hooked in the portable monitor.

Seth crossed the threshold and veered toward the consoles nestled against the left wall, fumbling to pull his program from the shirt's pocket. He slid the QG into the computer and began scrolling. "Michael."

His friend joined him. On the screen, a group of security personnel arrived at the transport. They fanned out, questioning nearby people. It was only a matter of time before the guards made their position.

"I'll take care of them."

"Michael, you can't." Seth yanked his QG from the console and rushed after Michael, who headed for the door. He grabbed Michael's arm and jerked him to a stop. "It's a suicide mission. There are too many of them. There's a back exit. We can take it and work around to the ship."

Michael looked down at him. "You need a distraction. That's the only way for you to get your children home safe, Seth." He disengaged Seth's hand and turned toward the window, watching the guards glance up and scan the area. One waved toward three men at the far side of the port and gestured toward the station. "This is where our paths will part."

"Michael, I can't let you. You'll be killed."

Michael turned his bright gaze to Seth. "I loved Sierra and Stephen as an uncle would. And my love for them is the same as my love for you—and even for Tamara." He returned to his vigil out the window and sighed before shaking his head. "In Genesis 6, it is written, 'And the Lord said, *My Spirit shall not strive with man forever, for he* is *indeed flesh: yet his days shall be one hundred and twenty years.'* It doesn't matter how young I look or how healthy, relatively speaking, my body is." Michael chuckled and gripped his abdomen a bit tighter. "I'm an old man, Seth. I've lived a long life—over half a century before your children came into this world. And I swore to protect them the day they were born."

Seth glanced back at his children. Sierra concentrated on the readouts of the portable monitor as Stephen lay in his induced coma. A knot formed in his chest. "Michael, I can see how much she loves you. And Stephen considers you more than an uncle or mentor. You mean a great deal to them—to all of us."

"I know. But time will heal the wounds. It always does." Michael straightened and dropped his hand to his side, resting it on the butt of his gun. "She will need you and Tamara, even Stephen, in the near future."

Seth frowned. Michael had been holding back from him for a while. Ever since their escape from the facility. "What is it that you know, Michael?"

A ghost of a smile drifted across the older man's lips as he continued looking out over the port beyond the thick glass panes. "Things will change soon. You know there is only one way out of this."

The older man turned from the window and faced Seth. Gone was the light in Michael's eyes. A hard and lethal look replaced it. In his hand was the slim dagger from the gazebo guard. Seth accepted it as Michael continued speaking. "I was once Zulu. Let me be Zulu one more time. It will give you the time needed to escape to the ship. Use the Quantum Ghost to create a new IF."

Seth embraced his friend. "I know I can't talk you out of this. But know that we all love you, Michael. You were always there for us!"

Michael returned the hug and then stepped back, his hands on Seth's shoulders. "You are a lot like your father. And so are your children. The good that was in him is in you and your children. Remember that. It was my honor to fight side by side with Jules. It was my privilege to watch you and your children grow into people Jules would have been proud of." He lowered his arms and took a step back. "Take care of your family, Seth. I'm going to meet mine."

Michael's gaze turned toward Sierra and Stephen. Seth followed it. Sierra looked up and began crying. When Seth turned around, Michael was gone. The door slid closed once more.

Sierra stood at the door, one hand on the medbed's handle and the other shading her eyes as she and her father watched Michael through the window. The older man—her longtime guardian angel— engaged two guards, his sword swiping across their chests in one slashing move. Then he was running down the walkway, ducking and twisting out of the way of plasma bolts. The contingent of guards that had been heading their way were now chasing Michael, who jogged more than ran as he disappeared down a narrow alleyway.

The comm on the console hissed. "Subject is fleeing between sectors five and four. Additional reinforcement is needed."

The abandoned transport and the newly arrived one stood unattended. The signals around the dock reengaged, and people began their normal routines. Her dad pushed open the door and stepped out, glancing around.

"Let's go."

She swallowed against the brusque tone. Anger shimmered around him, like an electrical current. His body was strung taut, almost to the point of snapping. Sierra brushed at the wet tracks on her cheeks and squared her shoulders. All this could be dealt with soon enough. They just needed to make it to the ship.

She gripped the handle, and then she gave the medbed a gentle nudge. The hover-skids activated, and the bed's motors hummed as she guided it through the door and behind her father. Around them, people cast wary looks at guards, including them. Whenever possible, they would skirt around them, giving them a wide berth. She glanced around.

They did it to all guards and Midland personnel. When she and Stephen were enjoying the sights in Golden Plaza, she had felt an undercurrent of hostility and fear but was so enthralled by the new sensations that she hadn't paid attention to it. Now that her senses seemed to be on high alert, it was evident.

There was fear, wariness, even a weariness. Some people held a look of defeat. Some of the faces were drawn tight in fury, but a hidden fury. A shift in her father's demeanor caught her attention.

She returned her gaze forward. They were now approaching the *Depthfinder's* docking access. His hand motioned her to a stop near the docking access of a smaller craft, so she pulled the medbed to a stop.

He turned to her. This couldn't be her father. His eyes had hardened. The planes of his face were stone. A coldness rolled off of him in great waves. "Stay here. Stand beside the medbed as though you are awaiting for the rest of your group to arrive. Tuck your hands at the small of your back, soldier's stance."

He spared her not another glance as he spun and marched toward the ship, keeping to the outside edge of the walkway. The nearest guard tightened his hand over the butt of his plasma rifle as her father neared. Her father gave the man a curt nod and continued past.

The guard returned the nod, resuming his watchful gaze across the port. He gave the same reaction as he passed the next guard. She studied the formation—four guards in front, three in the middle, four more in the back yet set two to each side, leaving the lowered ramp between them.

It was a flash of light that alerted her to her father's action. Even to her, it seemed slightly blurred with how fast he moved. The sword swung up the chest of one, across the neck of another, and through the chest of the third, where it seemed to become lodged. He let go and gripped the vest of another guard. He twisted around and let the plasma bolts slam into his human shield.

Three plasma bolts from the gun in her father's hand downed the guards. He dropped his shield, jumped toward the furthest two who had begun to react, and slammed into them, driving their bodies hard into the tarmac.

He rolled to the side, narrowly avoiding a plasma bolt, and fired a bolt into the man's chest. The last guard rushed toward him, but her father had already regained his footing and had a slim dagger in his hand. He raced toward the guard, ducked under the gun, and sent it flying into the air with a bat of his hand. The guard howled at the pain; but his yell ended in a gurgle as her father gripped the man's neck, digging his fingers into the muscles and tendons, and raised him inches from the ground.

The look on her father's face was beyond chilling. It was . . . diabolical, almost hellish. The white irises seemed brighter. His expression almost held a bit a glee as he pushed the dagger into the man's chest with agonizing leisureliness. He pressed the man against the side of the ship by the hatch. Then with a shove, he drove the dagger completely into him. The guard's feet kicked once before her father let him drop to the ground.

She didn't wait for his command but pushed the medbed as fast as it would go to the ship. Sierra ignored the bodies that littered the ground, averted her gaze from her father as she hurried up the ramp, and paid no heed as her father hit the hatch's panel and rushed to the small bridge.

A curse flowed from him as he shrugged out of his vest, inserted his program crystal, and bent over the console. Within moments, the ship began prepping for departure.

Sierra reached above her and grabbed the medical tubing, hooked them into the medbed, and activated the release of the controls. The ship's internal medical system would monitor Stephen until they made it home. She pushed the medbed against the side of the hull, deactivated the hover-skids, and allowed the weight of the bed to click itself into place. Above her, the control panel began displaying her brother's vitals and blood analysis.

Small movements, small thoughts, and a bit of nausea crept from her stomach. Sierra pulled a small seat from the recess on the hull and lowered herself onto it. From a storage underneath, she removed a thin blanket and draped it over her shoulders, pulling the edges tight around her chest. It was more than weariness that claimed her. She was utterly exhausted.

It was the nudge that brought her back. Sierra raised her head from the top of the medbed and regarded her father.

He was back to looking normal, though with a bit of guilt and sorrow tightening the corner of his mouth and eyes. His gaze was watchful, yet he avoided looking directly into her eyes. "Here." He held a box of rations. "You need to eat."

She gasped and began frantically patting down her pockets. "My metabolic pills!"

"I searched your pockets, sweetie. They aren't there. But we will be home soon enough. We are flying under a new IF, and I used the QG to give us a false manifest and destination. Once we reach the ocean, we can submerge and head home without any further trouble."

Sierra accepted the rations and opened the small box, surveying the contents—protein bars, a nutritional drink, two biscuits with dried fruit. It would be enough to keep her going.

He gripped a support beam above him and leaned against his arms, observing as she began nibbling at the food. "I'm surprised you lasted this long. I'll run a few diagnostic tests once we get home. Did Anya experiment on you, too?"

Sierra shook the drink bottle before opening it. She didn't meet her father's eyes as she nodded. It was his sigh that seemed like a punch to her gut. Remorse at her actions, her decisions, all that led to this flooded her heart. There would be no going back; that she knew.

His hand smoothed across her hair. "Eat up, Si. Then rest. You and Ven are safe now." He placed a kiss on top of her head, then retreated back to the bridge.

Silence governed the interior of the ship as Sierra consumed her rations. They were heading home. Without Michael. Without Jason. And deep down, she knew—she felt it. They had initiated a change that would cost them more than they could ever anticipate.

Nausea rolled around her again. Sierra sighed, finished her meal, and rested her head against folded arms across her brother's medbed. One step at a time. Just one step, then another. Eventually, the shock would wear off. Sleep slowly claimed her.

As a pillowy darkness surrounded her, her father's muffled moan reached her ears.

Chapter Eighteen
LOSS AND GAIN

Soft light. Bright light. Then darkness. The pattern repeated itself numerous times, burning through his closed eyes. Pain and scalding heat flooded his veins. Yet he was trapped, immobile, a prisoner in the darkness that surrounded him.

Stephen pushed and pushed against it. More red filled his vision. *No!* He hated that red. Another round of pulsing light drenched him, then a softness, as though a cool, cotton sheet had fallen upon him.

Voices filtered through. A man. A woman. Then two more men. He knew those voices. One rose in a heated exchange before calming down. The words were garbled, muffled, incoherent. Light surrounded him.

Smells invaded his senses—vanilla, a spicy resin, sterile air, the sharp odor of medicines.

Stephen blinked against the brightness of the medlab scanner as his vision blurred against the burn.

"Welcome back, Stephen."

He let his head fall to the side. Medtech Danvers and Elder John stood at the side of his medical bed. Stephen tried to lift his arms. Restraints held him down. He glanced around.

No other medbed was in the room. The glass between medlabs had been darkened for privacy. A guard stood at the entrance. He blinked again—no red vision.

"It will take a while for you to gain your bearings. The damage done to you was reversible, yet there may be some residual side effects. We will monitor those over the next several months." Medtech Danvers unfastened the restraints. Her hands were gentle as they slid under his shoulders. "Can you sit up?"

With a groan, Stephen pushed himself to a sitting position and rotated until his legs hung off the edge. "I don't understand."

Was that his voice? It sounded like gravel on stone. John pressed a nutrient drink into his hands.

"Drink up." He motioned for the guard to leave and pulled a stool toward him. "Give us a moment, Danvers."

She nodded and moved away to the far side of the room, giving the console her full attention. Stephen swallowed another sip of the drink. He was home. And what he remembered from Midland, from the rail transport, from Yukon . . . he let all those memories rush through him. But Medlab Twelve-twenty. There was something there he couldn't remember. It was all red—washed in a reddened haze.

Stephen set his drink to the side and gazed at his hands. Weren't they supposed to be red?

"Your memories will start to return soon enough." John leaned forward, elbows on knees. Stephen studied him. His mentor and leader seemed to have aged in the last week. Had it been just a week? It seemed like more. "Once Danvers gives the all-clear, you will be moved to a holding cell in security. Your actions before you left were in direct violation of our laws and faith."

"And I will be held on trial." At John's nod, Stephen cut his gaze away. Remorse enveloped him. He had disappointed John. "Sierra?"

"She's suffered enough. Although her actions were reckless and immature, she broke no laws. And the consequences of her actions will be with her for a long time."

"What do you mean?" Stephen began to rise from the bed, but the room twirled about him.

John placed a hand on his chest and guided him back down onto the medbed. "I'll speak with you again on this matter. Right now, we need you to rest and heal."

"Heal?"

Confusion danced through him. He was forgetting something—something important, something that he did or allowed to happen, something he was responsible for.

"You've been through a lot, Stephen. Once you are ready, I will have a report sent for you. Between it and your father's anti-serum, it will help you remember."

It was then he noticed the intravenous tube attached to his arm. A mild sedative entered him, and Stephen let himself sink into the softness of the bed. John's compassionate eyes held his gaze until sleep claimed him. Yet it wasn't a calming sleep. Images, bathed in red, brushed against his mind. He could see himself yelling, screaming at his own reflection that stood there sneering in return. A whirlwind of people, hands, weapons, and screams flowed around him. Then it all began to fade to a soft gray.

He woke to a not-so-soft bed. Weak lighting greeted him. Stephen pushed himself into a sitting position and surveyed his surroundings. He sat on a narrow cot. Across from him were the bars. Above was dim lighting, indicating nighttime. A small partition walled off a refresher unit.

The vague memory of being moved from meblab to the holding cell barely registered. He could remember the shadowy figures of his parents as they talked with John and Jackson while Stephen was led to the cot. His father's eyes were worried, sorrowful, hard. His mother's face shone full of love and fear. But Sierra hadn't been there. Then he was falling asleep, hearing his father tell John that the anti-serum would continue working yet would make him drowsy.

Stephen held his head in his hands. On a small table attached to the right wall was a datapad. John had said there would be a report for him. He guessed this was it.

Stephen grabbed it and opened the file. He skimmed past the beginning. Those memories had already resurfaced—his hacking and theft of the program, leaving Alaska, involving Sierra, meeting the woman on the rail transport. Stephen swallowed against the sickness that rolled in his stomach: the club.

He suddenly rose and raced to the refresher. His stomach emptied itself as the memory of what had transpired at the club flooded his mind. He turned on the water and rinsed his mouth, trying to wash away the vileness, wishing the same could be said about the memory and the imagined filth that seemed to coat his skin.

The memory of their capture stung as if he was being hit by those same darts. Then came the red, the hate, the killing. Over and over, every scene played out before him. The fight with his father replayed in his mind.

Stephen squeezed his eyes shut. His heart tightened in his chest as the tears fell down his cheeks. He had almost killed his father.

He blew out a ragged breath and scrubbed at his face. Time to see what John had on the datapad. He returned to his bunk and began reading.

More guilt consumed him. Michael was gone. Michael had come with his father to save him and Sierra. Now, his friend was missing. And Jason—Anya called him Alpha Zero. He was a prisoner, just as they were. No word had been received on his whereabouts. Jinx and Batch were missing in action. Their last known update was somewhere near the Ecuadorian Territory.

The last section had him slumped against the wall and his heart hammering heavily in his chest. Sector Gray, an offshoot of GFT Military, knew about them, the enhanced.

Anger rose within him—anger at himself and his own stupidity. He had caused this. He was solely responsible and to blame for what may transpire in the future. Stephen set the datapad to the side and studied his surroundings.

According to the calendar at the top of the datapad, his trial was set for two days from now. No, it wasn't going to happen.

Stephen rose and approached the bars. A guard stood at the end, reading the Holonews. "Could you let Elder John know I would like to speak with him?"

The guard looked up and smiled. "Sure. Hold on." He bent over a nearby console and called Main Command. John answered after a few seconds. "Stephen Williams wishes to speak with you."

"Give me about fifteen, and I'll come over."

The guard keyed off the comm and turned toward Stephen. "He said—"

"I heard. Thank you." At the guard's nod, Stephen retreated to his bunk and waited.

He leaned back in the corner and gazed at the ceiling. Soft, whisper-like memories bounced through his mind. His father said that the anti-serum would reverse what Anya did. The changes within him may not be permanent. They had caught it all in time.

Sierra's scans showed a fetal heartbeat. Stephen buried his fingernails into his scalp. What had happened to his sister?

He picked the datapad back up and began a new file. Starting with the decision and the reasoning behind it, Stephen entered his report—every minute detail and thought, even the evil he had committed and the longing to erase the abominations of the enhanced. Minutes passed by. Shadows lengthened. As he closed down the report, ending with his last gaze being of his sister with a knife in her shoulder and his father rising from the floor, he became aware of John waiting in the hallway.

"Stephen?" John stood at bars that separated them. Concern filled his gaze.

"Before I speak to you about what I wanted to say, I remembered Dad's voice saying that he detected a fetal heartbeat in Sierra. Tell me, John, what happened to my sister?" Stephen rose and met the elder at the bars. He threaded his hands through and propped against the metal rods. The coldness cooled his hot skin.

"She was subjected to in vitro fertilization. From what your dad discovered and through Sierra's own accounts, she and the one named Jason had been subjected to Anya Bastion's experimentation. In Sierra's account, which I can send to you, Anya had many vats that seemed to have at one time contained fetuses. And she thinks she was used as an incubator. Your dad has been monitoring her, and she is doing well. The genes of the baby seem to be a combination of Sierra and possibly Jason."

How much more guilt and remorse could he take? His stomach clenched into a hard knot. Stephen's knuckles turned white from the death grip he had on the bars. "Will she be okay?"

"She will. Miriam is with her, counseling her. She's healing." John placed his hand over Stephen's. "You can't change the past, Stephen. But don't worry about Sierra, nor your dad. They will be fine soon enough."

"My dad?" He swallowed against the lump that rose in this throat. "What happened to my dad?"

"A lot. But that is for him to tell you." John removed his hand and crossed his arms. "What is it you wanted to say?"

"I don't want a trial."

"That's not negotiab—"

"No, you misunderstand." Stephen let go and began pacing the small enclosure. "I want to forego my trial. I accept whatever punishment the committee assigns. My sin, my ill-thought actions, my stupidity put not just the enhanced in jeopardy, but also, all of Alaska. My arrogance of being an enhanced, thinking I was so much better than everyone . . . I deserve whatever is meted out."

"Do you realize what you are saying?" John furrowed his brows. "I mean, we will abide by your wishes, if you truly understand the magnitude of your request."

Was this what he wanted? No. But it was what was needed and deserved—a just punishment for all he had committed. Stephen picked up the datapad. He twirled it between his hands for a few seconds before walking back to the bars and handing it through the space between. His breath hitched for a second. "I understand completely. I put my report on here—every action, every thought. No matter how atrocious. John, I deserve this punishment."

John accepted the datapad. "I'll pass along your request."

"One more thing." Stephen sighed and rested his forehead against the metal once again. His heart tightened in his chest with a violent twist. "I don't want my family to visit me. Let me serve my punishment in solitude."

He deserved the loss of his family for all that he had committed.

Seth—his shirt lying forgotten by his side—sat on the edge of the bed, flipping the slim dagger over and over in his hand. Flip. Catch it by the hilt. Flip. Catch it on the tip. Over and over.

It was clean now—no blood. Yet it was the one that he had used multiple times. Lives were taken. One pierce of the blade and their souls were sent to their eternal destination.

Maybe that was what was wrong. He didn't know if he had sent them to a fiery anguish or if they were covert believers, yet he seriously doubted that. Flip. Catch by the hilt. Seth held it up. The overhead light in their bedroom glinted on the folded steel. It was a remarkable piece of art, yet this blade had doomed so many souls and removed their chance in this life to ever know Christ.

Was that what bothered him? Or was it that he had become what his father was: a killer?

"Seth?"

He drew in a sharp breath at Tamara's voice. He had been so involved with his own internal thoughts, she was able to come in unawares. That had been happening too often over the last couple of days.

When her weight pressed down on the mattress and her hands began their smooth caress across his bare shoulders, he tensed. She slid her arms around him, embracing him from behind. Slender and cool fingers spread across his chest. Her lips placed a soft kiss on the back of his shoulder.

Seth twirled the blade between his fingers. He had been ignoring her since they arrived home, since their son was taken into custody. For two days, he had either wandered the Hill, strolled the beach, or hidden away in the bedroom away from people, away from anyone who may be able to see what ran through him: rage, fury, aggression. The need was still there to tear things apart. The fragile control he held to keep himself from releasing all that had built up inside him threatened to shatter. And what was within him was an unquenchable, consuming fire that raged within his soul.

Her hands tightened on his pectoral muscles as she nestled her chin in the crook of his neck. "Speak to me, sweetie."

Speak to her. He closed his eyes. "About what?"

Seth almost didn't recognize his own voice—harsh, guttural.

Her sigh tickled his ear. She slipped off the bed and stood in front of him. When he didn't look up, she nudged his arms open and stepped into them, placing her hands on the sides of his face. She forced him to look up, and he allowed it.

Her amber eyes held sorrow and pain, yet also love, along with a touch of anger. "You can't keep hiding away. Tell me what is wrong with you."

"I'm not hiding—" He flipped the weapon through his fingers.

"Don't lie." She ripped the dagger from his hand and threw it at the wall. It embedded itself a fourth of a way up the blade. Now, he would have to repair the wall. "I hate that thing."

Seth tamped down his frustration and fury. He hated the thing, too. "Tamara." He stood and pushed her back a step.

Her hands slammed against him and shoved him. The back of his knees hit the bed; and he toppled, catching himself midway through the fall.

"Don't 'Tamara' me." She knelt over him as he began to push up from his position. The force of her hands against his chest held him down.

He didn't want to hurt her—not his Tamara. But she was pushing him over that edge, the edge he had been trying to run away from.

Seth fell back onto the soft covers and grabbed her wrists, pulling her arms out to the side until she was flat against him and looking down upon him, her mouth just inches away from his. "Stop this. Please."

"No." She twisted out of his grip and rolled away from him to stand at the end of the bed. "You have to let whatever this is out. You need to speak to me."

"No!" Seth roared and jumped from the bed. His hand grabbed her around the bicep. Then she was pressed against the wall by the door and dresser. He flattened his body against her, pinning her against the bedroom wall. She needed to leave him alone. "Leave it, Tam. Just leave me alone for a while."

"No!" Her hands slapped against his cheeks and clenched around his face. She forced his head down until their foreheads met. She always did this—tried to distract him with a loving touch, a gaze, or a kiss. Sometimes, even with a bit of roughhousing. But not this time.

He let go of her and slammed his palms against the wall, feeling the give in the structure at the force of the blows. There would be indentations left and one more thing he would have to repair.

He couldn't do this! Seth squeezed his eyes shut. He had to hide away what he knew she would see in him. She could never know what he was becoming.

He ripped himself away from his wife. "Please. Go." Seth turned away, aware of the tracks of tears that ran down his face. His fingernails dug into his palms.

Soft, tender touches surrounded his clenched fists. "Seth, you can never hurt me. I know this. You know this. You *know* this."

He shook his head. "I'm not supposed to be like this, Tam."

"You aren't meant to hold it in either—whatever it is that is driving a wedge between us." Her fingers forced their way into his grasp. "Just release what is within you. Let it go. Tell me."

Tension threaded its way throughout his body once again as he focused his gaze on the wall across from them. "No. I can't."

Her hands let go, encircled his waist, and pulled him closer. Soft kisses landed on his back, where the muscles bunched and corded.

"I know you, Seth. I've loved you since we were children. I know every part of you, inside and out." She slipped under his arm and stood in front of him, gazing up at him. "You will need to face this soon. But for right now . . ."

He looked down at her then.

"Seth." She reached up and touched his cheek.

And that was his undoing, his wife unconditionally loving him and trusting him—a woman who knew every inch of him and every dream, failure, and desire. His true half . . .

Seth buried his hands into her tight curls. His mouth crushed hers. He fell further into her embrace. And in the back of his mind, the thought that this was just the start of a dangerous path skittered through his mind. He was on an extremely narrow ledge.

He was lost. She wanted to help him, to love him, but it was only fueling the fire inside. But she couldn't know that. She could never know that. For the time being, though, he would hide the beast that was living within until he could gain a way to control it.

Chapter Nineteen
WHAT LEGENDS BECOME

Rolling golden brown hills stretched into the distance underneath a gray sky. Some of the trees had lost their leaves and stood bare, their limbs stretched high and silhouetted against darkening clouds. The rest were tall and green, enhanced even more by his unnatural vision. Their lush branches filled the air with the most heavenly scent. Jason breathed deeply.

So fresh and chilled was the air, it seemed to hurt his lungs. He hoisted the pack up onto his shoulder a bit more and trudged up the hill of waist-high grass. So much land and yet none were occupied by people.

He paused and turned a circle, surveying his surroundings. Canadian Province was expansive. And the people lived in the cities or along its edges. From what he had gathered from the history files, no GFT subject was allowed to own land. Midland and some of the more southern non-GFT countries were different. Would Alaska Country be different as well?

He smiled at the thought. It wouldn't take long to find out. He pulled out his compass as he resumed his trek up the hill. A small holographic projection rose from the circular surface, giving him a rough layout of the landscape and his direction. According to his calculations, he would arrive in Alaska in about a month, given his present pace.

He would have been there much sooner, but the citizen cards he had collected off the soldiers and medical personnel at Medlab Twelve-twenty had been flagged. He had trashed those cards back in Saskagina. Traveling was better this way. The longer he stayed under GFT's radar, the better and safer he and those at Alaska Country would be.

When he reached the summit, he paused again. In the distance, under a copse of Douglas firs stood a dilapidated building. He glanced at the ever-darkening sky, scratching at his full beard. Night would fall within the next twenty minutes. It would be nice to stay within walls instead of a cave or in a tree as he had been doing for the last three weeks. And it would be a warmer. Winter was coming sooner than he had anticipated.

Jason hurried to the building. What was once boarded windows now hung with decayed wood. Shards of stained glass clung to the frames. The roof held strong, yet some of the eaves had toppled to the ground long ago. A steel construction of a cross laid half buried in rubble, dirt, and grass alongside the destroyed eaves.

He stepped through the opening and into a wooden cavern. Startled birds flew down from the rafters and passed his head. Somewhere in the corner, a small critter scurried away.

Rotted benches littered the floor. Jason walked down the middle of the room. Some of the wooden benches still stood at the front but were covered in vines and animal nesting. The raised platform before him seemed sturdy. He tested it with a few jumps before walking across it. Along the back wall were the same kind of benches. Yet they were covered by a tarpaulin. Jason reached down and lifted a corner of the heavy canvas to peer under it. No critters.

Dust and dirt flew upward as he pulled it off the benches. If the wood had been cared for, it would have gleamed. But years of unuse and neglect left it dull and coated with grime, despite the covering that was placed on it.

Jason ran his hand along the seat. It was smooth, though. He placed his pack on the bench and ventured further down the raised area. A stack of three crates stood in the corner—broken boxes, crushed vases, and bottles. He raised the lid of one crate—nothing but dirt and spiders. He pushed it to the side and opened the next one to find much of the same. It shattered a bit as he pushed it off the bottom crate. This last one had the lid nailed firmly closed. He studied the edges and sides—no holes, no openings. The wood had been treated to withstand the elements, yet time was slowly beginning to eat into it.

He grabbed the top and yanked. The plank pulled away. It took two more forceful jerks to pry off part of the top. Jason reached in and pulled out a heavy sack. Mold spores flew into his face, eliciting a violent sneeze from him.

The material was a type of oilcloth, tied tightly with cording. He felt along the sides—books, it seemed. Jason pulled his knife from his pocket and sliced the bag open. The fading light gleamed against the black, leather-bound books. He angled one toward the window and read the cover: *The Holy Bible.*

Excitement flooded through him. If what Sierra had said was true, then this was the book that would answer all his questions—the book that would save him. He reached in and pulled out four more.

His heart thumped in his ribcage. Sierra had said these books were rare, and the printing press in Alaska Country were hard-pressed to produce enough copies for their people. He stuffed them back into the bag and hurried back to his own pack. He could read one after he settled in for the night.

The search for dry wood was relatively easy this time. He used the rotted benches and created a small pit in the middle of the large room. Soon, he had the vegetables he had collected throughout his travels in the wilderness roasting over the fire. The food he had filched from Medlab had slowly been waning. All that was left were a few meat cubes and highly preserved foodstuffs. Jason placed a small pot near the fire and added a meat cube and water. He had discovered after the first week of hiking that the cubes made a good broth. Add the roasted vegetables, and he had a meal that kept him sated for hours.

Jason pulled the surviving benches around the fire and flipped them onto their side, creating a wall that bounced the heat and light inward. Once finished, he settled down on his pallet and selected one of the books.

As the broth bubbled and the roasting vegetables filled the air with a delectable aroma that caused his stomach to growl, he opened the Bible and flipped the thin pages until he came to a chapter titled, "The Gospel of John" and read the first line.

In the beginning was the Word, and the Word was with God, and the Word was God.

Φ

Sierra shut down the medical file and rose from her chair when she heard her grandfather call out from the main room. "I'm in here, Granddad."

She met him halfway and stepped aside as he passed through the opening and into the study. His strong arms wrapped her into a hug. "How's my beauty today?"

Sierra leaned into his embrace. A spicy scent rose from his skin. He had been in the forest lately. "I'm well. Just starting to tire more quickly."

He stepped back but kept his heavy hands on her shoulders. Concern highlighted his dark eyes. "The baby?" His gaze fell to her rounded belly. Just a little over three months along and yet she was beginning to show.

"*Babies*. And they are doing fine. Actually, more than fine. Their growth is exceedingly swift." As if to emphasize her statement, one of them somersaulted inside the womb, causing a queasiness to flood through her.

"They?"

Sierra smiled and led her grandfather to the console. She pulled up the medical file she was perusing. "Mom and I ran a scan yesterday. I was just going over the data—fraternal twins. And boys. I'm thinking of naming them Cass and Zeke."

Her grandfather leaned down and pulled up the genetics file. She swallowed the lump in her throat when he paused over the data on the genes. Would he see what she saw?

Her sons carried the T-C 574 and the T-C 575 genes, which meant they would be more than she and Jason, even more than Grandfather Jules was designed to be. And that would account for the swiftly growing babies within her—another advancement of enhanced?

Her granddad straightened and cast a side gaze to her before closing down the file. "They are going to be more?" At her nod, he shook his head. "This Jason you told me about—does he know what Anya did to you?"

"No." Sierra sighed and lowered herself into the chair. "I think Michael knew." Her heart lurched. No one knew if Michael had survived. No word from Jinx, Batch, nor him had reached them. "He had this strange expression on his face when he looked at us. But all the data that Anya had has been destroyed by Dad's program. So, I will never know the true extent of what she did."

"What do you mean? I thought it was just in vitro fertilization that was performed." He drew in a deep breath. "Please tell me she didn't manipulate you or the babies."

"I don't know, Granddad. So far, there isn't any evidence of gene manipulation. From what we believe, Anya just used Jason for his genes and me as the incubator. But I do know she used the Serum Seventy-seven on both of us. At Dad's best estimation, the babies' growth were accelerated, and gestation time shortened."

"What was her game plan if not a soldier?"

"To cheat death was what Jason said." Sierra shook her head. "She was dying. Jason said she kept experimenting on him in order to harvest stem cells. When we came into the program, she decided to create a more advanced version of us, I guess."

A bit of anger crossed his face at the mention of Jason. "This Jason was the reason for you and your brother's capture."

"True." Maybe she should have been angry. Maybe she should have let bitterness override the forgiveness she gave Jason. Yet Jason was a victim, too. "But if you learn of his story, you will see that he was put into a difficult situation; and most of the time, he was under the influence of Paxolin-X and then the Paxmedlin. And we were able to help free him."

Her granddad turned away and walked to the window to look out at the water that flowed past. His shoulders slumped a bit. The initial anger seemed to have faded. "I understand, Sierra. More than most people would. Jules and I fought to leave that life behind. Experimentations, manipulations, torture. Jason's ordeal may have been slightly different, but the abuse he suffered . . . " He cleared his throat. "How are you handling it all?"

"I'm managing." Sierra shrugged. "I really haven't thought much about it, I guess. I do still have nightmares, at times. And when I arrived home and found out I was pregnant, it seemed as though my world just fell apart. But then . . . Granddad, it's not the babies' fault. They are victims of Anya's—two of many lives touched by GFT's assassin program. What started all those decades ago filtered down to us."

He turned from the window as Sierra continued. "And when I realized after the first scan that Anya had used Jason for the father, it just seemed as though this act that started as evil will eventually be used for good." She blew out a short breath. "I really can't explain it. Having a child wasn't my choice. It was forced upon me, yet I love them. I cherish the thought of seeing them soon."

The door slid open, and her mom walked in, cutting off whatever he was about to say next.

"Dad! I wasn't expecting you today." She dropped her bag on the side table and hurried to him. He lifted her into an embrace and squeezed tightly.

"Spur of the moment."

Her mom laughed and smacked his shoulder as he dropped her back onto the floor. "Sure. You never do anything spur of the moment. Mom didn't come?"

"She is with Mandy at some function of theirs. She said she would swing by later." He propped against the curvature of the window. "I came by to check on my girls. And to see where my boy was."

A frown pulled at her mom's mouth. "He's at the Hill."

"How is he doing?"

Sierra pursed her lips, allowing her mom to answer. Her mom shook her head so hard that her tight ringlets bounced around her head. "He's . . . not good, Dad. He's angry that Stephen won't allow anyone to visit. And I know there is something else, but he won't tell me. I can see it in him. Something haunts him. It's growing stronger each day."

Her granddad scowled. "I was afraid of that."

Sierra's heart lurched at the sadness in his voice. She brushed at the tear that began to fall. "He's been watching the videos Grandma Abby left him and constantly going over the medical data on me, Stephen, and the babies. Then he disappears to the Hill and never comes back until late at night."

"Sometimes, not even then, Dad." Her mother settled down in the other chair beside Sierra. "Lately, it's been almost three or four o'clock in the morning before he comes home. And when he does sleep, nightmares plague him."

"I know you read our statements." Sierra paused. Only her mom knew this part. She had left it out of the testimony she had given to the elders. No one needed to know how close her father had come.

"But there's more?" Her granddad walked over to the couch and sat down. His joints audibly popped as he crossed an ankle over his knee. His left hand absently rubbed at his knee as he waited. "I assumed as much. Seth had been changing a bit at a time over the last year."

Her mother slid an arm around Sierra's shoulders. "Go ahead and let him know, honey. Your granddad will be able to help him once he hears the full story."

Sierra nodded and fought back the tears that threatened to escape. "I didn't tell the elders everything, Granddad. I didn't want them to think that Dad had become something to fear."

She took a deep breath and began, leaving nothing out—from the slaughter at the facility to the near killing of Stephen in the corridor, then the battle at the ship and the heated rage that had burned in her father's eyes. The fears, the horrors she saw, and the awakening that happened in her father and in Stephen came tumbling out of her. They had become more. But what that was remained to be seen.

Seth stood far back from the headstones. After learning that Stephen had forewent the trial and accepted his sentencing and hearing that his son refused to allow them to visit, he had begun returning to the headstones. But they offered him no solace. Even the videos of his father gave him no answers. Yet he saw himself in those battles that his father fought. Only, his father fought for freedom. What did he fight and kill for? Sure, he saved his children and Jason. Sure, he fought in order to survive. Yet there was the one secret he had to keep buried—the one truth that would destroy him, his family, and their way of life: he enjoyed the killing. It gave him a release he never knew he needed. A part of him reveled in it. The other part rebelled against the slaughter at his hands.

Seth held out his arms and viewed his scarred and callused hands. Years of masonry and gardening and building had left their marks. Yes, they were clean. But he could see it—the blood that dripped from his hands, blood that was buried beneath his fingernails and stained the creases of his palms. He lifted his right hand to his nose. He could even smell the blood.

Logic said it was post-traumatic stress disorder that caused him to relive his memories. Reality said it was a natural coping mechanism. But his mind said he was a monster, and his soul said nothing. Only a deep, aching nothingness lived within him.

The wind blew against him. Seth dropped his hands and stuffed them into his back pockets, causing his coat to bunch around his waist. "Tam send you?"

Uncle JJ halted behind him. "No."

Seth turned to face him. JJ's eyes had darkened. Concern, worry, apprehension. Apprehension at what? At him? Seth's lip curled. Why couldn't they leave him alone? Couldn't they see there was nothing to talk about anymore? He became what they all feared he would be.

"There's nothing to talk about." Fury crept into his voice. And he couldn't stop the next barrage of words. "Why even bother? Do you think I would not have psychoanalyzed myself? Performed a self-assessment? Evaluated my thoughts and emotions?"

JJ huffed. "Of course, I knew you would. But none of that will help you one iota."

Seth stalked to his uncle and glared at him. "There's nothing that can help me!"

"You're wrong, my boy—"

"I'm not your boy!" Seth whirled and began his retreat into the forest.

"You are! Not by blood, but you are my family. Have been since your birth." JJ's hand landed on his shoulder, halting his flight.

Rage filled Seth. He flew backwards, slamming his back into JJ's chest; and reaching up, he wrapped his arm around JJ's neck and pulled. The older man flipped around and landed on his back, yet his hands had latched onto Seth's legs and yanked them out from under him. Seth hit the ground, sending dead leaves and dirt upward.

Red colored his vision. He spun around, rammed his knee onto JJ's chest, and drove his fist toward the man's face. Two meaty hands grabbed his fist and squeezed. Seth brought his elbow down, sinking it deep into his father-in-law's hard, flat stomach. Then Seth was thrown clear.

He rolled with the momentum for a second before halting his tumble and rising from the ground, meeting JJ halfway. Hands countered his moves. Thuds and grunts filled the air. Seth sent a fist into JJ's side and groaned when JJ's hit landed in his stomach. He spun around and drove an elbow at JJ, but it was blocked. Seth ducked JJ's hand that aimed for his back, whirled, and drove his fist into the man's chest. But JJ had anticipated him. The man grabbed the hand, but Seth was already spinning under the grip, his leg flying upward and into JJ's side.

Seth didn't think, only reacted. He let his fury guide him. JJ blocked some of the blows; yet Seth was younger, faster, had more stamina. JJ's age had slowed him.

An opening arrived. JJ had been retreating a bit at a time as Seth pummeled against him, trying to gain the upper hand. His father-in-law's left foot slid on wet leaves and a patch of snow-covered ice. He faltered and Seth pressed his advantage.

He grabbed JJ and yanked, driving the older man down to meet his rising knee. But the connection never happened. Milliseconds before his knee would have crushed JJ's face and nose, the times spent with the man flashed through his mind—the laughter, the heartaches, the love.

The man who had called his father a brother—who had stood at Seth's side and helped raise him, who today had sought out Seth to help him—stumbled back as Seth let go. Horror at his actions flooded Seth's body. Tremors shook him. A powerful fist gripped his heart.

Seth fell to his knees, burying his head in his hands. "What have I become?" He wrapped his arms around his midsection and pressed his face into the wet leaves. "Tell me what to do. I'm so sorry! So sorry!"

JJ knelt next to him. "Look at me, Seth."

He lifted his head and gazed back into eyes filled with love. "I tried to kill you."

His father-in-law gave a half grin, and his hand gripped the back of Seth's head and held on. "*Tried* is the operative word. I've had a little more than three decades of training and missions than you have had. You would not have gotten this far if I didn't let you."

Confusion rock Seth. "What?"

"You needed an outlet for all the anger and hurt, son. You are so much like your father—a flair for the dramatic. That was the reason we had our exercises—to purge that aggression, give it an outlet." A sad smile drifted across his father-in-law's dark face and into equally dark eyes. "And to answer your question, you have become a warrior. There's no shame in that."

"But I killed. And at times, I enjoyed it!" His hiss filled the air around them. "I know that the Bible has instances where God's people killed to protect. And I know I did that, too. But, Dad, I almost killed my own son! How do I come away from that?"

JJ's eyes brightened at the "Dad," but he only gripped Seth's head harder and pulled him into an embrace. "Do you think Abraham worried about almost killing Isaac?"

Seth shook his head, his hair rasping against JJ's coarse coat. "No. God provided the ram in Isaac's stead. Abraham trusted God to provide the substitution. But my fight with Stephen wasn't a test of my faith."

"In a way it was, son." JJ let go and sat on the wet ground. Seth followed suit, bringing his knees up and draping his hands over them. JJ hooked his arm around Seth's shoulders. "You trusted God with Stephen, trusted that God would show you the way. Sierra told me that you had prayed just before you and Stephen fought."

He could see where JJ was going with this line of reasoning. "And God brought Sierra there to keep me from stabbing Stephen."

"Yes." JJ sighed and gazed up at the afternoon sky. "I know that the fights and killings awakened something within you, Seth. And it will only grow as the days pass. But there's a difference between bloodlust and the need to protect."

"Stephen is facing the same. If I can't help myself, how will I help my son? How do I tell the difference?"

"You'll learn. You'll know." JJ returned his gaze to Seth. "You were raised in faith, and I know that the Lord will guide your footsteps. You are a child of God, Seth. You only need to give it all over to Him."

Silence reigned for long moments. Leaves scuttled about in the wind. Behind them, the sound of an elk stalking the forest faded away. A bird hopped in the bushes nearby. Voices from the compound hummed. And there, in the distance and barely audible, the windchime laugh of his daughter filtered through the air.

Seth forced the lump that rose in his throat back down. He wasn't gone yet. There were many instances in the Bible where men had to kill and where God had instructed them to take a life. Even some women had killed. Logically, it was the condition of the heart that determined if it was a sin or not. But what was the condition of his heart during those fights? If he was to heal, then he would have to face some cold, hard facts about himself and about his son.

But would he have to do it alone? Without looking at his father-in-law, Seth hung his head and closed his eyes. "Will you sit with me?"

"For as long as it takes, my boy." JJ crossed his legs and leaned on his hands, closing his eyes.

The sounds of the forest surrounded them as Seth silently called out to the Lord.

Φ

SEVEN WEEKS LATER

"Dinner!" The bell clanged to emphasize the shout.

Stephen laid his shovel next to his pickax and stepped across the drainage ditch he had been clearing. Rocks and hard-packed snow were piled high on the opposite side, where he had thrown the loads. There were still large amounts needing to be cleared before they could run the next segment of water lines.

He caught up with the other workers, hopped up onto the open-air transport, and settled down onto the bench. Two correction officers went down the seated line of inmates and scanned their labels. Once they reached the end where Stephen sat, they signaled the driver and stepped off. Two more officers climbed aboard, and the transport began moving.

The landscape slid by as they moved away from the worksite and to the walled-off area that had been erected as their temporary housing. Stephen propped his elbows on his knees. This part of their country was quiet. Trees zipped by them. The rocks and gravel underneath the transport crunched. Chilled air cooled his heated skin. The smells of pine and snow filled his lungs.

Within moments, they arrived. Stephen waited until the light above their heads indicated they could disembark. He stepped off, slid into the food line, and stood with his hands at his back, waiting. The food tables dotted the small clearing. And at each table stood a missionary from Alaska Compound's mission board.

Correction Officer Daniel Sellers slowly worked his way down the line, scanning the labels on the uniforms before signaling each man to their table. He stopped in front of Stephen and smiled.

"How's today going?" His scanner gave the green light.

"Tough. Hit a pack of ice. But I'm getting through it. Probably another day and I'll have it cleared."

Sellers nodded. "Good. You have table three-four. And I'll drop around your bunk about nine."

"Determined to lose another hand, aren't you?"

The man laughed and shook his head. "We'll see!"

Stephen smiled and left the line, heading for his solitary table. After two months in, he was allowed to have short visits with friends and family. But he had declined. No family. No friends. This was his self-induced punishment for all the horrors and wrongs he had brought upon his people. Only, Sellers didn't care. The man came by three times a week to play a game of cards with Stephen. Their conversations were stilted at first, until Stephen had asked him questions about Christ and forgiveness. Then those nights playing cards had become his tutelage. And Sellers had become his mentor.

His steps faltered as he approached his table. Peony stood at the end of it, setting out his covered dish and pouring his drink. She looked up as he settled on the bench.

"Hi, Stephen." She sat at his table and waited.

Stephen glanced around. Other missionaries were seated at the tables. Some already had their Bibles out and were reading to the inmates. For his first few weeks, he'd had a variety of missionaries at his table. Most of them were those he knew only in passing, people he had seen in church service or in the main lobby of Central Hub.

Peony was always around but not at his table and never on this side of the prison. And he had been watching.

Stephen picked up his glass and sipped the tea. Orange pekoe was the choice today. "You usually serve Darwin."

Peony's pale pink lips stretched in a small smile. Her blue eyes shone. "He was released three days ago. I asked to be your missionary."

That caught him off guard. Had she noticed him watching her all those weeks since he was assigned to the water-workers compound?

"Why?" He removed the lid to his plate. Before him was seared elk, sprigs of butter lettuce, fried potatoes, and a huge helping of lima beans. "I thought you would be one of the ones to hate me. It was my stupidity that cost us."

"True." She leaned on her elbows and regarded him. "But I've been observing you. You've changed."

He glanced back down at his food and began eating. The elk was seasoned perfectly and so tender that he didn't need a knife. Silence passed between them as he ate a few bites before setting his fork and knife down. "How have I changed?"

She ignored his question. "Why won't you let your family come see you?"

"You're blunt." Stephen laughed. "Is that why you're here? They want to know how I'm doing?"

"That—and, as I said, I requested it."

He finished his meat and beans in order to silence the rumble in his stomach before answering her. "I don't want them to see me like this. And I don't deserve to have their company—not until I've paid my dues for my sins."

"Daniel said you came to Christ three weeks ago. Your sins are forgiven, Stephen."

"By Christ, yes. But not by me." He leaned back and regarded her, truly looked at her. Her light brown, almost blonde hair glistened in the Alaskan sun. Red highlights ran through the strands, giving it a coppery tone. Her skin was delicate, porcelain-like. A small mole under her left eye accentuated her beauty. What seemed like blue irises were more a deep sapphire color. And there in that smooth, alabaster skin was his Golden Ratio.

He let his gaze travel over her hands. They were small but strong. Tiny scars and burns marred the smooth skin—grease burns and what looked like puncture marks or needle marks.

"What else do you do, Peony?"

"How do you mean?"

"You don't come here every day—at least, not from what I've seen." He cocked his head at her as he picked at his lettuce. "You are an enhanced. Why choose this kind of job?"

"Because it helps others." Her mouth quirked in a lopsided grin. "But I also do other things."

"Like?"

"Your food." She propped her chin in her hand and regarded him as he ate the potatoes. "I cook and teach culinary arts. I also run a tailor exchange. Your uniform—that's one of my designs."

Stephen ran his hands down the lightweight fabric. When he had first donned it, he was amazed at the comfortable fit. And after working in it, he realized it was designed to keep him warm, yet still cool enough as he performed hard labor.

"It's an amazing garment. I noticed the first day how it kept me from overheating, yet still warm enough to work in the cold."

Peony blushed. "It's my best accomplishment, so says Father."

"Well, I agree with Jackson." Stephen pushed his plate away and drained his tea. "But really, you don't need to come here for me. I'm fine without a missionary, since Sellers became my mentor."

"I came to be your friend."

That gave him pause. He didn't have friends. He didn't deserve friends. "Why?"

"Because you need one. I'm also Sierra's friend."

A deep ache formed in his chest at his sister's name. He had never been away from her for so long. He fought against the frown that pulled at his brows. "How is she?"

"She's good. And the babies are healthy. She's having no complications with her pregnancy."

A bit of shock rocked through him. "Babies?"

"She's carrying twins."

Shame filled him. If he hadn't abandoned his home, Sierra would have been safe. She wouldn't have been subjected to any violation. Peony's hands covered his.

"Stephen, don't let your thoughts dwell on the negative."

He shook his head and blinked back hot tears. "If it wasn't for my actions, she wouldn't have been enduring this, wouldn't have been subjected to IVF and experiments." Her hands tightened over his clenched fists. "How do I reconcile myself with the consequences? If you want to be my missionary, then tell me how to do that."

Compassion flooded her eyes. Those beautiful blue orbs gazed deeply into him for a few moments. "You accept it, that's all. Sierra didn't have to follow. So, blame can be at her feet, too. And she accepted that. Now you must accept that you made mistakes. And the cost of your sin was dear. Yet even King David had to deal with his consequences, too. God never left him. He only turned David back to Him. So that is what you must do. Turn your life back to God. Give Him control. Let Him deal with your anguish and guilt."

Stephen let his gaze travel around the courtyard. The other men were slowly rising from their tables, shaking hands or nodding at their missionaries. Dinner was ending. Time to return to work.

"I'm afraid." Stephen whispered that confession. Whatever it was about Peony, it brought to the surface every hard truth he had been trying to deny. He looked at the older woman again. No, she wasn't that much older—only five years. Yet she had an innocence about her, a softness, a balm that soothed his soul. He pushed away from the table and stumbled to his feet. "I gave my life to Christ, yes. But I'm afraid to completely let go. Look at what I did."

Her hand landed on his arm, stopping his flight. Stephen gazed at the hand and then down at her. Time to end this before it began.

"I'm a killer, Peony. I was a fornicator, reveled in debauchery. I did things that would make Sodom and Gomorrah blush. I cursed God. I even tried to kill my own father. I'm—" He fought back the tears. He only meant to gloss over it all. Why was he confessing everything? Pouring all this out to her? She needed to know the true him. Then she would understand that he didn't deserve her friendship. She would understand that he was tainted. "My grandfather died, sacrificed his life, in order to protect us. And I destroyed it all—put every one of us in danger. I'm horrible, Peony— dirtier than swine. Unworthy."

"We all are." Her hands gripped his, holding him in place. Around him, the courtyard began clearing. Sellers stood at a distance, waiting.

"I don't understand."

"We are all unworthy. No sin is greater than another in God's eyes." She took a step closer to him, gazing up at him. "Every one of us commits some kind of sin, each horrible in God's eyes. Yet Christ wipes that clear. Yes, some of us commit acts that are unlawful and land us in prison, such as you. But it doesn't make you less than."

Tears fell off his cheeks and landed on their clasped hands. "I didn't want my family to see me like this. That's why I don't want them here. I'm a disappointment. I brought such grief to them."

"I know." She reached up. Soft, cool palms rested against his hot, whiskered cheek. "But you will be released in six months, yes?"

Stephen nodded.

"Then take this knowledge with you: Christ makes all things new."

"'Therefore, if anyone *is* in Christ, *he is* a new creation; old things have passed away; behold, all things have become new.'" Stephen gave her a small grin. "Second Corinthians chapter five, verse seventeen. Yeah, that Scripture has been in my mind lately." At her soft smile, Stephen pulled away. "Will you come again tomorrow?"

Her gaze bored into him. "If you want me to."

Seconds passed by. A cloud moved in front of the low-hanging sun. A soft shadow danced across them as they stood facing each other.

Stephen gave her a small nod. "I do." Sellers waved for him to head his way. "I have to go now. And thank you for dinner. It was really delicious."

Her smile seemed to lift a heavy weight from him. He turned from her and walked away, yet she called out to him. "Stephen?"

He paused and looked back, soaking in the sight of her as the sunset backlit her body. A halo of light formed around her. "Yes?"

"Will you reflect on one thing for me?" At his nod, she continued. "You are now a child of God. It doesn't matter what you were. All that matters is what you become."

COMING SOON

WHERE

LEGENDS

LIVE

Chapter One
HOM≡COMING

Stephen's heart thumped against his ribcage. He slammed his hand on the exit button, causing the automatic rickshaw to stop. Cool air surrounded him when he flung open the door and stepped out onto the soft ground. Pines towered over him.

"Stand by."

The automatic controls beeped its comply and lowered itself to the small roadway, shutting down primary systems until Stephen was ready to resume his ride. He walked to the edge of the roadway, grateful that no one was out and about this time of day.

Already three hours post-release and he still couldn't find the courage to return home. For all his sins and wrongdoings, he had brought too much grief and pain to his family and cost his people far more than they could afford.

Global Federated Territories now knew they existed. More sanctions had been enacted, more embargoes on their trade. Trade routes had to be rerouted, and their freedoms were now in jeopardy. According to Peony, Elder John said not to worry; this was just politics. But Stephen did worry. Was it possible he had brought a potential war to their borders? Did he completely destroy everything his grandfathers had fought for?

And to think that he would be welcomed back home—no, there wasn't a possibility that he could be forgiven so easily and so readily. He lowered himself onto the soggy ground. Knee-high grass partially concealed him from the road.

Summer was near its end, and the ground had become saturated to the point that it could no longer absorb the rain. The wetness slowly soaked through his pants.

He looked up into the sky. Faint hints of the aurora borealis were beginning to show. Maybe he could just camp out here for the night, try again in the morning.

The purr of a hoverbike reached his ears long before the vehicle rounded the curve. He didn't have to look to see who it was. That purr had been coming around to each of his prison camps for the last six months, and she would have known the rickshaw route he would take. Stephen lay back among the tall grass and waited.

In moments, the engine shut down; and Peony's voice ordered the automatic rickshaw to depart. Still, he waited. Movement behind him indicated she was pulling something from the bike—probably a blanket. She hated getting dirty, and lying on the ground was too dirty for her.

He smiled at that thought. Peony didn't care about food or dye that stained her clothing or hands, but she drew the line at mud. He breathed in deep, inhaling her scent as it floated across the air—a mixture of strawberries, citrus, and the earthy, aromatic smell of pine—a strange combination, yet one he found intoxicating.

"I knew you wouldn't make it far." She spread the blanket on the ground beside him, plopped down, and then patted the area next to her as she lay back. Her blonde hair fanned around her.

He scooted over until his arm brushed against hers. "I can't. Not yet, anyway."

She rolled to her side and gazed at him. Her dark sapphire eyes studied him. "You don't plan to sleep out here tonight, do you?"

"Is that so bad?" He turned and propped his head on his hand, facing her. With his free hand, he traced her face, running it over the Golden Ratio pattern that he saw in her.

"You can't put it off indefinitely." She captured his hand and brought it down to the blanket between them. "So, I came to collect you and take you home. But we can linger here for a while, if you would like."

Stephen sighed. She always allowed him to touch her face, trace the pattern, but never more than that—no hug, no kiss. Every once in a while, she would clasp his hands. And throughout those months, he learned that he enjoyed it. He enjoyed her presence, never knowing what the day would bring when she came to the prison three times a week as his missionary.

"You're thinking again."

He smiled. She echoed Michael in a lot of ways. The thought of the former assassin brought a wave of sadness to him. No one had yet to hear from him, Jinx, nor Batch. Nor was there word from Jason, who had stayed behind at the medlab in order for them to escape.

"Too many thoughts, really—Michael, Jason, Jinx and Batch. And then you."

"Me?" She smiled as she settled back onto the blanket, watching the clouds overhead.

Her smile widened when he began to trace her profile again, this time from forehead down her pert nose and under her chin. "You came to see me at the prison. And I feel as though we have grown closer and closer each time, but you never let me go any further than this."

"That's because, dear Stephen"—she captured his hand, pressed it against her chest, and held it over her heart—"I was your missionary. It would have been improper to allow anything other than mentoring." Her eyes twinkled in merriment.

Under his hand, the beat of her heart thumped against him. And he could hear the *thump-swish* of it. Would she ever tell him about her condition? He had always been able to hear her heartbeat, see the pulse at her neck. After her first few days as his missionary, he had started sitting closer to her so that he could hear her heart and feel her pulse when she touched his hand.

"And now?" He scooted closer and peered down at her.

She gazed deeply into his eyes for long seconds before responding. "I know you can hear my heart, Stephen—in more ways than one."

"When were you going to tell me?"

"Whenever you asked." She reached up and cupped his cheek.

"Can't we do anything for you?"

"No. Your dad has tried. He used the plasma treatment, but nothing takes. My heart defect is permanent." She dropped her hand and let it rest on her stomach as she continued. "I'm not as enhanced as you or your sister. I don't have the healing abilities you and your father have. He thinks that may be why it doesn't work on me."

Stephen propped himself above her, letting his leg and hip lean against her body. "I guess I should have asked long ago. What did you inherit from Jackson?"

"Higher learning, enhanced eyesight and hearing—that's about it." She grinned. The little mole under her left eye almost became lost in the laugh lines. "But I will still have a fulfilled life. Your dad said fifty or sixty years, if not more. I just can't take a lot of excitement."

"Such as?" He lowered himself a bit more toward her. Her eyes darkened, and her hand flattened against his chest, holding him back.

"Fear, for one thing, great stress—things like that. It increases the adrenaline, and my heart can't handle it. The possibility of it giving out on me is too great."

"But what about . . . " He began to dip closer, but she grabbed his face and brought him down to her.

Her lips were soft and gentle, full against his mouth. And she tasted of strawberries, too. He pressed his hands against the blanket on either side of her head, keeping his desire under control. He couldn't let that part of him awaken again—not yet. It was not yet time for that.

She broke the kiss, placed a small one on his lower lip, and then smiled up at him. "But this is fine."

He grinned. "I can hear your heart, you know. It's definitely swishing around pretty quickly."

Peony laughed. "Shut it." She pulled his head down until it was pressed against her chest, his ear over her heart.

The one thing he had learned about Peony, despite the delicate nature she presented, was that she was forceful when she wanted something. She was a force to be reckoned with. He smiled as he listened to the heavy *thump-swish*. She was exactly what he needed and wanted. He hadn't realized it at first; but now, he couldn't imagine his life without her around.

"It sounds like music to me," he whispered, capturing the feel, smell, and sound of her in his memories. He tightened his arms around her and relaxed in her embrace.

"Music for you." Her hand buried itself in his hair, curling against his scalp. "We'll stay like this for a little while longer, but then I take you home."

He tensed. "Argh. Do we have to? There's so much I will have to face, and I'm not ready yet."

"The moment your foot touches your pathway home, my mentorship with you officially ends."

Stephen whipped his head up and looked at her. She was saying what he thought she was saying, right? "And?"

Her only answer was a smile and pushing his head back down over her heart. She might have said that was all she had gained from her father, but heightened observation and the ability to read people were there, too. How else could she have known that he loved the sound of her heart and the smell of her skin? It was a comfort to him.

She had shown him compassion and love long before he understood it. She was there guiding him through Scripture. He remembered Scripture, knew the words, but had never allowed it to soak into his heart. And she—along with Sellers, the prison guard— helped him mature in his faith.

As her heart thumped against his ear, he closed his eyes and lifted a prayer to the Lord, asking Him to guide him along this untraveled road and into a mysterious future.

Ω

Seth paced to the other side of the room and stood before the shelf that was covered with old books and framed images of their family. He reached out and touched the photo of Stephen and Sierra, captured when they were only ten. They were in the process of jumping into a small pool of water. Sierra held Stephen's hand, coaxing him to try. The image looped them from nodding at each other to leaping into the air; Stephen's eyes were tightly squeezed shut.

The next frame was one from five years ago—a random capture with Stephen's drone as they were eating dinner—five seconds of them being a family, smiling, joking, laughing. Even Stephen, so carefree then. And innocent.

Seth traced his son's face with a forefinger and sighed. Where had he failed his son?

That question had haunted him for the last nine months. He would need to figure out where he went wrong and correct course. Maybe he could salvage their relationship. Would Stephen be able to forgive or even willing to forgive Seth for almost killing him?

Seth turned from the shelf and paced back to the window by the outside door.

"Seth?" Tamara's voice floated toward him.

He stuffed his hands into his back pockets and rocked back on his heels. "Yes?"

Her arms encircled his chest, and she pressed her face against the back of his shoulder. Seth slid his arms over hers and held on. He needed her support.

"It's been almost three hours. You plan on pacing here until he comes home? Peony said it might take a while."

Peony Mills—the woman had become his son's mentor. But even Jackson had agreed with him that there was more between Stephen and Peony. Seth bit at his inner cheek. If they became a couple and had children, that would be another descendent from two offspring of the GFT assassin line—

"Stop." Tamara let go and moved around to stand in front of him. "Stop thinking. I can feel the tension in you."

He dropped his forehead to hers, wrapping one of her curls around his finger. "There's a lot to think about."

She cupped his cheek. Her amber eyes searched his. Worry laced her expression, creasing her chestnut-toned face. "Seth, my dear, there isn't anything you can do to change the past. And I know what transpired has stuck with you all these months—and that the nightmares won't leave. But please, just relax today. Our son is coming home. Let's take this one step at a time."

Her lips covered his in a soft kiss before pulling back from him. Then she was walking back into their main living area. Throughout their marriage, she had never expected him to carry a conversation when he wasn't ready. She only imparted her words of wisdom and then left him to ponder her words.

Tamara, his wife, a woman of wisdom, worth more than rubies or pearls, yet a warrior to reckon with if he ever crossed her. A small smile drifted across his lips. Only three times in their lives had he crossed her. Once, when they were children. He carried a scar from her strike across his face for a long time. Of course, her father had punished her, not allowing her to visit with Seth. So, he came to her, sneaked into her room where they would play chess or a game they had developed and called Tri-checkit. The second time was while they were dating.

His only betrayal of her trust had happened then. He had allowed another woman to kiss him. Tamara walked around the corner of the park and found them behind one of the columns. The bruises on his ribs had ached for hours, and it took months to make up for his mistake. When he had asked why she struck him and not the woman who kissed him, she had replied that he didn't have to allow it. It was his decision to let it happen.

The last time was four years into their marriage. The twins were three and a handful. Seth had become so distracted by his projects that he had ended up being away from home for two days. Not only had Tamara reamed him, but he had also received an earful from his mother, stepfather, and in-laws. There were no hits against him. She had matured enough to realize that her actions before were wrong. But the coldness that poured from her cut him more deeply than any of her punches ever had. And he had learned to never cross Tam.

The soft purr of a motorbike broke through his reminiscing. Seth whipped his head up and palmed opened the door. The hatch slid back, and he stepped out into the bright Alaskan daylight and onto their bricked pathway.

Peony gave him a small wave and waited until Stephen climbed down from the bike. His son stood with his back to him, talking with Peony. He seemed to have gained more muscle, becoming more trimmed and angular. His stance was stiff and rigid, until she reached forward, ran her hand down the side of his face, and smiled. The tightly strung muscles seemed to relax at her touch. Stephen turned his head with eyes closed, pressing his hand against hers, holding it against him for a few seconds before stepping back.

Peony pulled away and headed down the roadway that led to the central hub of their city. And he and Stephen both stood there for long seconds, not moving. Seth took a small step forward.

Stephen turned and squared his shoulders. And in that moment, seeing the glistening tears that highlighted his son's green eyes, noticing the softness of his face hidden behind a day's growth of beard, and watching the faint light that seemed to surround him, all of Seth's fears and hesitations fell away. This was his son—back home with them.

Stephen began to slowly walk toward him. Seth took one more step, and then he was racing down the pathway. He plowed into Stephen, grabbing his son and crushing him against his chest, wrapping his arms around him and holding on, burying a hand into his son's locks.

A raw sob burst from Stephen as he gripped Seth's shirt at the back and leaned into him, barely able to stand. "Dad?"

Seth held him tighter, supporting him. "You're home, Ven. You're home. That's all that matters." He pressed his lips against Stephen's temple.

Stephen broke down then. Collapsing in Seth's arms.

Tears ran down Seth's cheeks and into his thick beard. His son's heart was beating in time with his own. And yet they didn't let each other go. The sun overhead kept on its path as he stood there in the middle of the pathway, holding his son against him and feeling Stephen's arms around his chest.

His son was finally home.

For more information about
Daphne Self
and
What Legends Become
please visit:

www.authordaphneself.blogspot.com

For more information about
AMBASSADOR INTERNATIONAL
please visit:

www.ambassador-international.com

Humanity has spread and colonized regions of the galaxies. As their reach expanded, countries, colonies, and planets joined to form the Federated Nations, providing a centralized government among the stars. In this dystopian anthology, follow along as humanity discovers new beings, wondrous worlds, old temptations, and strength in horrendous trials.

Rune has lived her whole life in the mountains of Kansanai. When everything is turned upside down, will she be able to let go of the life she thought she deserved for something far greater than what she could have ever imagined? Rolf goes through the motions of everyday life yet, his routine is disrupted when a voice claiming to be the one true God speaks to him. While listening to his heart, he is thrown temptation after temptation on his journey. Will he be able to resist the temptations?

How far would you go to protect the ones you love? During the apocalyptic final days of Noloro, three orphaned teens have nothing left in the world but each other. A sardonic sorcerer offers them a way off their dying world, but at what cost? Family, courage, and faith are at the heart of this end-of-the-world adventure.